The Reel Sisters

A novel about a group
of women fly fishers.

Michelle Cummings

The Reel Sisters
By Michelle Cummings
© 2017 Michelle Cummings

ISBN-13: 978-0692970935
ISBN-10: 0692970932

To Dame Juliana Berners, who in 1496
wrote the first book ever to be published on
fly fishing. Her courage and tenacity over five hundred
years ago has inspired me to write this book and
encourage more women to go fly fishing.

Also to my soul sisters
(*you know who you are*),
those of you who know my soul,
I love you for pushing me and encouraging
me to pursue my dreams. Thank you for
your thoughts, help, and dedication to seeing
this project through--and for keeping my
wine glass half full.

And to my husband, Paul, and our boys, Dawson and Dylan.
Thank you for being on my life adventure team.
I love the way we laugh, explore together, and love each
other. Thank you for supporting me in my long hours of
writing and fishing in pursuit of "the big one."

The Reel Sisters

Sophie- Rose- Veronica-
Amanda- Melody-

Many people fish all of their lives
not knowing it's not the fish they
are after...
~ Henry David Thoreau

What are you wading for?

Section 1: Gearing Up

"When it comes to the tools of the fly-fisherman's trade, it all begins with a rod and a reel. In company with the line, leader, and fly, they provide all the items needed to catch a fish. Anything else constitutes an accessory, though as we will see in time, many of these accessories enhance the fly-fishing experience."[i]

Beginners Guide to Fly Fishing
by Jim Casada

Sophie

In any proper adventure, everything should be a bit of a challenge, so it seemed appropriate that I had to pee the moment I put my waders on. Rule #1 of Fly Fishing: always go pee before you put your waders on. Period. That's it. End of story. Once you slide your feet into those two dark holes, wiggle the waders up over your hips, and finagle the shoulder straps over your shoulders, you do not want to take them off again until you are finished for the day. Mainly because after you are geared up, it's a pain in the ass to push your waders down around your ankles to assume the appropriate peeing position. Not to mention that those shoulder straps are pee magnets once in said peeing position. Yes, the art of peeing outdoors takes practice to perfect, and it is ten times harder with waders on. In short, follow Rule #1. You'll thank me for it later.

Rose and I are fishing the Arkansas River downstream from the cabin today. I love spending time at Rose's place. She owns a cabin up in the mountains where we girls often retreat to. It might be for a fishing weekend or just to get away from it all. It is a simple, three-bedroom cabin, tucked back in the pines near Salida, Colorado, and sits right on the Arkansas River. Rose and her husband built this cabin together back in the '60s during their first year of marriage. It has been a refuge for her for years, and lucky for me, she shares it with the rest of us. No reservations necessary, there is room for everyone. We all know where the hide-a-key is located, and it is open 24/7. The cabin has weathered a little over the years; however, the external structure is not the only thing that has changed. Internal changes have been made, too—literally and figuratively.

The first time I met Rose we were in a fly shop. She saw me gazing over the hundreds of flies all neatly tucked into their little glass boxes. I giggled out loud at the names of some of the flies: Wooly Bugger, Bitch Creek, and Two-Bit Hooker. She heard me giggle and exclaimed, "That Bitch Creek caught me six brown trout in about two hours last week. That was the best two-dollar hooker I ever bought!" I fell in love with this woman instantly. In a ten-minute timeframe she told three fish stories and dropped two f-bombs. A soul sister indeed.

Rose emerged out of that fly shop and into my life when I didn't even know how badly I needed a friend. She invited me to go fishing on the Arkansas River with her that following weekend. Since I was new to the sport, I was thrilled to have an invitation from a veteran angler, especially one who seemed like so much fun. That was the beginning of our lifelong friendship.

Rose is one of those people you just feel special to know. I truly look up to her and admire the time we spend on the river together. She has taught me so much about fishing and life in general. She's old enough to be my mother, yet I consider her my best friend. Often, our trips together aren't about catching fish but about building our friendship. Fly fishing seems to be our escape into another time, a simpler time. I look forward to the trips ahead and cherish the memories of the trips that have come and gone.

This particular sunny April morning we are downriver a bit from the cabin. Generally, this time of year the fishing conditions are fairly stable as the water levels don't move much. Spring runoff from the mountain snow is just around the corner, and we are anxiously awaiting the Mother's Day caddis hatch. The Mother's Day hatch is a phenomenal event. Each spring, caddis flies by the thousands fill the air, as prevalent as dandelion tufts on a windy day. They call it the Mother's Day hatch as it always happens sometime around the last weekend in April to the third week in May. Sometimes it coincides with Mother's Day. The caddis itself is a fly-like bug called a Brachycentrus caddis. It is the bug of choice this time of year for the fish, so we try to "match the hatch" by presenting imitation flies on a hook to the fish. All fly fishers hope we can trick the fish into taking *our* fly rather than a live one. There is a saying in fly fishing that goes, "The tug is the drug," and it's true. The first time you get a good tug on your line and you land your first fish . . . well, there's nothing quite like it. And so the addiction begins . . .

There are two types of caddis that could be hatching this time of year, so I make sure I have both kinds of flies in my fly box. The entomology that goes into fly fishing fascinates me and allows me an outlet to "get my geek on." I always loved school, so the "scienc-y" stuff lets me be a student again. Now that I'm in my forties, I like doing stuff that makes me feel like a kid again. The Brachycentrus caddis is black to dark gray in color and with a hook size of 14 or 16. The secondary caddis hatch (Hydropsyche Occidentalis) is slightly smaller and more of an olive to olive-gray color with a hook size of 16 to 18. I just call them all caddis flies and make sure I have lots of different colors and sizes in my fly box. You never know what the fish are biting on until you get down to the river anyway. Usually I hunt around the riverbanks to see what kinds of bugs are around and then pick out flies in my fly box to match. If these are the bugs that are out, these are the bugs that the fish are eating right now. And if there are no bugs on the shores, then I turn over a few rocks in the river to see what types of aquatic insects might be hatching. If nymphs are on the menu, I'm serving imitation nymphs.

There is still a nip of winter in the air, and that means no caddis hatch today. The caddis flies hatch when the water temperature hits a magical 52 degrees; it is overcast and cloudy today, a crisp 41 degrees outside, so a Blue-Winged Olive day it is. We are in a section of the river where the current is swift. I like to fish in the current seams, where the fast water and slow water meet. I fish the edge of the fast water directly in front of and behind the boulders. This is where you find the fish. This time of year, you don't have to wade through the water much as the fish are in shallow water and near the surface. Whenever you see bug shells on the rocks on shore, your boots do not need to get wet. The fish will be near the surface and wading in to cast will scare them away. I wear my waders anyway as experience has taught me I am clumsy and have taken a few unexpected "dips" when attempting to net a fish. Rose has given me a few "River Rat" patches for my fishing vest. If you take an unexpected swim without losing your fishing hat, she presents you with a silly patch. She had a few dozen of these patches made up one time at a local embroidery store. I am the proud owner of three of these. You almost feel like a Girl Scout getting a patch for your sash that you worked very hard for, especially with all of the pomp and circumstance she puts on when awarding it to you. I wear my badges with honor.

I love fishing with Rose. Watching her cast is like watching a painter stroke a masterpiece. Her lines are flawless, and she can lay down a fly that would make any fish want to gobble it up. Sometimes I will stop fishing and just watch her cast. It really is a beautiful sight. The hypnotic motion of her line whistling through the air makes her appear to be in complete synchronization with her surroundings. Her precise motions are evidence of years of practice, timing, and discipline. I hope to match her casting ability someday. After several satisfying hours on the river, we pack up our gear and head back to the cabin. We haven't caught very many fish today, but any day spent on the river is a day well spent.

I got into fishing when I was a kid. I grew up on a farm in the great state of Kansas, and we had an awesome fishing pond in our pasture near the house. My brothers and I would hike down the draw and go fishing whenever the mood struck, but especially on Sunday afternoons after church. For some reason, we always seemed to catch more after spending a little time with the big man upstairs. My dad would stock our pond once a year to keep us from growing bored with fishing. We also hunted deer and pheasant, not to mention the occasional barn swallow or prairie dog if it dared show itself on our property. I come from a long line of hunters and gatherers. Opening weekend for pheasant season was often a bigger event than Christmas at our house. Friends and relatives from all over the United States would travel to Kansas each November and get up at the butt crack of dawn to hunt these beautiful creatures. I enjoyed being one of the only girls going on the hunt with them. Being a bona fide tomboy came easily to me—I had two older brothers, neither of whom showed any interest in playing with dolls. I excelled at my hunter education courses and shot my first pheasant when I was nine years old. I still have one of the tail feathers from that gorgeous bird. I still remember the look on my beaming father's face as I ran up to him, bird in hand. He plucked one of the tail feathers off my bird and stuck it in my hat, saying, "Nice job, Sophie! I'm so proud of you!" To this day, this is one of my favorite childhood memories.

As I grew older, I still enjoyed the hunt, but the brutally cold mornings and the demise of my opponent started to wear on me. Although we always cleaned and cooked what we killed, I felt like I was taking away something beautiful from the land. Then in 1992, the movie *A River Runs Through It* came out and it changed my life. At twenty-six years old, I had never seen anyone fly fish before (not to mention I had never seen a fisherman as cute as Brad Pitt!). I was used to spin casting with my fishing pole in the family pond. I was mesmerized by the pristine setting and the beauty of the fly

13

casting technique. The quiet of the wilderness and the sound of the water rushing over the rocks called my name like the suppertime bell Mom would clang each evening calling us home for supper. I was hooked before I even bent my first rod.

The very next weekend I drove to Colorado. The six-hour drive had me eagerly anticipating holding that long, sleek rod in my hand and feeling the heft of a big fish. There was a romance in the mountainous setting that I was already falling in love with. The highway on I-70 seemed like it would stretch on forever before I finally saw those magnificent white peaks spike the horizon. My stomach was jittery, partly because of the thirty-two-ounce Big Gulp of Mountain Dew I had downed without eating lunch, but also in anticipation of what lay ahead of me. I rolled down the windows in my truck to breathe in the crisp Colorado air. It smelled adventurous. I couldn't wait to get there.

I drove straight to Breckenridge, as that was the mountain town I knew best. My parents had taken us there every summer for vacation as long as I could remember, and in my opinion, that was God's country (and of course it is geographically situated right next to God's other country with its wonderful Kansas wheat fields). I boldly walked into a fly shop, sauntered up to the cutest employee the shop had to offer, and asked if they gave casting lessons.

"Excuse me, do you give fly fishing lessons here?" I asked, feeling a little intimidated by all of the fishing gear neatly displayed on the racks and shelves, tugging at my attention.

"We sure do. Were you thinking of getting lessons for your dad or boyfriend?" the handsome clerk replied.

With a smile I added, "Actually, the lessons would be for me. I'm interested in learning how to fly fish."

With a surprised look on his face he said, "I see. Well, we can certainly teach anyone how to fly fish. We don't get a lot of women in here wanting to learn how to fish. In fact, you might be the first! We just opened shop this last year. I'm Buck." He extended his hand.

"Sophie," I said as I firmly shook his hand in return.

"Welcome, Sophie. Have you ever been fly fishing before?"

"Not fly fishing. I've fished all my life in the family pond, though, just not with a fly rod. I enjoy it a lot. I just saw the movie *A River Runs Through It*, and I have never seen anyone fly fish before. It looks amazing and I'd love to give it a try."

"Ah, another Brad Pitt convert. That movie is doing wonders for business," he said with a chuckle. "Well, now's as good a time as any, let's get started. Learning the basics of fly casting isn't too difficult, and you'll be catching fish in no time. To get as good as Tom Skerritt or Brad Pitt will take a while, but your casts don't need to be perfect to catch enough fish to keep you happy."

I bought my first rod and reel, hired Buck as my guide, and started my casting lessons. I was surprised when the casting lessons initially took place in the backyard of the fly shop. I assumed we would hop in a truck and drive immediately to the river. But on grass you can actually see where your fly lands and it is easier to correct your line if you are casting incorrectly. This allowed me to practice not only the style and timing of my cast but also different rod, line, and leader setups. Buck laid down a few hula hoops about fifteen feet away from me, and I practiced for a good hour landing a hookless fly in the bull's-eye. Learning to cast with a fly rod was considerably challenging and a little intimidating. However, Buck was wonderfully patient with me and took the time to help me learn the physics and mechanics of casting

15

well. Back in the '90s, fly shops were not used to women coming in and asking for lessons, so I was grateful for his kindness when he saw the passion in my eyes for learning this craft.

Within a few hours we were out on the river. I felt a little clumsy with the first few casts, but as my confidence grew, so did the accuracy of my casts. I remember that first tug I felt on my line. The jolt of electricity it sent through my body was enough to power a small town.

I was giggling so hard when I was reeling in. Buck must have thought I had lost my mind. We were there a total of six hours, and I caught seven rainbow trout on a Beadhead Pheasant Tail fly. Seemed fitting I had caught my first fish on a fly that included feathers from a pheasant.

From that weekend on I was hooked. I moved out to Colorado a few months later and never left. After working odd jobs for a few years, I finally saved up enough money to purchase some land and started a greenhouse and nursery business. Evidently you can take the girl off the Kansas farm, but you can't take the Kansas farm out of the girl. I really missed farming full-time, so instead of planting a wheat and corn crop every year, I would plant seeds of a different kind. I bought enough land to start small with annuals, perennials, and landscaping plants. A few years later I expanded into exotic culinary greens and herbs. Eventually I vastly expanded the business as a fall festival destination with a huge pumpkin patch and apple orchard. We encourage families to come pick their own pumpkins and apples and make it a full day of family fun. I could not be happier with my profession.

Colorado really suits me well. And after all these years, I can't find much I don't like about it. Plus, I'm only a five-hour drive from my mom and dad's farm. I've now lived here almost twenty years, and you couldn't pay me seven figures to move away. I'm officially a transplant now, but I'll always consider myself a Kansas farm girl. I still help my mom and dad on the farm about five to six times a year, so my roots are still firmly planted there. My brothers and I will keep the farm in the family when my parents decide to retire. It means too much to us to let it go.

The one thing I would change would be the fact that I have not found anyone to share my life with. I find it ironic that I can grow any plant on the planet yet cannot seem to cultivate a meaningful relationship with a man. I thought I had found my true love when I was in college. His name was John. He was a gorgeous military man I met while I was attending Kansas State University. He was stationed at Fort Riley, and he stole my heart the moment I laid eyes on him.

In an instant, I knew my life would never be the same. After long-distance dating for several years through a few deployments and job separations, we became engaged. When he had served his term and left the military, he committed to move to where I lived but had a hard time finding a job before he relocated.

During this time he met someone else and fell in love, and they were married within six months—leaving me heartbroken and depressed. He even had the gall to ask me to stand up with him at his wedding. He said I was his best friend and couldn't imagine getting married without me by his side. I told him I could not stand there and listen to him say his vows to someone else when those words were supposed to be said to me. Several months of deep depression took its toll on my self-esteem and self-worth. I felt left behind and bewildered. Most days I gave up trying to understand and developed a seething layer of resentment towards him.

Thirteen months after the two were married, his wife was tragically killed in a house fire. Grief-stricken, he called me and asked me to come and help him through this devastating time. With my backbone and self-esteem finally back intact, I told him no. I didn't want to be anyone's second choice and knew I would get hurt all over again. Feeling empowered, I finally moved on with my life. I had a string of dates during an optimistic '97 but never allowed myself to fall in love again. Part of me wonders if I will ever fully recover from my relationship with John. I know my heart would not survive another heartbreak of that magnitude.

`·.,¸,.·´¯`·.,><((((º>`·.,¸,.·´¯`·..><((((º>`·.,¸,.·´¯`·..

Veronica and Amanda are coming up to the cabin today, and I am excited to see them. I haven't seen Veronica in a few weeks and Amanda since before Mike was deployed—which was a few months ago. I am looking forward to connecting again this weekend with some good fishing and cabin time.

I met Veronica a few years ago when I sat next to her on an airplane while headed out on a fly fishing trip. She saw me put my fly rod in the overhead bin and was intrigued by what it was. We immediately struck up a conversation that lasted the entire flight. She was traveling to a conference where she was giving a speech to a women's professional group. She is CEO of her company, Executive Coaching for Women, where she coaches top-level women executives to be better leaders. She couldn't believe I was taking six days off from work just to fish! She had never been fly fishing before and peppered me with question after question about the sport. We exchanged information, and she called me a few weeks later. I took her fishing and introduced her to this amazing sport. At first I was unsure if she enjoyed it. There is a lot to learn, and it takes time to feel confident in your abilities. I could tell that she was not used to being out in the wilderness away from her usual corporate setting. The bugs bothered her, she worried about getting dirty, she broke a nail in the first twenty minutes, and she refused to pee outside. I had my work cut out to conform this city girl! She struggled with her casting at first, but throughout the course of the day she began to get the hang of it. Over the years she has become quite skilled at fly fishing. It's fun to see how far she has come.

Veronica has been in Portland, Oregon this week for work and flies into Denver today. She is picking Amanda up in Colorado Springs on her way to the cabin.

I met Amanda one October when she and her husband, Mike, came to my pumpkin patch on Military Appreciation Weekend. We host a free weekend for local soldiers and their families to come and have a fun family outing every fall. Mike is in the army and stationed at Fort Carson in Colorado Springs. Amanda was pulling her two kids in one of our Radio Flyer wagons when Parker, their son, randomly bailed out of the wagon and scraped his knee. I happened to be the staff member who saw the incident, cleaned up the scrape, and applied the appropriate pumpkin-shaped bandage. This seemed to be the miracle cure for Parker, and he, his sister, Jordan, and Mike trotted off to get lost in the kids' corn maze together.

Amanda and I stood and chatted for at least another thirty minutes. She told me all about her kids and Mike's upcoming deployment to Afghanistan. I told her all about our kids' gardening club, both for the sake of her two kids and for that of the fifth grade class that she teaches. That following spring, she brought her class out to the greenhouse for a field trip. Somewhere along the way I mentioned that I was a fly fisher and invited her to come along one weekend. I picked her up on the way to the cabin, and she fell in love upon her first cast. She was a natural. She now ties her own flies and meets us to go fishing as often as she can. With Mike deployed she is single parenting, so it's harder for her to get away. The kids are too young to teach them to fly fish just yet. Her mother-in-law lives nearby and watches the kids from time to time so she can sneak away for a little river time.

`··,,.·´¯`··,><((((º>`··,,.·´¯`··><((((º>`··,,.·´¯`··

Veronica

I cannot wait to get off this plane and head up to the cabin this weekend. I have been on the road a lot this month and could really use a serene fishing weekend with the girls. It's funny how I can look out the airplane window, see a river down below, and wonder what kinds of flies the fish are biting on. If you would have told me ten years ago that fly fishing would change my life, I would have laughed right in your face. A bona fide city girl complete with a weave and manicured nails, I had never been in the woods in my life. Then one day I sat next to Sophie on an airplane. I had no idea that one two-hour conversation would change the course of my career and my life.

When I met Sophie, Thatcher and I had been married for two years. I met him one evening during a bachelorette party in downtown Denver. My girlfriends and I started our evening with drinks and appetizers at his restaurant, Noire, before hitting the clubs. I caught his eye as we checked in at the hostess stand. He was strikingly handsome—no, scratch that, he was damn fine, that's all there is to it. There was no way to *not* notice him. His dark, creamy skin glowed against his gleaming white chef's coat. I got busted staring at him and tossed him a quick smile and head nod as we were ushered to our table. He came out to check on us and sent over a round of drinks in honor of the bride-to-be. He asked us where we were headed to next, and he magically appeared there a few hours later. We began dating soon thereafter, dated for ten months, were engaged for another ten months, and have now been married for ten years. I could not love this man more! There are times I wonder why I became the lucky girl who gets to call him my own. He complements me in every way. In an odd way, my busy travel schedule helps keep us closer. The time we spend apart makes us appreciate the time we spend together more. He works evenings and a lot of weekends. I am more of a Monday-through-Friday, nine-to-five girl. We text one another fifty times a day, so the banter and love notes help keep the spark alive. There are times I wonder how it is possible that I landed a man as fine as Thatch. I could stand to lose a few pounds here or there, so the fact that he loves every ounce of me makes me love him even more.

I started an executive coaching business after spending many years in Human Resources. I found that the more team-building classes and leadership seminars I ran, the more I realized that if there was not strong, clear leadership from the top, anything I did with the middle managers had no lasting effects. I got so frustrated with the lack of focus and goals coming from the executives that I decided to start my own company called Executive Coaching for Women. I wanted to work with top-level woman leaders to help them lead with passion and help them achieve their professional and personal goals.

The first two years of my business were just okay. I had a few clients who were helping me pay the bills, but I was having a hard time getting my name out there. And then I met Sophie. I had not met anyone so passionate about fishing before in my life! Especially a woman. She was going on an all-expense-paid fly fishing trip she had won at a fly fishing convention. The excitement for her trip was oozing out of every ounce of her being. I couldn't help but catch the fever. I'm still not sure how, but she convinced me to give fly fishing a try. A few weeks after meeting her I found myself out in the woods in a huge pair of fishing waders waving this big, awkward stick in the air. I'm sure I looked absolutely ridiculous, but lucky for me there was no one else around. After I got over the bugs, the broken nails, and the fly getting stuck in my weave, I found the fishing to be very fun and relaxing. Now that I have been fishing for a few years, I am quite passionate about it. Fly fishing offers me a wonderful escape: a chance for a few precious hours or days to leave behind the mad pace of today's society. A chance to savor the simple, satisfying pleasures to be found in my line whistling through the air or my rod bent with the gratifying heft of a good fish.

It did, however, take me a while to make that realization. I found fly fishing to be a lot tougher than I had expected. I nearly gave up. I am used to picking things up very rapidly, and I was astounded by how much there was to learn about fly fishing. I was hopelessly discouraged after my initial exposure found me overwhelmed by what seemed to be an endless array of complexities, hundreds of different flies, dozens of casting techniques, and enough knots to hold Houdini captive. I wondered if it were possible to teach an old dog new tricks. Well, if early forties are considered old.

But Sophie kept pushing me. She called every time she was heading up to the cabin. "We'd love to have you join us! Even if you decide not to fish, just come up and escape the concrete jungle." I could hardly turn down an invitation like that. Especially since Thatcher works every Friday and Saturday night, I wouldn't be spending time with him anyway. So I went, kept trying, my pissy attitude along for the ride. Then one day I realized that I could improve my casting by focusing on my goals, adjusting my techniques, and following through with commitment—all things I instruct my clients to do to meet their business objectives. That realization inspired me to write a book that illustrates how effective strategies in fishing can also help people achieve success in business. I called it *Reel Leadership*, and it became a best seller in the corporate executive world. I now have more clients than I know what to do with and several staff members to help share the workload. I'm quite thankful that Sophie was sitting in seat 4C that day. You never know when one conversation can change your entire journey . . .

`·.¸¸.·´¯`·.¸><(((º>`·.¸¸.·´¯`·..><(((º>`·.¸¸.·´¯`·..

Amanda

I am so excited to go fishing with the girls this weekend. Parker and Jordan are going to "Grandma Camp" and staying with my mother-in-law, Lorraine. She moved out to Colorado Springs from Oklahoma when Jordan was born and helps out quite a bit. Especially while Mike is deployed. The kids call her Mimi, and it's so helpful to have her nearby when I need to take a little me-time like this weekend. I'm calling it a Mommy's Time Out, and boy do I need one! Mike has been deployed to Afghanistan for two months now, and I haven't taken any time for myself since he left. Having him gone stresses me out terribly, but I try not to let the kids see it. We're able to Skype with him about once a week, so it makes it a little easier when we get to see his face and hear his voice. Before he left, I had him make several videos of "stuff I want my kids to know" so in case anything tragic happens, the kids will have some nuggets of wisdom from their dad. We get them out and watch them often so they have a visual of their dad on a regular basis. It was actually a harder project to tackle than we thought, but now that it is done, we are both happy to have it. When I am missing him, I'll pop one of the videos in and fall asleep watching it. It hurts my heart and warms it all at the same time. I miss him so much.

Mike and I met when we were sixteen years old. We were high school sweethearts and have literally grown up together. Well, as grown up as twenty-three-year-olds can be. Everyone called us "Mike and Mandy" and told us to wait to get married, but we didn't listen. Mike joined the military right after high school so we would have a steady income. We were married when we were nineteen and had Jordan ten months after we were married. Parker followed just eighteen months later, so we have been very busy the last few years. I took night classes to get my teaching degree, and I teach fifth grade at the elementary school on base. I absolutely love teaching, even when it wears on me by the end of the day. It's not an easy job, and we struggle financially every month with our two small incomes, but I really love teaching. We have two healthy children and a roof over our heads, so we are grateful and thankful every day. I just pray that Mike stays safe while he is deployed. I don't know how I would live without him. Some days are harder than others. I feel brave and sorry for myself all at the same time. Whenever I start to worry too much about him, I wake up early and see if he is on Facebook or Skype. If he's not online, then I will stand in the doorway of my kids' rooms and just listen to the sounds of them breathing. It's a quietness I carry with me the rest of the day. It seems to help when fear takes over my mind.

I cannot wait for Veronica to pick me up today. One of the girls usually picks me up on the way up to the cabin as my vehicle is old and does not do well on the mountain roads. I can't afford to get a new one, and they basically drive right by my house on the way to the cabin anyway. I love carpooling with Veronica or Sophie as it gives me a little more one-on-one time with them. I feel a tremendous life force when I am around these women and when I fish. My day-to-day routine gets exhausting: morning routine of getting kids dressed, fed, diaper bags packed, papers graded, rush hour traffic, drop the kids at day care, drive to school; teach thirty fifth graders all day; evening routine of drive home, make dinner, eat dinner, do a load or two of laundry, do dishes, play with the kids, story time, bath time, snuggle time, prayers, and finally get kids to sleep. I'm exhausted just thinking about it! Plus, Parker is not sleeping well right now, so I am always a bit sleep deprived. He was sleeping through the night just fine until Mike was deployed. Now he wakes up once or twice a night. Part of me wonders if he is waking up to check and see that I am still there. It's hard for him to understand where Daddy is and why he isn't around every day. So fishing is worlds apart from my daily routine, which is another reason why I need this girls' weekend.

This is my first trip of the new year but back in an old, well-known place: Rose's cabin. I haven't been fishing in months, so I am excited to toss in a line again this weekend. I'm not a cold-weather girl, so I don't fish much in the winter. Plus, with Mike getting deployed in February, I wanted to spend as much time with him as possible the weeks and months leading up to his leaving. It didn't feel right going up to the cabin for a weekend with the girls when I could be spending time with him and the kids.

As much as I'm looking forward to the fishing, I'm also looking forward to spending time with the girls. The evenings of downtime hanging out in the cabin are some of my favorites. The stories that get shared are hysterical! Rose seems to have lived three lifetimes with the stories she tells. Even though I don't see them as often as I'd like, I still feel closely connected to these women. They generously share their fishing expertise and, more importantly, their friendship with me. Even though I am much younger than they are, they don't seem to mind. Sophie took me under her wing when we met at her pumpkin patch and has helped me ever since. Fly fishing is not necessarily a cheap sport to get into, and I've been fortunate that the girls share their gear and their knowledge with me. I have learned how to tie my own flies to keep my costs down. Some flies are two to four dollars apiece at the fly shop, and when you lose several each trip, it adds up fast. Once you have a wide assortment of the essential materials needed, you can tie a fly for a few pennies a piece. A far cry from what you pay retail. Plus, I'm notorious for losing flies in the trees. Sophie teases that if she ever needs a new fly, she will just go shopping in one of the trees near where I have been fishing. "Free danglers! Get 'em while they're hot!" she would joke. One weekend I lost a record twenty flies! Fifty bucks' worth! That's three boxes of diapers for Parker. I can't afford to do that, so I started tying my own. I was lucky enough to hit a good garage sale last summer where a woman was getting rid of her husband's fly tying supplies for a whopping five dollars! I was thrilled to find a vise, hooks, feathers, string . . . basically everything you would need to get started in fly tying. I later learned these fly tying materials are called hackle. I checked out a few how-to books at the library and searched YouTube for fly tying videos. Rose gave me several private tying lessons and pointers as well. Before long I had tied several dozen and became hooked on tying flies. I picked up my waders, rod, reel, and boots at that same garage sale for under a hundred dollars. The entire outfit should have cost well over $1,000, so I counted my lucky stars that day I stumbled across that sale.

At first I started tying my own flies because I didn't have the money to buy all of the flies I needed for each trip. Plus, as soon as you got to the river, the fish would be biting on something that you didn't have and I'd have to bum flies off one of the girls anyway. I find fly tying very therapeutic, and I find myself daydreaming of the fish I will catch with each fly I tie. Now that I am pretty good at tying my own, I bring my hackle supplies with me and spend the evenings in the cabin tying whatever bugs the fish were biting on that day. It gives me a feeling of power tying these flies, to make something practical and beautiful just by using my own skill and creativity. It's hard to describe the feeling I get when I catch a fish on a fly that I tied myself. A sense of pride and astonishment all at the same time, that I could trick something wild to believe my fly is the real thing. The girls now ask me to tie flies for them. They purchase the materials and I tie the flies. Works for me! There are hundreds of different fly patterns and materials, so having a variety of materials to work with is handy. Some of the fly tying patterns are very intricate and require several different types of hackle to get them right. My confidence is growing in my ability to tie. I try to create new patterns too. Seems there is a never-ending quest to find the perfect fly. I've spent a lot of the winter stocking my fly boxes for this upcoming season. I'm looking forward to catching a big fish on one of my flies.

`·., ,.·´¯`·.,><((((º>`·., ,.·´¯`·..><((((º>`·., ,.·´¯`·..

Rose

Tonight will be the first night all four of us have gathered at the cabin since before the first snowfall. Sophie and I have been here a handful of times this winter to fish and to check in on the cabin. Winter is Sophie's downtime at the greenhouse and nursery, so she has more free time to fish. Veronica and Amanda are more fair-weather fishers, so I see them less often in the colder months. I am very much looking forward to my girls all being together again.

Sophie, DJ, and I came up a few days early to get the cabin ready. DJ, short for Dame Juliana, is my beloved dog who goes everywhere with me. I named her after Dame Juliana Berners, a nun from the 1400s who wrote the first book on fly fishing ever to be published. Imagine that, a woman! In the 1400s women in publishing was absolutely unheard of. Most women in that time would use a pseudonym of a man's name for it even to be considered. Not Dame Juliana Berner! I bet she was a fiery rascal. I found a copy of her book in my grandmother's attic when I was a young girl, and it inspired me to take up fly fishing. My grandfather took me fishing, and I still fish with the bamboo rod he gave me all those years ago.

DJ is a wonderful fishing partner as she loves all things outdoors. She sits and scouts the banks for me and warns off any threatening wildlife that may be near. I've been

31

fortunate never to have crossed paths with a bear in all my years of fishing in Colorado, or at least none that I know of. She seems to know that deer are nonthreatening and allows them to cross the river when I'm fishing. I think she senses that an encounter with these wild beauties actually enhances the fly fishing experience. And squirrels, beware! If DJ is in the woods, you *will* be chased up a tree. How I love to watch her.

She's the cutest black Lab with a little white patch of fur above her eyes. She almost looks like a little nun, which is another reason her name suits her so well. She has a profound love affair with retrieving. One might call her a full-blown Frisbee addict. The happiest part of her day is when she is retrieving this UFO-shaped object. If there is a Frisbee in the room, she can sniff it out, dig it out of whatever bag it is concealed in, and drop it at your feet. It doesn't matter if it is 20 degrees and snowing; DJ would still prefer to be out sailing through the air attempting to nab her plastic prey. Watching her race out, make a spectacular leap, and snag the flying disc from the air is a fantastic sight. I swear she is actually grinning as she runs back eager for the next throw. She is not as fond of tennis balls or any other flying object— the Frisbee is her thing. I wonder if it's because the Frisbee is so unpredictable. It can hover in one place, get caught on a wind gust, or even reverse direction. She doesn't catch it every time but seems to learn from her mistakes and keeps on trying. She seems to thrive on the challenge of it all. *Hmm, sounds a bit like me and my fly fishing . . .*

She provides the best company and I love her dearly. I rescued her from the pound a few years after Bob died. I was ready for a new companion, and I can't imagine life without her now. Life is too short not to have someone to share it with.

I love the process of preparing the cabin for a gathering of dear souls. I like to make sure everyone is as comfortable as possible, bringing in special, personal touches for each guest: favorite foods, some drinks, and fresh flowers in each room. The more comfortable the environment, the easier it is for them to leave their hectic day-to-day routines at the door and enjoy the weekend. I also made several new quilts this winter, one for each of the girls. Quilting is another hobby of mine, and if I can't be on the river fishing, I like to be in front of a sewing machine stitching up a storm. I'm in a quilting club called the Stitch-n-Bitch, and that keeps me busy if it's too cold to fish.

This last winter, keeping the girls' favorite colors and personalities in mind, I went on a quest to find the perfect fabric for each of their quilts. For Veronica, I found a lovely, sophisticated African print, bursting with color and depth. It has a stunning array of patterns and is very pleasing to the eye. The fabric's sheen alludes to raw silk, while the fabric maintains the fine weave of finely spun cotton. It's just beautiful, if I do say so myself. For Amanda, I pieced together a bright, cheery geometric block print. I found a fun print in a fabric shop that just screamed energetic, youthful teacher. It is lightweight, soft, and perfect for cuddling up with those two babes of hers. For Sophie, I did an earthy, autumn-leaves block-print quilt. The fabric was made with natural dyes from tree barks, flowers, and roots, perfect for my green-thumb friend. The earthy colors blend so warmly together. It might be my favorite quilt of the three.

I can't wait to see the looks on their faces when they realize they get to take them home on Sunday evening.

I've just finished tidying the rooms, making the beds, and arranging the flowers on the bedside tables. I still need to start a fire in the fireplace to take the nip out of the air. Veronica and Amanda should be here in about an hour, so I need to get supper warming as well. I made my grandmother's beef stew recipe a few days ago at home and brought it up in the cooler. It is Amanda's favorite. I need to put a pot on to simmer so it's good and hot when they arrive. I hear Sophie chopping firewood outside trying to build up the woodpile. She is such a hard worker, and I appreciate her strong back and muscles. As I enter my golden years, I still enjoy chopping firewood, but today I'm happy to let Sophie take a swing at it.

`·.¸¸.·´¯`·.¸,.·><(((º>`·.¸¸.·´¯`·...><((((º>`·.¸¸.·´¯`·..

Sophie

I feel so empowered and Nordic whenever I chop wood. I channel my inner Paul Bunyan with every grunt and swing. There is great satisfaction in a good axe swing overhead and a CRACK when you make a perfect strike. The sound of the log splintering, cracking, and breaking in two echoes through the pines with every swing I take. I feel about as burly as a tomboy can feel when I'm chopping wood. I'm even wearing plaid.

We need to build up our dwindling winter woodpile for the full weekend ahead. Rose and I burned quite a bit of wood the three or four times we've been to the cabin this winter. DJ supervises from the porch while I bust out my favorite lumberjack tune to keep my swings in rhythm. Some words sound more like grunts when I am on the downswing. ♪♪♪ *"SHEEEEE'S a lumberjack and SHEEEEE'S okay, she SLEEPS all night and she WORKS all day... I CUT down trees, I EAT my lunch, I GO to the lavaTREE. On WEDNESDAYS I go SHOPPING and have BUTTERED scones for TEA."* ♪♪♪[ii]

I belt out this Monty Python song every time I chop wood. It makes me giggle. I will not be getting any awards or accolades for my singing ability, but I entertain DJ, a few squirrels, and the occasional bird during the process. When

35

my back muscles start to tire, I sit and make kindling. Making kindling is one of my favorite cabin chores. It's repetitious and very therapeutic, and feeds my inner geek. You take a triangular piece of wood that you just chopped, one with an even grain and no obvious knots. Then you stand it on end on a hard surface. Using a small, handheld axe you position the blade so the cut will make a half-inch-sized piece of kindling. Knock the axe on top of the piece of wood a few times, and the log will split down its length, splintering off the piece of kindling. In the hour or so it takes to fill the kindling box, my mind wanders from subject to subject. What is happening at the greenhouse, what each one of the girls is doing at that moment, why I didn't catch many fish earlier today, what I might do differently on the river tomorrow, what else I need to help Rose do before the other girls arrive . . . just random thoughts to pass the time. That's one of my favorite things about spending time at the cabin. There's time just to sit and think. Away from the busyness of the real world, in the quiet of the woods, it's just you and your thoughts. Well, and wine. There's always a lot of wine, which I believe helps a great deal as well.

Just as I am finishing up the kindling, Veronica and Amanda pull up in Veronica's Lexus SUV.

"Yay! You're here! Welcome, girls!" I exclaim as they both bound out of the car.

"Hey, Sophie! Good to see you!" Veronica says as she gives me a big hug.

"You too, world traveler."

"Ugh, I still have jet lag. *Soooo* ready to be out on the river tomorrow. I see Rose has you busy on firewood chores this evening. Nice lumberjack shirt."

"You like it? It's very Paula Bunyan," I reply as I point my toe and pull on my pretend suspenders.

"I love it," Amanda chimes in as she engulfs me in a hug. "It is so good to see you! I have been looking forward to this for months!"

"Me too. It's been way too long since the four of us have hung out. Winter always seems to get in the way of our fishing time! You know, because you two are winter wussies and won't go fishing unless it's over 50 degrees, but whatever."

"Oh, it's going to be like that this weekend, huh?" Veronica sparks back with a bit of attitude.

"Would you have it any other way?" I say coyly.

"I'm watching you, Ms. Bunyan," Veronica playfully sneers as she points two fingers at her eyes and then points them back at me.

"Rose is inside, let's head in. How was the drive?"

"Went pretty quick, only a few crazy mountain drivers out tonight," Veronica replies as she holds the screen door open for us.

"Yourself included, I'm sure, city girl," I jab again.

"Oh, it's on, Soph. You'd better watch it."

"Bring it, chica. I've got four months of pent-up ornery to get out this weekend."

Amanda giggles and lightly punches me in the arm as we head inside.

"Are you hungry? Rose made your favorite."

"She didn't!" Amanda gasps in disbelief as she bounces up the stairs and into the cabin. "Now I'm really excited!"

We are welcomed by the scent of dinner the first step into the cabin.

"Oh my goodness, that smells divine!" Amanda announces as she rushes into the kitchen and throws her arms around Rose.

"I made it just for you, dear. I'm so glad you are here."

"It is my favorite! Thanks, Rose."

"You are most welcome," she says as she winks Amanda's way. "Where's my Veronica?"

"Here I am," she says as she comes in for a hug. "So good to see you, Rose."

"Oh, I have missed you. You know, you can always come and join us for a weekend in the winter even if you don't fish," Rose says wryly.

"Jeez, you too? You and Sophie are on a roll tonight. Guess I'd better be on my toes this weekend."

"Indeed, you should," Rose replies with just the right amount of sass. "Supper is ready. Who's hungry?"

All three of us raise our hands like school girls, and Rose immediately ladles out bowls of stew for everyone. Amanda instinctively slices the French bread while I fill water glasses and set them on the table. Veronica retrieves a few bottles of wine from her car, and we all sit down for the start of our weekend together. After a nice glass of red is placed in front of each of us, Rose clinks her fork against her glass and stands.

"Ladies, a toast. To three of my favorite women I share my life with, thank you for coming this weekend. Here's to a weekend full of love, laughter, and tight lines."

In true tradition, we all chime in, "We got this!" We smile and raise our glasses to begin our wonderful weekend together.

`·.¸¸.·´¯`·.¸¸>´´)><(((º>`·.¸¸.·´¯`·..·><((((º>`·.¸¸.·´¯`·..

Melody

I don't remember the last time I saw the sun. You know, that big orange fiery thing in the sky? Yeah, that sun. I have photographed more nightclubs and restaurants in the last two months than I care to admit. Being out all night, sleeping during the day, and then processing pictures on the computer for hours at a time does not bode well for a nice suntan.

I fucking love photography. I really do. I shoot in nightclubs and concert venues mainly—bands, performers, venues, dancers, groupies, and for publications. I like to shoot specialty clubs and bands, everything from reggae to Latin to Asian punk. I sell my work online and do mainly freelance work. I get paid okay for it. I basically make enough money to cover the new camera gear I want. That shit is as expensive as cocaine, and the addiction is just as bad. My grandparents are loaded and paid for my downtown loft, so I don't have living expenses, just the monthly association fees, which aren't that much. I like the club scene: it's fun, the music is loud, and the reverberation of the bass pulses through my veins. I like the challenge of shooting in an environment that is emotional and *alive*. Nightclubs are difficult to shoot and that's another reason I like it. You can't hear jack shit, people are always banging into you, the lighting is terrible, and I'm a tiny Asian chick, a little on the

Goth side, who people often don't take seriously. I have to be aggressive to get the shots I want.

Music creates community. It unites people of all walks of life; young, old, rich, poor, gay, straight, white, black, brown, and everything in between. The self-expression of dance with any kind of music brings out sensuality, and with that sensuality comes heat. The heat in the room, the heat of the moment, the heat of the people dancing to the music, and the warm rush of satisfaction knowing I just nailed a shot. When I'm in the moment working the camera angles and capturing those emotions and expressions at the exact right time, something magical happens. In my head I'm always thinking about light and movement, movement and light. I bounce to the beat of the music waiting for the perfect timing, where the artist or dancer might be frozen for a mere millisecond so I can catch the shot without blur. I start to memorize the hand motions of the DJ so I know the precise moment to click my shutter to get the best shot. I study a couple and the way they move with one another on the dance floor so I can capture the perfect glance, look, or expression. I love being able to narrate the night through my creative process. I get a little high just thinking about it.

Photography can be a very solitary profession, which is one of the reasons I love it. I love my solitude, and the less interaction I have with other humans the better. I usually take pictures by myself and then process photos at my computer. Very little interaction with others is necessary to be a good photographer, especially if one does landscape or still life photography. Even when I'm shooting people at a night club, I don't have to interact with them much. It's amazing the distance that a simple camera can put between you and your subjects. You can be in a crowd of several hundred people, and no one will speak to you if you are holding a serious camera. I find that fascinating. Plus, it's usually too loud to have a conversation anyway. Unless I'm in a Goth crowd— then I blend in and more people approach me. They aren't

42

scared of me like most of the general population. I love my tats and piercings, but I think a lot of people are scared of me.

Lately there has been enough happening in the Denver downtown nightlife that I have been out most every night for the last several months. It's starting to wear on me, and I need a change of scenery. Shit, if I see one more strobe light or black light, I might slit my wrists. I'm in need of some serious Vitamin D sun therapy. I'm headed up to Salida tomorrow to drop off some of my prints to an art gallery where I showcase and sell my work. I'm staying over for the music festival going on this weekend as well. With the vampire life I lead, I sometimes forget how beautiful it is outdoors. I may even attempt a few outdoor, nude self-portraits along the way. I need some variety in my view finder before I fall into a photographic slump.

`·.¸¸.·´¯`·.¸.><((((º>`·.¸¸.·´¯`·.¸.><(((º>`·.¸¸.·´¯`·.¸.

Amanda

I wake to the smell of bacon and fresh-brewed coffee wafting into my room. Who needs an alarm clock when you have bacon? A warm smile washes over my face as I bury myself a little deeper under the cozy, weightless cloud of warmth that is my down comforter. I stretch awake and look at the alarm clock: 8:00 a.m.! Holy crap! I slept for nine full hours! Unbelievable. I actually cannot remember the last time this happened. I feel invincible. I bet I will feel even more invincible once I consume some bacon . . .

I roll over and check my phone. *Good, no 9-1-1 texts from Grandma.* I resist the urge to call and check on the kids, knowing they are in great hands. This weekend is supposed to be my me-time. Although it's still hard not to think about my babies 24-7.

I step into my slippers, wrap a quilt around myself, and shuffle wearily into the kitchen. Rose is in the kitchen making her ritual: two eggs over easy and bacon. Lucky for me, she makes enough to share.

"What's shakin', bacon?"

"Good morning, dear," Rose says sweetly. "I heard you rustling around, so I took the liberty of starting your hazelnut latte."

"Rose, you are a goddess. Why haven't you moved in with Mike and me? I could get used to lattes on demand."

"Well, if I ever become homeless, I'll keep your offer in mind. Until then, cheers," she says as we clink our coffee cups together.

I take my first sip and the flavors explode on my taste buds. "Perfection, Ms. Rose. I don't know how you do it."

"*Ms.* Rose? I thought school ended yesterday, *Ms.* Amanda," she jokes.

"Sorry, sometimes it's hard to shut my teacher brain off. Give me a few more sips of this awesome coffee and I'll start to wake up." We both smile and she gives me an affectionate nod.

I take another sip and the warmth surges through my veins. The bold aroma has notes of roasted hazelnuts, coffee beans, and a hint of last night's campfire. It goes down with a milky smoothness that causes me to close my eyes, tilt my head back, and get lost in the moment. *Ahh . . . Starbucks should take some lessons and learn to bottle what Rose has got going on here. It is complete perfection.*

"Where's Sophie and Veronica?" I ask as I slurp down another sip.

"They are already on the water. Both of them were up before dawn to get a good start to the day. They are just downriver a bit, so they aren't far."

"Well crap, why didn't you wake me?"

"Because you haven't had a full night's sleep since Mike left, and I'm pretty sure you needed the rest. Take your time and take care of yourself a little bit, the fish will wait."

Rose has this wry smile that she gives when, once you've seen it, you know she's right and there is no room for argument.

"Thanks, Rose." I say as I give her a hug. "It's nice to have someone take care of me for a change."

"You're welcome. Now here, eat some breakfast. Protein is an excellent way to start the day," she says as she motheringly hands me a full plate.

"Yes, *Mom*." I shove a full piece of bacon into my mouth.

`·.,  ,·´¯`·., ><((((º>`·.,  ,·´¯`·..><((((º>`·.,  ,·´¯`·..

After breakfast and dishes I pull out my apparel for the day. I always follow the "layering rule" when planning to be outside standing in a river all day. Sophie, the great woodswoman, has taught me well. *Always wear two pairs of socks, the first layer polypropylene socks, the second layer wool socks.* I hear her voice echoing in my head as I dress. *Wearing liner socks underneath wool socks helps to prevent chafing since the friction is between the two pairs of socks, not between the boots and your feet.* Last fall I decided to test her theory and wore cotton socks instead of wool socks. Big mistake on my part! My feet were frozen popsicles within an hour of standing in the river. The cold temperatures of the water penetrated my waders, and I have never been more uncomfortable in my life. It took several hours by the fire for me to warm up my core. When it comes to outdoor clothing,

47

Sophie knows best. One miserable afternoon was enough to teach me that lesson.

After I put on all of my layers and my waders, I go outside to put on my boots. The air is still crisp and cool, and I shiver as I quickly slide my boots on. I am so excited to get back on the river today. The stress of our family situation has been wearing on me lately, so this distraction from the real world is a real gift. I hope I have a good day on the river so I can recharge my draining batteries.

`·.¸¸.·´¯`·.¸><((((º>`·.¸¸.·´¯`·..><((((º>`·.¸¸.·´¯`·..

Rose, DJ, and I hike down the trail in search of Sophie and Veronica. The Arkansas River Valley is so beautiful. Rose and her husband, Bob, really did find an amazing spot to build their cabin on. I feel fortunate that I stumbled upon this group of friends and look forward to every opportunity to spend time with them. After several minutes of hiking we come to a clearing and see the girls wading in the river. They are both in a wide, curving section of the river casting to different sections. Veronica seems to be very focused and relaxed. She has a big smile on her face, and you can tell she has had a good morning on the river. Sophie seems to be struggling a little bit with her cast, and you can see the frustration on her brow. We watch for several captivating minutes before we make ourselves known.

"What are they biting on?" I ask as we get within hearing range, hoping they would get my *River Runs Through It* reference.

"Don't ask me, ask Veronica. I haven't caught a damn thing all day," Sophie retorts, her voice dripping with disgust. "I can't figure out what I'm doing wrong."

She didn't.

"Flies in the air don't catch fish, Sophie. You're casting too much," Rose offers.

Sophie fires a glare back in Rose's direction, and you can tell that she knows Rose is right.

"Remember, it's timing, not strength, that produces the best cast. It looks like you are heaving that line out there. Your flies are hitting the water so hard you are probably scaring off the fish. Work on mending your line rather than recasting and see if that works," Rose coaches.

Sophie takes a big deep breath and tries to refocus herself.

Rose looks at me and winks. "We'll see if she can hear me through all of that stubbornness," she whispers my way.

I smile back and nod carefully so as not to let Sophie see that we are talking about her.

A few minutes go by and you can see the tension in Sophie's brow soften. She takes in a few long, deep breaths and resumes the motions. Her casting seems much more fluid, and her fly starts landing softly right where she wants it. She casts fewer times and works on mending her line in the water instead of recasting. You can tell she is trying to put Rose's advice into practice. It is fun to watch.

"FISH ON!" Sophie yells as her rod rapidly bends with the weight of a big fish. She starts reeling in like crazy, keeping tension on the line without pulling in too sharply.

"Well, she *was* listening! Or maybe the fish were." Rose laughs as she steps into the river to watch. DJ races up next to Rose, splashing into the water and barking in excitement as Sophie continues to reel. "Stay here, DJ, let's watch from the bank." DJ heels and whimpers with excitement.

The fish fights hard, changes direction, and races downstream. Sophie lets him run the line out so it doesn't break. The reel screams as he runs quite far before he pauses to rest and then changes direction again. Sophie feels the pause and begins reeling him back in giggling like a little schoolgirl. "Damn, this is fun!" She says as she continues reeling in. Her line slaps against her rod sending an impressive spray of water droplets all around her.

"Oh, no you don't!" Sophie screams through clenched teeth as the fish runs again and pulls the line out. She has him in the seam of the current, and it doesn't seem to be tiring him out much.

"Keep him on! Don't lose him!" I holler with excitement, a giant smile on my face, as I watch her reel in. I start praying that her line will hold and not snap under the pressure. There's nothing worse than losing a fish right as you are about to net him.

She plays the fish well, wading up and down the stream, whooping and hollering the whole time. You can tell she is in fish heaven. Eventually she plays the fish into the shallow waters and close enough to net him. Rose bounds out with her net and helps scoop him up out of the water. "We got this, Sophie!" It's a nice brown trout.

"Nice work! Look at that big guy! A fine job, dear," Rose beams as she pats Sophie on the shoulder. "He's a fat one! He's obviously been eating some stone flies lately."

"Look here for a picture!" I say as I fumble my waterproof camera out of my vest and snap a photo of them with Sophie's sixteen-inch brown trout. They lean in together and assume the "cheese" position, holding the trout up proudly.

"That will turn my frown upside down," Sophie says as she gleefully releases the fish back into the wild. "Man, I needed that. After not catching anything yesterday and seeing Veronica pull in four fish already this morning, I was starting to doubt my skills."

Rose replies, "Don't put so much emphasis on catching a fish, just enjoy yourself!"

"Well, I enjoy myself more when I actually catch some fish!" Sophie laughs back.

Rose wades back out of the stream and starts rigging up her rod to start fishing. DJ finds a spot to sun herself and lies down to take a nap after all of the excitement.

Sophie inspects her fly to make sure the knots will hold another fish and tosses the line back out in the water. She inhales a big, deep breath and casts again. I hear her quietly state, "I'll sleep much better tonight."

`·.,｣.·´¯`·.,｣.·´¯`·.,｣.·´¯`·.,><((((º>`·.,｣.·´¯`·..><((((º>`·.,｣.·´¯`·..

I scramble downstream through the brush and scout a good place to start my day. I put on my polarized sunglasses so I can see below the water's surface and try to spot any feeding fish. I scan the river from side to side and finally spot a few rainbows in the deep pool of water behind a large rock. They are hovering, just waiting for an unsuspecting morsel to float by. I step cautiously into the water careful not to let my shadow fall across these beautiful creatures.

As I tie on my new leader, I feel rusty and dull. It has been several months since I've been fishing. *Crap, what knot do I use when I connect my leader to my tippet? Oh right, the double surgeon's knot.* I'm struggling not only with retying a couple of knots but also with life itself. The past several weeks have also been rusty and dull. I am missing my spark, and I hope the stream will rekindle my fire today—my fire for teaching, for maintaining a strong long-distance relationship with my husband, for being a good mother, and also for fly fishing. It is not that I have lost the fire to fish, but rather I need to fish to add oxygen to my flames. The first match will be lit today on the Arkansas River, and hopefully it will burn long and bright.

I tie on a size 16 caddis fly that I tied over the winter. I can't wait to catch a fish on a fly I have tied myself. When I am sitting at the tying vise, I always try to imagine what type of fish I will catch with each fly I tie. I get lost in the vivid imagery and sometimes even close my eyes and watch the scene unfold in my mind. I actually remember this exact fly when I was tying it as I had to retie it after Jordan decided to "help" with this one. I stepped away from the vise for mere moments to fix Parker a bottle, and when I returned, Jordan had added a sparkly ribbon from one of her dolls to the fly. I picked her up, sat her on my lap, and let her watch me mend her addition. I backtracked to her starting point and pulled a small, silvery piece of thread from the ribbon. I began to weave this piece into the fly, and I let her do a few wraps of the thread around her glittery piece. She seemed pretty proud of herself that she had helped, and the fly actually turned out pretty good. I can't wait to teach her to fish someday.

There is too much brush along the riverbank to do a full backhanded cast. I do a quick roll cast upstream and let the fly gently float down with the current. I miss the pool with my first cast, so I pull out a little more line and cast again near the same spot. My fly floats convincingly along with the current and through the pool where I see my fish friends.

"Come on, little fellas, I know you're hungry," I say coaxingly.

My fly floats through the pool again and still no movement from the fish. I know they are there, as I can see them. I cast again, and this time I add a little action to my line. A few quick jerks to imitate a swimming bug and WHAM! The rainbow strikes and I have my first fish of the day. "Wahoo!" I scream as I start reeling this amazing creature in. He isn't that big, and much to my chagrin he doesn't put up much of a fight. I reel him in gently and snag my net off the back of my vest. I tuck my rod under my arm and scoop him up in my net. I am giddy beyond words. I have netted my first fish of the spring.

I wet my hand before picking him up so I won't damage his skin. His colorful speckled skin radiates in the sunlight. I quickly reach for my hemostats and tug the barbless hook from his pink lip. I smile as I note the silver, sparkly thread that Jordan added to this fly. I can't wait to tell her that her fly helped me catch a fish! I marvel at his colors as I measure him against my rod. A ten-inch little rainbow trout is not a bad start to my season. I bend down and hold the fish underwater and face him upstream to force the oxygen back into his system. Once he has his wits about him again, I let him go and watch him dart away. "Thank you, my fish friend." Today is already a great day.

I fish this same hole for about an hour. My fishing steadily improves and so does my confidence. It's crazy how my attitude affects my casting ability. If it feels right, my casts seem to do what they are supposed to do. If I question myself, I end up in knots. Today every third or fourth cast hangs a long time in the air and falls lightly onto the top of the water, almost without making a sound, just like it's supposed to. I catch five fish in my first hour back on the river. Not too shabby. Feeling pretty good about myself, I decide to head upstream towards the other girls. I fish the deep, eddying pools I cross as I go, thoroughly enjoying myself the entire way.

`·.,¸,.·´¯`·.,¸><((((º>`·.,¸,.·´¯`·..><((((º>`·.,¸,.·´¯`·..

Section 2: Fly Fishing in a River

"When you're fishing in a river or a stream, your fly is moving downriver with the current. You'll typically cast upstream, putting your fly upriver of the place where you think the fish are, so the fly can drift to them. The drift of your fly may take it past several good places for fish, so let it drift until it drags or gets close to you before you cast again."[iii]

River Girls: Flyfishing for Young Women
by Cecilia "Pudge" Kleinkauf

Melody

I'm looking forward to being outside today. Anytime I find myself getting into a rut or get bored with my photography, I head to the mountains. It forces me to see things differently and think outside the proverbial box. Shooting in nature has its own challenges and limitations, and not just the ones I place on myself. The terrain, the weather, the wildlife, the time of day and lighting—all of these components come into play when photographing landscapes. The great outdoors often represents a feeling of escape from the real world, so if I can capture that in a photograph, that's gold.

I have submitted some photos to a few travel and adventure magazines that have gotten published in the past. It's a kick-ass feeling to see your work sitting on the magazine rack— an excitement and satisfaction like none other. I submit a lot of my work to websites providing stock images for purchase and do fairly well with that. I also sell several prints at a few select art galleries. I enjoy the challenge of capturing wild moments of extreme outdoor action in a still photo that can take one's breath away. There is something about a beautiful scene that evokes deep emotion in people. I love being the reason behind that emotion. Outdoor photography is fun; however, one of my favorite, more underground subjects to photograph outdoors is myself.

I stumbled on an online group of girls a few years back called the Suicide Girls. Within five minutes of being on their website, I felt like I had found my long-lost best friends. These girls look like me, act like me, and seem to have the same sense of humor as me. Think 1950s pinup model meets the mainstream Goth culture. Beautiful, tatted, and pierced girls take sexy, creative nude or seminude photographs of themselves and submit them to the SG website in hopes of becoming an actual Suicide Girl. I was lucky enough to get selected a few years ago and have built quite the online fan club. I can interact as little or as much as I want with my followers, so for the secluded, loner type like me it's an absolute dream arrangement. I haven't posted any new pics in about a month, so today I'm searching for a perfect spot to meld human form into a luscious, wild landscape. I'm pretty good at combining landscape with an artistic interpretation of the human form. The hard part is that I'm the photographer and the subject, which means the shoot takes two to three times longer than it would if I had someone else photographing me. What I love about being the photographer is that I can control how other people see me. If I don't like a shot of myself, I can simply delete it and no one else ever had the chance to see it. I can hide my flaws and insecurities and control my image—at least my external image anyway. Not many people know the real me, but I pretty much control that aspect of my life as well.

Today I'm looking for the perfect spot for some nude shots— secluded, rocky terrain with the perfect number of trees, next to the river with no bugs. Outdoor photography does not always lend itself to be a comfortable naked experience. There are bugs, rocks, and other scratchy things you do not want in or around your nether regions, but I enjoy it anyway.

My early morning drive up to the mountains is pretty easy. As I get closer to the Salida area, I spot a private dirt road that seems to meander off in an interesting direction. I decide to give it a try and see if it connects to the river.

As luck would have it the winding little road leads straight to the river. I pull over right before a little bridge and park the car. Bridges make great tripod bases for my camera, but they are also right on the road, making it not as private as I would like. I get out of the car and assess the scenery. I walk downstream a bit and through a small thicket of willows. About sixty yards downstream I stumble upon a unique rock out in the middle of the river. The water is low and clear in the eddies, so my reflection is sure to be caught. It's fast and furious in the main current where the big, fat rocks are. I might have some challenges getting to the rock itself, but I'll figure that out in due time. The lighting is perfect, just a little overcast, which makes the light more natural. The spring plants and colors are just starting to manifest alongside the river, contrasting nicely with the tall pines on the opposite side of the river. I believe this spot is just perfect.

I head back to my car and open the hatchback. I start prepping my camera gear: lenses, tripod, remote camera trigger, memory cards. You can't really take decent photos of yourself with your camera wavering all over the place, so the tripod and remote trigger are pretty important pieces. I trek everything down the makeshift trail to my perfect spot. I first set the tripod up on the rocky shore line aiming directly at the big rock in the rapids. I check the settings and take a couple of test shots so I know my limitations once I'm out there. The rock has a nice curvature in it that I think will work symmetrically with the curves of my body. I have pretty good kinesthetic awareness of what will work and what won't, but trial and error is always the name of the game when you are the photographer and the subject. Seems I have the best angle and lighting from this vantage point, so I'll give it a whirl and see what I get. Normally I like to take a few test shots, just to make sure my poses look good and that the angle and lighting are working well together. I also like to check that there are no weird shadows across my face or other parts of my body, but today I'm going to have to take my chances.

After the tripod is set up, I walk down to the river and quickly glance around me to see if anyone is around. With the coast all clear I quickly undress and chart out my rock-hopping pattern to get out to the big rock. Even though I am off the beaten path a bit, I am acutely aware that I am naked. Too bad the perfect rock is not closer to the shore. I've never been one to mind getting a little bit dirty to get the best shot and in this case a little bit wet.

I look out at the big rock and watch the roaring white-water rush in front of it. My heart sinks into my stomach when I realize I will either have to wade out to the rock through this crazy white water or find another spot for my shoot. I ponder the situation for a minute and make my decision. The rock is just too perfect for this not to work, so I have to figure out a way to get out there.

I step onto the first rock and my toe dips into the water. I immediately shudder as the cold races up my body and my nipples immediately harden. *Holy shit! This water is fucking cold!* The little voice in my head starts screaming at the top of her lungs. *This is going to SUCK! Am I sure I want to do this?* I feel the cold mist graze my skin causing massive goose bumps to crawl all the way up both legs. I try to shake it off and convince myself that this is the right thing to do. *At least I will be properly nipped out for the photo shoot.* I giggle. One less thing to prep before the trigger, no tweaking required.

Maybe I should find a new rock. Honestly, this is the first place you looked. Surely there's another rock that will work along this river somewhere. Looking up into the sky and assessing what soft, morning light I have left, I know otherwise. I tell my little voice to shut the fuck up and just do it. *Don't be such a wuss and get your ass out there!*

I slowly ease both feet into the water and feel the cold, round river rocks below my feet. *So. Damn. Cold!* I'm careful to hold my remote trigger for my camera above my head so it does not get wet. I would hate to get all the way out there and then not have my trigger work. I place each foot carefully before transferring my weight. The current is very strong as it pounds against my legs. I look down and see my skin turn an instant red before my eyes. It takes full concentration with each step to maintain my balance. I swear this is the coldest water that has ever lapped my thighs. My toes are numb and the cold of the water is getting painful. *Oh my God, I have to get out of this water!* I quicken my pace in my final steps and finally make a bold leap onto the rock. Success!

I brush the loose gravel off the top of the rock and try to find a comfortable spot to sit. I shudder as my naked bum meets the cold rock beneath it. Once seated I hug my knees to my chest and rock back and forth trying to absorb the sun's warm rays. I attempt to massage some warm blood back into my toes as I sit and think about my shoot for a few minutes. When I finally feel a little warmer, I start posing and begin my shoot. *Okay, Melody, work it . . .*

For some shots I stare right at the camera. Others I stare off into the sky for more of a profile view. I experiment with several different poses and angles, accentuating my best assets and hiding my flaws. I'm always careful to show the woman's body as an artful, beautiful work, not as something perverted or anything that would be considered soft porn. I firmly believe there is a difference. I feel myself slip into the hypnotic zone I get into when I am the subject of my own work. I want to be captivating and intriguing, sexy and vulnerable, yet convey strength and passion. I slither and shift in every way I can think of as I capture each moment on film. I disguise the remote trigger discreetly with each shot. I pose and shoot for about thirty minutes and work every

61

angle that this rock can possibly offer. Feeling pretty good about what I have done, I sit and ponder my icy baptism back into the river to get back to shore. I hope my camera settings are still the way I originally set them, because I am *not* wading out to this rock ever again. Feeling finished with the shoot, I stand to determine the quickest and safest route back to shore.

Deciding I am finished with my remote trigger, I heave it over onto shore. No need to risk getting it wet and it's one less thing to worry about. I'm worried enough about wading through this rapid to get back on solid ground. I note its exact location and begin to lower myself back into the water. *Holy shit, this is so cold!*

Suddenly I hear a loud burst of laughter come from downriver. *What the fuck?* Catching me off guard, my foot slips and I unexpectedly plunge into the icy, rapid stream. The strong current sweeps me downstream, and I am unable to regain my footing. *Shit!*

`·.¸¸.·´¯`·.¸><((((º>`·.¸¸.·´¯`·..><((((º>`·.¸¸.·´¯`·..`

Amanda

Every once in a while Rose gets a certain look in her eye, an ornery look. And once you see it, you know that someone is about to get it.

"Psst, Amanda! Watch this."

She picks up a small pebble and tosses it in the river right in front of Sophie, who's facing the other direction. Sophie snaps her head around quickly when the tiny splash makes a gurgle in the river. Sophie strains her eyes trying to catch a glimpse of the fish that she thinks just rose to the surface. Rose quickly turns the other way and giggles under her breath. Sophie casts to the exact spot where the pebble landed. One, two, and three casts to that very spot. You can almost *feel* Sophie *willing* that fish to take her fly. A few minutes pass and Rose picks up another pebble and tosses it a little bit behind Sophie, who whirls in the direction of the splash and whips her line to the new location. The look of determination on Sophie's face is fierce. Come hell or high water, Sophie is going to land this imaginary, hungry fish.

Veronica, waist deep in the water upriver from Sophie, tunes in to what is happening and is now in on the joke. "He's there somewhere. You can do it!" she falsely encourages. We all choke down laughter as best as we can. I feel like one of my fifth graders giggling in class and trying not to get caught. I actually have to cross my legs so I won't pee my pants.

Then Rose picks up a giant rock, lifts it straight up over her head and hurls it right in front of Sophie. Kersploosh! The water spray from the heavy rock sends a tidal wave of water right into Sophie's face. She lets out a blood-curdling holler as the icy water invades her soul. We all fall on the ground screaming in uncontrollable laughter. Realizing she had just been had and that we are all in on it, Sophie sprints out of the water, screaming and crazy-eyed. "I'm going to get you, Rose!" she screams as she beelines it straight for Rose and tackles her to the ground. They both roll over onto their backs and laugh until they cry. We lie there for a few minutes just giggling and enjoying the moment. God, I love Rose.

All of a sudden DJ starts barking wildly and rushes the river. Confused, we look around and wonder what is wrong. A panicked scream pierces the air.

"What the hell?" Sophie says as she rapidly sits up and looks upstream.

"Help!" the girl screams. "PLEASE HELP ME!"

We all look upstream to see a girl getting tossed and turned by the rapid current. She screams out another desperate cry for help. "Somebody help me!"

"Holy shit, there's someone in the water!" Sophie yells. "Quick, someone grab her!"

"Oh no," Rose exclaims as her hand rushes to cover her mouth. She immediately starts rocking back and forth as she continues to repeat, "no, no, no, no." over and over again.

We all jump up and race out into the river. Veronica is already knee-deep in the stream in her waders.

"Veronica, there's someone in the water! Grab that girl as she comes near you!" I yell in a panic as I see this poor woman being swept downstream, struggling against the current.

Veronica heaves her rod onto shore and lunges out with an outstretched hand towards the girl.

"Here, grab my hand!" Veronica shouts. The woman's eyes look like a deer in the path of an oncoming train as she flails about trying to maneuver closer to Veronica.

"That's it . . . almost there . . . you can do it . . . gotcha!" Veronica coaches as she firmly grips the woman's hand. Veronica quickly jerks her out of the current and pulls her closer to shore.

"Jesus, you're naked!" Sophie yells out as she escorts her out of the water.

We all rush out to her and hold her by the arms and help her stand. The girl is finally able to get her feet planted underneath her and she stands up out of the water.

"Sophie, take off your fleece jacket and get it on her," I exclaim as we quickly get her onto shore. Her small limbs were turning purple from the cold water. "Does anyone have any extra shoes or pants?"

"Here, rip this open," Sophie barks as she pulls something out of her fishing vest. "It's one of those plastic rescue blankets. We can wrap it around her to get her back to the cabin."

"Are you okay? Can you talk?" Veronica asks.

"Yes," the girl says slowly, her teeth chattering wildly.

"We've got to get her back to the cabin quickly and get her warmed up before hypothermia sets in," Sophie instructs, her outdoor skills coming into play. "Who knows how long she's been in the water. Quick, let's go!"

"She's bleeding," I exclaim, having noticed a small gash on her forehead. "There, above her eye."

"Shit," Sophie yells as she stops and looks at the girl's face. "It's not a bad cut. Let's get her back to the cabin and we can get it taken care of there."

We all start bustling about, grabbing gear and helping the poor girl walk. In all of the chaos I look around and notice Rose still sitting on the bank in the same exact spot where Sophie tackled her. Her hand is still clasped over her mouth, and her skin has turned a pale, ghostly color. She is just staring out into the river with a lost look on her face. DJ is nestled up next to her with her head resting on Rose's leg.

"Rose? Are you okay?" I ask as I softly approach her.

She doesn't respond, she just sits and stares blankly out at the river, shaking her head back and forth.

"Rose, what's wrong? Are you okay?" I ask again, my worry growing with each moment.

Again, nothing. She just sits and shakes her head back and forth.

"Rose? You are scaring me. Are you okay?" Tears start to prick the corner of my eyes. I have never seen my friend like this.

"Run along, Amanda. DJ and I will follow in a bit," she says solemnly, not looking in my direction at all.

"Are you sure? Can I help?" I really don't want to leave my friend in this state.

"I said run along," she snaps back.

I wince, as I have never heard Rose use a tone like this before. A bit stunned, I turn to Sophie and Veronica, and shrug. They shake their heads, indicating they don't know what is going on either. Each of them grabs one of the girl's arms and help her walk down the trail to the cabin. I scoop up as much gear as I possibly can and start up the trail after them. I turn once again to check on Rose, and she is still sitting in the same spot. Fear sweeps over me, and I decide to linger behind and wait to see what happens. I wait down the trail and out of sight to give her some space. I can still see her as she sits quietly on the riverbank. Suddenly, she buries her face in her hands and a sob erupts from her chest. I'm not sure what is going on, but it doesn't look good.

`·.¸¸.·´¯`·.¸><(((º>`·.¸¸.·´¯`·..><((((º>`·.¸¸.·´¯`·..

Veronica

The rushed walk back to the cabin is a little awkward. We try to make small talk with the girl to ease the weirdness.

"Are you hurt? Is anyone else with you?" Sophie asks.

"No, I'm fine." The chattering in her teeth subsides some as we rush her down the trail. The rescue blanket makes a loud, crinkling sound with every hurried step we take.

"What were you doing out in the river?" I ask.

"I just . . . I just fell in upstream," she replies as she shakes her head.

"What happened?" Sophie asks as she leads the way up the trail. She holds back the branches of the reeds as we pass by them so they don't snap the girl's legs.

"I was just taking some pictures upstream." Her teeth were still chattering like crazy. "Sorry . . . sssomething caught me off guard and I ssslipped on a rock and fell in."

"Where's your camera?" I ask.

"Um, hopefully ssstill on my tripod on the bank. I need to get back there and sssecure my gear."

"You need to get warmed up first. Hypothermia is nothing to mess with," Sophie suggests as she helps the girl hop over a downed tree. "Were you naked when you fell in or did the river rip your clothes off?" Sophie asks, looking for more clarifying details.

"Um . . . well . . . I was naked when I fell in," the girl replies sheepishly.

Sophie's mouth actually drops open as she shoots me a *what-the-hell?* look. "I see . . . um . . . and . . . and you were by yourself?"

"Yes."

Our pace quickens as the awkwardness increases. "What were you doing?"

"Just taking some pictures," she says, obviously leaving out some major details.

"Oh . . . I see," Sophie replies. Without much tact she utters back, "Actually, no, I don't see it. What the hell were you doing?"

"I was taking nude photos of myself," the girl replies rather directly.

"Ah, okay, now I get it. I think . . . well . . . a little, okay, maybe not," Sophie stammers.

Shooting Sophie a *pull-it-together* look, I ask, "Is this part of your job?"

"Kinda. It's not a big deal. I post the pictures online and people pay to see them," the girl explains.

"Oh," Sophie murmurs back with a confused look on her face, struggling to make sense of what she is hearing.

Unable to control myself I blurt out, "I'm sorry, WHAT?! What kind of site is this?"

"I'm a model for an online group of nudes. It's called the Suicide Girls. It's a pretty cool site actually."

"Suicide Girls? Why are you called the Suicide Girls?" I ask.

"The founder goes by the name Missy Suicide."

"Oh," Sophie murmurs again, still trying to figure out what to make of this girl.

"Can you tell us your name?" I ask, realizing we haven't even asked this yet.

"Melody."

"I'm Veronica, this is Sophie."

The girl gives a slight nod of acknowledgment. "Thanks for rescuing me. Sorry to intrude."

"No worries. I'm just glad I was out in the river when you floated by."

"Me too. I also hit my head on a rock when I fell in, so I was a little disoriented at first."

"That must be where you got that gash over your eye," Sophie says as we near the cabin. Melody reaches up and touches the wound. "Doesn't look too bad. More of a scrape than a gash. Probably won't need stitches," Sophie determines. "Let's get you to the cabin and warmed up in a hot shower."

"Thanks. Sorry."

"Here it is," I say as we round the corner. We escort her up the steps to the cabin. "Let's get you inside. The bathroom is straight ahead." I open the door and lead the way.

She follows us into the cabin. She stops and looks around, assessing her surroundings. She rubs her hands together and blows warm air into her fingers.

"Let's get you into a hot shower. Follow me." I start the hot water and then grab some linens from the closet. "Here's a towel and a robe for when you get out. There's soap and shampoo in the shower, so help yourself."

She stands there, not saying anything.

"I'll figure out some clothes for you to change into and make you some hot tea. Any preferences?"

"Whatever. I'm not picky."

"Sophie will get the fire going again in the fireplace. We'll have you pinked up in no time," I say with a smile.

"Take a good, long hot shower to get your core warmed back up," Sophie shouts from the other room.

"She's the mother hen of the group," I say with a wink. Melody attempts a smile and nods her head.

"Need anything else?" I ask.

"No, I'm good."

"Alright, well, have a good shower." I close the door behind me.

As soon as the door is closed, I turn and shoot Sophie a crazed look and mouth, *What the hell?* to her as we both choke down the giggles. Sophie shrugs her shoulders making a clueless facial expression back at me and pulls me down the hallway. We both run back into the back bedroom, stifling down laughter. Once inside we close the door and fall on the bed laughing.

"I cannot believe we just fished a naked chick out of the river! What the hell?!" I whisper loudly. We both grab pillows and bury our faces in them to conceal the sounds of our laughter.

Doubling over, Sophie replies, "That is the craziest thing I have ever experienced!"

"Seriously! Me too! Oh my God, I know I shouldn't be laughing at this poor girl's situation, but holy hell! What just happened?"

"I have no idea! This will definitely go down in the history books as one of the funniest things I have ever pulled out of the river."

"I think I actually get credit for that since I'm the one who pulled her out."

"True, I'll let you have that one. Too bad you can't stuff it and put it on your wall!" Sophie jokes. "You going to hang it over your mantle? That will be quite the conversation piece!" she says as she bursts into her pillow.

"Oh my God, STOP! I'm going to pee my pants!" I say as I laugh uncontrollably. I bury my face in my pillow even harder to release the pent-up laughter. Sophie follows my lead, and we both lie there giggling like two school girls for several minutes.

"So what is it that she does? Photographs herself in the nude and then posts the pics online? Have you ever heard of this before?" Sophie asks.

"Um, just *PORN*." I say. "Not sure what to make of this yet. There is obviously more to the story."

"Absolutely."

"Did you see the tats on her legs? They looked pretty intense."

"I didn't see any on her legs, but I saw one crawling up her neck. Looked like some detailed work."

"Pretty interesting girl, can't wait to learn more about her," I say as I roll onto my back.

Suddenly Sophie sits up, "Wait! Where's Amanda and Rose? What was going on with Rose when we left the river?"

"Oh crap, that's right. I had completely forgotten about that. I don't know what that was about," I say as I sit up as well. "Quick, let's find something for Melody to wear and then let's go find them."

We bolt from the bed and spring into action. I grab some sweats, a T-shirt, a hoodie, and warm socks and leave them in front of the bathroom door, impossible for Melody to miss. I make a quick cup of tea and leave it on the end table next to the couch. Sophie stokes the fire in the fireplace, adds a few logs, and then quickly jots a note that says, "Went to find Rose and Amanda, be right back. Make yourself at home." We leave everything right in front of the bathroom door and then dart down the trail towards the river in hopes of finding out what is going on with Rose.

`·.,,.·´¯`·.,><((((º>`·.,,.·´¯`·..><((((º>`·.,,.·´¯`·..

We hustle down the trail in a panic.

"What was Rose doing when we left?" I ask Sophie, trying to recall the time line of events.

"Just sitting there staring off into space. She wasn't really responding to Amanda either."

"She was fine up until the girl floated down the river, right?" I ask.

"Yes, before that she played that trick on me and I tackled her on the shore," Sophie recounts.

"Oh, that's right. She was laughing hysterically until we heard the girl scream for help. What do you think that was all about?"

"I'm not sure," Sophie says as she pauses to think a moment. "Do you think she knows someone who was drowned in the river? It looked to me like she was in shock."

"Hmm, maybe. That definitely looked like someone in shock. Maybe it drudged up an old memory for her? Ugh, I'm worried."

"Me too. I've never seen Rose like that before. She's always so in control."

"Let's approach cautiously, in case they are in the middle of something," I advise as I hold up my hand to slow our pace on the trail. As we near them, I can see Amanda sitting next to Rose on the ground. Her arm is around Rose's shoulder, and they look to be talking and in good spirits. We are too far away to hear what they are saying. We contemplate revealing ourselves when DJ suddenly notices us, barks loudly, and runs towards us.

"Hey there, girls, everything okay?" Sophie asks softly as we creep out from the bushes.

"Oh, we're fine," Rose replies, with a hint of exasperation in her voice. She lets out a big, cleansing sigh and says, "I was just telling Amanda about how Bob and I found this wonderful piece of property."

"It's a pretty cool story, maybe you can tell it again tonight over a glass of wine," Amanda says as she gives me a *she's-okay* look.

"Are you feeling okay, Rose?" Sophie asks.

"Yes, I'm fine. I just had a moment there, nothing to worry about."

"That was some moment. You sure you don't want to talk about it?" I ask, really wanting to know what was going on with her.

"No, I don't. At least not right now," she says as she pats Amanda on the leg and gives her a smile. "I'm fine, really."

"We're here for you, Rose. Whatever you need," Sophie replies.

"I know that, girls. I'm blessed to have you in my life," she says as she starts to stand. DJ rushes to her side, wagging her tail back and forth. "Let's get back to the cabin and tend to our guest."

"Everything okay with the girl?" Amanda asks, helping Rose to her feet.

"Yes, she's fine. We started a hot shower for her and made some hot tea. I left her a note telling her we would be right back, so we shouldn't be long. We were worried about you two and wanted to find out what was going on," Sophie says as she steps forward to give Rose a big hug. "You sure you're okay?"

"Yes, dear, I'm fine," Rose says as she embraces Sophie back. They embrace for several moments, and then Rose lets out a big sigh. "Let's head back and meet this naked girl."

We all laugh at the memory of Melody's nakedness.

"Why again was she naked?" Amanda asks with obvious curiosity.

"You know, doing what everybody does on a brisk Saturday morning, taking outdoor nude pictures of herself."

We all laugh out loud as Amanda blurts out, "I'm sorry, what?!"

"She's a photographer of some sort, takes nude pictures of herself, and then posts them online," I say, giving what little information I have out to the girls. "We didn't get a lot of details."

"I'll never forget the look on Sophie's face when she realized the girl was naked. So funny!" Amanda blurts out laughing.

"That is the weirdest thing that has ever happened to me! It's crazy enough that we pull someone from the river, but the nakedness totally threw me off."

"Well, that was obvious," Amanda adds sarcastically.

"Veronica gets credit for the biggest catch of the day," Sophie sings out.

"Woo hoo!" I reply as I fist pump into the air. "Rose, do you have a patch for that?"

"Oh girls, you make me laugh," Rose exclaims. "I may have to create a new patch just for this!" It is good to see her smiling.

"Let's head back," Sophie says, leading the way.

`·.,,.·´¯`·.,><(((°>`·.,,.·´¯`·..><(((°>`·.,,.·´¯`·..

Melody

This hot shower feels freaking amazing.

I stand and let the warm, steamy water pour over my cold, purple body. I lean down and put the drain stopper in the bottom of the enormous claw-foot tub to allow it to fill as the hot shower water rained down on me.

So fucking stupid. Can't believe I did that.

My red, frozen toes need some constant warmth to recirculate the blood to my extremities. I squat down and hug my knees to my chest, much like I did earlier today when I was trying to warm myself on the rock in the river.

Thank God these women were out fishing in the river when I fell in. Who knows what would have happened to me had they not been there.

I wiggle my toes and cringe at the sharp pains shooting through them. The painful pins-and-needles feeling subsides within a few minutes.

I'd probably have hypothermia by now if this cabin wasn't so close by.

I catch a glimpse of my reflection in the water. I slap the top of the filling bath water with my hand thinking of my foolishness for falling in. *What were you thinking?* My inner voice screams at my strong-willed independence. *Such a stupid move wading through that rapid to get to that rock. So fucking stupid.*

I take a few deep, cleansing breaths and shake my head at the crazy events of my day so far. *Damn perfectionist photographer . . . I know what I was thinking. I was thinking that I was losing my best chance at natural lighting for the day, that's what I was thinking. One of these days my risky decisions are going to get me killed.* I punch the side of the tub in frustration.

I rise and stand in the shower for another twenty minutes before I finally start to feel the hot water turn lukewarm. Still pissed at myself, I turn the antique knobs to the off position and pull the stopper to drain the very full tub. I carefully step out onto the cushy floor mat and grab a rolled-up white towel from an old barrel laid on its side. I begin to dry off and then wipe the fog from the large antique mirror hanging on the wall. I stare at myself for a few moments. *You're fuckin' lucky.*

Irritated with my reflection, I look away and pull on the soft, terry cloth robe Veronica had left me. It weirdly felt like a warm hug as I slipped it on. I pulled the waist belt tight and suddenly felt like I was at a high-end spa, ensconced in luck and luxury.

I look around to get my bearings and notice the decorations. The dark hardwood floors feel warm beneath my feet. There are fresh purple flowers in an old blue Mason jar on the counter next to a picture of four ladies. I get a whiff of lavender as I pick up the frame to get a closer look at it. I recognize the two girls who brought me back to the cabin in the photo. The other two I'm assuming were the other women on the shore when they pulled me out of the river. I didn't really get a good look at them. I put the frame back on the counter and peer around the room.

Two of the walls are covered in rustic, red barn siding. The towel rack on the back of the door has hooks that are antique forks with their tines curled back into spirals. The light fixtures looked like old kerosene lanterns I've seen in the movies. There are bath salts, cotton balls, and lotions in apothecary-type jars lined up on a vintage corner shelf thing made out of old chicken wire and reclaimed wood. Oddly it made me feel at home.

As the fogged-up mirrors start to clear, I wrap my hair up in my towel and open the bathroom door. I pad out into the hallway and see a pile of clothes, a cup of tea, and a fire going in the fireplace. *Wow, this is really nice.* I see a note on the top of the pile that reads "Went to find Rose and Amanda, be right back. Make yourself at home." I take a sip of the hot tea. *Chamomile.* I plop down on the big couch in front of the fireplace. I gaze around the room and try to catch a glimpse of whoever lives here.

There are quilted blankets everywhere, neatly draped on the back of every seated surface possible. They are really done well in lots of colors. The dark hardwood floors are covered with tons of cozy, colorful rugs. The river rock fireplace stands stately against the far wall while the fire crackles and burns. There is a guitar propped up in the corner and more photos framed on the mantle. *Hmm, someone must play.* There are two antique fishing rods mounted up high on the wall of the fireplace. On the walls are various fishing signs, my favorite reading, "Fisherman's prayer: Yeah though I walk through the valley of the shadow of the lodgepole pine, I shall fear no trout, for fly art with me. Thy rod and thy reel, they comfort me." *That's funny.* I snuggle a little deeper into the couch and take another sip of tea.

After a few minutes, I decide to get dressed so I at least have clothes on the next time I see these girls. No need to be naked in front of them twice in one day. *So much for first impressions. Not that I care, but still . . .* I slip into the clothes and hang my towel and robe up in the bathroom. I wander into the living room and sit on the couch to wait for them to come back.

Suddenly I come to a quick realization that I have never felt this at home even in my own apartment. A strange sensation surges through my veins as I acquaint myself with this feeling of being "comfortable." I feel lucky to have stumbled upon these women and I haven't even formally met two of them yet. *This day is proving to be very odd.*

`·.,,.·´¯`·.,><((((º>`·.,,.·´¯`·..><((((º>`·.,,.·´¯`·..

Sophie

We head back to the cabin and find Melody warming herself by the fire.

"Hey there, we're back!" Veronica announces. "Oh good, you found the clothes we left for you."

"Yes, thanks. These are great."

"Hello dear, I'm Rose," Rose says as she immediately walks over to Melody and introduces herself.

"Hi. Um, I'm Melody."

"And I'm Amanda," Amanda yells out from across the room.

"Welcome, Melody. You gave us quite a scare back there. Are you okay?" Rose asks her.

"Yes. Sorry. Thank you for helping me."

"Well, it was Sophie and Veronica with all of the manners this time. Did they take good care of you?"

"Yes, they were great."

"Good girls," she says to Veronica and me as she shoots us both an approving eye.

"Thanks *Mom*," I tease back.

"Oh, you hush," Rose sparks back towards me, then turns back to Melody. "Are you hungry, Melody? We were just talking about having an early lunch and then getting back out on the water. These big ole dumb trout haven't seen my tasty flies in too long. It's time they got reacquainted." Rose laughs at her own humor. It's pretty cute to watch.

"A few of them got to meet you yesterday, might I remind you," I toss out.

She puts both hands up in the air and exclaims, "I need to meet his friends! Is that too much to ask?" We all laugh at her silliness.

"Who's making lunch?" Veronica asks.

"I made breakfast, you're on lunch," I tell her.

"Leftovers it is!" she announces.

"Laziness! Do you do this to Thatcher?" I say as I wash my hands in the kitchen sink. Everyone starts bustling about pulling out plates and cups and anything else needed for a quick lunch.

"Girrrl, we have an awesome arrangement: he cooks, I clean. I'm a rock star at reheating."

"You are so lucky! With Mike overseas I cook *and* clean," Amanda chimes in as she makes a pitcher of lemonade.

"Yeah, V is spoiled. She's the *only* one here who doesn't have to cook. The rest of us girls bring home the bacon *and*

84

fry it up in a pan," I say as I pull the leftover stew from the fridge and pour it into a microwave safe bowl.

"And then do the dishes," Amanda mutters. "I hate dishes!"

"Girls, do I need to implement a chore chart? Because I'll do it!" Rose teases as she sets the table with five place settings.

"Is there a 'Does Dishes' patch, Rose?" Veronica questions. "'Cause I would rock that patch."

"Sounds like I have several new patches to design for this summer," Rose adds.

I put the bowl in the microwave and give DJ a dog treat. "Melody, Rose gives us patches for different things like we are in Girl Scouts. I'm most famous for earning the River Rat patch."

"Oh, I love it when you earn that patch. Means you went for a swim!" Rose says as she laughs. "If Melody would have had a hat on today, she might have earned that patch herself!"

We all awkwardly pause and giggle since Melody had *no* clothes on let alone a hat. "To earn the River Rat patch you have to fall in the river but retain your hat," I tell her, not wanting her to feel left out.

"Maybe next time," she says as she looks away, a hint of embarrassment in her voice.

"You have to be on your toes around this group. Guests are not immune to being the butt of our jokes," Rose informs her as she pats DJ on the head.

"Good to know," Melody says as DJ runs over to her, finally realizing there is someone new in the room.

"This is DJ, she's the real queen of this cabin," Rose announces.

DJ immediately greets Melody by shoving her nose right into her crotch.

"DJ! Cut that out," Rose scolds. "Where are your manners? You can say hi without doing that. So sorry."

"That's okay. At least I have my clothes on this time."

We all bust out in a little giggle at the obvious elephant in the room. Secretly I'm glad she is bringing it up so the awkwardness doesn't double in size.

"Sorry about the, uh, state in which you found me earlier today. It definitely was not in my plan to fall in the river," she says somewhat sheepishly as she looks down at the ground. She leans down and gives DJ a good rubdown.

"Oh, it's okay," I reassure her. "Don't worry about it at all. We've all been skinny-dipping at some point in our lives, right, Rose?" I say as I shoot her a knowing look.

"Sophie Myers! You shut your mouth!" Rose playfully fires back at me. "No need to tell stories on me in front of our guest!"

"She'll learn all on her own in due time. She just needs to know she's in good company," I inform her with a playful tone.

"Girl, you have no idea what you just fell into. Welcome to the club," Veronica says as she pulls out a chair for Melody to sit in.

Amanda leans in towards Melody and whispers, "They're harmless, don't let them scare you."

Melody takes her seat with a bewildered yet comfortable look on her face, soaking us all in. The microwave ding pierces the air, and Veronica scoots across the kitchen and pulls the steamy bowl out.

"Look! I did it all by myself," she proudly announces as she holds up the bowl.

"Oh, whatever, V," I lightheartedly fire her way. "Just dish it out."

"Oh, I plan to, Soph. You just wait," Veronica sparks back with just the right amount of attitude.

"Ladies, are manners a lost art around here?" Rose says as she takes her seat.

Taking the seat next to her, I lean over and give her a big zerbert on her cheek. "Apparently so!" Everyone erupts in laughter.

"Cheese and Rice! Sophie, cut that out!" Rose yells loudly.

"No swearing at the table, Rose!" Veronica roars from across the table, shaking wildly with laughter.

Amanda leans over to Melody again and whispers, "That's how Rose says Jesus Christ when she wants to swear."

"Lord, what kind of hooligans have I invited up here this weekend?" Rose says as she wipes Sophie's spit off her cheek, everyone still giggling uncontrollably. "Melody, you might want to get out now."

The girl smiles and says, "Noted."

"Well, I obviously have no control over the maturity level of this group, so enter at your own risk," Rose says as she sticks her tongue out at me.

I lift my lemonade and proclaim, "To never growing up!"

"Hear, hear!" everyone exclaims as they each clink a glass with someone near them. The giggling finally starts to subside, and everyone ends with an audible sigh of laughter overload.

"Can you pass the bread, Soph?" Amanda asks.

"Sure thing," I instinctively reply and pick up the basket of bread.

"What flies were you guys using earlier today? I caught a nice brownie on a number 12 Parachute Adams," Amanda says as she takes the bread from me.

"I'm using nymphs and dries, just because I can," Veronica says as she inhales a big bite of stew.

"Nymphs?" Melody asks, with obvious surprise in her voice.

"Yeah, nymphs. Like insect nymphs. Not nymphos, like nymphomaniacs, that's a very different kind of fishing."

Everyone explodes in laughter again, and Amanda spits her mouthful of food across the table, all over my shirt. "Ew! What the hell?" I exclaim. "Amanda!"

"Sorry! Jeez, so sorry!" she says as she jumps up and attempts to wipe up the mess. "Serves you right, madam comedian!"

Everyone doubles over in laughter, unable to control themselves.

"What? There *is* a very big difference in the two," I reply, still wiping off my shirt.

"Pull it together, girls," Rose exclaims. "Our guest will never want to visit again with all of these shenanigans."

"Shit! My camera gear!" Melody screams out as she leaps up from the table. We all freeze in place at the tone of her voice. "My camera gear is still on the side of the river! Shit! I have to go." She hurriedly leaves the table, looking for something.

"How far is it? Do you want me to drive you?" Veronica asks, wiping her mouth and getting up from the table.

"Fuck, where are my keys?" she says as she continues to look around. "Dammit! They are with my camera gear!"

"I can drive you. Come on. We'll find it," Veronica says as she heads out the front door.

"Fuck, thank you. I mean, shit. Sorry. I'd love a ride. I have no idea how far it is. It was by a little bridge?" she recalls, trying to remember the details.

"Oh, Old Man Hagerty's bridge. I know right where that is," Veronica replies. "It's not far at all. Come on, let's go." And out the door they went.

The rest of us sit for a few seconds in silence and smile at each other across the table. As soon as my eyes meet Amanda's, we both bust out in laughter again. This is seriously the oddest, most fun day I have had in a long time. I can't wait to see what the rest of the weekend brings! I let out a big, fulfilling, breathy sigh and shake my head in disbelief of the morning events thus far.

`·.,¸,.·´¯`·.,><((((º>`·.,¸,.·´¯`·..><((((º>`·.,¸,.·´¯`·..

Section 3: Little Rivers

"For me, the jewels of the outdoor experience are the little rivers. The famous, broad rivers that we fish and then brag about are big and public, like the face we show to others. Though we can get to know a small section of such a river pretty well, we can leave it feeling somewhat dissatisfied or lost.

Little rivers, brooks, and streams, on the other hand, are easy and intimate, the flip side of the fishing experience, the private world. They feel safe."[iv]

Little Rivers, Tales of a Woman Angler
by Margot Page

Veronica

We easily found Melody's gear and were back at the cabin gearing up to get back on the water.

"Okay, girls. I only get a few weekends to fish this summer, so I'm not wasting it sitting in this cabin. Let's get back out there!" I announce, ready to hit the river again. I tighten up my boots, grab my rod and get ready to head down the trail. "Melody, you are welcome to join us. We are bona fide gear whores and have plenty to share."

"Whoa, who you callin' a whore?" Sophie playfully yells back as she pulls on her waders. "Takes one to know one."

"If the boot fits . . ." I spark back. "Exactly how many pairs of fishing boots do you have?"

Sophie stands and puts her hands on her hips. "Hey, a girl needs options, ya know."

"Um, I'll just watch today. Maybe I'll take some pictures if you don't mind."

"Oh, Melody, that would be splendid," Rose replies as she bends down and pats DJ on the head. "What are your plans for this week? Do you have a job to get back to?"

"No, I set my own hours, so I can head back whenever I want."

"Well, I plan to stay here all week. You are welcome to stay and I can give you a few fishing lessons if you'd like." DJ smiles from ear to ear as Rose gives her a good rubdown.

"Oh wow. Uh, okay," Melody replies, checking the settings on her camera. "I'm so glad my camera and tripod were still there, completely untouched. I can't tell you how freakin' lucky I am." There is obvious relief in her voice. "This shit is expensive," she says, as she holds up her camera.

"So is this," Sophie exclaims, as she holds up her custom titanium rod and reel. "We're sorry in advance if you end up falling in love with this sport. It's not cheap!"

"Hey, you can do everything on the cheap if you want to," Amanda adds. "I have a similar outfit that you do and I didn't pay near what you did."

"Yeah, but you are the luckiest garage-saler I have ever met! I stand corrected. But seriously, buying this stuff retail can be crazy expensive."

"Craigslist and garage sales are your friend!" Amanda calls out. "You just have to be patient."

"I can be a patient fisher, but I lack serious self-control when it comes to buying new toys," Sophie adds.

I really have to hand it to Amanda. She and her husband don't have a lot of money, but you would never know it. She is the thriftiest person I know and is always on the lookout for the best deal. Her kids are dressed to the nines, yet she doesn't spend much on them at all. She's a huge garage sale shopper and finds designer brands for twenty-five cents apiece. She scored big time on her fly fishing gear at a garage sale. The lady was going through a divorce and sold her soon-to-be ex-husband's entire fly fishing outfit for mere pennies. He must have been a small man because his gear fit Amanda's little frame perfectly. I think she actually has nicer gear than I do, and I spent well over $1,500 for my full outfit. I think she spent eighty dollars total. I'm so happy she found that sale. I could always tell she felt self-conscious about borrowing gear from us before she had her own. Not that any of us cared. We all have way too much gear and plenty to share, but her attitude and spirits definitely rose once she had her own stuff.

"Okay, girls, are we ready?" I ask, really wanting to get back on the water.

"I think so. If I forgot anything, I'm sure Sophie will have extras," Amanda says. "She always has enough gear on her for three people."

"Hey! I'm prepared for anything!" Sophie replies.

"Melody, see that backpack there? It's full of ibuprofen, toilet paper, extra flies, sunscreen, water bottles, and the kitchen sink," I say, giving Melody a few more details about my friend Sophie.

"I'll remember this teasing the next time you need toilet paper, V," Sophie teases back.

Attaching my net to the back of my vest I reply, "You know you leave it on the bank when you're fishing, right? It's not like it's under lock and key."

"So now you're a thief and a whore? Wow, you are making quite the first impression on our guest," Sophie says with a chuckle.

Ignoring her comment I giggle back, "Are you ready to fish yet? I'm tired of waiting on you."

"I've been ready for five minutes!" she says as she starts down the trail, rod in hand. DJ darts past her like a lightning bolt down the trail.

Amanda picks up her gear and walks over to Melody. "They're just playing with each other, they love each other like sisters."

"Yeah, I can tell," Melody replies as she puts her camera strap around her neck and starts to follow them down the trail.

"Don't let them scare you off," Amanda adds.

"Okay."

"Let's see if the caddis are going to hatch today. It feels about the right temperature," Rose announces as she heads down the trail. "And remember, we got this."

Walking down the trail we look like we had just walked out of a giant fishing store. Everyone is decked out in muted tans and greens in every brand name available on the market. Fortunately for us, the fly fishing gear manufacturers have finally figured out that women have different gear needs than men do, and we'll spend the money to buy gear that fits. It has taken a little while for this trend to catch on, and I am thankful I have a pair of waders that fit my feet and my ass at the same time and not one or the other.

We hike downriver much farther than where we were this morning. I hadn't fished one of my favorite holes yet this trip, Roosters Cove, and I am leading the way so I get to choose. We nickname each of our favorite areas near the cabin, just in case we want to fish alone. We usually leave notes for one another on our general location, just to be safe. Even though this section of the river is on Rose's private property, you never know who you might run into out in the wilderness.

Once at Roosters Cove we each spread out to give each other some space. Proper fly fishing etiquette is to give your fellow fly fishers plenty of room and not crowd their space. Tangling your line with another angler just takes time away from catching the fish.

Since our rods are already assembled and ready to go, Rose wastes no time stepping out into the river and making her first cast. Amanda heads the farthest upstream, followed by Sophie, then Rose, then myself. Melody and DJ find a spot on the bank to watch while Melody gets her tripod set up.

Within a couple of casts, Rose hooks and lands a nice brown trout. I just stand and shake my head at how easy she makes it look. She ties on another fly, casts a few more times and *boom*, another brownie hooks on. It's amazing that just a few casts in the same damn spot and she lands another big trout. Sometimes her skill renders me speechless.

Filled with fishing envy I cast my fly. My first few casts are a little sloppy. I notice Melody taking my picture out of the corner of my eye, and it makes me nervous. Suddenly I want to cast like casting champion Joan Wulff so I can have a picture-perfect cast captured on film. I glance over at Rose and watch her casting technique again for tips.

Suddenly, I have a strike myself, but the fish was gone in a flash when I didn't set the hook. I was too busy watching Rose's perfect casting that I forgot to watch my strike indicator. Pissed at myself and my lack of focus, I turn away from Rose so I won't be distracted. Thirty minutes pass and then all of a sudden, *WHAM,* I hook a heavy fish. I can feel him shaking his head against my line. Suddenly he leaps out of the water in an impressive attempt to get away.

"Keep him on, Veronica!" Rose hollers at me from upstream.

He furiously shakes his head to and fro, and my rod bends at the gratifying weight of this big boy. Suddenly he bites off my tippet with his sharp teeth and is gone.

"Damn! I wanted that fish!" I yell out, disappointed.

"We'll call that one an LDR."

"An LDR?"

"A Long Distance Release! You'll get him next time!" Rose yells out.

I smile and shake my head as I lift up my rod tip, hoping that he would still be attached to the end of my line. Sadly, the line slithers effortlessly back through the water as I reel in.

"Stupid fish," I mutter out loud to myself. No one is close enough to hear me, but there's some satisfaction in being able to say it out loud. I pick another fly from my fly box, this time a number 16 Elk Hair Caddis, and tie it on. I also tie on an emerger hoping to double up my chances. "Okay, Veronica, let's change your attitude and actually land one of these bad boys," I say out loud, not that anyone can hear me. I cast several more times, my confidence soaring as my loops do exactly what I want them to. "Yes!" I whisper with proud satisfaction. I feel my mind and body making one simple, fluid motion with each cast. I'm nowhere else but standing right here in this river.

Suddenly I see a swarm of bugs lap the top of the river. At first there are just a handful here and there. Within fifteen minutes there are swarms of them everywhere. Several fish start rising and leaping out of the water, catching mouthfuls of bugs in midair.

"Rose! Look at this!" I yell upstream.

Rose turns my way and hollers, "It's the caddis hatch!" Rose has told us stories about the famous caddis hatch, but I have never witnessed it before. She says bugs by the thousands will hatch all at the same time. So many that it will look like it's snowing with all the white tufts flitting through the air.

I look around me and the fish are now going crazy, rising and leaping out of the water feeding off the hatch. Realizing there are too many real bugs for the fish to even attempt to take my artificial fly, I stop casting and just stand in the middle of the river. Rising fish are everywhere. There have to be fifty or more fish rising all around us. I stand there in awe enjoying this National Geographic moment. I look upriver at the other girls, and they are doing the same thing, standing there mesmerized by this incredible sight.

I look over at Melody, and she is snapping picture after picture of this amazing display of events. She is beaming from ear to ear behind her lens, and I can't wait to see the pictures that she is getting.

In the span of forty minutes the hatch starts at my location and works its way upstream to where Amanda is fishing. Bursts of white tufts explode like fireworks off the water's surface every few feet, and continue to work their way upstream.

After the hatch passes, the fish are still as active as ever. I tie on flies that match the hatch that has just happened and start casting my little heart out. The other girls follow my lead, and we all start landing fish after fish after fish. We hoop and holler like a bunch of schoolgirls as we collectively catch and release at least fifty hungry trout over the next several hours. It is unlike anything I have ever experienced in my life.

Three hours later my arms finally start to fatigue, and I feel accomplished and full. I wade out of the water and sit on a big rock to rest. Melody comes over to join me.

"That was fucking cool!" She exclaims.

"I can't believe what just happened. I'm totally stunned! I have never caught that many fish in one day."

"I got a lot of great pictures of you guys," Melody says with a little excitement in her voice. It was the most emotion I have seen from her yet. "I can't wait to get home and process these."

"I hope you got some good ones. I actually don't have very many pictures of me fishing, so I'm so happy you got some. Thank you so much."

"Cool," she says. "This could be my way of saying thank you for pulling me out of the river."

"Oh, you would have done the same thing if the roles would have been reversed. I'm just glad you are okay," I say, and I squeeze her arm.

The other girls emerge from the river and come and join us by the big rock.

"I'm pooped!" Rose exclaims as she walks up to us.

"Me too!" Amanda says as she rests her rod against a tree. "I think I caught more fish today than I have caught in an entire year. That was crazy!"

"Girls, we were very blessed today. Not many fishermen get to experience the caddis hatch like we just did. She's usually very elusive. In fact, I've only witnessed a few in my forty-some years of fishing."

"Really? Wow, that surprises me," Sophie says as she takes out her water bottle and chugs half of it in a few big gulps.

"Well, if you think about it, we were in the right place at the right time. If we would have fished a different location today, we might have missed it," Rose replies.

"Good point. I'm thankful we were able to experience this today. I think this calls for a nice glass of red back at the cabin," I suggest.

"Music to my ears, dear," Rose replies as she stands up. Turning away from the rest of us, she lets out a piercing whistle that rings out across the Arkansas River Valley. Moments later, DJ bounds out of the woods and darts over to Rose.

"Good girl, DJ. Have you been out hunting squirrels?" Rose coos as she pets DJ's shiny black coat. "Great job today, girls. Let's head back."

`·.,,.·´¯`·.,><((((º>`·.,,.·´¯`·..><((((º>`·.,,.·´¯`·..

Back at the cabin we hang on the front porch as we take off our boots and waders. Rose has a rule that only fish stories are allowed inside; fishing gear is grounded to the porch. Which is just as well, no need to bring any river residue into the house. I leave my rod assembled and snap it into the rod holder attached to the cabin wall so I'm ready to go fishing first thing in the morning. The other girls follow suit, and before long we are all lounging on the couches in front of the fireplace, a glass of red in hand.

I always bring a few bottles of wine that have flies on the label each time I come to the cabin. I love shopping around for new varieties, and the girls seem to get a kick out of the names of the wines.

"Great day, ladies!" Sophie exclaims as she collapses onto the big, brown leather couch. "That is one for the record books."

Amanda sits next to Sophie. "You said it. That was awesome! I can't wait to tell Mike all about it."

"How is Mike, have you heard from him recently?" I ask, hoping it is okay to bring up the subject.

"He's doing okay. We Skyped last Wednesday and he looked pretty good. Tired, but good. The kids got to say hi to him too, so he enjoyed that."

Rose leans over and squeezes Amanda on the arm. "Oh good. It's so good that those kids get to see their dad while he is gone for so long, especially with them being so little. And his wife too. How are you holding up dear?"

"I'm okay. It's hard, but I stay strong for the kids." Her voice trails as she finishes her sentence. Then she turns to Melody. "My husband is deployed in Afghanistan right now."

"Oh wow," Melody says, as she tucks one leg underneath herself on the couch. "How long has he been gone?"

"Since February twelfth. Three months already."

"How long will he be over there?"

"He's scheduled to be there until next February, so we have about nine months to go."

"How old are your kids?"

"Parker is eighteen months and Jordan is three. They are still a little young to grasp where Daddy is, but it's still hard on them."

Sophie chimes in, "Remind me what does he do over there?"

"He's in small weapons repair, so he follows behind the front line and picks up any weapons that get dropped due to malfunction. He's not on the front line, but he's runner-up."

"Oh Amanda, that must keep you awake at night," I say. Sophie shoots me a look that seems to say I shouldn't have brought this up.

"It does. It scares the hell out of me. I don't know what I would do without him. I've never loved anyone else." A tear rolls down her cheek, and all of us well up right along with her.

"You know we're here for you, whatever you need, Amanda," I say as I walk over and give her a big hug.

"I know, thank you, V." She hugs me back, lets out a big sigh, and then proclaims, "Okay, let's change the subject. Who needs some more flies in their fly box? I brought my vise with me."

"Girrrl, you know I'll never turn down free flies."

Amanda goes back into her bedroom and brings out her fly-tying hackle and vise. She sets up shop on the coffee table in front of her and begins to work on a new fly.

"What are you making tonight?" Sophie asks her.

"Figured I had better get a few more caddis flies in my fly box after a day like today," she says as she tightens a hook into her vise.

"I used several of your flies today. I think they were good luck, Amanda!" Rose says as she takes a sip of her wine.

"Oh, thanks, Rose. That's sweet," she says as she pulls out some tan thread and matching hackle.

"How did you learn to tie flies?" Melody asks, moving over next to her to get a better look.

"Rose was my first teacher. She showed me how to tie several different patterns. I also checked out several books from the library as well." She keeps working as she's talking. The tan thread is on a special spool, and she wraps the thread up the length of the hook and then back down again. "Actually, my biggest tutor lately has been YouTube. There are how-to videos on about every type of fly out there now." She lets the thread dangle on the spool as she picks up another type of material and starts wrapping it around the long part of the hook.

"She could teach me a few lessons now with the quality of flies she can tie," Rose throws in.

"I doubt that, Rose. Don't you know everything about fly fishing?" Amanda asks.

"One will never know everything about fly fishing, dear. There is always something new to learn," Rose replies humbly.

"Wow, you are fast at that," Melody exclaims as she watches Amanda work.

"I didn't use to be. I've had a lot of practice at the vise lately," she replies as she weaves the tan thread back up the length of the hook, tightening down the elk material she's just applied. Her focus is impressive as she answers questions and ties at the same time. "When I can't sleep at night, I sit up and tie flies," she says as her voice drops.

Everyone but Melody looks around the room and gives a knowing glance at what Amanda is talking about.

"That's cool," Melody says, mesmerized by what Amanda is doing.

Amanda adds some elk hair "wings" to the fly and wraps the thread tightly around this material as well. She whips a few knots into the thread and then snips off the excess.

"Voila! An Elk Hair Caddis fly," Amanda says as she holds it up proudly.

"Nice," Melody says.

"Here, you can have this one," Amanda says, handing the fly to Melody.

"Really? Um, thank you," Melody says as she takes the fly from Amanda. She studies it intensely and a smile washes over her face.

"Stick around and you'll have a fly box full of them," Sophie chimes in. "If you buy the hackle, she'll tie the flies."

"That's the arrangement," Amanda says as she loads her vise with another bare hook. "I get free hackle and the girls get cheaper flies than buying them at the fly shops."

"How much are they?" Melody asks, full of curiosity.

"They run anywhere from two to four dollars apiece. I figure I can tie them for about twenty cents apiece. A pretty good savings. Plus, I really enjoy tying them," Amanda adds. "It takes me about four to five minutes to tie a fly. At least the simple patterns anyway."

"We still support the local fly shops by buying our hackle from them. I buy from the little guys as often as I can. They are such a wonderful source of knowledge for the local rivers and what the fish are biting on," Sophie adds.

"The big box shops usually have more gear designed for women, like waders and boots, so I bought that stuff there, but I bought my rod and reel from the local shop just up the road," I say as I pour a little more wine into Sophie's glass.

Rose raises her glass towards me indicating she would like a refill as well and says, "I still fish with the bamboo rod my grandmother gave me. She's an old girl, but she still gets the job done."

"I noticed your rod looked different from everybody else's. What are the rest of them made of?" Melody asks.

"They range from bamboo to titanium to carbon fiber graphite, to boron. It really just depends on how much you want to spend on them. You can get a rod for a hundred dollars, or you can get one for a thousand dollars or more. It really just depends on what you like to fish with," I add as I take a sip of my wine. "Dang, this tastes good after a fun day of fishing."

"Indeed," Rose says as she raises her glass to agree with me.

"Who's making supper?" I ask as my stomach growls.

"I threw some lasagnas in the moment we returned. Should be ready in about thirty minutes," Rose says as she rises to check the oven. "They look and smell good!"

"You think of everything, Rose. I usually don't think about making anything until I'm too hungry to think," I admit. Rose opens and closes the oven door and the lasagna smell wafts through the room, causing my stomach to growl even more. "Oh, that smells amazing!"

"Here, Veronica, come and butter up this garlic bread. Let's get it ready to throw under the broiler," Rose instructs.

"Yes, ma'am," I reply and rise off the couch to do as I'm told. As I scoot past Melody, I glance down at one of her tattoos on her leg and have a total flashback. "Oh my God, I've been racking my brain ever since we met you why you look so familiar. I think I just figured it out. Do you live in a loft in downtown Denver above Noire restaurant?"

"Um, yes?" Melody replies with an odd look on her face.

"I knew it! I knew I had seen you before. My husband owns and operates Noire."

"Really? I love that place. Their pear and walnut salad is really good."

"That's one of my favorites as well. Thatcher is my husband, he's the owner and head chef. I'll tell him it's a favorite of yours."

"Cool."

"I think I sat at the table next to you one time. I remember pointing out one of the tattoos on your leg to Thatch one time."

"This one?" Melody asks as she pulls up her tights a little further and reveals her tat-covered legs.

"Yes, the ivy crawling up the back of your leg. I love that, it's really nicely done."

"Thanks. My grandmother's name is Ivy, so this one is for her."

"Cool. How many do you have?"

"Tattoos? Um, around nineteen. It's kind of an addiction."

Rose pipes up from the adjoining kitchen and joins the conversation. "Okay, what's with that metal stuff in your face? Did that hurt?" We all snicker at her lack of discretion.

Smiling, Melody says, "Well, it did at first, but it doesn't anymore. My neck piercing hurt the worst." She turns and lifts her hair up off her shoulder to reveal the inch-long barbell stud she has implanted in the back of her neck. We all scream in horror.

"Oh my God! I've never seen anything like that! Why the hell did you do that?" Sophie shrieks out. I shoot her a *shut-the-hell-up* look, but she keeps going. "Can I touch it?" We all burst out in laughter at Sophie's request.

"Sophie!" I scold.

"What?! I want to touch it. It's crazy looking," she says, completely engrossed in Melody's piercing.

"Um, sure," Melody obliges.

Sophie rubs her finger over the area where the barbell is underneath her skin. "Oh my God, that feels weird!" she says as she shudders. "What made you think of doing that?"

108

"I saw it in a magazine and I thought it looked cool."

"I'm all for looking cool, but holy crap, that is pushing it for me," Sophie says. "Not that I'm against it for you, it's just not for me."

"No worries," Melody says, as she shrugs her shoulders. "I'm not for everyone."

"Well, we don't care what anyone looks like around here," Rose chimes in. Moving over to Sophie she puts her arm around her shoulder and says, "If we did, Sophie never would have made it past the threshold."

"Rose! You meanie!" Sophie screams as she playfully elbows her in the ribs. We all erupt in laughter at Rose's joke.

"Oh I'm just kidding. You know that," she says as she gives Sophie a hug. "Now, Veronica, didn't I tell you to butter the bread?"

"Right, sorry," I say as I spring into the kitchen. "Let's get this supper finished up. I'm starving."

`·.,¸,.·´¯`·.,><((((º>`·.,¸,.·´¯`·..><((((º>`·.,¸,.·´¯`·..

The rest of the evening is spent in front of the fireplace, telling more stories and just enjoying one another's company. Rose gets on a roll and has all of us in stitches with the stories that she tells. I swear she has lived three lifetimes with everything she's been through. DJ curls up in her dog bed at the base of the fireplace hearth and looks up disapprovingly at us whenever our laughter gets a little too loud. We get to know Melody a little better as she tells us a

109

few details about what she does. I think Rose gets the biggest education of all of us on what online nudity is all about. Her eyes are as big as saucers as Melody tells us about the online nude group she belongs to. She actually pulls up her site on her laptop and shows us her profile. It's actually very artistically done, and in the end it didn't seem weird to us anymore.

We all drink just a little too much wine and then finally start dispersing off into our bedrooms. Rose shows Melody the spare bed in my room and helps her get settled. Sophie collapses onto her bed and is out like a light. I go in and help get her under the covers so she doesn't freeze her butt off all night long. I then head into my room and start to get ready for bed myself. Realizing how thirsty I am, I go out into the kitchen to get a glass of water. In the dark shadows, I see Amanda slip out the front door and out onto the porch. Deciding to check up on her, I pull my sweater tight around myself and throw on my flip-flops. I wander out into the dark and see her down by the river sitting on a rock in the cool evening shadows. I shuffle my way towards her, making enough noise for her to hear me so I won't startle her.

"Care if I join you?" I ask as I sit on a nearby stump.

"Not at all," she says, looking out at the river.

"You okay?" I ask, knowing something was up.

"Yeah, I'm fine," she replies as she looks down and kicks at the dirt below her feet.

"You're a terrible liar, you know that, right?" I say, pulling my sweater a little tighter.

"That bad, huh?" she says with a smirk.

"Worse than Sophie!"

"Oh jeez, I must be terrible at it then."

"What's up?"

"Just processing things from today, it was a pretty full day."

"No doubt. What was up with Rose on the riverbank? Did she share anything with you?"

"Um, a little. I'll let her share the details with you. I think she's okay for now."

"What do you mean?"

"She's . . . um . . . Today brought some stuff up from the past for her. It's not for me to share, so I'll let her tell you if she wants."

"Wow, um, okay."

"Sorry, I don't want it to be weird, but I really feel like it's not my story to tell."

"Okay, I get it. No worries."

An awkward silence builds between us.

"So how are things with you?" I finally ask, wanting to change the subject.

"Well, nights are always hard for me. My mind starts racing with all of the what-ifs with Mike, and my anxiety shoots through the roof."

"I can imagine. What do you do when you are at home?"

"I mix it up. Sometimes I watch TV, sometimes I cruise Facebook or Pinterest, sometimes I work on the kids' scrapbooks. The time zones between Mike and me are so different he's sometimes online around two a.m. my time."

"Can you instant message him then?"

"Yeah, depending on how much time he has, we can get in about thirty minutes of chatting. Sometimes that helps me sleep, sometimes it keeps me up longer. Just depends on what we're talking about."

"How's he doing over there?"

"Actually, he loves it. He hates being away from me and the kids, but this is what he was trained to do. He's a bona fide soldier."

"I couldn't do it. I'm so glad we have people like him in the world who are willing to do what he does."

"He's one of a kind. I miss him so much," Amanda says as she pulls her knees up to her chest and rests her chin on top of them. "I also tie flies to keep my mind from racing. I have tied a crap load of flies in the last three months. It's the one thing that actually takes my mind off of it. It's like it transports me to a different time."

"Probably because it's so intricate. I would think it would be hard to concentrate on anything else."

"Yes, it is. I really love tying."

"Well, I'm glad you have an outlet. Plus, I love catching fish on my 'Amanda flies.' It always makes the experience that much richer since I have a piece of you right there with me."

"Ah, thanks, V. That's really nice."

"I'm serious. I swear I catch more fish on your flies than any of my store-bought ones."

"I'm sure it has *nothing* to do with the skill of the angler using those flies," she teases back.

"Maybe a little," I say with a grin. "But the connection is there."

"Thanks."

"How are the kids?"

"They're good. Jordan is potty training right now, so that's a joy."

"Yeah, I bet that's a ton of fun."

"It's not too bad. She's pretty responsive to her reward chart system I created for her. Every time she pees in the potty, she gets to put a sticker on her chart. Once it's all filled up, she gets to pick a prize out of a treasure chest. She's really into ponies right now, and I scored an entire box of them at a garage sale this summer for ten dollars!"

"You are the luckiest damn garage-saler I know! Seriously, do you just drive around town every Saturday morning looking for the best deal?"

"Sometimes. I also check Craigslist to see if there are any nearby that have kids stuff."

"Well, you amaze me with what you find."

"Thanks. It's kind of a necessary evil, but I'm also kind of addicted to them."

"How's Parker?"

"He's good. So stinkin' cute right now. He misses his daddy so much."

"I'm sure."

"We have pictures of Mike up all over the house. Plus, I pop in the videos we made with him so he can see himself and Daddy interacting. He runs up to the TV screen and gives Daddy kisses. It's cute and heartbreaking all at the same time."

"I bet." A cold shudder runs the length of my spine. "Dang, it's getting cold out here!"

"I agree. Let's head back inside," Amanda says as she rises to her feet. "Thanks for following me out here."

"Of course. Had to make sure my girl was okay." As we stand, we hear the sound of a stick crack out in the meadow. A deer and two fawns are walking by, looking for a place to bed down for the night. "Hey, look," I whisper as I point towards the deer. They don't notice us, so we watch them find a safe, comfortable spot and disappear in the tall grasses. It was a nice, gentle encounter that made both of us smile. I give Amanda a wink as we turn and walk quietly back up into the cabin.

`·.,,.·´¯`·.,><(((º>`·.,,.·´¯`·..><((((º>`·.,,.·´¯`·..

Sophie

The morning sun spills into my window early. I pull my pillow up over my head to attempt to block the blinding barrier to my slumber. I assess my sleeping position, and I swear I did not move the entire night. After almost nine hours of nonstop sleep, I'm in the exact same position as I went to bed. Rose's cabin has a way of making me do this, so comfortable, so relaxing. Worries seem to fade away while I am here. Plus, there is wine.

I wrap myself in a blanket and wander out to the living room to see who is up. The cabin always has a slight nip to it early in the morning. Rose is usually up early and has the fire started already. I don't see any sign of her, so I dutifully begin to gather the kindling and wood to get it started. I stack the layers of logs alternating in direction, making a little log cabin shape like I used to do with my Lincoln Logs. I put my kindling and pine needles in a teepee shape in the middle, making sure there is enough space for air to circulate through. I light a match and stick it through the cabin walls and ignite the pine needles. A pleasing *whoosh* sound pierces the air as the fire engulfs the teepee. I throw the match into the teepee as additional kindling and assess whether I need another match. I always try for a one-match fire, and today it seems I am successful. Once the fire catches, I draw in a deep breath and blow slowly and steadily to intensify the flame. The fire begins to burn with a crackle and a pop, and a little plume of smoke unfurls up the chimney. A small amount of smoke enters the cabin, and I adjust the flue so the air forces the smoke up the chimney. I inhale a deep, intoxicating breath of musky, smoky pine needles and plop myself down onto the couch. *Ahh. Good morning, self.* I hug myself for a job well done and snuggle deeper into the cushions.

After the fire has a steady roar, I sit and watch it burn. I find myself drifting off into a mesmerizing state while I watch the glowing yellow-and-orange kaleidoscope show dance in front of me. The wood smoke curls up into the still morning air, and I can feel the cold nip turn into a warm embrace. The heat washes over my face, and I feel my cheeks pinking up almost immediately. The morning is very quiet, so the sizzling pops and hisses from the burning wood are amplified off the cabin walls.

I sit for about twenty minutes and drink in the glow from the fire. I peek at my watch—6:10—and decide to test the "early bird gets the worm" theory. And in my case I hope it's a fish and not a worm.

After getting dressed I leave a quick note on the kitchen table. "Gone fishing, upstream near Old Man's Beard. ~Sophie." I head out to the front porch and get my rod assembled, carefully lining up the line guides as I go. I stare down the rod like a shotgun to make sure that all of the guides are lined up properly. I pull the line through each guide and prop my rod up against the cabin. The morning air smells of pine cones and wet grass warming in the morning sun. Heavenly.

I pull out my fly box, peer over the brightly colored imitation bugs and carefully select a Yellow Sally. This is a favorite fly of mine as I usually have a lot of success with it this time of year. After my rod is assembled, I pull on my waders and boots. I do so quietly so I don't disturb the sleeping beauties

116

inside. I haven't fished by myself in quite some time, so a little private river time sounds pretty good. I decide to stick close to the cabin and go to my lucky watering hole. There is usually a nice Rainbow that likes to hang out behind this one particular big rock, so I head upstream and scout my location.

This morning the valley is bright and clear and the evergreen mountains are painted pink and orange in the morning sunrise. The sagebrush scent is wildly intoxicating this morning as I hike my way upstream. I'm careful to carry my assembled rod above my head as I weave through the sage bushes so I don't catch my line on an outstretched twig. I hate tangling my line before I even step foot in the river.

I reach my destination after a brisk ten-minute walk. I double-check my knots to make sure I won't miss a feeding fish due to a poorly tied knot.

I carefully wade out into the water so I don't disturb any nearby fish. I release my Yellow Sally from the fly catch on my rod and gently toss it into the water. I pull out enough line to make my first cast and get into position. I cast several times and watch my strike indicator float by a small pool of water behind a large rock. If there are fish in this part of the river, they are going to be hiding behind that rock. I cast several times, each time mending my line so it floats perfectly with the current. I feel the current pushing at my legs, and I readjust my feet on the slippery, round river rocks. Feeling balanced, I cast again letting the fly float down the pocket seam with the current.

I notice my strike indicator is a little too close to my fly, so I pull the line in to investigate. I always have the darnedest time with my strike indicators. They always seem to sneak down the line and get too close to my fly. *I will have to remember to ask Rose if I need to attach them to my line differently.* I slide the strike indicator up above the knot

117

where the leader and tippet are connected, thinking that the knot might hold the indicator in place. Suddenly, I lose my balance and wave my arms vigorously to keep my balance. In doing so, I accidentally let go of my line and, due to my not-so-graceful arm swing, it ends up in a giant tangle. *Crap.* Simultaneously I become acutely aware that in my attempt to keep my balance, a small section of clothing above my waders dipped below the water's surface, and an icy gush of water races to my toes. *Shit.* This is not a good start to my day. I haven't even been out here fifteen minutes . . .

Upon further inspection, my fly is now above my strike indicator in a hopeless knot. *Damn.* I put my reading glasses on to attempt to untangle this mess. *Should I just cut my line and start over or salvage what I have?* I always struggle with deciding which would take less time, starting completely over with new tippet and a new fly or untangling my mess. I'm not the fastest knot tier, so I decide to untangle my mess as this is a brand-new leader and I haven't even caught a fish with it yet.

As I work through the knots, my stomach growls. *Dang, I forgot to eat breakfast. Why do I always do that?* I make sure that everyone else has eaten and is taken care of, but I forget to take care of myself. Irritates me.

Something in the water catches my eye; I look down and see a fish swimming at my knees. Of course there is, as I am in no position to catch him at this moment. *Well, hello, little friend, fancy meeting you here,* I say to myself as I watch him swim. *Taunting little sucker, aren't you?* It's a beautiful cutthroat. I stare at him for the longest time, his color gleaming against the sun rays piercing the water. Such a beautiful creature. I know as soon as I move he will bolt away, so I resume detangling my line, keeping as still as I possibly can. Twenty minutes go by and I am still detangling. *Stupid knot.* My fish friend is still near my knees, swimming to and fro in the current. I look down at my knot, audibly let

118

out a big sigh, and simultaneously the fish darts away like lightning. He disappears behind the very rock I was casting to, and I glare at him with my pessimistic attitude.

At this point I don't feel like I am any closer to knot freedom and my toes feel like icicles, so I decide to head back to the cabin to untangle my mess and to fix some breakfast for the girls. My stomach growls in agreement, and I slowly back out of the water. Maybe I can return to the river with a better attitude and my fish friend will still be there.

`·.,¸¸.·´¯`·.,><((((º>`·.,¸¸.·´¯`·..><(((º>`·.,¸¸.·´¯`·..

"Morning', Sophie! What are they biting on this morning?" Veronica asks as I walk in the door.

"Not sure. I only casted a few times before I lost my balance and tangled my line. I have a terrible tangled mess to deal with."

"Oh darn. I hate it when that happens."

"Yeah, me too."

"You going to cut your losses and start over?"

"Probably. I just hate cutting off so much of the leader when it's brand-new. I haven't even caught a fish with it yet!"

"Ugh, that sucks. You'll get it done this afternoon. I have faith in you."

"Glad somebody does. What's for breakfast?" I say as I put another log on the fire.

"Depends on what you're making me," Veronica sparks back as she sits on the couch with a mug full of hot tea.

"Touché, Mrs. Reed," I say. "Probably something eggy. With bacon. Definitely with bacon." After stoking the fire, I head into the kitchen and stick two pieces of bread into the toaster.

"I always tell Thatcher that bacon should be served with every dish that comes out of his kitchen and he'd be a millionaire. Who doesn't love bacon?" Veronica states from the adjoining room.

"It should be its own food group!" I pull the eggs and bacon out of the fridge and put them on the counter. I adjust the knobs on the stove and get two burners heating up.

"Agreed," she says as she sips on her tea.

"How is Thatcher these days?"

"He's good. Works too much, but that's what you do when you own the joint."

"I know that feeling all too well." I add a dollop of yesterday's bacon grease into my egg pan and watch it start to melt in the pan.

"I'm sure you do. How are things at the greenhouse? Are you gearing up for spring?"

"Oh yes, we've had things planted for months now in all eight greenhouses. I love it when people place their orders in January for their summer hanging baskets. It's usually a good indicator of what kind of summer we're going to have." I line up bacon slices side by side in my favorite cast-iron skillet and put it on the hot burner.

"How's it look so far?"

"So far, so good! We have tons of orders for baskets. Plus, our hothouse winter vegetables are selling well with the local grocery stores and restaurants. That helps pay the bills through the winter."

"Thatcher loves his fresh produce from you. His customers rave about it!"

"Good! So glad to hear that. I will be sure to let the boys know." The toaster pops out the two pieces of bread, and I quickly butter them with real cream butter.

"The boys?" Veronica asks.

"Two of my winter staff, Duke and David. I call them 'the boys.' Brothers from Iowa who came out to Colorado when they pulled an elk tag and then never left. They keep the joint running over the winter while I take a little time off. I work so much in the spring, summer, and fall, so I need a little downtime in the winter. They are fantastic employees, which makes all the difference in the world." I bring a slice of toast over to Veronica on the couch.

"Oh yum. Thanks," she says as she takes the hot piece of toast from me. "That is so true. Thatcher says the same thing. It can be hard in the restaurant business to find good staff, but he pays better than most restaurant owners, so that usually lets him retain more quality people. He invests in them, they invest in him. A definite win-win."

"Absolutely. I do the same thing. I can't do it by myself anymore, it has literally grown out of control for just one person to manage. And that's a good thing."

"I just love what you have done with your property, Sophie. It is so beautiful and there is so much to do! That corn maze is so dang fun every fall. Thatch and I had a blast running through it last year."

"Well, good! That's what it's supposed to do! I love it too. It's been fun to grow over the years." The bacon starts to sizzle in the pan, and its tantalizing scent starts wafting through the cabin.

"How long have you had it now?" Veronica asks.

"Let's see, I bought the property in 1996, and then the lot next to it in 1998. Guess that makes it sixteen years now. Dang, longer than I thought! It really started taking off when I added the pumpkin patch and corn maze. The fall festival experience has exploded over the last few years. I got into it at just the right time."

"Well, you have done it up nicely, Sophie. People will come back again and again for the fun! I know we will."

"Well, good! Always glad to provide the venue for a good date night with the hubby." I crack four eggs into the hot bacon grease, and they instantly sizzle and start turning white. "I wish I could have a good date night. Over easy okay?"

"Absolutely," she says as she takes another bite of her toast. "Speaking of date night, are you seeing anyone these days?"

"Nah. No time for such nonsense."

"Oh, whatever, Soph. Are you putting yourself out there? Have you tried the online dating sites?"

"Yes, of course. I don't like them, though. Seems I always get the creepers."

"I need to look at your profile. Something isn't right. You should have been snatched up a long time ago."

"I've been thinking of taking my profile down, at least for a few months. I'm too busy in the summertime to date anyway." I pull a few plates down out of the cupboard and set them on the table.

"What about that Troy guy you went out with last month?"

"Oh, he was a gem. He actually had a big ole wad of chew in his mouth the entire date."

"Ew, gross!" she yells out. "Some guys just don't get it. What about Thatcher's friend Greg? Did he call you?"

"Yes, he did, but we never went out. I was too busy at the greenhouse," I explain. I turn over each piece of bacon, careful not to splatter myself with the hot grease.

With obvious irritation in her voice she exclaims, "Soph, he's a nice guy! Why don't you give him a chance?"

"I've just been too busy," I reply, hoping she will drop the subject and sorry I accidentally brought it up.

"Maybe we should double-date one night, just so you can get to know him in person."

"V, I don't want it to be awkward," I reply as I pull the orange juice from the refrigerator.

"Awkward? Why would it be awkward?"

"What if it doesn't work out? He's a friend of Thatcher's, I don't want it to get weird with us." I pour two glasses of orange juice and set them on the table.

"Sophie, you are ending the relationship before it even begins! Why don't you give him a chance?"

"You don't get it," I say without looking at her, flipping the eggs over in the pan.

"I don't get it? Hardly, Sophie. I'm just pointing out the facts."

"Listen, *Coach*. I don't need the lecture," I say, accentuating the word coach to let her know I'm not one of her clients.

"Whatever, Sophie. I'm just as busy as you are, yet I find time for the things that are important to me."

"Can we drop this?" I yell back, shooting a fiery look her way.

"Sure, we can avoid it some more, just like always," she fires back.

"Hey! Watch it, missy," I spark back at her, pointing my bacon-turning fork in her direction. "What the hell is this all about, Veronica?"

"It's about *you*, Sophie, always making excuses for yourself. You say you want a good date night, yet you avoid going out on a date. You are not even giving yourself a chance! You are ending things before they even begin, assuming that they are going to flop."

"I don't want to waste my time if it doesn't feel right."

"And how will you know if it feels right if you don't even try? Honestly, Sophie, I never see you being negative about anything in your life except for dating. Why do you have such a doomsday attitude about it?"

"It's not the same now as when you and Thatcher dated. You've been together for, what, like twelve years? It's

124

different," I say, my hands defensively on my hips, my anger flaring.

"Excuses, excuses," Veronica mutters under her breath.

"Morning, girls," Rose sings out as she shuffles into the kitchen. "Smells divine, Sophie." She walks over and gives me a big morning hug, oblivious to the spat Veronica and I are having. When my hug is not warmly returned, she looks at me and asks, "What's up?" I roll my eyes and shake my head in annoyance.

"Oh, you know, Sophie avoiding issues, taking care of everyone else but herself," Veronica jabs as she coyly takes another sip of her hot tea.

"Wow, you're on a roll this morning," I say hotly back in her direction.

"It's true, Sophie. Every time we talk about this, you make excuse after excuse and I'm sick of it! If you're not going to help yourself, then quit bitching about it!" she yells.

"Who's bitching? It seems like it's a bigger problem for you than it is for me!" I say as I pull the eggs off the burner and put them on a plate. "Here!" I say as I shove the plate of eggs at her and storm out of the kitchen.

"Ugh! She drives me crazy sometimes," I hear her say as I stomp down the hallway.

"What was that all about?" Rose asks.

"Oh, nothing," Veronica replies. Then I hear the front door of the cabin slam shut.

Back in my room I pace around the bed, so mad at my friend. *What the hell was that all about? Why was she*

125

pushing me like that? I say to myself in quiet anger. I look over at Amanda who is still sleeping in the bed next to mine, also oblivious to the tiff that just unfolded in the kitchen. I silently fume to myself for several minutes before wandering back out to the kitchen. Rose is sitting by herself at the table, finishing up the eggs I had shoved at Veronica.

"The eggs are delicious, Sophie. Care for a cup of coffee?" she asks, avoiding the obvious.

"No, thank you," I mutter as I grab a piece of bacon and shove it in my mouth. I sulk around the kitchen trying to act busy to avoid what I know is coming next.

"Everything alright?" she asks nonchalantly, already knowing that it's not.

"Can we not talk about this right now? Please?" I say with a bit of exasperation in my voice.

"Talk about what?" she asks coyly.

"Oh stop. You know what," I say as I roll my eyes at her in frustration. "I don't want to talk about it right now."

"Then don't talk about it," Rose says as she takes a sip of her coffee. "You sure you don't want a cup of coffee?"

"Sure, I'll have one of your famous hazelnut lattes," I say as I sink into a kitchen chair.

"Good girl. Coffee always helps." She stands and walks over to her espresso maker. "Did I hear you leave early this morning?"

"Yes, I attempted to go fishing this morning, but all I caught was a tangled mess."

"Oh? What happened?" she asks as she starts the drip on my espresso.

"I was out in the middle of the river and I lost my footing. I flung my arms around to catch my balance and ended up getting my line in a terrible tangle."

"I see," she says as the espresso machine dispenses two steaming-hot streams of coffee into two shot glasses. Once full, she pours the two shots of espresso into my coffee mug. She turns the machine to the steam setting and pulls the milk from the fridge. "Did you cut your losses and start over?"

"No, I stood there freezing my ass off in the river trying to untangle my mess," I admit.

"Hmm . . . ," she says as she pours some milk into the milk-frothing container. "Did you catch any fish?"

"No, I just told you all I caught was a tangled mess," I say with a hint of frustration in my voice. "Actually, a fish came and swam right by my knees, but I couldn't do anything about it since my line was all tangled."

"How did that make you feel?" she asks, her back still to me as she starts the noisy milk-frothing process of my latte.

"Pissed off. Frustrated. I could see the fish but couldn't catch it," I recount, playing the scene out in my mind again.

"So let me get this straight. You went out to catch a fish, but because you were so busy trying to detangle a mess that happened *twenty years ago,* you couldn't take advantage of the opportunities right in front of you?" she says pointedly as she spins around and looks me straight in the eyes.

Suddenly, I realize we are not talking fishing anymore. I look away and shake my head in frustration. I sit there speechless and stunned, not having a witty retort in my defense. I stare out into the fireplace in the next room and let Rose's words sink in. My eyes instantly well up with tears, which start to stream down my face.

Rose brings my finished latte over and sits it down in front of me. "Veronica is right, Sophie. You are sabotaging your own love life.

I say nothing as I wrap my hands around the warm, fragrant coffee mug, tears continuing to fall down both of my cheeks. I stare down at the creamy froth on the top that is ironically in the shape of a heart.

"She just cares about you and wants what's best for you as her friend. Her delivery of the message was not very elegant, but what she was trying to say is that you say one thing and then do the exact opposite. It's like you don't want yourself to have it," she says as she puts her hand on my shoulder. The moment her hand touches me, I burst into a sob.

"I'm just scared of getting hurt again, Rose. It took me years to get over John, maybe even decades. I just can't imagine feeling that way for anyone else."

"You haven't given yourself the opportunity," she says as she pulls up the seat next to me.

"I know. It's just so risky. The pain was indescribable."

"I'm sure it was. Loss always is," she says as she wraps her hands around mine. "At some point along the way you have told yourself that it's not worth the risk to try it again. And by doing that, you have robbed yourself of multiple opportunities for love." She squeezes both of my hands as she stands, and then goes to start another latte. I sit in silence soaking in everything she has just said. Several minutes go by, and just as she puts the final touches on the second latte, Amanda wanders into the room.

"Mornin', girls!" she cheerfully announces as she walks over to Rose and gives her a morning hug. "You are the best hugger!"

"Here, your morning latte," Rose says as she hands her a hot, steamy cup.

"Oh, Rose, you spoil me!" she squeals as she takes a sip. "Mmm, that is heavenly. Thank you so much. Is everybody up?" She pulls out a chair and sits across the table from me.

"Everyone but Melody," Rose says as she looks out the kitchen window. "Here comes Veronica now."

Moments later Veronica opens the front door and walks right over to me. I stand to greet her as she says, "I'm sorry for being such a bitch this morning, Soph."

I throw my arms around her in an embrace. "It's okay. I get it now," I say as I glance over Veronica's shoulder and smile at Rose. We stay in the embrace for several moments. It feels good to hug my friend.

"Are we okay?" she asks as she pulls away and looks me in the eye.

"Yeah, we're okay," I say as I punch her lightly in the arm. We both smile and then sit down at the table. I look over at Amanda, and she has a very confused look on her face.

"I obviously missed some drama this morning," she says, her head cocked to one side.

"Maybe a little," I say, smiling at Veronica.

"Are you going to make me some more eggs?" Veronica asks as she playfully bats her eyes at me. "My other ones got cold."

"Your other ones got eaten," Rose adds. "They were delightful."

"You're impossible," I say as I rise out of my chair. Rose instinctively grabs the carton of eggs off the counter and hands them to me as I walk across the kitchen towards the stove. "Over easy okay?"

"Absolutely," she replies, exactly as she had earlier this morning. We both let out a small laugh, and we both know that everything is A-OK.

`·.,¸,.·´¯`·.,><((((º>`·.,¸,.·´¯`·..><(((º>`·.,¸,.·´¯`·..

After the drama of the morning, all of us were eager to get out on the water and get a good day of fishing in. Veronica, Amanda, and I have to leave tonight as we all have to work tomorrow. Rose and Melody are staying on a few extra days. Melody opted to save her fishing lesson for tomorrow so she can take pictures again today. Secretly I think she is just waiting for the rest of us to go home so she doesn't have to fish in front of us. I don't think she quite knows what to make of us yet. We are an eclectic group, that's for sure. Of course, she's pretty eclectic herself.

The afternoon flies by way too fast, and before we know it, we are all packed up and standing on the front porch saying our good-byes. Before we leave, Rose gives each of us a quilt she made over the winter. Each quilt is personalized beautifully, and it turns into a cry fest as she gives them to us. The hug marathon finally concludes, and we pull away in our respective cars.

I already miss them . . .

`·.¸¸.·´¯`·.¸><(((º>`·.¸¸.·´¯`·...><((((º>`·.¸¸.·´¯`·..

Section 4: Sharing

"Aside from fishing itself, perhaps the most popular pastime for fly anglers is sharing information. Because the sport has so many facets—entomology, unusual casting methods, tying techniques, specialized lines and customized leaders, high-tech rods, endless kinds of fly-tying materials—fly anglers appear to be especially drawn to these more social aspects of the sport."[v]

"Shows, Events, & Schools,"
by Sandy Rodgers, in
The Elements of Fly Fishing:
A Comprehensive Guide to the Equipment,
Techniques, and Resources of the Sport
by F-Stop Fitzgerald

Rose

I love spending time with the girls at the cabin. This cabin has been a source of retreat for me all of my adult life. When Bob and I were married, it was 1965 and we were in our early twenties. We decided we wanted to build not just a life but an adventure together. We thought that having a cabin in the woods to escape to whenever we wanted or needed to would be the icing on the wedding cake. So for our honeymoon we traveled just 130 miles from home to the Upper Arkansas River area. We scouted for the perfect nirvana to build our rustic cabin.

We began to look around, to explore the area for possibilities. Bob and I talked with a few realtors and walked through a few old, rustic cabins that had been standing for decades. There was one on a nice piece of property, but the roof was caving in and it was showing obvious signs of decay. We decided we wanted to start with a little more solid foundation. We then visited a few newer cabins that had several bells and whistles. Nothing we saw really felt like home, or the property was too far from the river. Finally we decided to just explore. The two of us hopped into our old, brown Ford pickup and just drove. We began to explore the unique countryside, driving down old mining roads into abandoned clearings, always watching for the perfect spot, wandering through the mountains on tiny dirt roads that followed the river. It was important for us to be near the water, both for a cleansing feeling and also for our love of fly fishing. After several hours of driving around on bumpy roads that should have had Sports Bra Necessary signs posted, we pulled over and decided to get out and hike. We were both getting a little frustrated with not being able to find the right place.

As we got out of the pickup, I noticed a small rock formation in the shape of a person pointing down a trail. It seemed a little strange at first. I had definitely seen rock cairns left on the river before, but I had never seen one that was in the shape of a person. It was almost as if that little rock formation was pointing us in a certain direction. Intrigued, we grabbed our packs and trotted down the trail like giggly schoolkids hand in hand. The area was beautiful, the stand of pines was stately, the large boulders and rocky shelf formations sat solidly at the base of the mountain, the wildflowers in full bloom left a floral scent on the breeze, and the view of the Sangre de Cristo Mountains with the billowing clouds behind them was just breathtaking. We followed the trail into the tall forest. You could tell the trail had not been used in a very long time and was a little overgrown, but the path was well worn and easy to follow. There was comfort in knowing that someone had been here before.

After a mile of hiking we came through a clearing and met the river. The sound of the rushing water over the rocks was deafening as we got closer. We dared not speak to one another so as not to disturb this wilderness symphony. We sat on a large boulder together and just watched the water, the way it raced downstream over the rocks and pooled on the sides. It felt nice to sun ourselves on the warm, smooth rock surface. I couldn't help but reflect over the water, both literally and figuratively. I was so excited to begin my new life with Bob—Mr. Robert K. Bradbury.

After an hour or so of quiet reflection we felt a gentle connection to this place, a place of tranquility and beauty that our previous searches had not found. Without saying a word we held hands and smiled at one another, knowing that this was the place.

As we scrambled off the rock, we turned to ramble through the wildflower clearing. It was such a nice flat clearing, and it burst with blossoms of columbine, fairy trumpet flowers, and longleaf phlox. I felt the wind blowing on my face as we danced through the field. The smell of the flowers was intoxicating. We skipped and ran and played as if we didn't have a care in the world. This place felt magical, and I wanted to drink in as much as we could. We lay down in the lush wildflowers and felt the warmth of the sun on our skin. We decided to keep exploring and see what else this area had to offer. As we were nearing the edge of the clearing, we noticed another rock formation in the shape of a little person again; however, this time there were two of them. Two figures of stone perfectly stacked and shaped to look like humans with outstretched arms. One of the figures was slightly taller than the other. We couldn't help but notice that the arms of the two figures were touching one other. It was as if these formations were a sign of togetherness and they were pointing us to this very spot.

I later learned that this rock formation is called an inuksuk, pronounced in-ook-shook. The inuksuk is an ancient symbol of Inuit culture traditionally used as landmarks and navigation aids in the Baffin region of Canada's Arctic. It is the Inuit word meaning "in the Image of Man." The inuksuk were and still are magnificent lifelike figures of stone in human form with outstretched arms and serve as a well-known symbol of northern hospitality and friendship. They are still built along treeless horizons, these landmarks helped travelers navigate on land and water. They endured as eternal symbols of leadership, encouraging the importance of friendship and reminding us of our dependence upon one another. The traditional meaning of an inuksuk was to act as a compass or guide for a safe journey. The inuksuk, like ancient trackers, helped guide people seeking their way through the wilderness. They represent safety and nourishment, trust and reassurance. The inuksuk guided people across the frozen tundra and gave them hope in barren places to handle hardships they encountered. These primitive stone images showed the way ahead . . . pointing travelers in the direction they wanted to go. These beacons of the North have now been adapted as symbols of friendship, reminding us that today as in yesteryear, we all depend on one another. It seemed a little odd to find these inuksuk in this clearing that day, but I know they were placed there for Bob and me. Some unknown person knew that this pristine wilderness location would be the place of someone's lifelong dream of serenity.

For the entire day I floated in my own imagination and walked with Bob. We walked the entire area and even outlined where we wanted the cabin to be with river rocks. We didn't even own the property yet, but we knew this would be our home away from home. We decided to camp out in the wildflower clearing that night, next to the inuksuk couple. We hiked back to the pickup to get our tent and necessities for a campout. Being the outdoorsy type, we had planned on spending a night or two on the potential property before purchasing it. We wanted to get to know the land and let it get to know us before making a lifelong commitment.

We set up the tent while there was still daylight. Bob built a rock fire pit, and I gathered firewood from downed trees and plenty of dried pine needles to use as a fire starter. Our meal that night consisted of canned soup heated over the fire and a loaf of bread I had baked earlier that week. There's nothing like a hot, wood-smoked bowl of soup on a cool Colorado evening.

That night in the tent we made love and touched in a marathon I wanted to last for the rest of my life. That night we created a connection to one another, to the land, and to the dream of starting our adventure together in that very spot. When the night faded and the entire world dipped into the arms of the night, I knew we had christened the exact location of where our cabin would be built and where we could live comfortably ever after.

As the moon lingered, we listened to the river, listening for any secrets or stories about this amazing place. The river always tells the story of the region. These woods are the same as they were over four hundred years ago. Like the flowing waters of the Arkansas River, the people who have settled along its banks throughout history have had their ups and downs, experiencing both prosperity and devastation. Although the river has been somewhat tamed, it remains a powerful storyteller, thanks in part to the artifacts it has left behind. I couldn't wait to explore its banks the next day.

The sounds of the night whirled around me. Threads of peace and happiness ran through my veins. I remember falling asleep that night with a smile on my face, even though no one else noticed.

I awoke the next morning greeted by a few mosquitoes, a warm fog, and the morning sun shining on my tent. I found my newlywed self in a gorgeous mountainous setting. Stepping out from a tent rather than a honeymoon suite made me feel a connection with the land. I had slept gloriously and woke up feeling like a forest creature getting an invigorating start to my day. Birds flitted around us through the branches, squirrels scurried over the rocks, and there were soft rustlings in the fallen pine needles. There was an invisible breeze that kept every branch moving just a little. It made it seem as if the trees were whispering to us. All I heard was the wind in the trees, Bob's breath, steady and even as he slept, and the constant gurgling of the river rushing over the rocks. The sun was just stretching awake, and I knew we were in the most divine place on earth this fine morning. We were home.

We emerged from our tent feeling refreshed and renewed. The sky was a crystal-clear blue, the trees and flowers were practically bursting at the seams, and the temperature was just right. The mist rising from the river was a beautiful gray and cast a tranquil spell over me as I sat and watched the river flow. Bob built a campfire to warm some water for coffee and to make breakfast. Campfire-smoked bacon and eggs were on the menu for the morning. One of my absolute favorites.

Later that day we packed up camp and headed into town. We did our research to find out who owned that beautiful piece of property and if they would be willing to sell. We learned that the property had been owned by a well-known local man who had passed away a few months prior. He had no family to pass the land to, and it was coming up for sale within the next year.

Bob was one of the lucky ones who had purchased some original IBM stock when it first went public. His small investment early on rewarded him kindly within a few years. We paid cash for the land and began the two-year process of building our dream cabin. Nothing too fancy, but large enough that we could bring a family here in the future. We spent many weekends building our cabin with our own two hands. There was a lot of love, sweat, and tears in the foundation of that magical place. When it was first built, it was an amazing blond wood. Over the years it has grayed a bit, but then again who doesn't? When we built this cabin, we built her so she blended closely with the rocks, pine trees, and wildflowers. We knew that she would change over the years and so would we.

`·.¸¸.·´¯`·.¸><(((º>`·.¸¸.·´¯`·..><((((º>`·.¸¸.·´¯`·..

Melody

"Ready for your first fishing lesson?" Rose asks.

"Um, I think so." *I really hope I can do this.*

"Okay, let's head out to the backyard," she says, smiling. Her dog DJ bolts out the backdoor as soon as she opens it.

What?! "The backyard? What the hell? Shouldn't we go out to the river?"

"Patience, dear. To teach the basics of the cast, it's actually better to do it on dry land. You can actually see what your line is doing. And watch your mouth, no need to swear," Rose replies with an ornery grin. *That damn grin.* We walk out the front door to the cabin and put together our rods in the front yard.

Hell is swearing? Jesus. I'm gonna have to really work on what comes out of my mouth around here, I guess.

"To get started I'm just going to tie on this piece of cord. No hooks just yet. If you are going to smack yourself or me in the face with the line, I'd rather it didn't have a hook on it. Plus, the cord will help you understand the movement of the line. It will feel a little different when you have a fly on the end, but this is a good start." Rose ties on the piece of cord, then tosses the line off to the side. "Take a good grip on the handle of the rod, keeping your thumb on top like this."

"Like this?" *This feels weird.*

"Yes, perfect. Good job. Now, to get the line out, play out the leader until you see a little of the fly line going through the last guide loop." *What the hell is a guide loop?*

"What's a leader?" *Damn, I don't know shit, and apparently I have to watch my mouth too.*

"The leader is this part here," she says as she shows me the leader. "It's the nearly invisible line between the fishing line and the fly. See how it's thicker at the top than it is at the bottom?"

"You mean the clear line is not called fishing line?" *Why did they change the name of it for fly fishing? That seems dumb.*

"No, the fishing line is actually this fluorescent-colored line here. The leader is the clear line."

"So basically forget everything I have ever known about fishing in the past?" *Seriously.*

"Pretty much. You'll catch on. Before you know it, even you will be hooked."

I smile at her attempt at humor. She's a funny old lady.

"Pretend you are shaking hands with the rod. Using only your wrist, keep an eye on the tip and the line." She shakes the rod like she just described. "See how the rod moves? You don't need much pressure to make it curve slightly. See?" She demonstrates with her rod.

I try to imitate what she is doing with her rod. "Like this?" *I think I got it. Feels right.*

"Yep, good. With your other hand, pull the line three or four times from the reel while you continue the shaking-hands motion." She watches me intently as I do as she instructs. "Good job. This is known as stripping."

I gasp out loud completely caught off guard by Rose saying the word stripping. "Stripping? I know stripping as something else," I say, giggling. "Depending on the place, it might even have hooks and poles." *Shit, too much?*

Smartly, she replies, "Poles are for stripping, rods are for fishing." My mouth falls open in disbelief, and I laugh out loud. *Evidently not! I can't believe she just said that!*

"Nice."

"Okay, focus dear," she says with a smile. "Now stop and take a look at what you've done. Did the fly line go through the guides on the fishing rod?"

"Yeah, actually it did," I say with disbelief in my voice.

"Well, good! You'll be an old pro in no time."

"Yeah, right."

"I laid down my hat in the grass about twenty feet away. Hold your rod in your casting hand, point the opposite foot towards your target, and place your other foot at a slight angle to provide a solid footing."

"Wait, don't we need to tie the hook on?"

"A hook? In fly fishing we call them flies. And no, we're not ready for flies yet, just cord at first. Didn't I just say that?"

"Sorry, I must not have heard you." *Damn, chill out.*

"Women usually have an advantage over men in fly fishing because of three things: listening, patience, and observation." She holds up a finger for each of the three things as she lists them. "Women will usually take the time to learn how to do it right the first time. Most men just want to catch a fish." She has an ornery grin on her face as she finishes her sentence. "I can see that you are not cut from an ordinary mold, though, so that listening piece may not apply to you? Hmm . . . I might have my work cut out for me."

I smile and say, "Point heard. Next?" *Moving on . . .*

"Alright, lift up the tip of the fly rod quickly using your wrist and stop your arm's movement when it is pointing straight up. You should feel the line's weight start to pull the tip of the rod back. As soon as you feel this, snap the rod forward at a forty-five degree angle. You should see the line make a small loop and flip at the end. The flip will tempt the fish. If you snap the end, your fly will smack the water and scare them away instead."

"Well, that wouldn't be good."

"No, it wouldn't, especially if you are fishing near me," she says with a grin.

Dang, I like this lady. She has some spunk to her.

"Put your arm at a forty-five-degree angle. Make a quick one-two movement by barely bending your arm at the elbow, bringing your wrist back over your shoulder and then back towards the front. Keep your wrist straight. No floppy wrists. That's a bad habit that is hard to break. That might feel weird at first, but give it a try." She gives me a quick demonstration and makes the fly hit the hat beautifully. "See how the line makes a loop and then snaps to the front?"

As she demonstrates her cast, her sleeve rides up just a bit and I catch a glimpse of something on her arm. *No way!*

"Is that a tattoo?" I exclaim out loud, although not really intending to.

"Well, yes it is. Surprised?" *Hell yeah, I'm surprised.*

"A little. What is it?"

"It's an old faded rose. Got this one years ago when I was on vacation." Her voice trails solemnly as she finishes her sentence.

"What do you mean 'this one'? Do you have more than one?"

Narrowing her eyes and grinning at me, she says, "Hmm, a lady never tells."

"Oh really? I must not be very ladylike then. I have nineteen."

"Nineteen?! Well, you're a colorful thing, aren't you?"

"I like to think so," I say as I put my hands decidedly on my hips. *More than you know . . .*

"Well, we'll have to do a show-and-tell later. I'm intrigued."

"As am I." *I wonder how many she has.*

"Are you still interested in learning how to fly fish? Because I'd like to get out on the river sometime today."

"Yes I am," I say emphatically. "Let's do this!" I surprise myself with my enthusiasm. *Okay, chill Melody.*

"Not so fast, dear. I need to see you hit my hat at least five times before we hit the water. Now try again."

Feeling like I've just been scolded, I cast again, this time nailing her hat twice in a row.

"Hey, look at that! I'm doing it!" *Sweet!*

"See! Nice job. Just takes patience, darling. Now keep practicing for another five minutes and then we'll head downstream," she says as she steps back to watch. I see her out of the corner of my eye as I cast, and it makes me nervous. My next three attempts are miserable and nowhere near her hat. *Damn.* Rose says nothing as she sits and watches. I fumble through for several minutes and start to get frustrated. I look over at Rose, and she is just smiling and nodding, eyebrows raised as if I should already know what to do. *This must be my lesson in patience . . .*

I try to remember what Rose said as she was showing me. *Arm at a forty-five-degree angle, a quick one-two movement, bring my wrist back over my shoulder, keep my wrist straight.* Right. I adjust my technique and wham—I nail her hat. "Finally!" I say out loud.

"Don't be so hard on yourself. This is your first time and you haven't even made it to the water yet," she says with a smile. "Try a few more casts, then we'll go."

I keep trying and eventually start hitting her hat consistently.

"See! You are doing great, Melody. How does it feel?"

"Um, a little awkward, but I think I'm starting to get it. I'd really like to try the real thing."

"Would you now? Well, let's see what we can do about that," she says and smiles. "Okay, let's get suited up first. Here's an extra set of waders that I think will fit you. Go ahead and put them on. What size boots are you?"

"I'm a size six and a half."

"Okay, I think I have some sevens in the closet. I'll be right back." She disappears into the cabin.

I fumble my way into the too-large waterproof overalls and get the shoulder straps snapped together and into place.

"Is this right?" I ask Rose as she reappears out onto the porch, boots in hand.

"Look at you! Looks great. You're halfway there. Here, try these."

"What's special about these boots?" *They look weird.*

"They have felt soles on the bottom that help grip the slippery rocks in the river. They are about to be outlawed, though, so I'll have to have them re-soled with rubber soles."

"Outlawed? Why is that?"

"Some people think that the felt can transfer bacteria and other algae to other rivers, which would harm some fish. I'm not so sure I agree with that, but what do I know? I always leave these boots here at the cabin, so you're safe to wear them today."

"Don't get me arrested for breaking some fish law I don't know about!" I crack back.

"Not to worry, dear," she says as she smiles back at me.

After I get my boots on and laced up, she hands me a fishing vest. "Here, this is yours to keep."

"Really? Are you serious?" I ask, stunned. *Is this lady for real?*

With a big grin on her face she replies, "Yes, welcome to your first fly fishing lesson."

"Oh wow. Thanks so much!" I put the vest on and examine each of the dangly surgical-looking instruments hanging from it. *What the hell is this stuff?* "What is all of this stuff for?"

"We'll get to those once we get on the river. Now come along," she says over her shoulder as she heads down the trail. "Don't forget your *pole!*"

Ha, she's funny. I scoop up my stuff and trot down the trail after her. *I can't believe how excited I am to try this. I'm actually giddy. Never in a million years did I think I would be fishing this weekend instead of taking photographs. I guess I need a little variety in my life. Plus, I really like Rose. I'm glad she invited me to stay a few days and learn how to fish.*

We wander down the trail, hopping over rocks and raising our rods over our heads when we near any brush alongside the banks.

"Try not to get your line caught in the branches. There's nothing worse than tangling your line when you're not even fishing."

I feel like a chipmunk scurrying down the trail. Well, a chipmunk in giant, trash-bag overalls carrying a big stick, but a chipmunk nonetheless.

"So tell me a little about yourself. Where did you grow up?" Rose asks.

"I grew up in Denver," I reply, a little reluctantly. I'm not a big fan of sharing personal details.

"Oh yeah? What part?"

"Cherry Creek."

"That's a lovely area."

"It was alright." *Nothing special.*

"What do your parents do?"

"They are both well-known musicians in the symphony." *Uh-oh. Don't really want to go there.*

"Really? Who are they? I've probably heard them perform. Bob and I used to have season tickets to the symphony."

I need to change the subject. "Who's Bob?" I say, trying to direct the conversation away from the topic of my parents.

"He was my husband of forty-three years. He passed a few years ago."

"Oh, I'm sorry," I say quietly. *Shit. Nice job, Melody.*

"It's okay. How were you to know?" she says as she hops over a fallen tree covering the trail. "He was the love of my life and I miss him dearly. Thank goodness I have DJ and my fishing girls to keep me company. What do your parents play?"

"My father is a concert cellist, and my mother plays the violin."

149

"Do you play as well?"

"Um, I can play, although I don't enjoy it like they do." *That's an understatement.*

"What do you play?"

"You name it, I can play it."

Rose stops and looks at me quizzingly. "Really? Are you kidding?"

"Nope. I can play just about anything," I state matter-of-factly.

Rose pauses on the trail and looks at me. "And you don't enjoy it? Seems like that many instruments would require some passion and a lot of practicing."

I don't stop and keep walking down the trail. "I was given the talent without the passion. Plus, my parents *want* me to pursue music, which is why I won't."

"I see," she replies as she heads after me, her voice hinting with a bit of discovery. Coyly she adds, "I sense an ongoing battle there."

"Perceptive of you," I mutter back. "Can we change the subject?" *Seriously.*

"Of course," she replies, and an awkward silence falls between us. We keep hiking down the trail, rods in hand. Rose seems to be scouting out a good spot as she keeps watching the river.

A few minutes pass before she asks, "How did they choose the name Melody for you?"

Seriously, lady? "I thought we were changing the subject?" I reply hotly, dumbfounded that she has brought up my parents again.

"I thought I did," she replies, frowning.

"We're still talking about my parents," I say coolly, wondering if I should say more or try to change the subject again.

"I asked about your name," she says, obviously not wanting to drop the subject.

I pause to collect my thoughts before I give in. *She is starting to piss me off.* "My grandparents gave me the name Melody. They named me after my parents' musical career." *There. Can we move on now?*

With obvious surprise in her voice she asks, "Your grandparents named you?"

"Yes." *End of story.*

"I see," she replies. "Well, it's a beautiful name, Melody."

"Thanks," I mutter back as I draw in a big, cleansing breath. "Can we please not talk about my parents?"

"Of course. Are you ready to fish?" she asks as we make a hard left towards the river.

"Yes," I say with a hint of exasperation. *Finally.*

"Good, this is my favorite spot."

`·.,¸,.·´¯`·.¸><((((º>`·.,¸,.·´¯`·..><((((º>`·.,¸,.·´¯`·..

Once at the side of the river, Rose gets busy tying on a fly. She pulls out some clear line from her vest and ties a small section onto the leader.

"I'll teach you how to tie knots later this evening in the cabin. I'll get you rigged up this morning, then we'll backtrack and cover more of the basics tomorrow."

"Whatever you say." I stand and watch her do her thing. "Is that another leader you're tying on there?"

"No, this is called tippet," she says as she holds up the nearly invisible thread. "It's a small piece of line you can add between the leader and the fly. Leaders can get expensive when you are starting out. Mostly because you chew through the end pretty fast when tying on your flies. I'll tie your first ones on to get you going."

I stand there and watch in awe. She is very fast at her knots. She starts to pull the knot tight, and then to my surprise she spits on the knot. *What the hell?* "Why did you just spit on that?"

"Good question," she says, smiling. "The spit lubricates the knot and allows it to tighten. The line is too slippery to stay in a tight knot without the spit."

"So lube is a good thing," I say, giggling out loud.

"Indeed it is," she says with a grin. Holding up a fly she explains, "This is a size 16 Parachute Adams."

"What is?"

"The fly. This fly is a size 16 Parachute Adams."

"The flies have names?" *That's weird.*

Giggling, she replies, "Yes, just like us, they all have a name and a story of how they got their name. Would you like to hear about how this one got its name?"

Niiice. I pause as I see the correlation she is making. Giving her a teasing glare I reply, "Do I have a choice?"

"You always have a choice."

Giving in again, I reply, "Do tell."

"Back in the 1920s a young man by the name of Leonard Hallady created this fly pattern. He named it after a man he looked up to and respected by the name of Charles Adams. Mr. Adams brought Leonard some insects he wanted imitated into a fly." As she tells the story, she adds a bobber-looking thing to the line. Later I learn this is called a strike indicator. I watch with curious interest as she continues, "Leonard imitated the bugs as best he could into a fly pattern and gave it to Charles to try out. Charles caught a mess of fish with it the first time he used it and asked Leonard what the name of the fly was. Leonard named it after Mr. Adams as he was the first to catch a fish with it."

"What about the parachute part? Why is it called the Parachute Adams?"

"The Adams fly is undoubtedly the most tied fly in America. Probably every fisherman that has ever caught a trout has used an Adams fly of some kind—yourself included after you catch one today," she says with a wink. "The parachute part of the name is after the style of tying that is used. There are dozens if not hundreds of Adams variations out there, but the Parachute Adams is one of the best for matching hatches."

"Hatches?" *Seriously, there is so much new shit I don't know.*

"Yes, hatches. Bug hatches. There is much to learn about this amazing sport," she says with a smile. "These flies are tied to match bugs as that's what fish eat. When bugs emerge from their egg state, they hatch. We try to match the hatch and try to trick the fish into eating our fake bugs. Kind of fun, eh?"

"I'm getting quite the education today, aren't I?"

"We both are, *Melody*," she says, emphasizing my name, obviously referring to our previous conversation. Without looking at me, she tosses the fly out into the water and stands back. "Okay, you're ready to start fishing."

"Really? That's it? So I just cast it out there?" I ask, standing there with a dumbfounded look on my face.

"Almost. First, let's read the water and see what it can tell you. Fish have somewhat predictable hiding spots, and it's good to put your fly in or near those spots."

"Read the water . . . now there's a term I've not heard before," I say as I stare at the top of the glassy surface of the river, uncertain of what I am supposed to look for and what it should be telling me. I pan the river from side to side, no clue what I am doing.

"What do you see?" Rose asks.

"Um, not much. Just the surface of the water."

"Okay, here," she says as she hands me a pair of sunglasses. "Look at one section of the river without them first, then put on these and see if it's different."

Before putting them on, I scan the top of the river.

"Do you see any fish?" she asks.

"No, I just see the sun reflecting off the surface of the water."

"Okay, now put on the glasses."

I put on the lenses and stare down at the water. *Holy shit!* Suddenly, everything looks dramatically different. I can see *into* the water and below the surface. "Holy cow! I can see all the way to the bottom!" I exclaim as I rapidly scan the river from side to side. "That is amazing! Are these polarized or something?"

"Yes, exactly."

"I have some camera lenses that do the same thing. I didn't think about them being used for fishing, though. That's really cool." *I'm digging all of these little lessons.* "Holy shit, there's a fish!" I scream as I point at a fish hovering behind a big rock, excitement soaring through my veins.

"Exactly. Now you know where one of their hiding places is. Fish like to hide out behind big rocks as they provide shelter from the strong current. What we need to do is cast upstream from this rock and let your fly float down past the fish. That fish is just waiting for a tasty morsel to float by for him to gobble up."

"Well, let's do it!" I exclaim loudly, exuding pure excitement.

"Shh, not too loud. Fish can hear very well," she says quietly. "Okay, first we need to carefully wade out into the river just a bit. We want to avoid all of that brush behind us so our line doesn't get caught on the back cast. Step carefully and cautiously, we don't want to scare off that fish with any sudden movements."

Rose carefully wades out into the water first, and I follow her every footstep. Once in a good spot, she pulls out some of the line and gets into position. Rose demonstrates how to make an upstream cast. She beautifully tosses that fly fifteen feet above the big rock and lets it float downstream with the current. She takes up the slack in the line as the fly gets closer to her. Quietly she says, "See how I take up this slack as the fly gets closer to us? You don't want to have too much slack in your line when the fish goes for your fly. If there is too much slack, you won't be able to set the hook and the fish will spit out your fly once it realizes it's not the real thing." Rose plucks the fly off the water right before it floats by the rock. "I don't want that trout to consider this fly until you offer it to him," she says with a smile and hands the rod to me. "Did you see how I did that?"

I nod in silence, taking the outstretched rod. Rose steps back and gives me a nod, indicating it is my turn to try. I strip out a little of the line and give it my best shot.

I cast the fly upstream, attempting to mirror what Rose has just demonstrated. The fly skims the surface of the water, causing a small splash of water. Rose gives me an approving look, and I strip in the excess line as the fly floats down the current. *Okay, I guess that was right.* The fly floats right past the big rock and tumbles downstream. "Good job. That was near perfect. Do the exact same thing again."

I get my line set and cast again. I send the fly sailing upstream. It lands softly on the surface again and begins its journey downstream. I strip in the excess line, hoping that I will get a bite. I watch the fish glance at my fly as it floats by him once again. *Why didn't he bite it?*

"You're doing everything right, Melody. Give it another try."

I repeat the motion a third time and watch the fly ride the current once again. Wham! A jolt of electricity shoots through my hands. *Holy shit!*

"Rod tip up!" Rose screams as she wades over to my side. "Keep it tight and let him run with the line if he starts to swim away."

My rod bends with an impressive arc as I feel him shake the line from side to side. He turns and runs upstream. "Oh my God, I caught a fish! I actually did it!" *I'm actually doing it!*

"Good job! Let him run! Don't force him to come to you or it will snap the line and you will lose him," Rose exclaims excitedly. I do as I'm told, and I can feel myself smiling from ear to ear. "Good job, Melody, keep playing him just like that. When you feel him pause, start to reel in your line."

I wait for said pause, and when I feel it, I start to reel him in.

"Bring him over into the slow water. Good, just like that. Come here, little fella!" I see Rose tug her net off the back of her vest. She leans over closer to the fish as I finish reeling him towards her. She scoops him up in the net and then brings him over to me.

"Oh my God, look at him! He's beautiful!" *Look at all of those colors! I wish I had my camera gear nearby.*

Rose swoops her left hand around his tail and gently picks it up under its belly with her right. The eleven-inch fish dances in her hands as she lifts him out of the net. "Nice job, Melody! Look at him!"

"Wow. Look at his skin!" *Oh, the shots I could be getting right now . . .*

"Beautiful, aren't they? This is a rainbow trout. You can distinguish it from other trout because of its coloring. See how beautiful those freckles are?"

"It's awesome." *Completely amazing.*

"Here, wet your hands so you can get a hold of it."

"Why do I need to wet my hands?"

"Fish have a protective, slimy coating on their skin. Dry, human hands can damage the skin. Wetting your hands helps keep more of the coating on the fish rather than on your hands. You'll still get some on your hands, but not as much as dry hands would." The slippery fish is still wiggling about in her hands.

"Okay, cool." I wet my hands and take the fish from Rose.

"That's a good hook set, right in its lip. Great job, Melody!"

"Thanks, although I just did what you told me to."

"You'll get the hang of it soon enough, and I won't always be here standing right next to you telling you what to do."

Rose grabs one of the shiny objects from her vest and shows me how to push the hook back through the side of the fish's lip to release the hook. "Next time you catch one, you get to do this on your own, so pay attention."

I nod, watching her every move.

"These are called hemostats. They're perfect for helping dislodge the fly from the fish's mouth. You don't have to use them, but I like them. Just backtrack the hook out of the mouth until it is free." She releases the fly perfectly and then places him back in the net. "If the hook is down deep in the

158

fish's mouth, you're better off to cut the line and let him have the fly."

"Why is that? Wouldn't a hook left in the fish's mouth hurt it more?"

"Actually no. Fish have strong digestive acids that dissolve metal. Within a day or two, that hook would be gone."

"No way! That is awesome. It's like a fish gets a piercing." *Cool.*

"He'll end up with a small scar, and your memory of catching him will last forever," she says as she picks up the fish and looks it straight in the eye. "Your first fish!"

I'm beaming from ear to ear. *This is so fun.* Rose then holds the fish underwater and faces it upstream. "Before letting a fish go, you need to face it upstream so it forces oxygen back into its system. Always make sure the fish has its wits about him again before you let it go."

"Why is that?"

"Otherwise the trauma of getting caught may kill it. You'll be able to tell when he has his wits about him again. Usually they dart off like lightning." She stands there smiling as the fish darts upstream. "See, just like that!"

I gaze out over the river and realize I am smiling as well. I have caught my first fish, and it was awesome.

"Thank you, Rose. That was amazing!"

She wades over and pats me on the shoulder. "You're a good student, Melody. It's pretty fun, isn't it?"

"Absolutely!"

"It's fun when you catch them, but there are days when you will get skunked, too. There's always something new to learn, which is why I love it so."

"How long have you been fishing?"

"Since I was a young girl. I found a copy of a fly fishing book in my grandmother's attic when I was twelve. I showed it to my grandmother, and she told me it was the first book ever written about fly fishing." She closes her eyes and pauses her story. It's as if she is seeing the story unfold all over again in her mind. I can tell she is lost in a childhood reverie so potent I can almost smell the attic dust right along with her. "It was written by a woman by the name of Dame Juliana Berners in the 1400s."

"Whoa, that's cool."

"What makes that so significant is that the 1400s women did not publish using their real names. If anything, they used their initials or a surname as it was definitely a man's world back then."

"Oh, that's true. I wouldn't have thought of that."

"Once the book became so successful, there were many men who surfaced trying to take credit for her work. They claimed she was the scribe for them, instead of the author."

"How did she retain it as hers?"

"She was a nun and many people vouched for her as being a woman of her word who lived with the utmost integrity. They claimed there was no way she would lie about such a thing. It was the only reason her name is still on the cover of that book today."

"That's frickin' awesome." *Oops, does that count as cussing?*

"I remember the exact place where I was when my grandmother told me that story," she says as she closes her eyes again. She pauses and a smile washes over her face as she relives the moment again. When she opens her eyes, she looks at me and says, "Her story inspired me to take up fly fishing and I've been doing it ever since. I really do love it."

"I can see that. You're also a very good teacher. Sorry if I was a little bullheaded."

"No worries. Thank you, dear," she says as she pats me on the arm. "I believe I have a responsibility to pass this craft down to the next generation of fly fishers. Otherwise the wisdom doesn't get passed on. Plus, fly fishing is a sport you never master. You will never learn all of the secrets."

"Really? You don't consider yourself a master?"

"I may be good at it, but I'll never achieve mastery. But that's just as well, I'm a big fan of puzzles and figuring out a good mystery. I look forward to days I get skunked so I can try to figure out what I did wrong."

"You don't sound like any fisherman I have ever known."

"No? Well, I probably don't look like any fisher*man* you've ever known either," she says as she playfully elbows me in the ribs.

"Well, that's true. So are you a fisher*woman* then? What do you call yourself?" I ask out of curiosity.

"I call myself a fly fisher. No need to bring my sex into it."

"Got it. Well, unless we start talking about stripping again, then we might bring sex back into it," I say with a giggle.

With a burst of laughter she exclaims, "Melody! You are a rascal, aren't you?"

"Maybe a little."

"Maybe a lot. I guess we shall see . . ." She draws out the word "see" as she tilts her head and gives me an ornery finger-shake gesture. She then winks at me and says, "Are you ready to catch your next fish?"

"Absolutely. Let's do this."

"Alright then, try again. Take a few steps downstream to cover different water. You've got this."

Yeah, I do.

We fish the rest of the day. We barely even remember to eat lunch because we're having so much fun. We close out the day catching a total of twelve fish. I can feel my confidence growing with each passing hour. The more I reflect on the day, the more I realize the river has its own rhythm, nature's symphony that I get to learn how to conduct. With music I wasn't told when or how to play from my parents; it was up to me to figure out the pace of each song and which instrument to play. Today maybe Rose was the conductor and I was her student . . . I obviously still have a lot to learn, as I don't remember what the names of the flies were that I used or the kinds of fish I caught, but I will remember this amazing day for the rest of my life.

`` `·.,.·´¯`·., ><((((º>`·.,.·´¯`·..><((((º>`·.,.·´¯`·..

Sophie

My alarm clock Monday morning goes off way too early. I struggle getting out of bed and down two lattes before making it to work around 9:00 a.m. Duke and David have been there since 6:00 a.m. getting the produce trucks loaded for deliveries. They wave and smile as they see me pull into the parking lot. David looks down at his invisible watch, smiling with his eyebrows raised, and taps his wrist indicating I'm a little late this morning.

"Must have been some weekend!" he exclaims as I open my door.

"I know, sorry. I could not drag my ass out of bed this morning!" I say as I hop out of my truck and walk over to them.

"Catch anything?" Duke asks, his hunter-gatherer side eager to hear about my fishing weekend.

"I'm not sure you want to know. You might explode with envy," I smile.

"Oh, come on. I was stuck here watering plants all weekend! Throw a guy a bone here!" he pleads.

Joyfully I share details. "It was amazing! We hit the caddis hatch on Saturday afternoon. It was like nothing I had ever seen before! Flies by the thousands swarming everywhere. The fish were leaping out of the water all around us! Completely amazing." His eyes grow wide with jealousy as I tell the story. "It looked like a blizzard of snowflakes there were so many."

"No way! That sounds awesome," David exclaims.

"It was. After the hatch passed, the fish were still feeding like crazy. I lost count after I had caught twenty or so."

"Are you kidding? Oh man, I've never caught that many in one day. You lucky duck!" Duke replies with envy in his voice. "You're right, you shouldn't have told me."

"It still kills me that you don't keep any of the fish." David adds. "I'd be a fat and happy fisherman after a fish fry like that."

"Catch and release is the name of the game for me. Lets me catch the same one over and over again!" I say, smiling. "You guys are going out on Wednesday this week, right?"

"Yeah, can't wait," says Duke.

"Where are you going?" I ask.

"I think we're going to head up to Spinney Reservoir. We haven't fished up that way in a while, so hopefully they are biting up there," David replies.

"Oh nice. I was there a few months ago, but it was colder than crap. Didn't catch much, but that was before the spring runoff started. They should be feeding much better now."

"I hope so," Duke says.

"Me too," I say. "Okay, I'll make sure I'm here early on Wednesday since you'll both be gone. Where are we with deliveries this morning?"

"We've got the Brown Babe all loaded and ready for City Harvest and Noire," Duke tells me.

"Okay, cool. Thanks for getting that ready for me," I reply.

"You'd better get going pretty soon. You don't want to keep your boyfriend waiting too long," David cracks at me. "He'll be worried about you if you're not there by 10:00 a.m."

"Oh, that Virgil. He's such a cutie," I say with a smile. "Let me check in with the girls in the office and then I'll head out in a few."

"Okay, sounds good. Welcome back, Sophie," David says.

"Thanks, guys," I say as I head towards the big red barn where my office staff works.

Today is my City Harvest delivery day and I always like being the one to make the delivery. I donate fresh produce to this local food bank once a week and their receiving guy, Virgil, is one of the cutest little old men I have ever met. He reminds me of my grandpa, whistling everywhere he goes and always wearing a smile on his face. Every time he sees my truck, the Brown Babe, pull up, he flashes a huge smile and waves vigorously like a little kid. He is good to his core, and just being around him makes you feel better about the world. He donates his time accepting and organizing the fresh produce section for City Harvest five days a week. He always brightens my Monday mornings.

I check in with the office girls for a few minutes and then sit at my desk to write a quick note to Virgil. Today is his

165

birthday and I bought him a card last week. I add my own little personal note to the inside:

"In friendship as in gardening, you need patience, generosity, and the willingness to get your hands a little dirty. Thanks for all you do for City Harvest and for brightening this world with your smile. My Monday mornings are always a little bit better because I get to see you. I'm honored to know you and call you friend. Sincerely, Sophie."

I make up a gift certificate for $200 worth of produce from our farmers' market booth near his home. I jot a note on the certificate that says, "This is for YOUR family, not City Harvest." He is such a kindhearted man, he has a hard time not giving everything he earns right back to the center. I stick the certificate in the envelope, lick it shut, and get on my way.

The morning goes by quickly. After I make my City Harvest delivery and get my Virgil fix, I head downtown to Noire, Thatcher's restaurant, for his delivery. These are the only two deliveries I do each week, and I do them because I love the people. It's usually one of the only times I get to connect with Thatcher, so the two of us always have lunch together after I make my delivery to him.

"Hey, Soph! How's it going?" Thatcher says as he meets me at the delivery dock.

"Thatcher! I'm good, how are you?" I exclaim as I hop out of the cab and unlock the back door where the produce is.

"Can't complain too much since my wife came back to see me last night," he says as he gives me a big bear hug. *Wow, he's strong.*

"Well, that's good." I pull away and hop up into the back of the truck. "I told her to send me a text when she got home, so I knew she made it okay."

"You're always the checker-upper, aren't you?" he says as he grins at me.

"Can't help it. My dad was the same way. It's pure habit now." I hand him my clipboard with his order attached to it. "Look this over and make sure this is what you ordered."

Peering over the numbers he replies, "Yep, this looks good!"

"Okay, you're my last stop, so all of this is yours. Any chance you have some muscle in that kitchen?"

"You mean other than these guns?" he says as he flexes his arm muscles at me.

"Oh, if that's all you have, then I can manage," I spark back.

"Oh, no you didn't!" he yells with a big belly laugh. "V said you were on a roll this weekend, guess you're still on it."

"Yeah, sorry. I have a hard time shutting it off after I've been giving crap to your wife all weekend," I say as I hop out of the back of the truck.

"I'd have it no other way. V had a blast this weekend. How about you?" he asks as he holds the door open for me. I enter the back door and into the kitchen area where his staff are bustling about.

"An absolute blast. Always do when I'm with my girls."

"I'd love to be a fly on the wall of that cabin sometime."

"I'm not sure that would be a good idea," I say with a hint of sarcasm in my voice.

"Yeah, you're right. I'm probably better off not knowing what you guys are up to," he says as he gestures one of his staff over. "Hey, Todd, can you and the guys get the truck unloaded while Sophie and I have lunch?"

"Sure thing. Good afternoon, Sophie," he says with a smile.

"Hi, Todd. Thanks for doing my grunt work," I say with a wink.

"My pleasure," he says as he walks out the back door.

"I have a little surprise for you today," Thatcher says as he leads the way out into the restaurant.

"Oh? What's that?"

"More like *who's* that," he says as he directs me to a table where Veronica is seated.

"Hey girl!" Veronica exclaims as she rises from the table to give me a hug.

I hug her back and say, "V! What a nice surprise! I thought you were headed to Orlando today?"

"Not until tomorrow. I needed a day in the office to catch up on emails. The conference I'm speaking at doesn't start until Wednesday," she says as she takes her seat.

"Ah. Well, this is a fun surprise. I feel spoiled since I just got to spend the weekend with you."

"Well, I figured I needed to spend as much time with Thatch as I can this week before I leave again, so I figured I would crash your Monday lunch date and get to see both of you at the same time," she says as she leans over and kisses Thatcher on the cheek. "I don't travel again for a few weeks after this trip, so he'll be sick of me by Wednesday of next week."

"Not true!" he says in his defense. "I love it when you are home." He snuggles up closer to her in the booth. "I used to see a lot more of her before you introduced her to this fishing stuff." He glares playfully at me.

"Yeah, sorry about that. Didn't mean to turn you into a fishing widower."

"That's okay. It's what launched her career," he says as he puts his arm around her. "I wouldn't have it any other way."

"All in the name of 'research,'" she says as she gestures air quotes with her fingers. "Plus, I met the best friend a girl could ask for." She reaches across the table and squeezes my hand.

"Aw shucks," I say, and squeeze her hand back. "You're still saying that after I called you a bitch this weekend?"

Giving me a dumbfounded look she says, "You called me a bitch this weekend?"

"Oh wait, maybe I didn't say it out loud. My bad," I say with a sly grin.

Her eyes flare as she sticks her fingers in her water and then rapidly flicks the water droplets at me. "Sophie Myers! *You're* a bitch!" she exclaims as we both giggle like schoolgirls.

"Ladies! This is a fine dining establishment. Can you please control your behavior?" Thatcher says, playfully scolding us. "I have a reputation to uphold here."

"Oh yes, sorry, Thatcher. We'll behave," I say apologetically as I flick water back at Veronica.

"You two are impossible," he says as he shakes his head. Just then Todd comes out from the kitchen, my clipboard in his hand.

"We've got everything off the truck and checked in," he says as he hands me the clipboard. "Those currant tomatoes look awesome."

"Don't they, though? We tried several new exotic varieties this winter in one of our greenhouses. They have been doing really well. Have you tried the yellow beets yet? Those are my new favorites," I say as I take a sip of my water.

"I did! Thatcher put those on special for lunch last week, and we sold out in an hour! I saw that he put some more on the order this week. I can't wait," he says as he glances down at his watch. "Well, I'd better get back and get ready for the lunch rush. It was really nice to see you, Sophie."

"Thanks, Todd. Good to see you, too," I say as he turns and walks away.

"What did you do with the yellow beets? Sounds like they were a hit!" I ask Thatcher after Todd has walked away. They are both looking at me with funny looks on their faces. "What?"

"He likes you," Veronica says, cocking her head to one side.

"Oh stop . . . ," I gasp with a hint of disbelief in my voice.

"This is what I'm talking about. You have no idea when someone takes an interest in you."

My face flushes red with embarrassment, and I put my palms up in the air. "*That* conversation was supposed to tell me that he likes me?" My mouth gapes slightly open.

"It's not what he said, it's *how* he said it," Thatcher chimes in as support. "Plus, I don't think I've *ever* seen Todd out in the main dining area as long as he's worked here." He smiles in amusement at my uncomfortable state.

"You are the worst flirt I have ever met," Veronica teases.

"Ugh, I'm terrible at this stuff," I say as I shake my head. "Maybe I should double-date with you two so you can show me how to do it." I look over at Veronica and the excited, shocked look on her face grows with each second that passes. "Wait, I can't believe those words just came out of my mouth. Scratch that, rewind, *erase*!"

"No way, you just gave me permission!" Veronica exclaims. "Hmm, Todd or Greg? She sneers as she internally plots out our date. "I'm calling Greg to see what night he has free next week. When I get back, we'll have the two of you over for dinner at our place. Nothing crazy, just dinner."

"He did call you, right?" Thatcher asks me.

"Yes, he did. I was just too busy the night he wanted to go out," I say, embarrassed, looking down at my silverware.

"Well, good. Otherwise, I would have to kick his ass," Thatcher teases.

"Are you sure it won't be awkward?" I ask, looking Thatcher's direction. "I mean, what if it doesn't work out?"

"See? There you go again," Veronica blurts out. "You're ending it before it even begins."

"It will be fine, Sophie. Greg is an old friend. He can take care of himself," Thatcher says, reassuring me. "It's not like he's my best friend or anything. Then, it might be awkward." He grins.

"Ugh. Okay, fine," I say, giving in. Desperately wanting to change the subject I say, "Can't a girl get anything to eat around here?"

"Right-O," Thatcher says as he waves over one of the waitresses. "Miss Kate, will you please bring us our lunch?"

"Of course, Mr. Reed," she says, and turns and heads back into the kitchen.

"I took the liberty of ordering ahead and making your favorite. Hope you don't mind," he says with a smile.

"Perfect! One less decision I have to make on my own."

"What night next week do you want to have dinner?" Veronica asks as she looks at her calendar on her iPhone. "I can do Tuesday, Wednesday, or Thursday."

"Any day but Wednesday. I am going to start watching Jordan and Parker on Wednesday nights for Amanda for a few months."

"Oh yeah? What is she doing?" Veronica asks as our soup, salad, and bread are served.

"I asked her this weekend what I could do to help while Mike is deployed. She said she needed one night a week where she could go and get the weekly shopping done without having to tote two little kids around with her." I gaze down at my soup and pick up my spoon. "She said the last time she took them to the store, Parker had a meltdown and she wasn't able to get everything on her list. I just think she is

172

under a huge amount of stress, so anything I can do will help."

"I can't imagine that kind of stress. I mean, he's basically right behind the front line. I would stay up and worry every night," Veronica says as she takes a bite of her salad.

"I think she does. She talked a little bit about it this weekend," I say as I take a bite of my soup.

"Yeah, some."

"I think she needs a shoulder to cry on more than anything. She feels pretty alone," I say, completely enjoying my appetizer. "I don't mind driving down there one night a week. I'm looking forward to it, actually."

"Do you know what kind of diapers Parker wears? She talked about them being a special brand. I was thinking about picking up four or five boxes of them and mailing them to her."

"She would love that. I have it written down at home. I can text it to you," I say, taking a bite of bread.

"That would be great. We'd love to help out too."

"Thatcher, this soup is awesome!" I exclaim, dipping a corner of my bread in my soup and biting off a piece.

"Good. I made it the special today just for you. Cream of mushroom is your favorite, right?" he asks, smiling.

"Yours is, none of that crap that comes in a can, though," I add.

"Homemade usually is a little more flavorful," Thatcher says, taking a bite of his salad. "So when does Mike come home for his visit?"

"I think sometime in October. She was asking me about bringing the family up to the Corn Maze when he's back, so that would have to be October-ish."

"We'd like to have them up to the restaurant for a special date night when he is back," Thatcher says. "We'd like them to stay in our guest suite as well."

"They will love that." I slurp down another bite of my soup. Changing the subject, I ask, "What did you think of our new friend, Melody?"

"Thatcher knew exactly who I was talking about when I described her. Isn't that wild that she lives upstairs?"

"Totally random. Think she'll stick around?" I ask as our main entrees are served.

"Not sure. We're all a lot older than she is, except for Amanda. Not that that matters, but hopefully that doesn't bother her. I suppose it might depend on whether or not she likes fishing," Veronica adds, admiring her plate.

"Rose will see to that. That's a given," I say as I stare down at my plate of yumminess. "Thatch, this seared Ahi tuna looks awesome! Will you ever show me how to make this at home?" The first bite I take explodes on my taste buds. "Mmm."

"And give you a reason to put someone else on my Monday morning delivery? Never!" he says as he watches me devour my first few bites. "You're so easy to please. That's the easiest thing on the menu to make. Now Miss V, on the other hand, makes me work for it."

"You love it and you know it," she says as she feeds him a

bite of her meal. They are incredibly cute together.

"I think it will be nice to add someone new to our little group," I say, returning to the topic of Melody. "She seems pretty cool. I'm looking forward to getting to know her."

"I told her to let me know when she gets back from the cabin so we could meet up for dinner. I want to introduce her to Thatcher. He is just getting ready to hire someone to take pictures of his menu items for his website. Aren't you, honey?" she asks, looking at Thatcher.

"Yeah, I'd like to look at her portfolio and see what kind of work she does. If it's good, we'll give it a try. She's in here quite a bit, so it would be nice to give her some work," he says as he takes a bite of his tuna.

"That would be nice. I hope that works out."

We sit and talk a while longer as we finish our meal. The restaurant starts to buzz with the lunch rush, so we head into Thatcher's office to release our table. Before we leave, Veronica pins me down for Tuesday of next week for our double date. I give them each a big hug before saying good-bye and heading out the back door to leave. I hop into my big truck surprisingly optimistic about my upcoming dinner with Greg.

`·.¸¸.·´¯`·.¸.><((((º>`·.¸¸.·´¯`·...><((((º>`·.¸¸.·´¯`·..

Amanda

"Mike! Hey! Oh my gosh, you look great, babe!" I scream as Mike's image appears on my computer screen when Skype connects us.

"Hey baby! How's it going?"

"Everything is going great. Look, Jordan, it's Daddy! Say hi to Daddy!"

"Daddy!" she yells as she hops in my lap. "Look at my picture I made you. Do you like it?

"I love it, Jordan. You did a great job! Hold it up so I can see it closer." She moves it into view of the camera, and Mike squints to take a better look. "Oh wow, sweetie, that is really good. I'm very proud of you."

"Mommy is going to put it in a box for you," she says as she squirms on my lap.

"That will be great. I can't wait to get it," he says as he smiles. "What have you been doing? Have you been reading books with Mommy?"

"Um, I like *Mr. Brown Can Moo!* Can you read it to me?"

"Yes, I sure can. Why don't you go get the book and bring it to Mommy so I can read it to you."

"Yay!" she squeals as she hops off my lap and runs into her bedroom.

"Good thing you memorized this one before you left!" I say, smiling.

"No doubt. I think I've read that one at least a hundred times to her tucking her in at night. I could probably recite it in my sleep!"

"I love it when she hoots like the owl when it asks if you can do it too. Totally cracks me up," I tell him.

"Ah, me too. That's one of my favorite parts."

Running back she leaps into my lap with the chunky board book. "Here it is, Daddy!"

"Okay, you turn the pages as Daddy reads."

"Yay!" she says as she opens to the first page.

Just then Parker wanders into the room, and I catch a whiff of his poopy diaper.

"Whoa, Parker! That is awful!" I say as my face contorts with the pungent smell surrounding my son. "Poopy diaper alert."

"Oh yuck! I don't miss those," Mike says, laughing.

"Yeah, thanks a lot!" I playfully sneer back. "Oh wow, that is bad," I almost gag. "Here, Jordan, you sit here and let Daddy read you *Mr. Brown Can Moo* while I go and change Parker. Be right back."

"Okay, Mommy," Jordan replies cheerfully.

"Ugh, sorry about that, honey," Mike says, empathizing with my gross task.

"You're on full-time diaper duty when you get back!" I holler as I walk into the living room.

"Are you ready, Jordan?" Mike asks.

"Yep!"

"Alright, let's do this. You turn the pages. 'Oh, the wonderful sounds Mr. Brown can do! He can sound like a cow. He can go Moooo Moooo.'" I hear Mike reciting the book and mooing like a cow as I get a diaper and wipes and chase down Parker. *He is such a good daddy.* I get Parker cleaned up as quickly as I can and into his jammies.

As I get back to the computer, Mike is finishing up the second time through the book. "'Tick Tock *Knock Knock* BOOM BOOM *Splat!* Last a *whisper whisper* and that is that.'[vi]

"Yay, Daddy!" Jordan says gleefully as she claps her hands at the end. "Can you take me to the park tomorrow?" We both wince a little at her request. I pick her up and put her on my lap.

"No sweetie, Daddy will still be at work tomorrow. I'll take you to the park when I get home, though!" he says with enthusiasm, trying to keep her spirits high.

"Okay, Daddy. Love you, bye-bye!" she yells as she hops down and scampers away.

"Ugh, sorry about that. She still doesn't understand that you won't be home next week. She misses you so much, Mike."

"I know. I miss her too. Breaks my heart."

"I know, sorry . . . ," I say as I bite my bottom lip to prevent myself from tearing up.

Mike clears his throat, his tell-tale sign he is tearing up as well, and blurts out, "So, how are you? Is everything going okay?"

"Yeah, it's busy, but everything is going fine. Parker is still getting up a few times a night since you left, but his cold is better now. How are you? How are things over there?"

"Oh, pretty good. The mission is going well. The captain has big expectations of us, so we're trying to get everything done that he wants us to do."

"Are you staying safe? Have you seen any combat this week?"

"Oh, a little. Nothing major."

"Not like you'd tell me anyway," I spark back.

"I just don't want you to worry. I'm doing my job and I'm fine," he says with a somewhat exasperated tone. Changing the subject, he continues, "Let's not talk about that. Tell me about Parker. What new trick does he have this week?"

"Fine," I mutter, then move on. "His newest trick is his train sounds. He absolutely *loves* the train set you got him. He plays and plays for hours with it. He has to have a Thomas the Tank Engine in his possession at all times—even when he goes to bed! He calls it Tomman instead of Thomas. It's totally cute."

"Oh good, I'm glad he likes it. Where is he? Hold him up so I can see how big he is!" he exclaims.

"Where else but at his train table? Parker! Come here and say hi to Daddy!" Parker looks up from playing and then runs over to me. I pick him up so he is in view of the camera. "Look, Parker, there's Daddy! Say hi to Daddy!"

"Oh wow, he's huge! What are you feeding him? Hey buddy, it's Daddy! How's my little man?" he says, beaming from ear to ear. "You are getting so big! Have you been playing with your trains?"

"Daddy?" he asks as he points his chubby little finger at the screen.

"Yes, Daddy is right here! Say hi to Daddy!" Mike replies as he waves at the computer.

"Daddy, wook it. Tomman!" Parker says as he holds up his train.

"Is that your train? That's a cool train, buddy. What sound does a train make?"

"Toot toot!"

"Oh, good job, buddy! Are you having fun playing with your trains?"

"Bye, Daddy!" he yells as he bolts off my lap and runs back to his train table.

"Bye, buddy. Daddy loves you."

"*Annnd* off he goes. That's about the attention span of an eighteen-month-old."

"Yeah, no doubt," Mike says, smiling. "He looks awesome. I can't believe how big he is getting! I miss you guys so much."

"We miss you too, baby. I love you so much," I say as I put my hand up on the computer screen. "If I could will you here, I would."

"I know. Nine more months. Three months have already gone by, so hopefully the next nine will go just as fast," he says sullenly. "Hey, how was your fishing weekend with the girls?"

"Oh Mike, it was so awesome!" I tell him.

"Did you catch anything?"

"I did! I caught a ton of rainbows and browns. It was so much fun. You remember that fly that Jordan helped me tie? The one with the sparkly ribbon?"

"Yeah, I remember."

"I actually caught a fish with it! The first fish of my trip. I couldn't believe it. I basically added the ribbon just to appease her, but I actually caught a fish with it! So fun."

"That's so cool. I bet she was excited when you told her about it."

"Yeah, she was. It was cute. Oh and get this, Rose made each of us girls a quilt! She gave it to me this weekend. It is so cool!"

"Oh wow, that's awesome. Be sure to tell her I said thank you."

"Here, I have it right here." I lean over and pick it up off the floor and hold it up for him to see. "Look at this, aren't the colors amazing?" I say as I show him the beautiful patterns and colors.

"That is amazing. How big is it?"

"Big enough for two to snuggle under," I say coyly.

"Sounds good to me!" he says excitedly.

"I thought it might."

"Well, that is awesome. Tell her thanks. I can't wait to see it in person. How was the rest of the weekend?"

"So much fun. I love those women so much. I really needed a weekend off to just unwind a bit. It's nice to wake up and have someone else make you a cup of coffee and make you breakfast."

"I can relate. You make some mean eggs."

"Ha ha, Mr. funny guy," I say playfully. "But seriously, we had a great weekend. Rose was up to her usual shenanigans on the river."

"Oh Lord, what did she do now?"

"She threw a couple pebbles into the water near Sophie to trick her into thinking it was a rising fish. Sophie totally fell for it too."

"Oh dang, that's funny."

"Then Rose picked up a huge rock and hurled it into the river right in front of Sophie and drenched her with water. It was hysterical!"

"Ha! That Rose is something else."

"But wait, it gets better," I say as I continue the story. "Right after this we heard a woman screaming and splashing in the river. There was a naked chick being washed downstream!"

"Um, what?! She was naked? What the hell kind of waters were you fishing in?" he says, laughing. "And why haven't you taken me to any of these fishing holes?"

"I know, right? It was so bizarre," I say, laughing along with him. "Evidently she's a photographer and was out taking nude pictures of herself in nature. She lost her balance and fell in the river."

"Oh wow, that's crazy."

"She's just damn lucky we fished her out when we did. She was already blue. That water was just snow not too long ago, it was freezing!"

"I bet!"

"We threw a jacket on her and ran her back up to the cabin. Sophie got a fire started, and Veronica made her some hot tea. She actually ended up hanging out with us for the rest of the weekend, which now that I think about it sounds a little strange."

"Yeah it does, who is this chick?" he asks.

"Some young photographer who lives in a loft downtown. We actually figured out she lives above Thatcher's restaurant."

"No way, that's random."

"Really random. She was pretty cool for the most part. Her name is Melody."

"Does she fish?"

"Well, she does now. You know Rose, always looking for a new project. Rose is staying a few extra days at the cabin with her to let her spend some time on the river."

"She'll be a pro in no time then, just like you."

"Well, I don't know about that, but the weekend was great."

"Sounds like it was fun. I'm so glad you went. You deserve it," he says with an adoring smile.

"Thanks, babe. I need that every once in a while just so I can have a little me-time," I say as I look down at my keyboard. "Helps to recharge my batteries so I can be the best mom I can be when I'm back in the real world."

"You're a great mom, Mandy. Our kids are so damn lucky to have you as a mom. Thanks for being there when I can't," he says as his voice drops off a little.

"Oh, you're here, baby. We just can't physically hug you right now." I put my hand back up on the computer screen, trying to touch him from a world away.

"I know. Thanks, love. I love you," he says as he puts his hand up to his screen.

"I love you too, Mike." We both sit in silence for a moment, both of us trying to choke back tears.

I hear a loud noise come from over his shoulder, and he sits up straight in his chair. Clearing his voice again, he says,

"Well, it looks like the captain is making some noise, so I'd better get going. Sorry this was so short."

"It's okay. It was awesome to see you." I feel the heat of tears flood my eyes as I realize our time is over.

"Sleep tight, love. I love you."

"I love you too, Mike. Have a great day, baby. Bye."

"I will. Bye."

It's pretty routine for me to shut my laptop after a Skype call and burst into tears. I stay as strong as I can while he can see me, but as soon as the laptop is shut, the flood of emotions come surging out of my body. Since the kids are still up, I hold it together until I get them down for the night. I kiss them good night, and the moment I close their bedroom door I burst into tears.

I wander around the house, not quite certain what I should do to calm myself down. I finally find myself in our closet, embracing an entire section of his clothes, aching for him to be there. I collapse on the floor in a sobbing mess and curl up into the fetal position, crying as if there were no tomorrow. Thirty minutes later, exhausted, I crawl out of the closet and into our bed. I bury my face in his pillow to smell where his head had touched.

I pop in a few of the videos that Mike made the kids before he left for Afghanistan. I love to see him throwing Jordan up in the air and hearing her big belly laughs. And watching Parker squeeze his daddy's neck tight with a big hug just melts me. Mike has such a unique sense of humor, and hearing him in the video give tidbits of advice to the kids in his own funny way brings tears to my eyes. "Parker, when you go on your first date, make sure you open the car door for her. Be a gentleman, and don't be too nervous—girls see right through that. *Always* remember the day of your first date. Give her flowers every month on that same date to show that you remember. Girls love that shit, er, I mean stuff." Realizing he just swore on video, he looks straight into the camera and grins that magical grin that I love so much. I hug his pillow a little tighter as the tears flow steadily down my cheeks. The thought of losing him is more than I can bear. I seriously do not know what I would do without him.

I turn off the video and cry myself to sleep.

`·.¸¸.·´¯`·.¸¸><((((º>`·.¸¸.·´¯`·..><((((º>`·.¸¸.·´¯`·..

Melody

I put the finishing touches on what I'm calling my Food Porn portfolio to show Veronica's husband today. I included food pics, people dining, and a variety of musicians in the moment. He has no idea that I snuck into his restaurant on Saturday and took pics of the jazz trio that was playing and his guests that night. It would be cool to shoot his food for his menu and website.

I also put together all of the photos I printed from the fly fishing weekend. I hope they like them. I really enjoyed processing them. It dawned on me that this is the first time in a long time that I did any kind of photography that was a gift. Most everything I do is for sale, for a client, or as a benefit to me in some way. It felt strange when I realized how much I cared about capturing everyone's personality and passion in each photo I chose to give them. I probably took two thousand photos that weekend, and I didn't even make it to the music festival. Figuring out which ones were the absolute best took hours if not days. *Not that I need their approval, but I do hope they are impressed.*

My favorite pic from the whole weekend is of Rose in an impressive back cast the evening after everyone else left. The bend in the fly line is just perfect, and her face exudes confidence and joy.   The rhythm and grace of her casting is like watching a dance, as if she's lost in the music yet keeping time at the same moment. It was even a little hypnotic as I processed her pics. *It's strange how much I like this woman, even though I hardly know her.* Such a weird feeling for me. I haven't cared this much about

189

anyone in a long time. *Other than my grandparents, of course.* Knowing the back story of the picture makes me like it even more. She spent the entire day teaching me, then still took time to step into the river to feed her soul as well. *I need to do more of that.* There are times I feel like I'm doing what I *have* to do and not what I *want* to do, like I have an image to uphold yet I'm doing it for all the wrong reasons. *Please your parents. Don't embarrass them.* My art gallery prints pay the bills, but I do them more to please my parents, so they have something to tell their friends about what I do. They aren't very web savvy, so they don't know much about my online life. If they ever find out about me doing Suicide Girls . . . I can't imagine the shame and dishonor it would bring to the family. I shudder just thinking about it.

It's funny how I felt my confidence in my photography soar after Rose spent time with me teaching me how to fish, which is weird since I already know I'm a talented photog. In a weird way that I wasn't expecting, being in the outdoors helped me see the rhythm of nature's music, a symphony that I could capture and conduct through my lens. I wasn't told when or how to play by my parents, but I could create my own masterpiece. Using *my* unique perspective rather than that of someone else, as if I'm writing my own song. *Your name is Melody, for crying out loud . . .*

I slide my prints into my portfolio sleeve and head downstairs to Noire. I briefly chat with Girard, the bellman, in the elevator on the way down. *I have to admit, I kinda like Girard.* He's a nice old man who always smiles at me. Most people seem to be afraid of me, but he seems to be able to look past my tats and piercings and see me as an actual person. *What is it about me liking old people? Weird.*

`` `..,.·´¯`·.,><((((º>`·.,.·´¯`·..><((((º>`·.,.·´¯`·.. ``

Veronica

I'm looking forward to introducing Melody to Thatcher today. I hope they hit it off, as I think there are opportunities for both of them. I researched some of her stuff online, and she is damn good at what she does. You can tell there is passion behind her purpose. She has a "local eats" blog that features hip restaurants that showcase musicians with a great vibe. Now that Thatch has added music on the weekends, I'm hoping she will highlight Noire. It would give him some great publicity, and she has an impressive following. I even noticed several food critics commenting on her stuff, so I'm hoping this introduction will be fruitful for both of them. He was so funny when his piano was delivered a few months ago; it was like watching a kid on Christmas morning. He was downright giddy as he skipped around the restaurant waiting for its arrival. *Could he be any cuter?*

I'm so proud of him. He works so damn hard. I think his passion shines through in his food as well as the experience he wants to create for his diners. He pours his soul into this place, so I hope Melody can see this as well. He's been wanting to upgrade his website with new pictures of his dishes, and I think Melody would be the perfect photographer for this.

"Hey, Melody! Great to see you again!" I say as she walks in the door with her large, black portfolio folder.

"Hey, Veronica. Thanks for setting this up."

"Of course. How was your time with Rose?"

"Oh, it was pretty good. I did catch a few fish, so I must have done something right."

"Well, that's Rose for you. She helped teach me, so I know she has the patience of Job." Just then Thatcher emerges from the kitchen. "Hey babe, good timing. This is Melody."

"Hello! Good to meet you, I'm Thatcher." He walks briskly towards her and shakes her hand. "V told me you stumbled into their group last month."

"Um, yeah."

"Oh sorry, I mean, well, that you met them last month."

"Yeah . . ."

"She was just telling me about Rose teaching her how to fly fish," I chime in, trying to break the awkwardness.

"Oh yeah? Did you like it?"

"It was good. A lot to take in, but I did like it."

"Yeah, V didn't like it much when she started, but man I'm glad she stuck with it. It really propelled her career."

"Yeah, I love it now, but I pretty much hated it when I started. Rose and Sophie had to talk real hard to get me back out on the water after the first day, but I'm glad they did. It took a little bit for me to get the hang of it, but I love it now."

"Cool," Melody says as she looks down at her portfolio and then around the room a little bit.

"Right, well, I thought it would be great for the two of you to meet, especially since you live upstairs, but also because I think the two of you can help each other out."

"I've definitely seen you in here at the restaurant. V told me you live upstairs, how long have you lived there?"

"A few years now. It's pretty cool. I like your food."

"Nice. Well, thanks. I'd probably be in trouble if my bed was stumbling distance from work. Too hard to leave when it's so close, or I'd be too accessible to my staff. We live over in the Riverfront Towers, so not too far."

"My parents live over there."

"Oh yeah? What part?"

"Just near there," she says, a little awkwardly. Changing the subject, she blurts out, "Um, here, I have some pictures of my work to show you." She sets her portfolio up on the table, and it must not have been zipped all the way shut as it falls open and her pictures spill out onto the floor. "Shit. Oh God, sorry."

We all spring into action to pick up the pictures. Thatch picks one up and exclaims, "Oh my God, is this Noire?"

"Yes. Sorry. Damn, I had this whole presentation. I . . ."

"Melody, these are fantastic. When did you take these? Oh my God, look at this, V. Was this last weekend?"

"Yeah, I, um, stopped in last Saturday evening when you had the jazz band here."

"Look at this one! It's when we were sitting down with the Bosers and Koelpins having dinner that night. Look how she caught you laughing." I marvel at the photographs, trying to take in each one fully. "Melody, what a surprise, these are so fantastic."

"Thanks, I thought what better way to showcase what I can do than for you to see photographs from your own environment. Hope it was okay that I snuck in."

"How did I not see you?" Thatcher asks. "I'm supposed to see everything around here."

"Um, I can be pretty elusive when I need to be." She finally smiles, seeming to loosen up a bit.

Thatcher and I admire and stare at the quality of her photographs. She has captured guests having a lovely time, enjoying the atmosphere, the entertainment, and the food all at the same time. You can almost hear the music from the photos of the musicians. The lighting and ambiance make Noire look like the finest dining establishment in all of Denver. She even has a shot of our head chef through the kitchen window. What a cool thing for her to do. I knew she was going to be a good fit for Thatch.

"Well, if this is the quality of photos you can take, then you are absolutely the right person for the job. Let's talk about what I need done and what your rates are."

I left the two of them to talk shop as I slipped into the back room.

Section 5: Practice

"The preparation has been done. You've now got the right tackle and some confidence in the water you're going to fish. Remember that conditions can change from minute to minute—awareness and adaptability are the keys to successful fishing."[vii]

John Bailey's Complete Guide to Fly Fishing: The Fish, The Tackle & The Techniques
by John Bailey

Sophie

My phone vibrates in my pocket, and I fumble to get it out in time to answer it. It's Veronica.

"Hello?"

"Are you ready?" she exclaims as she hears my voice.

"No, I'm not ready. It's only three thirty and I'm up to my elbows in dirt!" I look down at my dirty, mud-stained jeans and shirt, and shake my head.

"What do you mean 'it's only three thirty'? What time are you coming over?" she asks.

"What time do you want me there?"

"Um, how about five thirty? Gives me time to get a few glasses of red in you before Greg gets here," she says, giggling.

"So, you're going to get me drunk before he even shows up? Awesome plan, thanks, V," I joke.

"Loosen up, Soph. It will just take the edge off. Wait, hold on a second," she says as she mutters something to someone near her. "Sorry, just leaving work. Trying to tie up a few last-minute details for tonight." She mutters one more thing, trying to cover the phone so I can't hear what she is saying. I giggle to myself as she sounds like Charlie Brown's teacher. Suddenly she's back and blurts out, "Are you seriously up to your elbows in dirt? You need to get in the shower! Get your hair done! You have to leave in an hour if you are going to make it by five thirty."

"Crap, I guess you're right. I'd better get out of here then." Now I suddenly feel rushed.

"Who are you and what have you done with Sophie? You are usually the biggest *planner* of all of us. Why haven't you planned your day out to the last minute? Are you getting cold feet?"

"No, why would I do that?" I ask, grabbing my truck keys and heading for the door.

"Oh, I don't know, maybe because you are notorious for ending things before they begin. Maybe because you can take care of everyone else but yourself?"

"Oh, shut up, V," I say with irritation in my voice.

"You drive me crazy sometimes," she mutters under her breath. "Why do I get the feeling I'm more excited about this than you are?"

"You're not! Cut it out! I just didn't know what time you wanted me there," I spark back as I jump into my truck. "I'm headed home now."

"Good. What are you wearing?"

Shit. I hadn't thought that far ahead yet. "Um . . ."

"You haven't even thought about it yet? Jesus, Soph."

"I'll figure it out. I have a couple of ideas," I lie.

"Wear your black cowl-neck shirt and your dark-blue Miss Me jeans. Your ass looks awesome in those. Wear your red heels and the necklace, earring, and bracelet set that Rose gave you last year. Wear your hair down and curl the ends using that big, four-inch curling iron so it frames your face. And for God's sake, put a little makeup on for once. Any questions?" she states matter-of-factly.

"Wow, how do you do that?" I ask, a little stunned.

"It's what I do," she says with a giggle. "You'll look hot. Now go!"

"I'm going! Sheesh!" I say as I go to hang up.

"Hey, Soph?" I hear her yell out as I'm hanging up.

Placing the phone back up to my ear, I say, "Yeah?"

"You know I love you, right?"

"Yeah, I know," I grumble. Not wanting her to have the last jab, I continue, "See you soon, *Mom*."

"Don't be late!" she yells as she hangs up, my comment obviously not registering. I love and hate her all at the same time.

I race home and quickly swim through the shower. I put on a black bra and panty set and sit down at my vanity. I quickly blow out my hair and curl the ends under as instructed. I apply some light makeup and a little lip gloss and look in the mirror. I hardly recognize the cute stranger staring back at me. I rarely take the time to do hair and makeup anymore.

199

Maybe tonight won't be so bad after all. I finish getting dressed and dust off my red heels before slipping them on. I don't even remember the last time I wore these! *I sure hope tonight goes well.*

`·.,ˌ.·´¯`·.ˌ><((((º>`·.,ˌ.·´¯`·..><((((º>`·.,ˌ.·´¯`·..

I arrive at 5:44 p.m.

The bellman greets me as he opens the door for me. "Good evening, ma'am."

"Good evening, sir. Sophie Myers for Veronica Reed, please."

"Mrs. Reed has been anxiously awaiting your arrival," he says with a smile, gesturing towards the elevator.

"I'm a few minutes late. That drives her crazy," I say as I awkwardly clop towards the elevator doors.

Following directly behind me, he replies, "Beautiful night tonight, don't you think?"

"Oh, yes it is. The sunset is gorgeous right now! I almost hated to come in so I would miss it," I reply.

"I'm sure you will still be able to see it well from the top floor."

"Oh right. True." I sometimes forget how nice of a place V and Thatcher have. She's so down to earth I forget that they live in one of the most expensive buildings downtown. "Have you worked here long?" I ask, trying to make small talk on the ride up to their loft.

"Yes, ma'am, since it was converted to lofts ten years ago."

200

"Do you enjoy it?" I ask, wondering what it would be like to walk in his shoes.

"Very much so. We're lucky to have very nice tenants."

"That's good," I say as an awkward silence falls between us. We both look up at the floor numbers and watch them light up as they ascend towards the top. The elevator dings when it gets to the top floor. The doors open and he gestures towards their front door. "Have a nice evening, Ms. Myers."

"Thank you, sir," I say as I exit the elevator. "See you later."

"You're late!" Veronica yells as she throws open the front door.

"Hardly!" I reply.

"Thanks, Frank!" she hollers as the elevator doors close shut. "Look at you, Miss Thang! You look good!" She eyes me up and down. "I can pick out a hot outfit, can't I?"

"You didn't do too bad," I say as I give her a hug hello. "Although these heels are killing me!"

"When was the last time you wore heels? 2009? I've never known someone to actually *wear out* a pair of hiking boots, Sophie."

"They're comfortable! Plus, I don't ever have a reason to wear heels."

"Well, hopefully after tonight you will," she says with a smile.

"Is Greg here yet?" I ask quietly, in case he is.

"No, not yet. Thatcher talked to him yesterday and confirmed the time, so he should be here shortly."

"Hey, Sophie!" Thatcher says as he walks out of the kitchen. He greets me with a kiss on the cheek. "You are looking beautiful tonight."

Blushing, I reply, "Thanks. It smells amazing. What awesome concoction are you brewing up tonight?"

"Oh, a little of this and a little of that," he says as he hands me a glass of wine. "I avoided some of the top-ten worst first-date foods: spaghetti, wings, shelled crab."

"Ugh, thank you! I didn't even think about that."

"Just looking out for you," he says as he pours a glass for Veronica. "Cheers." He clinks his wine glass to each of ours.

"Cheers. Thanks, Thatcher." I take a sip of wine and its hearty flavors go down nicely. "Oh wow, what is this? It's divine."

"I've been saving this one for a special occasion," he says with a smile. "I picked it up in France several years ago. It's a Château Lafite Rothschild, Pauillac from 1996." He puts his arm around Veronica and squeezes her closer to him.

"Wow, I don't know what you just said, but it's very good," I tell him.

He smiles and says, "I'm glad you like it. I like the dark, silky texture it has." He swirls the glass and inspects the side of the glass. He then holds it up to his nose and draws in a long, exaggerated inhale. "It sports aromas of mint and black currant. I love it."

"I love this one too," Veronica says. "I will be sad when we deplete our wine cellar of this one."

"What were you doing in France?" I ask, taking another sip of wine.

"I went there for a month and studied under Alain Ducasse at the Dorchester restaurant. I wanted to add some flair to my menu with some French cuisine. It was a fantastic experience," he says as he takes another sip of his wine. "Have you been to France?"

"No, I haven't. I'd like to take a few months some winter and tour several European countries."

"Winter? Why winter?"

"Because I'm busier than hell in the summer. You might recall I run this little thing called a greenhouse?"

"Okay, Miss Sassypants." He gestures towards the living room, and we both follow him in there. "Here, have a seat and enjoy that sunset before it's gone. I'll bring out some food."

I love the living room in their loft. The walls are decorated with beautiful and rare African art, a tribute to their ethnic heritage. Every shelf is a curated display of antiques and found items from their many travels. There are adornments such as her grandmother's china and angel collections and his dad's trumpet and clarinet. She has blended them very well for a sophisticated yet homey feeling. The floor-to-ceiling windows offer soaring views of the Rocky Mountains that make you feel like you're just inches away from the wilderness, instead of being downtown. The wraparound exposure makes you feel like you are living on top of the world. I could stare out the windows at that sunset all night long.

We settle down in their living room on one of their large leather couches. Thatcher refuses all offers of assistance in the kitchen from V and me, so we sit and chat away, waiting on Greg's arrival. We chat about fishing, travels, business, and the other girls. Thatcher brings out an amazing appetizer of smoked salmon and brie with crackers. I'm so hungry I dive in as if I haven't eaten in days. Two glasses of wine later, I'm thoroughly enjoying our conversation when I notice Veronica looking more and more irritated by the minute. She keeps looking at her phone over and over, presumably to check the time. I look down at my watch and realize that ninety minutes have passed since I arrived. She glances over at Thatcher looking for information. He shrugs his shoulders and disappears into the kitchen.

"I'm going to go check on dinner," Veronica says as she stands. "Here, have another glass of wine." She pours me another glass before heading into the kitchen.

I can vaguely hear their conversation as they whisper back and forth.

"Where is he?" she asks, irritation in her voice.

"I don't know. He's not responding to my texts and I've left three messages. I don't know what the hell is going on."

"He's not standing her up, is he? He wouldn't do that, would he?"

"No, I don't think so. As of yesterday he was on board. I don't know what the hell is going on."

"Should we go ahead and eat? I don't know what to tell Sophie."

"I don't either."

"What about our tickets? Should we still go to the game?"

"Have you told Sophie about it yet? Does she even know we were going?"

"No, I didn't tell her. I wanted it to be a surprise."

"Well, what she doesn't know won't hurt her."

"Was Greg thinking he was going to meet us at the game?"

"No, I specifically told him we were going to eat dinner here, then head to the game."

"I am going to kick his ass if he doesn't show up!" she whispers loudly. I shake my head knowing that this night is not going to turn out the way I had hoped.

"*You* are? I'm so flippin pissed right now, I could throttle him," he tells her. They both pause for a few moments, not really knowing what to say. "Let's go ahead and eat," he mutters, and he starts tinkering around in the kitchen.

"Okay, I'll tell Sophie."

Veronica comes back into the living room all smiles, trying to put on a straight face. When our eyes meet, I tilt my head to the side and give her an all-knowing look. She rolls her eyes, knowing that I overheard them, and says, "I'm sorry, Soph. I don't know what the hell is going on."

"It's okay, V. He's not coming. It's alright," I say as I look down at my wine glass.

"It is *not* alright. I'm flaming pissed off at him!" she shouts.

I shrug my shoulders at her. "It just wasn't meant to be, it's no big deal."

"Well, it's a big deal to me. I'm going to kick his ass the next time I see him." She slumps hard into the couch, almost spilling her wine.

"See, this is the exact reason why I didn't want to go out with your friends. Now it's awkward with you guys."

"Well, I don't need to be friends with assholes anyway," she says, seething.

We both sit for a few moments, not really knowing what to say next.

"Let's go ahead and eat," Thatcher says from the kitchen. "Everything is ready."

We head into the dining room and the table is now set for three, whereas earlier I had seen it set for four. We take our seats and Thatcher serves the meal. I pick at my food, and the overall mood of the evening dramatically declines. I lose my appetite after finishing off my fourth glass of wine. I decide to stay the night due to my inebriated state and retire early to their guest suite. By the time my head hits the pillow, I swear off men for eternity. Assholes.

`·.¸¸.·´¯`·.¸><(((º>`·.¸¸.·´¯`·.¸><((((º>`·.¸¸.·´¯`·..

Amanda

I'm really looking forward to Sophie coming over tonight. I haven't talked much with any of the girls since I got back a few weeks ago. I'm looking forward to going grocery shopping by myself, which crazily enough will feel like a one-hour mini vacation. No meltdowns to deal with or impulse items being thrown into the cart, which usually add another twenty dollars to my already strained grocery budget. I'm also looking forward to a little adult conversation with my friend over a glass of wine. Hanging out with ten-year-olds all day and then toddlers all night definitely impacts my sanity. I could use a little conversation that does not include rhyming words. I'm also looking forward to bending her ear about what has been going on with Mike. I just need someone to talk to.

Mike usually logs on to Facebook or Skype every day, and it has been seven days since he was last on. This is not the norm for him, so I've been worried sick for a week. I haven't slept well since our girls' weekend, and I am completely exhausted. I know I shouldn't assume the worst, but it's so hard when communication gets interrupted. He could be out on a mission, or a sandstorm could be blocking communication. There could be a million reasons why he's not logged on, but I just can't keep my mind from running through the worst-case scenarios. The unit will also go on a communication blackout if anyone in the unit is killed in action. This prevents family members of the deceased finding out secondhand information from a soldier's relative before being notified properly. Last month when he was out on mission and didn't contact me for a few weeks, I logged on to www.icasualties.org daily, which lists all the dead soldiers ranks, ages, where they were, and how they were killed. It doesn't list their names, but it gives enough detail to let me know if it's near his location. It seems a little sick and twisted, but it actually puts my mind at ease. It also lets me see where the real combat is happening. If it is far away from him, I don't worry as much. If it is close by, I don't sleep. Checking this site does, however, put reality right in my face that each one of those names has someone like me sitting at home. Each time the doorbell rings, I shudder in fear until I see that it's not someone in uniform.

At six o'clock sharp Sophie shows up on my doorstep with an armful of groceries.

"Sophie, what did you do?" I say as I hold the door open for her. She takes the bulging bags of groceries into the kitchen and places them on the kitchen counter.

"What, this stuff? A cute grocery store sacker put these in the back of my truck and asked me to bring them to you. Who am I to argue with him?" she says, smiling.

"Well, you shouldn't have. Really."

"Oh, it's okay. It's my little way of helping out. Plus, I've got four greenhouses full of veggies. I've got plenty to share."

"Oh my gosh, thank you so much!"

"One condition, though, you have to help me unload the car," she says with a smirk.

"Deal!" I say as we both head down the sidewalk and out to her truck. Once there she opens the door, and her backseat is overflowing with boxes of food.

"Wow, look at all of this. This is too much!" I exclaim, completely dumbfounded by the number of groceries stacked in the backseat. It is overflowing with boxes of produce, diapers, pasta, and more. It is obvious she hit Costco or Sam's Club on the way to see me.

"It's nothing, really," she says as she hands me a huge box of cereal.

"No, you have no idea how big this is." I am overwhelmed with her generosity. "Thank you so much."

"You are welcome," she says as she reaches her arm around me and gives me a side squeeze. "Well, this stuff isn't getting into the house on its own. Get busy!"

"Yes, ma'am!" I reply as I grab a giant box of diapers in my other hand and walk towards the house. Jordan wanders out the front door and meets us on the sidewalk. "Look at all this stuff Aunt Sophie brought us, Jordan!" Seeing Sophie, Jordan bolts down the sidewalk towards her.

"Aunt Sophie!" she screams as she jumps into her arms.

"Hey, big girl!" Sophie calls out as she embraces my daughter. "Oh, you give the best hugs!" She winks at me as she hugs Jordan tight. After a few moments she puts her down and asks, "Here, Jordan, do you think you can be a good helper and carry this?"

"Yep!" she says as she grabs a sack by the handles. "I'm strong!"

"Yes you are! Look at those big muscles," Sophie says, exaggerating her words. "Wow! You're the strongest girl I know! Take those in to Mommy." Jordan beams from ear to ear.

Parker toddles out as well, and Sophie pulls a bag of bagels out of a sack and hands it to him. "Here, Parker! Take this to Mommy."

"I help!" he says as he takes the bagels and staggers back into the house.

"Good job, buddy!" I say as I meet him on the sidewalk. "Let's go put these on the table."

Several minutes later we have the truck unloaded and everything in the kitchen. Sophie plays with the kids while I get busy putting things away, trying to find a place for what looks like a month's worth of groceries. My kitchen pantry is small enough that I have to stash some of it in the garage. My heart overflows with the generosity of my friend. I smile as I hear her wrestling around with my kids on the floor, both of them giggling and having a great time. Sophie becomes the human jungle gym while I uncork a bottle of red and pour two glasses of wine.

"You thirsty?" I ask, holding up a glass.

"You bet!" she says, holding Parker upside down and tickling his exposed tummy. He shrieks with laughter as she gently places him back on his feet. He immediately throws his hands up in the air and screams, "Again!"

"You know you will be doing that all night long now, right?"

"Oh, I know. That's half the fun!" she says as she zerberts Jordan on the neck. "I'm gonna get you, Jordan!" Jordan tries to run away, but Sophie grabs her and tickles her neck again. "Gotcha!" Jordan screams in laughter, and I watch and smile as my friend plays with my kids.

"I don't have the energy to roughhouse with them like that. They love it, though," I say as I observe the fun.

"That's what aunts are for!" she says as she is tackled by my toddlers once again. The laughter-filled chaos continues for a good twenty minutes. Everyone is having a blast, and it is fun to watch my kids be so happy. They finally start to tire, and I put on an episode of *Sesame Street* to give Sophie a break. The kids' focus immediately changes as they become entranced by the dancing and singing characters on the TV. Sophie sits them each on the couch and then joins me at the kitchen table.

"Figured I'd give you a little break," I say as I slide her glass of wine over to her. "I don't let them watch TV very often, so when I do they are glued to it."

"That's like the Pied Piper! Look at them!" she exclaims as we giggle at the expressions on my children's faces. Both of them have their eyes fixated on the characters with their mouths gaped open a bit.

"It saves me every once in a while. If I need a few minutes to fix dinner or even to pee, I'll put an episode on." I take a sip of my wine. "At least it's a little educational. I only let them watch one episode before it goes back off, though. I don't want the TV to become the babysitter."

"That's good of you, because I know a lot of people do that."

"It would be easy to let that happen. Believe me, there are times I'm tempted."

"Do you need to run any errands while you have me at your disposal? Bank? Gas? Oil change?" Sophie asks.

"No, I think I'm good. I think the only thing I really needed was Parker's diapers, but since I saw you picked some up for me, I can just sit and enjoy some adult conversation for a change."

"Well, good," she says, taking a sip of her wine. "What have you been up to since I saw you last?"

"The usual grind: work, kids, laundry, grading papers. You know, the glamorous life," I say, smiling. "What about you?"

"Work mostly. Although I attempted to go on a date last night."

"Oh yeah? How did that go?"

"It didn't. I got stood up."

"No way! What a jerk! Who was it?"

"A friend of Veronica and Thatcher's. Boy are they pissed at him now."

"Oh, I bet. I'd hate to get on Veronica's bad side. He'd better run. I've seen her pull out her street slang before, and it ain't pretty," I say with a giggle.

"Yeah, that's one reason I was hesitant to go out with him in the first place. I didn't want to screw up any friendship they had with him if it didn't work out."

"So what happened? If you don't mind talking about it, that is."

"Oh, I don't mind. It's not a big deal, really. V and Thatch invited us both over for dinner and he never showed up. So it's not like I sat and waited on him for hours at a restaurant or anything."

"Yeah, but still. That's totally rude not showing up."

"It is, but I'd rather not get attached if he's going to turn out to be a douche bag in the end," she says with a laugh.

Giggling, I reply, "True. That's so weird, though. I mean, Veronica wouldn't set you up with a jerk. I wonder what happened."

"Yeah, not sure."

"I'm just sorry you got disappointed."

"Yeah, me too. I was actually looking forward to it, so I was a little bummed. But I'm sure there will be another."

"Of course there will be," I say, reassuring her. "Hungry?" I ask as I stand and pull out a giant container of cashews she had picked up from the store and poured them into a bowl.

"These are my favorite. I could eat handfuls of them," she says as she tosses a handful of them into her mouth. After she swallows, she asks, "So how have you been lately? Everything going okay?"

I pause and scrunch up my nose a little, "Oh, it's been a rough couple of weeks."

"Why? What's up?" she asks, taking another handful of cashews.

"It's been seven days since I've had any contact with Mike. Usually he is online every day, so when he goes several days without contacting me, it freaks me out."

"Oh wow. Has this happened before?"

"Yes, and I've been told to expect it from time to time, but it doesn't ever get easier."

"I bet. Is there anything I can do to help?" she asks.

"You're already doing it, just by being here," I say as I reach across the table and squeeze her hand. "You have no idea how much I have looked forward to you coming tonight. Thank you so much."

"Of course. It's really not that far and I love playing with the kids," she says as she looks over at my comatose kids. Smiling back at me, she adds, "You're not so bad yourself."

Suddenly, my phone dings indicating I have received a text. I look down at my phone and roll my eyes when I see who it's from.

"What was that look for?" Sophie asks, seeing my reaction.

"Ugh, an ex-boyfriend from high school has been texting me lately. I have told him to leave me alone, but he won't take the hint."

"Seriously? What does he want? I mean, besides the obvious," she says with a smirk.

"I'm not really sure. I don't even know how he got my number."

"What has he been saying?"

"At first he asked how things were going, if I was happy in my marriage, and stuff like that."

"Uh-oh."

"I know. But I quickly squashed all of that, telling him how happy we are. I told him we have kids, jobs, and are doing fine."

"Who is this guy? What does he want?" she asks.

"His name is Chad. And I don't really know what he wants. He hasn't really said much about himself, like what he is doing or anything. He just texts random things and says he's thinking about me. He's starting to annoy me."

"You are going to have to tell him to stop texting."

"That's the thing, I have told him to stop. And now he won't leave me alone. I have quit replying to him altogether. I don't know what else to do."

"Are you scared of him?" she asks, going into detective mode.

"No, I don't think he'd hurt us. I just don't think it's appropriate that we are communicating. Mike and he were *not* the best of friends in high school, if you can imagine. He would *flip* if he knew he was texting me."

"You haven't told him?"

"No, I don't want him to worry about it while he's over there."

"Where does this guy live? Is he local?"

"No, he used to be. But his area code is from somewhere in Connecticut."

"And you've told him to stop texting you?"

"Yes, absolutely."

"I don't like it, Amanda. Seems too creepy."

"I know, I agree. I don't know what else to do without changing my number. Do you have any ideas?" I ask.

"Can you block his number?" she asks.

"Hmm, I don't know. That's a good question. I don't even know how to do that stuff on my phone. I'd really just like him to go away."

"Here, let me try." She grabs my phone and messes with the settings. "There, that might've done it."

"Oh cool. Thank you."

"I think you're right not to respond to him. Even repeating your request to stop texting might keep it going," she says as she takes another sip of her wine. "How did you guys break up?"

"He wasn't the nicest boyfriend. I broke up with him after he pushed me into my locker when he thought I looked at another guy. Mike saw it happen and came to my rescue."

"Did you know Mike before that?"

"I had seen him around at school, but I didn't know him personally until after that day."

"Does he know that Mike is in Afghanistan?"

"Yes."

"Ugh, Amanda. I don't like this."

"I'm sure it's fine. I just won't respond to him again, especially if you actually blocked him."

"I think you should tell Mike," she advises, staring me down across the table.

"I don't know. It's not like he can do anything from way over there. And I really don't think I'm in any danger."

"But what if something happens and he has no idea? Put yourself in his shoes for a second. Does he know where you live? Is your address listed?"

I sit and think about it for a moment. None of this situation feels good, but it's hard to know what the right thing to do is. "I don't know what to do. I'll think about it," I reply. I look over and realize the credits are rolling on the show the kids have been watching. Both of them are slowly sinking into a sleepy state. I look at the clock on the wall and see that it is seven thirty. "Oh wow, I'd better get these guys into a bath before they fall asleep. Want to help?"

"Sure," she says as she walks over and picks up Jordan.

"They can take a quick bath together," I say as I pick up Parker. "I'll go start the water."

I carry Parker into the bathroom and sit him down on the floor. I make sure the water is the right temperature and get the tub filling. I throw in a few toys and get Parker undressed and seated in the tub. Sophie works on Jordan, and in a flash we have two naked pair of buns in the tub. Before long, they are both splashing and giggling away.

"Can you watch them while I get their jammies laid out?" I ask her.

"Of course," Sophie says as she steps aside to let me out of the bathroom. She kneels down beside the tub and starts splashing and playing with the kids. "Who's little piggies are these?" I hear her sing out as Parker lets out a big belly laugh. She really is amazing with my children. I'm lucky to have such a good friend.

Once the kids are down, we sit and chat for another hour or so. About ten o'clock she decides she better head back as she has an hour-plus drive home. She advises me one more time to tell Mike about Chad. I tell her again that I will think about it and will let her know what I decide. In the back of my mind I know I have at least a week before I will see her again and get drilled on it once more. I really don't think it will go over very well, which is why I may avoid it. I promise to think about it and give her a hug good-bye.

`·.¸¸.·´¯`·.¸,><(((º>`·.¸¸.·´¯`·..><((((º>`·.¸¸.·´¯`·..

Rose

DJ and I are looking forward to having lunch with Miss Melody today. I had so much fun with her at the cabin when she stayed a few days extra. She caught on to fly fishing very quickly and will be a very good angler if she chooses to keep at it. I do hope she will join us again and get to know the rest of the girls as well. She would be a fun addition to our little group and bring an edgy, youthful vibe to our weekends together. As long as we don't bore the girl to death. She's used to a little more action than we would be able to provide.

She gave me quite a heart-stopping moment when she was flailing in the river. She looked exactly like my Clara: so small, so helpless, and black hair to boot. I have tried to avoid sharing that story for the last few decades; I haven't even told Sophie. I can't believe I told Amanda . . . Now that the cat is out of the bag, it won't be long before it surfaces on its own. Guess I better start mentally preparing for that . . .

`` `..,.·´¯`·..,><((((º>`·.,.·´¯`·..><((((º>`·.,.·´¯`·.. ``

Melody

"Hey, Melody! Great to see you again," Thatcher says as he opens the door for me. "The kitchen is getting all of the dishes prepped for you that we need new photos of."

"Ok, thanks. Um, any place in particular you want me to set up?"

"What do you think? You have complete run of this place. It's up to you and your artistic mind."

"Okay, sweet. Um, that table there would probably give us the best lighting. I brought some additional lights that will help showcase the food as well."

"Sounds good. Feel free to do whatever you need to do."

"Okay, cool. Um, here are those photos I was telling you about." *I still can't believe I forgot to give these to Veronica the last time.*

"Oh nice. You would not believe how excited Veronica is to see these. She told me you took pictures of them for hours while they were fishing."

Please don't look at them while I'm standing here.

"Do you mind if I take a look?"

"Sure." *Shit.*

I open my portfolio and pull out my favorite shot of Veronica.

"Wow. Look at that . . ." He pauses and studies the photo. "I mean, you have captured the very essence of her being in this shot . . . Strong, determined, gorgeous, fierce, yet vulnerable all at the same time . . ." He puts his hand over his mouth as he gazes over the print. He turns and looks at me with an astonished look. "This is absolutely incredible. Honestly, I have no words."

Um, yes you do. You just said like a thousand words. "Thanks. I really enjoyed processing these." *Ugh, embarrassed. Why can't I take a compliment?*

He slowly transitions to the next photo. "Oh man, look at Sophie . . . The colors are so vibrant! How do you do that?"

"It's all in the settings." *And a $2,000 camera rather than an iPhone.*

He pauses as he looks at one shot of the five of us. "Look at that, the perfect cast."

"Yeah, Rose insisted that there was one photo of all of us so she had a new one for her mantle."

He starts flipping through the photos, making expressive remarks at each pic he sees. "Incredible . . . Look at the size of that one! . . . Oh my God, stunning . . . Really impressive, Melody." I grow more and more uncomfortable yet stand there and try not to look awkward. As he gets near the last photo, his phone buzzes. "Sorry, I need to take this." He turns his back and puts the phone up to his ear.

"No worries." *Thank God that's over.* I head over to the table we identified for the shoot and start pulling my camera gear out of my bag.

"Hey man, what's up? Are you ready for tomorrow night?" Thatcher walks to the other side of the restaurant while he takes the call. "Wait, what? Are you kidding me?" Thatcher starts to pace angrily around the room.

Ugh. Awkward. I hate overhearing other people's phone calls.

"No. You can't do this! Which part are you missing? The pianist? Don't you have someone else?"

Shit. He needs a pianist for this weekend.

"What do you mean you don't have a replacement? You can't do this to me. We are sold out for both Friday and Saturday night! What the hell am I supposed to do?"

Ugh, this is painful.

"We only have thirty-six hours until you are supposed to go on."

Shit. They have been so nice to me, maybe I should step up . . . No. Stop. What are you thinking?

Thatcher paces as he listens, growing more and more pissed by the second, his voice escalating.

"I don't care what you have to do, but you find a damn replacement for your pianist! I have food critics showing up tomorrow. I *have* to have you here. Do you understand me? You have no idea what this will do to me."

As if I'm having an out-of-body experience, I slowly start walking over to the piano at the back of the room. *What the fuck are you doing? Don't do this . . . Don't do this!* My fingers slide over the tops of the ivories. *For the love of God, do not let Thatcher know that you can play.* I sit down on the bench and rest my fingers on top of the keys.

"Hey, Thatcher?" *What are you doing? Stop!!*

"Seriously, man, this will ruin me. *Please.*"

"Hey, Thatcher?" I say a little louder. *What the fuck are you doing?*

"Hold on . . . Yeah?"

"We got this." *Shit!*

"Wait, what? What do you mean 'we got this'?"

There is a hushed pause as I close my eyes, lean in, slightly lift my fingers as if a conductor was dramatically instructing his orchestra to begin. I press down on the keys and magically start to play Beethoven's Fifth. About ten stanzas in, I open my eyes and look over at Thatcher, phone still up to his ear, his mouth gaping open.

"Um, hold on one second," he says to whomever he is talking to. He has a shocked look on his face. "Seriously? You can play?"

I say nothing as I continue to hold his gaze and deliver a flawless performance.

"Can you play jazz?"

Can I play jazz . . .

Without even looking at the keys I transition to Duke Ellington's song, "Take the 'A' Train." Thatcher and I are locked in a trance as I soulfully play this famous tune.

"I think I found your replacement," he says into the phone and immediately hangs up.

I close my eyes and get lost in the music.

`·.,,.·´¯`·.,><((((º>`·.,,.·´¯`·..><((((º>`·.,,.·´¯`·..

Amanda

It's 2:15 a.m., and I'm up cruising Facebook. It's now been two weeks since I last talked with Mike. I'm starting to go out of my mind with worry. I haven't slept in days, and I'm reaching a point of exhaustion that is really affecting everything I do.

All of a sudden I look down and notice that he has logged on. "Holy shit! He's on!" I instantly start a message to him.

A: Mike! Oh my God! Where have you been? Are you okay?

I see the little jumping dots that indicate he is typing back, and a wave of relief washes over me. *Oh my God, he's alive.* I let out a huge sigh and instantly burst into tears. A floodgate of emotions overwhelms me. I have never been more excited to see those dancing dots.

M: Hey baby, can you FaceTime right now?

A: Of course!

M: Okay, give me a minute.

Oh my God I cannot wait to see him. I wipe the tears from my eyes and fix my hair quickly. *Need to look cute for my man!* A surge of excitement and adrenaline pulse through my veins. *He's alive!* The sing-songy FaceTime ring pierces the air, and slowly our video call connects. Nothing could have prepared me for what I see next . . .

He is in a hospital bed, his left side completely bandaged. There are IVs and bags of fluids hanging everywhere. His face is all scraped up, and his left eye is completely bloodshot and swollen.

"Hey there, beautiful."

"Oh my God . . . Mike . . . Are you okay? What happened?" My eyes fill with tears and instantly spill down my cheeks. My voice trembles with panic.

"We were ambushed, didn't see it coming."

"Are you okay? What happened to your shoulder?"

"I took a hit here." He points near his left clavicle, just above his heart. "Shattered my clavicle but missed any major organs. Got damn lucky . . ."

"Oh my God . . . Can you move your arm? What's the extent of your injuries?"

"I'm going to be okay. I have a long road of rehab ahead of me, but I'm going to be okay. I was one of the lucky ones . . ." His voice trails off as he finishes his sentence, and by the look on his face I know there is more.

"Is everyone else okay?"

He looks down and away from the screen and shakes his head. He just sits there for the longest time and finally chokes out, "We lost two . . ."

"Oh no . . ."

His bottom lip quivers, and I can see him struggle to choke back tears. He puts his hand up to his face and presses his thumb and forefinger into his eyes. His face clenches into a painful squint as he draws in a big deep breath to try to hold back tears. A primal sound erupts from his chest, and I simultaneously start sobbing as well.

"Oh my God, who was it?"

His body convulses as he cries. Seeing and hearing him sob is horrible. I want to reach through the screen and embrace him and hold him tight.

"I'm sorry . . . I thought I could do this. I thought I could be strong enough to tell you."

"It's okay, baby . . . I'm so sorry."

He clears his throat and tries to take a deep breath to gather himself. It is so hard to watch him struggle.

"It was Jacobi and Smitty . . ."

"Oh my God . . . Have they contacted Jenny and Nikki?" My heart feels heavy, like it's breaking out of my chest.

"They just did, which is why I was finally able to call you."

"When did this happen?"

"A few weeks ago. The colonel had a tough time getting ahold of Smitty's family."

"No wonder there hasn't been any communication from anyone. I can't even imagine what they are going through right now . . ."

We fall into a silence as our minds drift to the horror both families are experiencing.

"So how are you doing?" I ask him.

"I'm fine."

"*No really*, how are you doing?"

"Um, not great . . ." He looks down again and kind of shrugs his shoulder, then immediately winces in pain having forgotten briefly about his injury. "Damn, I forget I can't do that."

"Do you have to have any more surgery?"

"Yeah, they are doing more repair work next week. After recovery for a few weeks I may get to come home for a little bit."

"Seriously?!"

"Yeah, my injuries were severe enough they're going to let me recoup at home for a few weeks. Not sure how long right now. They'll let me know after they see how the surgery goes."

"Oh my God, I can't wait to have you here, safe and back with us."

"Even though I'm all banged up?" he says with that cute side smile of his.

"I'll take you any way I can get you. I love you, babe."

"I love you too."

We talk for another thirty minutes before he has to go. We both sob as we say our good-byes. Knowing I almost lost him and that he has another major surgery coming up before I can see him again is gut wrenching. As soon as we disconnect, I fall into a heap on the table. Grief consumes my entire body as I cry. *I came so close to losing him . . . My Mike . . . He is my everything . . .* I wish I could close my eyes and beam myself to his side. Thank God the kids are asleep so I can just let it all out. I slowly wander into our bedroom and curl up in the fetal position in our bed. I grab his pillow and cling to it, wishing with every ounce of my being that it was him.

I can't even imagine what Jenny and Nikki are going through right now . . .

In a state of exhaustion I have never felt before, I finally close my eyes and drift off to sleep.

`·.¸¸.·´¯`·.¸><((((º>`·.¸¸.·´¯`·..><((((º>`·.¸¸.·´¯`·..

Section 6: A Perfect Cast

"Throughout your fishing experience, you will have good casts and bad: some that are better than expected, others that will make you wonder if you'll ever get it right.

And there *will* be casts that are absolutely perfect! A perfect cast is a thing of beauty. It is like a note of music extended and held. In all other sports, the moment of impact separates you from the very thing you are projecting in beautiful flight—but the execution of the perfect cast can be seen and felt, from its inception until the fly touches down on the water."[viii]

Joan Wulff's Fly Casting Techniques
by Joan Wulff

Veronica

Finally, our annual fly fishing trip to the Fryingpan River is here. I have been looking forward to this for weeks! There are several reasons why I am looking forward to being in the woods for the next several days. One, I don't have to wear makeup. The fish really don't care whether I put my corporate face and hair on before I hit the stream. In fact, they may prefer the more au naturel look anyway. Two, I don't run into anyone I know. I like just hanging out with friends who don't care whether or not I shower every day. And three, I enjoy the friendships I have with these women. Each one is unique and different. They all fill me up, understand me, and complement me in different ways. I'm a lucky girl.

I really hope this is a good week for Amanda too. She has had so much drama unfold with Mike getting injured in Afghanistan last month. I hope she is able to relax and enjoy a little downtime before he comes home. I can't imagine the amount of stress she has been under, all while working full-time and taking care of the kids. She is one of the strongest women I know.

This trip is usually a blast, and the fish are pretty active, for the most part. We always stay at the same little campground. It is such a great campsite. It is a family campground that sits right on Ruedi Reservoir at an elevation of 7,800 feet. Rose brings Fly Girl, her trailer, and we camp out and fish for a week. It's like heaven on earth. We used to tent-camp together, but when Rose turned sixty she decided she was done sleeping on the ground, so she purchased a big trailer that sleeps five and named it Fly Girl. We like to call it glamping, or glamorous camping, which suits me just fine. I'd rather pee in an actual toilet than a hole in the ground any day. After all, I'm still a city girl.

The Fryingpan River is a fishing mecca this time of year. I envision this river in my sleep and can see myself bring fish to the surface. In doing so, I study both the air and the water, hoping to get a glimpse of the insects filling my trout friends, insects I will need to imitate to enjoy the marvel and absolute magnificence of such beautiful creatures.

In my first three years of fly fishing I was skunked three times. The first time was my very first outing after meeting Sophie on that plane. I felt completely ridiculous, like a fish out of water. Sophie had me bundled up in her dad's old, leaking waders in men's size extra large. They were way too big and I felt very clumsy. The boots were too big as well, and I felt I needed to shuffle my feet to keep them from slipping off. I wore a vest bulging with things I didn't even recognize: flies, leaders, extra tippet; lead weights; dangly forceps and nippers hanging from retractable wires. I had a fishing net dangling down my back, less-than-fashionable sunglasses, and a big, awkward fishing rod I was trying to keep from getting tangled in the bushes. I am sure that the fish were all enjoying laughing at my stupidity. After hours of fishing without a bite I grew frustrated and bored and suggested we call it a day. Sophie reluctantly agreed and we went back to the cabin. Needless to say, Sophie had a hard sell that evening to talk me into getting back into those waders the next morning. Somehow, she did and we had a spectacular day on the water the next day. I've been hooked ever since.

The other two times were both at the hands of the same stream, the Roaring Fork, a section of river we plan on fishing this week. I don't know what it is about this stream, but as soon as I tie on my fly, I act like I've never fished before. The stream is extremely narrow, and the fish are, too, in that they are narrow-minded in their selectivity. One of the local fly shop owners loves this stream but I am not sure why. I'm not saying I need to catch X number of fish to feel a trip was worthwhile, but catching *a* fish would be nice. I'm going into it with a different attitude this time, and hopefully that will be the difference I need to change my fate on this river. After all, that's what I tell my business clients all the time. Attitude can change your altitude. You can climb greater mountains if your attitude is in the right place. *Damn, I hate hearing my own advice . . .*

Tonight the moon is picture-perfect as I arrive at the campground. It lights up the night and silhouettes the mountains around me. This symbolizes the beauty of this land and the surrounding support I have with this group of women. A heavenly place indeed.

As I pull up to campsite number 16 where Rose indicated the camper is parked, I can see the interior light of the camper spilling out through the window. I can see Rose, Amanda, and Melody on the inside chatting away. Rose is obviously telling another one of her stories as the two of them are doubled over with laughter. Rose is doing her traditional cross-my-legs-while-I-laugh-so-I-won't-pee move. I giggle as I watch the animated scene unfold in front of me. It makes me all the more excited for the fun week ahead. It's nice to see Amanda smiling, and Melody looks like she is joining in as if she's been one of us for years.

I throw open the door and tease, "What the hell is so funny in here? I could hear you seven campsites away!"

"Hey! Rose was just telling a story of when she trampled three random people on a trail after seeing a big bull snake in front of her. It was hysterical!" Amanda wipes tears of laughter from her eyes.

"Oh great, starting the week off with snake stories? Really, Rose? Is that necessary?"

"Nothing like a good snake story to keep a city girl on her toes this week. How was your drive up?" Rose says as she gives me a hug hello.

"Pretty uneventful, which is the way I prefer it."

"Well, good. Sophie shouldn't be too far behind you. Now, can I pour you a glass of red?"

"You read my mind, Rose," I say as she pours me a glass. "Melody, thanks again for those awesome pictures you gave to Thatcher. You are so incredibly talented!"

"Thanks. I had a lot of fun with them." She smiles with a hint of pride.

"Look at this frame I found," Rose says as she pulls it off the shelf and hands it to me. It's the picture of the five of us already framed in the cutest frame. It has a tiny fishing rod on the top and a creel on the bottom next to the words The Perfect Cast. "Isn't it just perfect?"

"Oh my gosh, that is so cool! I love it!"

"I just couldn't love it more if I tried," Rose says as she beams at the photo. "I asked Melody to bring copies for everyone."

"Rose bought frames for all of us too," Amanda says as she points to the stack of frames.

"Of course she did."

"How could I resist? It is really just so perfect."

"I love it. It's so cool." Amanda says as she peers down at the photo again.

"How are you doing?" I ask Amanda.

"Oh, pretty good. Glad to be here, that's for sure. It's been a rough few weeks. Feels good to laugh again." Her tone changes, and she looks down into her wine glass.

"I'm sure," I reply, a little sorry I brought it up so soon into the evening. "You doin' okay?"

"I'm doing okay. I feel a little guilty about coming on this trip, but as soon as he gets back next month I won't be able to leave for quite a while. Every minute with him will feel like a gift since we almost lost him. Plus, I'm sure he's going to require some extra medical care as well."

"I'm sure. I'm so glad your mother-in-law could watch the kids this week so you could still come along. Do you know the extent of his injuries?"

"It's mainly in his left shoulder. I don't know all of the details, but he still has a few reconstruction surgeries to undergo. We're not sure of the timing of anything either, so I've got to make this week count! I need to catch *all of the fish*!" she sings out emphatically, obviously wanting to change the subject and lighten the mood.

"May they tremble at your knees," Rose chimes out. "To catching *all of the fish*!" Rose mimics Amanda's exact tone and raises her glass, and we all clink our glasses together.

It's going to be a great week.

`·.,,.·´¯`·.,><((((º>`·.,,.·´¯`·..><((((º>`·.,,.·´¯`·..

Sophie

"All good things—trout as well as eternal salvation—come by grace and grace comes by art, and art does not come easy." So if art equals grace which equals trout, then eternal salvation equals all good things. . .[ix]

I am moved as well as perplexed by the meaning of this quote from the book *A River Runs Through It*. I find myself thinking about what it is truly saying. I ponder it off and on while driving through the mountains today on my way up to the campground. Each time I think about it, my heart grows warm and my face turns to a smile.

The mountains and rivers are very spiritual to me. I feel much closer to God and feel his presence out in nature. I'm also a much better listener when I am away from the noise of everyday life. God's beauty is ever present in the color of the landscape, the sway of the trees, and the music of the water. Good thoughts fill my head as I think about being in this church. This is a place where I am judged only by my own abilities and desires. I am able to ask for forgiveness and cleanse my soul and spirit in this heavenly sanctuary. I think of all I have: a successful business, wonderful friends, a meaningful job where I make a difference in the lives of others, my health, and the ability to fish and pursue dreams. Fishing clears my head and reminds me of the beauty found in the surroundings of my endeavors. Just as in life, I can't take fishing for trout for granted. Bringing a fish to rise takes patience, dedication, and determination. Releasing a trout is an offering of thanks and a reminder of the above ingredients necessary for creating a happy life.

I am looking forward to the opportunity of spending time on the river with Rose, for she is an example of all the things I want to be. She is a kind, caring, generous woman who never has a bad thing to say about anyone and will do whatever she can for others, often putting their needs before her own. She truly is my role model and is the artist I long to be. I try to live up to her standards and ideals as much as I can, hoping to mold my actions as a model of hers.

That being said, as much as I love my girlfriends, I am still feeling a void in my life without a man to share my life with. I've been having some pretty big pity parties for myself lately. It drives me crazy when I get like this, but I can't help it sometimes. I do hope that someday I will find Mr. Right. I guess I just haven't found the right fishing hole yet. I get so envious of Veronica and Amanda and the love that they have for their husbands. Rose also tells some amazing stories of the life she and Bob had together. What if I am the one getting in my own way? What do I need to do differently? Am I really sabotaging my own life when it comes to relationships like Rose pointed out? I'm not sure. It's hard to trust God and know that he has a plan for me. Deep down I hope that a relationship is in God's plan for me someday.

As I pull into the parking lot of the campground tonight, I pause and say a little prayer.

> *Lord, thank you for this wonderful day, for the opportunity to feel closer to you and hear your voice. I pray that the river is giving over the next couple of days. I ask for the strength and*

courage I need to refuel and refocus my inner fight. I pray for the safety of my friends and for blessing us with this time together. Please help me to have patience and know that you have an ultimate plan for my life. Please help me to focus more on the blessings you have given me and less on the importance of making my line go tight. Amen.

`·.,¸,.·´¯`·.,¸><((((º>`·.,¸,.·´¯`·..><((((º>`·.,¸,.·´¯`·..

Amanda

I have found myself longing for this trip, a trip I didn't think would happen with Mike's injury last month. He's in Germany right now at the big military rehab hospital there. Such a scary time for us, and it puts life into perspective. I really need this time away to clear my head before he comes home next month. Lately I have found that the only way I can do this is by spending time on the stream and with my girlfriends. They are such a comforting lifeline for me. Sophie came rushing down to be with me when I called and told her about Mike. Rose made several crock pot meals for us, and Veronica had some groceries shipped straight to the house. Melody surprised me by sending me a text telling me she hoped he was doing okay and that she was thinking about me. We don't know each other very well yet, so it was definitely a surprise to hear from her. I want to hang out with her a bunch more this week so we can bond a bit more.

Because I get so few weekends to fish, I really want to make this one count. We plan on fishing on the other side of the Colorado divide this trip: the Fryingpan River and the Roaring Fork are the ones I plan on fishing. I might try to hit Gore Creek on the way home if the other two rivers aren't fishing well.

This trip will be a test for me, a test of my tying and fishing ability. To me, fishing these big rivers this time of year is a measuring stick of my ability to become an artist. Before Mike's accident, I had been practicing and fine-tuning my casting techniques in a few of the local streams that run nearby our home. Since the accident, I have spent *many* hours at my vise working through my anxiety, fear, and sleepless nights. I feel my tying techniques improving, so now I have the opportunity to test both skills on different streams, which I'm sure will present new challenges I'm ready to tackle. Bring it on.

`·.,,.·´¯`·.,><((((º>`·.,,.·´¯`·..><(((((º>`·.,,.·´¯`·..

Sophie

After a quick breakfast, Veronica and I load up my truck and head out to find a good spot on the Fryingpan. Rose, Melody, and Amanda are going to hit the Roaring Fork River today, so we are going to divide and conquer. Since all of us are going to be away from the campsite, we take everything we need for the day. Rose packed us all a bunch of sandwiches, fruit, and plenty of water. She even packed some Goldfish crackers so we could eat some "fish" on the trail just for fun.

This time of year, you have to get on the water early if you want to get a good spot. The public access is a little more limited in the section we want to fish, so we have to beat all the other fishermen onto the water. I wish I knew someone who owns riverfront property up here. *What I would give for fishing private waters today!* By seven o'clock we are at the river loaded with fly rods, day packs, and anticipation. There is a buzz in the air, and we can't wait to step in the river. I want to get in as much fishing as I possibly can this week, so an early start it is. We find a place to park the truck and start gearing up. We pass pool after pool of picturesque spots torn straight from the pages of a Trout Unlimited calendar. We finally settle into a nice open spot with several exposed rocks popping out of the water. A fish hideout for sure.

There is a rich smell of weeds, pebbles, and muck from the undercut banks that hang over with grass. I marvel at the granite cliffs that rise heavenward to my right and my left on both sides of the river, both crowned with stands of aspen. I have been looking forward to fishing this river all month, and the beauty of my surroundings makes it even sweeter.

Veronica called a few local fly shops yesterday to see what the trout are biting on right now, and they suggested Royal Wulffs and Yellow Sallys. V has tied on a perfect size 18 Royal Wulff and walked upstream about thirty yards from where I have stepped into the river. I watch as she unhooks her fly and wades into the water. She works out some line, casts to a rising fish, and hooks it straight away. *Lucky girl!* It is a nice, fat brown trout. She plays it for a few minutes, brings it in, and then lets it go. Greasing her fly, she takes two steps upstream and casts again. She hooks another one within a few casts and plays it well. I can see her grin span from ear to ear from thirty yards away. It is fun to watch. Now I can hardly wait to get my line wet! I hope I have the same luck she's having . . .

I decide to tie on a Yellow Sally, one of my favorite flies. I also add an emerger just to increase my chances. I gaze out at the river and try to read the water. I'm always trying to increase my water-reading ability by attempting to place my fly in the exact right spot. An exhilarating thrill rushes up my spine as I see a fish rise to the surface. I cast to this exact spot multiple times, patiently waiting on my fish friend to take my fly. Several casts later I still don't get a bite, but I'm bound and determined that my trusty Yellow Sally will work. I try again. And again. And again.

After an hour with not even a bite I decide to take a step out of the stream and watch the water. I begin noticing fish sipping on the top rather than feeding on the bottom, so I take off the emerger. I keep the Yellow Sally on and cast again, hoping for a different outcome.

Veronica wades down towards me and asks, "What are you using?"

Flatly I reply, "A Yellow Sally. How about you?"

"I've nailed three with a Royal Wulff already. Have you tried one of those?"

I roll my eyes and try to hide my jealousy. "No, not yet. I feel like the Yellow Sally will work."

She smiles wryly and says, "You know, the definition of insanity is doing the same thing over and over again expecting different results, right?" She turns and wades downstream. I glare back knowing she is right.

I switch to a Royal Wulff . . .

We fish for several more hours and I still don't catch a thing. Pissed off and a little dehydrated, I hike back to the truck to eat some lunch. I need a little mental break from my less-than-fun morning. I eat the sandwich and banana I packed that morning to refuel. Veronica joins me just as I am finishing up and eats her lunch as well. She goes on and on about how many fish she has netted already. I am happy for her and hate her all at the same time.

After lunch, we drive upstream a few miles to fish a different part of the river. We find a nice reedy area where we have to use the roll cast technique or risk spending most of the day fishing our line out of the reeds instead of fishing for trout. Maybe a different casting technique will deliver better results.

Alas, still nothing. The afternoon drags on.

As evening approaches, many insects are doing what insects do best: hatching, flying, scuttering, but most importantly bringing trout to the surface. They are popping the surface all dang day! And how many have I caught? Nada. Zero. Zilch . . . Completely sucks. I think Veronica has caught around ten fish this morning and seven more this afternoon. This afternoon she caught fish on a yellow/tan Elk Hair Caddis, a green little midge, light Cahill, a Quill Gordon, and a hair's ear nymph. I have tried them all and haven't even gotten a nibble! So frustrating. I was short stroking all afternoon. I used a nine-foot 5x leader and tried to concentrate on presenting the fly naturally to the fish, for that's what I thought would work the best. I also tried casting straight upstream and stripping my line in quickly, again presenting the fly as realistically as possible. Nothing. Flippin' nothing. I eventually just stuck to short stroking because I felt my line was causing a shadow unnaturally on the water. I don't know. *Why is Veronica catching them and I'm not?* Maybe Rose will have some advice for me this evening . . .

These words have never come out of my mouth before, but I didn't mind leaving the river today. The fishing was tough and the stream just seemed disappointing to me. I was turned on to this spot by a guide at a local fishing shop. She reported catching fish after fish after fish, big beautiful brown trout, and I was mesmerized by her tales. I had grand visions of beautiful brownies stacked up like cordwood in the stream, and I didn't even get a bite. Selfishly I don't even want to hear about Veronica's day. Stupid jealousy . . .

`·.,.·´¯`·.,><((((º>`·.,.·´¯`·..><((((º>`·.,.·´¯`·..

Veronica

Man, what a day! I think I ended up catching seventeen fish today. I actually lost count there were so many! Sophie bailed a few hours before I did and went and sat in the truck and pouted. Not sure what is going on with her today, but her attitude is definitely affecting her success—or lack thereof today. I was having so much fun I stayed out until my arms got tired.

When we got back to the campsite, Sophie walked straight down to the river and sat, probably reflecting on the day. I'm pretty sure she just needs some alone time to blow off some steam. I hope she can turn her attitude around, as it is definitely the biggest thing getting in her way.

I approach the camper and open the trailer door. I find Rose napping at the dinette table, her stockinged feet propped up on the seat across from her. She has a sewing needle still in hand atop an unfinished quilt binding in her lap. She is asleep, snoring lightly.

"Hey, Rose," I say softly, leaning forward to touch her grandmotherly, knobby hand. I sit down at the dinette across from her.

Rose comes awake slowly. Behind her old-fashioned reading glasses, her confused gaze finally clears, "Oh, Veronica, did I fall asleep?"

"Yes, do you want to move back to your bed? I can help you."

"Oh no, I'm fine . . . Just give me a minute."

"Are Amanda and Melody here?"

"Um, no. They went into town to grab something to eat. Not sure when they will be back."

"Okay, no worries. Did you catch anything today?" I ask her.

"Oh yes, I had a good day. Caught several nice browns. You?"

"One of my best days ever! I lost track around seventeen or so."

"My goodness! That is a good day. What fun it is when the fishing gods are smiling upon you."

"Indeed. Sophie had a tough day on the river. She's here, just out blowing off some steam for a little bit."

"Her bad attitude get the best of her, huh? She gets like that sometimes and then can't seem to pull out of it. Hopefully she'll have better luck tomorrow."

"What were you catching them on today?"

"I used a Yellow Sally most of the day and the brownies were gobbling it up. So fun when they do that."

"Funny, that's what Sophie was using and she couldn't catch a thing. I caught most of mine on a Royal Wulff."

"Oh yeah? Maybe I'll give that one a try tomorrow," she says as she puts her quilting materials away. "Amanda didn't have much luck today either. I think she has too much on her mind to be focused on the water. That poor girl has a lot going on."

"I agree. I'm so glad Mike is okay. Did you hear what day he is going to be home this month? We want to have everyone over for dinner when he gets back, make it a fun homecoming from all of us."

"Oh, that will be fun. I think it's in a few weeks, but I'm not sure."

"Okay, I'll be sure to ask her when she gets back. How did Melody do today?"

"She did pretty good. I gave her a few pointers on her casting technique, and her arc seemed much better by the end of the day. She's a quick study."

"Well, she has a good coach. She'll be off on her own before you know it."

"Indeed. She may go off on her own a little bit tomorrow. She mentioned wanting a little solo time. I think she just wants to prove to herself she can do it without me, which of course she can."

"I think it took me a year before I was brave enough to fish without either you or Sophie around."

"Yeah, but you could have done it much sooner. You caught on pretty quick as well."

"Did you have dinner?"

"No, not yet, but I brought some leftovers from last night I was going to reheat. Interested?"

"Rose, you know I am queen of the reheat. Show me the way."

Just then, Amanda and Melody throw open the trailer door and pile onto the dinette bench. "Whew! Glad to be back! We almost hit a deer on the road back from town. Melody has some mad evasive moves when it comes to driving."

"That thing jumped out of nowhere! I'm so glad I didn't hit it. That would have put a damper on my trip, that's for sure."

"Where did you all go for dinner?" Rose asks.

"We found some greasy burger joint just up the road a few miles. Amanda had grease trickling down her arm it was so greasy. It was awesome," Melody says, smiling. It is good to see her interacting with the group a little more.

"But it was dammmn good," Amanda says as she closes her eyes and relives the moment all over again.

"Ugh, that brings on acid reflux just thinking about it," I chime in, unfortunately coinciding with actual acid reflux, and I look in the cupboard for an antacid.

"Be grateful for your iron stomachs and metabolism in your twenties, girls. This will catch up to you when you get into your forties, right, Veronica?" Rose adds.

"You got that right. There's a reason I'm not a size two," I say as I clink my wine glass with hers. "How did you do on the river today?"

"I got skunked," Amanda says with a scowl. "I hate when that happens!"

"I only caught one, but only because Rose was right there telling me where to throw my fly. Not sure that one counts."

"Of course it counts! You netted it, didn't you?" Rose says emphatically, throwing her hands up in the air.

"Well, yes. But still . . ."

"Well, that counts in my books."

"So technically I didn't get skunked today, right?"

"Absolutely correct!" I say emphatically.

"Rub it in, why don't ya?" Amanda playfully retorts.

"Yeah, sorry . . . I think I want to try fishing by myself tomorrow, just to see if I can catch one without Rose having to tell me what to do."

"Of course you can! You know exactly what to do," Rose chimes in.

"How about you, V? How'd you do today?" Amanda asks with her big doe eyes.

"I'm not sure you want to know," I say with a sheepish grin, not sure if I should tell the truth and make them jealous or lower the actual number so they don't feel bad.

"You bitch, did you catch a lot? I seriously dislike you sometimes," Amanda jokes.

"Only seventeen." I say with the right amount of sass.

"Seventeen! Oh my God, I really hate you now," Amanda screams. "What were you catching them on?"

"Mainly Royal Wulffs. I threw in a few Cahills and elk hair nymphs in the afternoon. But the Royal Wulff was my drug of choice today."

"Ugh, I'm so jealous! Where were you?"

"We were on the Fryingpan, not too far from here actually."

"Can I go with you tomorrow?" Amanda asks. "I need to mimic whatever you are doing."

"Actually, I didn't do anything different than what I normally do. Sophie didn't catch anything today either, and we were fishing the same water."

"Good. At least I'm not the only one. Is that bad?" Amanda says, smiling.

"A little, but we'll let it slide. Misery loves company, eh?"

"You know it. I bet that pissed her off," she says, knowing our friend all too well.

"Um, yeah. She did not have a good day," I say as I recall her sour attitude. "You know what, though, I've been skunked twice on this exact river in years past, and this year I told myself that I was going to have a positive attitude no matter what. I swear that made a difference although I'm not quite sure why that works. But I'll take it!"

"Of course it makes a difference," Rose adds. "You've got to believe in yourself and your abilities or the doubt will win every time. Don't you teach this stuff, Ms. Leadership?"

"Oooooooh," Melody and Amanda call out in unison and then bust out laughing.

"Alright, Miss Smarty Pants Rose. You got me there. Damn, I hate hearing my own advice."

"Just making sure you're not too big for your britches," she says with a click of her tongue and wry smile.

"Oh, I gotch you. I'll show you who's not too big for their britches!" I retort and charge towards her as if I am going to tackle her. She stumbles back onto the dinette cushion, and we all erupt in laughter.

"Oh, you old coot, you!" Rose calls out as she attempts to regain her balance and laughs at the same time.

Just then, Sophie flings open the door. "What kind of racket's going on in here?"

"Hey, Soph!" everyone calls out, almost in unison.

"Oh, you know, Rose slinging insults and makin' fun, just like normal," I announce.

"You bite your tongue! I did no such thing," Rose defends, pushing her bottom lip out as if she were pouting. "I better go get my boots on. The shit's getting a little deep in here."

We all chuckle at hearing Rose swear. "Oh yeah? Is Veronica full of shit again?" Sophie teases, tossing a playful glare my way.

"Like hell I am! Rose is the one dishing it out," I cry, completely tickled by Rose and her one-liners.

"Speaking of shit, did you make another *socrifice* today, Veronica?" *Bwahahaha.* Everyone erupts in laughter at my expense, recalling my unfortunate less-than-funny story from a few years ago. Well, everyone except Melody, who wasn't in on the inside joke.

"A socrifice? What's that?" Melody asks with a quizzical look upon her face, giggling along with us even though she doesn't know what is so funny.

"Yeah, Veronica, what's a *socrifice*?" Sophie teases me as we all start laughing.

"Oh my God, seriously? You girls can't let that go?" I cry out, in between my cackles.

"You're the one who had to *go*," Sophie retorts, and lets out one of her enormous guffaws she is famous for when she laughs too hard. She starts slapping the table and doubling over from laughter.

"What? I was resourceful," I finally squeak out, defending my actions—smart ones, if I do say so myself.

"Oh my God, tell me!" Melody exclaims, wanting to be in on the laughter.

"Veronica was out on the river when, *ahem*, Mother Nature came to call."

"I had had a little too much to drink the night before, and, um, I had an urgent visitor." Everyone giggles while envisioning my unfortunate circumstance.

"Oh my God, you should have seen her try to sprint out of the river. You just knew what was going on by the look on her face and the way she was trying to run," Amanda recalls, laughing out loud. We all start to lose it, tears spilling out of our eyes.

"There was no way in hell I was going to blow ass in my waders! Can you imagine how long that would have taken to get the smell out? I would have had to have burned them." We all howl again at the thought and start crying and choking from laughter.

"So what did you do?" Melody inquires, wanting the full story.

"Well, I made it as far away from everyone as I could, unbuckling my shoulder straps and clinch-butt sprinting the whole way."

"Oh my God, we were dying laughing at her. She kept screaming, 'Don't you come near me! Leave me alone!!' We were seriously dying." Sophie adds.

"I was horrified. Seriously. Like, completely horrified. Can you think of a more horribly embarrassing situation? No, no you can't."

"But wait, it gets better!" Sophie chokes out in between her howls.

"So I was trying to play it off, like it wasn't a big deal. After I was done, I just nonchalantly rejoined the group as if nothing had happened. I stepped back in the river and threw out another line."

Sophie, unable to refrain from finishing the story, yells out, "Yeah, but then we get back to the cabin and as we're taking off our waders, I look down and notice that Veronica only has one sock on. So I asked, 'Hey V? What happened to your sock?' And you know what she said?"

"What? I made a *socrifice*."

"Oh my God, a socrifice!" We all scream in laughter as Sophie screams out this now-famous one-liner. "She wiped her ass with her sock!"

"Like I said, I was resourceful!"

Complete and utter hilarity ensues. No one can even get a word out, they are laughing so hard. I think we laugh about this for a full ten minutes. For the rest of the evening, anytime someone thinks about it, they start giggling and we all erupt in laughter again. My cheeks and my sides hurt from so much laughter.

We drink and tell stories into the wee hours of the night. There is nothing quite like a lively, rambunctious night of storytelling and laughter with a group of girlfriends. A soul-cleansing experience for sure. God, I love them . . .

Eventually, we all tire and one by one people start drifting off to their beds. I decide to take a quick shower before calling it a night, so I grab my shower stuff and head towards the shower house. Amanda decides to join me, so we take a quick walk along the river on the way.

`·.¸¸.·´¯`·.¸ ><(((º>`·.¸¸.·´¯`·..><((((º>`·.¸¸.·´¯`·..

Amanda

"Oh my God, I am jealous of your day!" I say to Veronica as we walk towards the shower house, shower supplies in hand.

"Nah, don't be. You'll get one tomorrow."

"I don't know what I was doing wrong. I could tell they were looking at my fly, but I couldn't hook any. It was so frustrating!"

"That is tough. This stream has skunked me a few times, so I get it."

"I just felt so awkward. I couldn't seem to concentrate on what I was doing. I kept thinking about Mike and wondering how he's doing. I felt very clumsy fishing, casting, and even tying knots, which I'm usually really good at."

"Of course your focus is off. How could it not be? I can't even imagine . . ."

"I tried not to think about it. I really did, but it's just so big. So real," I say as we see a fish jump out of the river. "Did you see that?"

"Cool, let's go down there." We detour and walk down to the river. We stand there and wait for the fish to jump again. We watch in silence for several minutes. My mind wanders again to Mike.

"The bullet missed his aorta by three millimeters . . . *three millimeters!*"

"Oh my God," Veronica exclaims. "That's crazy."

"He was so lucky . . ."

"Absolutely. I'm so sorry," she says softly.

"It's crazy how close I came to losing him."

"I can't even imagine. Did I hear that two of his buddies didn't make it?"

"Yeah, two of his best friends. It's been really hard on him."

"I bet."

"I talked with both of their wives this week . . . I have cried more tears in the last few weeks than I have my entire life."

"I'm sure."

We stand and stare at the river as we both reflect on what happened. I start to well up with tears again. I can tell she doesn't really know what to say, so I decide I need to change the subject. I hop up on a rock to change the energy in the conversation "Sorry, we can change the subject . . . it's just hard to focus on anything else."

"No, I get it. This is big stuff—the most important stuff there is."

Just then, I lose my balance and fall backwards off the rock. "Shit!" I fall into the deep eddy right at the edge of the river and get baptized in the stream.

"Oh my God!" Veronica exclaims as I come up out of the water. "Are you okay?"

When she sees that I'm fine, we both burst out laughing at the same time. "Yeah, just wet. Oh my gosh, I am so clumsy!" I'm dripping from head to toe. "Can this day be over already?"

"Lucky for you Rose already went to bed. You know she'd bust out one of her patches."

"Yeah, but I'm not wearing a hat. Doesn't count!"

"Come on, girl, let's go wash off this day with a good shower."

"Amen to that."

`·.¸¸.·´¯`·.¸><((((º>`·.¸¸.·´¯`·.¸><((((º>`·.¸¸.·´¯`·..

I wake up early the next morning with a new attitude. I am determined to change my focus so I can have a better day. I feel refreshed and renewed and ready to try a few tips that Veronica gave me last night. This morning I step into the river right outside the camper where my unfortunate baptism happened last night, tie on a number 16 Adams, and on my second cast catch a nice rainbow. Oh, how a couple of fish can turn my frown upside down! I hoop and holler loud enough that I'm sure I wake half the campground. I cast again and immediately catch another fish. After catching four fish in about thirty minutes, I am pleased with my casting and my focus.

All four of the girls have come down to the river to root me on. Melody has her camera out and takes a few pictures. Sophie immediately gets her rod out and joins me about twenty yards upstream. You can tell she wants some redemption from yesterday as well. Veronica grins as she watches me pull in fish after fish. Several other people at the campground pull up camp chairs and their morning coffee and enjoy watching as well.

As I reflect back on yesterday and my dip in the river, it felt like a shock to my system, more of a baptism if you will, or a rebirth of my attitude about fly fishing skills and everything I have going on. I've been fly fishing for several years now, and when I have confidence in myself, I tend to do really well on the river. When I'm distracted and I doubt what I'm doing, I tend to get skunked. I need to remember this more often, especially as I go into this next month with Mike coming home. I'm sure there will be times that he will struggle and I'll likely need to remind him of this as he recovers from his injuries.

I'm so thankful I have opportunities like this to get away from the real world, to broaden my perspective. They always seem to open my mind in ways I can't when I'm at home in the daily grind.

`·.¸¸.·´¯`·.¸><(((°>`·.¸¸.·´¯`·..><((((°>`·.¸¸.·´¯`·..

Rose

Oh, Miss Sophie, you are such a good angler. Why don't you trust your own abilities and instincts?

"Can you give me some pointers for today?" Sophie asks. "I hate getting skunked. I've tried so many different things this week and nothing seems to work for me."

"Sophie, why do you use a graphite rod?"

"Um, because I have one? I don't know. I've just always used one."

"Would you consider using one of my bamboo rods?"

"I suppose so, why?"

"Because I feel like you have too much artificial crap between you and the fish. You're a damn fine angler, but for some reason you're not catching any fish."

"Wow, um, okay . . ."

"I've heard you coach Veronica, Amanda, and Melody. You know what you're doing. You've tried everything else, why not try a different rod and see what happens?"

"Do you think the fish know the difference?"

"Well, if fish could tell the difference, that would imply they knew they were being hunted, and then they wouldn't take your fly anyway, now would they?"

"Good point."

"For me, I love my bamboo rod because there's a natural connection between me and the rod. Nothing synthetic or artificial. Just me and another once-living material, connecting me to a vivacious, majestic creature. I love the way the rod looks and feels, and I can lay down my line easier with bamboo than any other rod I've tried. Just give it a try for a day. You may hate it, but you won't know if you don't try. Who knows, maybe you'll catch the big one," I say with a sly, slight grin.

`·.,.·´¯`·.,><((((º>`·.,.·´¯`·..><((((º>`·.,.·´¯`·..

Sophie

Now that I'm a fly fisher, I don't really enjoy spin casting anymore. With fly fishing, there's always something to do: mend your line, cast to a specific spot, read the water, change your fly . . . My mind is always busy, so I don't get bored and it helps me focus. With traditional spin casting, you throw the line out one time and then you just sit. And wait. And wait. I get really bored with the whole process now. Other people really enjoy it, which is fine, but for me I like how active fly fishing is. It's like I'm actively pursuing a specific goal—usually trying to catch a difficult fish on a fly, instead of passively waiting for an opportunity to come along. Recreationally, I also only practice catch and release now, so it's more of a sport than wanting to bring in a big haul to feed my family. I might view it differently if I were keeping what I catch.

So, I guess I'm borrowing one of Rose's bamboo rods today. In my forever quest to pursue my goal, I'm going to try something different. It feels a little weird, but what the hell, why not? *Too much artificial crap between me and the fish . . . I mutter to myself. Humph.*

Today I decide to fish upstream from the campsite. That way, I can switch out rods easily if I don't like Rose's rod. I hike several hundred yards upstream and find a nice spot that has a little feeder stream coming into the Fryingpan. There is a significant bend in the river with some giant rocks right where the river bends. The eddy pools on the downriver side of the bend look pretty deep and epic, so there have to be fish in there. I decide to cast upstream above the rocks and let my dry fly float down the seam right by the eddy pools. That's precisely what bugs would do, which is why the unsuspecting fish will be hanging out in that exact spot waiting for them.

I find a good location and get rigged up. Before entering the stream I pause, take a big, deep breath, and say a quick little prayer. *Lord, thank you for the opportunity to be out in this glorious setting, doing something that I love. Please help me to have a better attitude today, and if it's your will, let me hook a big one. Amen!*

I laugh at myself for praying to catch a fish, but I'm certain I'm not the only fisherman who has done it. Especially right after getting skunked a few days in a row . . .

I decide to just relax and focus on what I know. Like Rose said, I am a pretty good fly fisher; I just need to believe in myself and not get so frustrated when things don't go my way. Maybe I'm a bit of a control freak after all.

I cast to this spot for a good thirty minutes. I get one nibble on my second cast, which is the first bit of action I've had all week! I am bound and determined to land one in this hole. Through my polarized lenses I can see a few nice-sized trout hanging out in the eddies. *You are mine, Mr. Fish. Come to me, you fine specimen, you.* I cast my line out a little further allowing it to float a little longer on top of the water. I can feel my confidence grow with each cast, rather than getting frustrated like I did yesterday. I'm kind of digging the casting arc that the bamboo rod is giving me, so I let it sail a good distance just to get the feel of it.

All of a sudden, I feel my line snag on something and think to myself, *Oh crap, what's upstream that I can't see around this big rock?*

Just then, a loud voice yells out, "Ow! What the hell?"

Oh, holy shit, I just hooked someone with my fly. "Oh my God. I'm so sorry! Are you okay?" Out of nowhere a drift boat floats around the corner, and I see my fly lodged into the arm of the fishing guide.

"Don't pull on the line! I'm hooked!" the voice yells back, his back to me.

Oh my God. Oh my God. Oh my God . . . "Oh my God, I'm so, so sorry! I didn't even see you coming!" *I seriously want to crawl inside myself right now.*

"It's okay, hold on. You got me pretty good." He egresses his boat over into the slow water and pulls out his nippers to cut the line. "Oh man, that hurts!" he exclaims. *I wish I could crawl underneath a rock and hide.* Once I see my line lying limp on the water, I reel the excess back in. I see him work on dislodging the fly from the flesh of his forearm, and I cringe when I see his face twist up as he works the fly out.

"Oh jeez. I'm so sorry! Are you okay?" I ask, embarrassed beyond belief.

"Yeah, I'm okay. Thank God you use barbless hooks!" he says, trying to lighten the mood.

"Again, I'm so sorry."

"No worries. I'm used to getting hooked a few times a season, just usually by a client and not someone in the river." He looks the fly over, wipes the blood off on his pants and hands it back to me. "I'm Buck," he says as he extends his hand out for me to shake, his boat floating right next to me. I grab onto the side to steady it so it doesn't continue floating downstream. "That's Jerry," he says as he points to his client in the boat with him.

"I'm Sophie," I say as I shake his hand. "Nice to meet you."

"Sophie Myers?" he asks quizzically, catching me completely off guard.

"Um, yes? How do you know my—"

"Holy crap, Sophie Myers. I always wondered what happened to you."

"Um, what?!" I cry, louder than expected.

"You walked into my fly shop about twenty years ago, and I gave you a casting lesson in the backyard."

"Oh my gosh, you're *that* Buck?"

"Come on, how many Bucks do you know?" he teases.

"True, come to think of it, you might be the only one." My heart races a bit, surprised by what is unfolding in front of me. "Um, why is it you remember me?"

"There are a few patrons that are hard to forget," he says with a sheepish grin.

"Um. . . okay, well . . . uh . . . I'm not sure how to respond to that."

"Sorry, don't mean to be creepy. You just . . . you just made an impression on me that day and I've thought about you a few times over the years. I wondered if you kept up with fly fishing and if you stayed in Colorado. That's all."

I look over at Jerry and catch him chuckling and shaking his head. "Okay, well . . . your answer is yes. I kept up with fly fishing and I stayed in Colorado. I live down in the front range, but I still fish on a regular basis."

"Well, good! Glad to hear it. You were one of the first women we had come through our shop wanting casting lessons, so you were memorable to me."

Completely embarrassed, I look down at the water and feel my face flush red. "Well, cool. Hopefully it's not such a rare occurrence anymore. Do you have a lot of women come through the shop these days?" I catch myself looking at his left hand. *Hmm, no wedding ring. Interesting . . . Oh my God, what are you doing?*

"Yes we do, actually. I would guess women are at least 25 percent of our customers now. There's been a huge surge of women fly fishers in the last five to seven years, which is awesome."

"Uh huh. I bet it is," I joke, instantly regretting it.

"No, not like that. I just mean it's cool that more women are fly fishing, that's all," he stammers, trying to recover.

"Sorry, I was just kidding. I'm glad to hear so many women are out doing it. I absolutely love it, so I'm glad it's catching on," I reply, trying not to sound ridiculous. "Thanks for giving me my first lesson. I obviously learned something that day."

"Well, the pleasure was all mine," he says as he looks away, obviously a little embarrassed. An awkward pause falls between us. We both look over at Jerry, and he's still chuckling and shaking his head. Buck finally pipes up and asks, "Didn't you have a farm or something back in Kansas?"

Wow, good memory . . . "Yes, and still do. My parents still live on the farm there."

"Oh cool. Do you miss it?"

"Well, yes and no. I'm now a farmer of a different kind. I own a greenhouse and nursery business in Littleton. I definitely miss growing big fields of crops, but I still go back and help out during harvest, so I still get my fix a few times a year."

"Nice! That's really cool."

"It's in my blood. You'd be hard pressed to keep me away."

"I wouldn't dare." Just then the boat surges forward a bit and makes me lose my balance. I let go of the side and it starts to drift downstream a bit. Buck also loses his balance and almost falls out of the boat. He quickly catches himself and grabs his oars and tries to paddle back up to where I'm standing.

"Well, we'd better get on downstream. It was really great seeing you again, Sophie."

"Likewise. So sorry for hooking you . . ."

"Ya know, I'm actually glad you did," he says, trying to keep his boat close enough to me so we could continue the conversation.

"Oh, yeah right. Well, I guess you'll have something to remember me by."

"You'd be pretty hard to forget . . ."

Again, an awkward tension builds between us. Not really sure of the protocol for saying good-bye to someone you just injured, I call out, "Thanks, Buck. It was really nice seeing you again." *Holy cow, I think those are butterflies in my stomach . . .*

"Ya know, back in the day, we didn't think to capture contact information for everyone who came through the shop . . . Any chance you'd want to go out on a date with me?"

Oh my goodness . . . Is this really happening? "Um, sure. Are you still at the fly shop in Breck?" I look over at Jerry and he is stifling down laughter now, trying not to be rude.

"Yes, same place," he replies, shooting his client a *shut-the-fuck-up* look.

Embarrassed and wishing Jerry was not overhearing our every word, I reply, "Great, I'll call the shop and catch you there."

"Cool. Sounds like a plan. Until then . . . ," he says, and starts to drift downstream.

"Until then . . . ," I repeat, and watch as they slowly float off downstream. I wave good-bye and dare not break eye contact with Buck as our eyes remain locked onto one another, drinking in the moment. We're both smiling, and I can feel the electricity in the air. I continue to watch until they are almost out of sight. In the distance I hear Buck say, "Shut up, Jerry!" and I giggle out loud.

What the hell, did that just happen?

I immediately gather up all of my gear, and I race back to the campground. I cannot wait to tell the girls . . .

`` `·.¸¸.·´¯`·.¸><((((º>`·.¸¸.·´¯`·..><((((º>`·.¸¸.·´¯`·.

273

Amanda

The anticipation and emotional buildup of Mike coming home has been overwhelming. When I finally see him step off that plane and our eyes meet, I burst into tears and run out to embrace him. I have Parker on my hip and Lorraine has Jordan by the hand. We race out to greet him, and we all collapse into one another's arms, as if we were clinging to life itself. We try not to squeeze him too tightly so we won't hurt his shoulder. Jordan wraps her arms around his leg and keeps shouting, "Yay Daddy! Daddy's home! I love my daddy!" We are an emotional mess. Parker is a little freaked out, not sure what is going on, but we stand there and hug and cry and don't care who sees.

That evening we all snuggle on the couch and hang together as a family. We are all exhausted after such an emotional day. We put on a movie, pop some popcorn, and just hold each other close. Jordan sits right next to Mike and will not let go of his hand. I sit on the other side of him and snuggle up under his arm. Parker doesn't get as close, but he sits on my lap and keeps reaching out to touch Mike's face, as if he doesn't believe that Daddy is right there rather than in a video. He does eventually lay his head on Mike's leg and falls asleep. After we put the kids down, we crawl into bed and curl up together. We don't say a lot, but we hold each other all night long. I am so happy to have him home safe in my arms. *Am I dreaming? I hope not.* I don't want the night to end.

I wake the next morning with a smile on my face. *He's home.* I reach across to his side to touch him and quickly realize I am alone. *Mike?!* I spring out of bed and race into the kitchen. There he is, sitting at the kitchen table on his laptop drinking a cup of coffee, his shoulder all bandaged up and his arm in a sling.

"Good morning, gorgeous."

"Oh my God, are you okay? I freaked out when you weren't in bed."

"Oh yeah, I'm fine. Just couldn't sleep. I woke up about three and my mind was buzzing."

"For a moment I thought I had dreamed up yesterday, that you weren't really back."

"Oh I'm back, baby. Come over here and give me a good morning kiss." He reaches his hand out, grabs mine, and pulls me onto his lap.

"Ew, I have morning breath. Let me—" I try to pull away to go brush my teeth, but he holds me and won't let me go.

"I don't care, just kiss me."

"Alright, you asked for it," I say, and passionately plant one on him, gross breath and all. *My God, it feels good to kiss him again.* His right hand is in the small of my back, and he pulls me tightly to him. I caress the back of his neck and run my fingers across his short, stubbly hair. I love the feeling of his rough, military-cut hair on my hand.

"God, it's so good to have you home," I say as I pull away from our kiss.

"You're telling me."

"I have missed you so much."

"When I couldn't go back to sleep, I lay awake and just watched you for the longest time last night. You are so beautiful, Mandy."

"Oh God, while I'm asleep? Hardly. You sure you didn't injure your head when you were over there?" I playfully jab as I brush my hand over his temples.

"Ha-ha, very funny. I'm serious." His tone turns a little more serious. "The moonlight was spilling in our bedroom window right onto your long blonde hair. I just couldn't help but look at you and wonder how I got so lucky. Felt like I was dreaming."

"Oh baby, that's so sweet." I blush and turn away, slightly embarrassed by the attention. "What woke you up?"

"Partly a dream, partly because I'm not adjusted to the time zone yet. It will take a few days not to feel like a zombie. I'm also a little stiff and sore from the plane ride. My shoulder was bugging me, so I got up and took a painkiller, then couldn't go back to sleep."

"How's it doing now? Do you need anything?"

"Nah, I'm good. I just want to sit here and stare at my smokin'-hot wife." He kisses me again, and we lock in a passionate embrace for several minutes. He finally pulls away, and then we just sit, my head on his shoulder, feeling the closeness of one another. A quiet stillness fills the room, and for a brief moment all feels right in the world.

All of a sudden, Jordan shuffles into the room, rubbing the sleep from her eyes. "Is Daddy still home?"

"Hey, big girl!" Mike exclaims and motions for me to stand. "Of course Daddy is still home. How's my girl this morning?" He winces and grabs his shoulder as he stands to pick her up to give her a morning hug. "Did you sleep well last night?"

She nods her head up and down, then rests her head on his shoulder, obviously still tired and not quite awake yet.

"Are you excited to go to Aunt Sophie's pumpkin patch today?"

"Can I get a caramel apple?"

"You bet, sweetie." Mike kisses her on the cheek and hugs her close.

"Can you make me cinnamon toast?" she asks softly.

He replies sweetly, "Can I make you cinnamon toast? Are you kidding? Of course I can!" He winces again as he puts her back down on the floor.

"I can do it, sweetie," I say, not wanting him to have to do too much.

"It's alright. I got it." He walks towards the pantry.

"No, it's not a big deal. Just have a seat so you don't strain your shoulder."

"Mandy, it's okay. It's just toast. I think I can manage." He peers around the pantry looking for the bread. "Don't we keep the bread in here?"

"Actually, it's in the cupboard over here." I walk across the kitchen and pull the bread from the bottom shelf. "Here you go."

"Thanks." He pops a piece into the toaster and presses the lever down. "What time do you want to go today?"

"I was thinking around two this afternoon, after Parker wakes up from his nap."

"Oh yeah, I forgot about his naps. When does he usually go down?"

"We definitely don't want to forget his naps. Otherwise we'll have Senõr Crankypants on our hands. I usually put him down around twelve thirty, right after lunch. He usually sleeps about an hour and a half. I thought we would head out right after that."

"Alright, that sounds good." When the toast pops up, he puts it on a plate. He grabs a butter knife from the drawer and fumbles getting the lid of the butter container off since he only has the use of one arm. It's a little painful to watch him struggle with getting the butter spread onto the toast.

"You need any help?" I ask, teetering between wanting him to do it himself and not wanting it to be difficult.

"Nope, I got it," he replies, a hint of frustration in his voice.

The butter is chunky and not evenly spread. I have a feeling Jordan will throw a fit, but I'm hoping she won't.

Mike starts opening several cabinets looking for something. "Where's the cinnamon?"

"It's right by the toaster. I keep it handy since this is a pretty routine breakfast for her."

"Got it." He shakes the cinnamon over the toast and then puts the plate in front of Jordan.

"Ew, look at the butter! This isn't the way Mommy makes it," Jordan blurts out. A look of hurt and disappointment washes over Mike's face.

"Oh, sorry, sweetie. Daddy had a hard time doing it with his arm like this."

"Mommy, can you make me my toast?" She looks at me longingly.

Horrified, I respond, "No, this toast is just fine. You need to eat the toast Daddy made you."

She says defiantly, "But I don't want to. The butter looks yucky."

"Just eat the toast, Jordan. The butter will melt in just a second and it will be just like Mommy's." *Please, for the love of God, child, just eat the toast.*

"Here, Daddy will eat the toast with you." Mike pulls up a chair beside her and takes a big bite of the toast.

"Noooooo! Now it's even more yucky," she cries.

"Fine." He stands, pushing his chair in swiftly. "You make the damn toast," he says, and he angrily leaves the room.

"Mike, she's just . . ." He is out the door before I can finish my sentence. Once I'm sure he is out of earshot, I look at Jordan. "Jordan, you need to be nice to Daddy. He just got home."

"I don't like yucky toast," she replies sheepishly, staring at her plate.

"I know, but Daddy tried very hard, and you hurt his feelings when you didn't eat his toast."

"But the butter!" she whines as she points to a clump of butter while her eyes start to fill with tears.

"I know, sweetie. Don't cry. It's going to take a little while for Daddy to learn all of your favorite things again. We need to be patient, and you need to say sorry to Daddy." She sits there and starts to cry. Oh, the irony of a meltdown over non-melted butter . . .

Clearly being rational with a sleepy, hungry three-year-old is not going to work in my favor. Knowing when to pick and choose my battles, I pop a new piece of bread in the toaster.

`·.¸¸.·´¯`·.¸><(((º>`·.¸¸.·´¯`·...><((((º>`·.¸¸.·´¯`·..

Sophie

I could not be more nervous for this date. I've had a million questions run through my mind. *Will he like me? Will I like him? Will I do or say the right thing or totally embarrass myself? Do we have anything to talk about besides fishing? If not, how will we get through the evening? Why am I analyzing every little thing? Will there be any chemistry between us? What should I wear? We're going hiking, should I kind of dress up or be practical and wear my quick-dry clothing? Do I wear my hair up or down? Should I wear makeup even though we're going hiking?* Ugh, my brain is on overload.

I was impressed that he asked me to go hiking, rather than out to eat or to a movie. A lot of restaurants are really noisy, which make it hard to hear and have any kind of conversation when you are trying to get to know someone. There was no way I would have suggested Noire, as Thatcher and Veronica would have been spying on us the whole night. At a movie, you aren't really talking, you're just sitting in the dark, so a hike sounds really nice. In theory, going out into the woods with someone you don't know for a first date is probably not the smartest idea. However, as Rose pointed out, he's a river guide. He goes out into the woods every day with strangers and to my knowledge hasn't killed anyone yet. Plus, he already took me out on the river by himself twenty years ago, and I didn't get a serial-killer vibe from him then.

We're meeting at the trailhead, so I pull my truck into the parking lot and check my mirror one more time. Need to make sure I don't have any cliff hangers or smudged eye liner . . . My stomach is doing summersaults, and I can't remember the last time I felt this giddy. *I really hope I'm not setting myself up for disappointment.*

I see him pull up in a shiny, black Toyota FJ Cruiser and park in a spot a few cars down from mine. *Hmm, nice truck, newer, well taken care of. Jeez, I'm already analyzing him.* He notices me and flashes a smile and a wave. *Oh wow, nice smile . . .* My heart rate quickens a bit. He opens his door and steps out. I instantly notice his tan skin radiating against his bright blue shirt, as well as his wavy, light-brown hair. *I don't think I even knew what color his hair is; he's always been wearing a hat both times I've seen him.* I notice the six locking fly rod cases mounted to the top of his racks. *Oh cool, I wonder what kinds of rods are in there . . . Sophie! Focus!*

I get out of my truck, grab my backpack, and walk over to his SUV. *Crap, do we hug? Shake hands? How do I greet him?* I point to the top of his truck and say, "Nice rack." *Oh God, you big dork. What are you doing?!*

"Hey thanks. Ha, that's usually not the first thing girls notice."

"Yeah, sorry. The addiction is real."

"That's alright, you've got good taste." He flashes another pearly smile, and my eyes light up a little bit. He opens the back of his truck and pulls out a few Nalgenes and his backpack. "I took the liberty of making us a picnic lunch. I hope that was okay."

"Of course. What did you bring?"

"It's a surprise, but I promise it's good," he says as he slings his pack over his shoulder. His bicep bulges and so do my eyes. "You don't have any food allergies, do you?" he asks, with a slight look of concern.

"Nah, I eat pretty much anything."

"Oh good. I didn't think to ask that earlier. Sorry."

"No worries."

"You ready to hit the trail?" he asks, as he motions towards the trailhead.

"Yep! Let's do this," I say with a little bit too much enthusiasm. *Please stop being a dork.*

"Have you hiked this trail before?"

"Yeah, a few times. I love the views from the top. You?"

"No, I'm not too familiar with this area, but a buddy of mine recommended it."

"Yeah, thanks for coming down the mountain for this," I reply, acknowledging the fact that we live two hours away from one another.

"Are you kidding? Wouldn't have missed it for the world. I still can't believe you hooked me."

"I know! So crazy. How's the arm doing anyway?"

"All good. Actually, makes me smile when I see it. You've scarred me for life, Sophie Myers!" he says with a chuckle.

Oh great. That sounds ominous. No witty retort comes to mind, so I don't say anything. *Shit.*

"Ha-ha, I'm just kidding. Seriously, it does make me smile."

"Okay, well, I still feel really bad."

"No, please don't. Had you not hooked me, I would have floated right by you that day. I'm really glad you did."

"I guess that's one way of looking at it."

The summit is about an hour hike from the parking lot. We talk about all kinds of things along the way: where we both grew up, how many siblings we each have, my Kansas farm, my greenhouse, my fly fishing girls, favorite places we've traveled, and favorite rivers to fish in. It is a nicely paced hike, and the conversation is very easy and natural.

When we get to the top, Buck pulls out a blanket and starts setting up a picnic lunch for us. My mouth gapes open as he magically pulls out a sumptuous meal for us. First, he prepares an exotic cheese board with five different kinds of cheeses, a few cured meats, and honey-and-fig jam served with crunchy toastettes. He has a small container of sweet Shuksan strawberries and another of fresh cherries tossed with mint leaves. He prepares a bright salad with spring panzanella, chicory leaves, and asparagus that makes my mouth water just looking at it. He finishes it off with slices of poached salmon from fish he caught himself on a recent fly fishing trip to Alaska.

"Oh my goodness, are those nasturtium petals in the salad?"

"Yeah, I found some at this great little greenhouse in Littleton."

"No way, you stopped by the shop?" *Niiice. Super big brownie points.*

"I sure did. Had to get the best ingredients possible," he says, flashing that sweet smile my way.

"Oh my goodness, that is awesome. I was actually admiring the chicory greens and mentally complimenting the grower." *Is this for real?*

"Now that's funny. Pat yourself on the back!"

"I'll be sure to tell Duke and David, two of my chief growers. They really work hard for me." *I cannot even believe he did this.*

"With your inspiration, I'm sure."

"I do like to try some more exotic varieties. It helps that Thatcher, Veronica's husband, will buy anything I ask him to. It's fun seeing the food critic reviews he receives knowing all of his fresh ingredients come from my farms."

"I bet. That is really cool." *His eyes are so, so blue . . .*

"Are the watermelon radishes from us as well?"

"Anything fresh came from your place."

"Thatcher requested those." I smile and shake my head, staring down at the well-thought-out feast in front of me. "Wow, this is really cool. Thank you." *Seriously.*

"You're welcome. I actually really like to cook, and I did know what a nasturtium petal was even before seeing them in your shop."

"Really? You're not just saying that?" I imagine pressing my lips to the curve of his jaw, and immediately goose bumps shoot down my spine. *Whoa. What was that?*

"No really! Have you ever tried them in omelets? Mix together some chives and either the leaves or petals, and add them to your eggs before you make them. So good! Mix in a little gouda? Heaven."

"Now you're just showing off." *But really, don't stop. Say more things . . .*

"Nah, I just wanted to do something special, something you would remember."

"Well, mission accomplished." *Um, seriously, like I could never forget this. Ever. Such planning, the thoughtfulness of it all. Huge. I can't wait to tell the girls . . .*

We sit and chat for another hour and watch the sunset start to light up the sky with pink hues, crimsons, and reddish oranges. As the sun dips below the horizon, the treetops cast dark shadows in the softened light of the evening. I don't want to leave.

We finally remember we have to hike back down to the parking lot, so we quickly pack the leftovers from this scrumptious meal back into his backpack and hike down the mountain. When we get to the parking lot, he gives me a hug, tells me what a wonderful time he's had, and opens my car door for me. I can tell he is hesitating, trying to decide whether to kiss me or not. He asks if we can see each other again, and I emphatically say yes. He thanks me for a wonderful time and says goodbye. I drive out of the parking lot and squeal as soon as I know he is out of earshot. *What an amazing day . . .*

`·.,,.·´¯`·.,><((((º>`·.,,.·´¯`·..><((((º>`·.,,.·´¯`·..

288

Section 7: The Joy of Going Solo

"Never travel alone—it's a rule found on nearly every list of wilderness dos and don'ts. It's also a rule I violate regularly.

There are immense practical advantages to traveling alone if you're comfortable doing it. All of the choices are yours. You hike at your own pace. When you're feeling strong, you can step out and really cover some ground. If you want to hike until dark, bolt down a cold supper, and hit the trail again at first light, you just do it.

Ultimately, though, hiking and fishing alone offer much more than practical advantages. Consider the things you go to the wilderness to find— independence, self-sufficiency, release from daily routines, the quiet to hear yourself think(or not think), the opportunity to see and absorb wild country. All of these experiences are enhanced by traveling alone."[x]

Fly-Fishing the
Rocky Mountain Backcountry
by Rich Osthoff

Melody

I've decided I'm going to go on a solo backpacking trip. I can't decide if I will tell anyone I am going or not. My instincts tell me that I should at least tell Rose; that way there is at least one human being who knows I'm out traipsing through the woods on some remote trail. I will definitely not tell my parents. I don't think they will even know I am gone. I've done a little research on different parts of Colorado on where I might find some rare fish. I want to go somewhere new that I can explore and get away from the overcrowded areas that are busy this time of year. I located an area in the San Luis Valley in Southern Colorado that seems to be pretty remote and inaccessible except by mountain bike or boots. *Away from the peoples.* Anyone on that trail would have at least a day hike in before they hit the river. The vision of the solitude and pristine surroundings excites me.

I have researched online what I would need for a four-to-five-day hike alone. It really is amazing what you can find on the internet these days. Why would anyone visit a library when you can find everything online? Rose says that she loves the library. I wonder what the allure is? Seems like there would be too many people for my liking.

I've made a list of what I need and ordered everything online. Within a few days everything will arrive at the front desk, and Girard will haul it up to my loft. He'll naturally assume it's more camera gear. *Wouldn't he be surprised as hell to find out it's outdoor shit?*

My plan is, once everything arrives, I will pack everything into the backpack and wear it around a couple times to get used to the weight. If I think it will be too heavy, I'll omit a few nonessential items. Heck, I should probably go walking around in Boulder. I would fit right in. No one would even look at me twice for wearing hiking boots and a thirty-pound pack with a sleeping bag strapped on.

I need to leave room in my pack for my camera and all of my fly fishing gear. Luckily, my fishing gear does not weigh much, thanks to graphite rods and tiny flies. I probably won't bring my fishing vest, just my nippers to cut line and my pocket knife for other essential tasks. Rose has taught me how to build a fire; plus, I downloaded several survival books to my iPad, which I will bring with me. It has a long battery life so it should last me for five days. I don't plan on using it much, but it will be there if I need it. I'll pack enough food for a couple of days, and then I figure I can eat a few of the fish I catch. I know that fly fishing is mainly catch and release, but I'm sure a few fish in the remotest part of Colorado will be fine to keep and eat. I checked online and found out the limit is two fish a day per angler. I watched a video online on how to fillet a fish, and it doesn't look that hard. Gross, but not hard.

Every book I have read so far says not to hike alone. I wonder if they mean that for people who are used to being around other people? I spend most of my time alone, so I don't know what the big deal is. I am keenly aware that there are dangerous things out in the woods—bears, mountain lions, crazy people—but I am also very good at self-defense. Both external and internal. As much as I hated martial arts training when I was a kid, I'm very glad for the knowledge and skill it still provides me. I'm sure I could kick some backcountry hillbilly's ass before he even knew what hit him. I'm also bringing one of my dad's Asian spears with me. If I do come in contact with any ferocious wildlife, I am trained in weaponry and I'm confident I could win a battle no matter the opponent. I'm really not afraid of anything like that. I may be small in stature, but I am a giant in battle. Unless it's against my parents. They always seem to win. Someday I hope to end the constant tug-of-war we play. It seems there is always something simmering below the surface with us, and I will never live up to their expectations. Part of me wants to please them and go to Juilliard to pursue music. Another part of me wants to scream myself hoarse at the thought of living up to their expectations. Maybe I'll find some clarity out on the trail.

`·.¸¸.·´¯`·.¸><((((º>`·.¸¸.·´¯`·..·><(((((º>`·.¸¸.·´¯`·..

It's been a few weeks since I decided to go on this trip, and now I am packed and ready to go. In that time frame I have been able to hit a few local trails with my pack and logged about ten miles carrying a thirty-pound pack. *Pretty impressive for a 115-pound chick!* The first practice hike I was pretty uncomfortable after about five miles, but looking at the map and the trail I'm going on, I should hit the river ten miles in. I have nothing but time. I can rest when I need to.

I am headed to the San Luis Valley in Colorado and can hardly contain my excitement. At the risk of sounding like an excerpt from the musical *Rent*, I have three days, seventy-two hours, and 4,320 minutes left until I leave. *Did I mention I was excited?*

I have made my list, checked it twice, packed my backpack, watered the plants in my loft, and I am ready to embark on this solo hiking-and-fishing marathon. *A forced march, if you will.* Hoping for a little clarity for my life. I have a few questions I want to think about while out on the trail: *What am I capable of? Am I equal to what nature has to bring? What should I do with my life? Will this trip actually help me answer any of these questions?* I'm sure Veronica could have added a few coaching questions to this list if I had bothered to ask.

It will be a little strange taking this journey without my new fishing buddy, Rose, but I think this is something I need to do for myself. I need to prove to myself that I am strong and capable of making good decisions. And not just the decisions my parents want me to make, decisions that feel right to me. There is a part of me that wishes Rose could accompany me on this epic path, or one that I hope to be epic. She really has been a fun addition to my life. It's been strange for me to enjoy the company of others lately. I've led a very solitary life, so having this new dependence on the fishing girls is a little weird. Spending time alone is not a strange feeling for me as it is for others. After meeting the girls, I have had more interaction with other humans than I have in the last five years combined. That's probably a good thing, but it's also another reason why I am looking forward to this solo trip.

And just like that I pull up my potential and all I have learned, grab my pack, and head out to change a few things.

`·.¸¸.·´¯`·.¸><(((º>`·.¸¸.·´¯`·.·.·><((((º>`·.¸¸.·´¯`·..

Amanda

We had so much fun last week at Sophie's place. We took it easy, not really knowing how much Mike could do without getting too fatigued. He did pretty well but had to sit down quite a bit. Jordan got frustrated a few times when we had to wait, which in turn frustrated Mike. Parker is starting to warm up to him, so that helps, but we were there for several hours, so we were all ready to go home by the end. I was surprised to see Sophie walking around with that guy, Buck, she hooked on our fishing trip. She even introduced him to Mike, which I thought was a pretty big deal.

Overall the last week has been pretty good. It's taken awhile for us to get back into a rhythm of being a family of four again. It's amazing how quickly we can fall into new routines. When you are single-parenting, you are just used to doing everything. Now that Mike is home, I need to learn to let him do some of the routine stuff. We're still not sure if he has to go back to Afghanistan or if he can stay for the remainder of his tour due to his injuries. We're supposed to find out this week after his next doctor's appointment.

He's supposed to see the psychologist next week as well. He's woken up several nights this week with night terrors. When I ask him about them, he just shuts down and doesn't want to talk about it. He's obviously not sleeping well, so I'm sure that's part of it. I have a hard time knowing when to push and when to let him be. I don't want to piss him off, but I'd really like to know what's going on in his head. I can't help him if he doesn't talk to me. We have about an hour before the kids wake up from their nap, so I attempt to see if I can break his silence.

"Mike, can we talk?" I ask cautiously, really wanting him to open up to me.

"Ugh, Mandy . . . I told you I don't want to talk about it right now."

"I know, but it's driving me crazy having you so closed off. I just want to talk again, like we used to."

"Fine. *Talk*."

"Come on, don't be a jerk about it. I just want to know how you are doing."

"I'm not being a jerk. You want to talk? Let's talk. What do you want to know?" The annoyance in his voice is telling.

"First, bring the attitude down a few notches. *I just want to talk.* Like, how are you?"

"I'm good, Mandy. I'm fine. Everything is fine. How are you?"

"It's not fine. You wake up in the middle of the night screaming, then you're up for hours on your computer, and when you do come back to bed, you don't sleep. I feel like you need to talk about this stuff or it's going to eat you up inside."

"I can't talk about it. I have so much guilt about what happened that talking about it just makes me feel shittier. I'm struggling enough with being a functioning husband and father in my own family right now. Talking about what happened over there is not going to help me here."

"Yes it will. Right now you're so closed off that we are all walking on eggshells around you. No one knows what to say or do so we don't set you off."

"What do you want me to do, Mandy? Spill my guts and cry? I'm supposed to be the strong guy, not the gimpy, one-armed fuck-up who feels like I'm intruding on my own family."

"What are you talking about? Why would you say that?" I yell back. "You were *shot,* Mike. It's just going to take time to heal. You are supposed to get full range of motion back in your arm. This is just a setback for a little while."

"Well, I feel like a damn invalid. I can't even butter a piece of fucking toast."

I let out a big, frustrated sigh, "This is just temporary. You know that. Stop beating yourself up for being injured. *You are alive. We still have you.* There will come a day when you will *rock* at buttering toast again." I attempt a little humor, to try to break the tension.

He rolls his eyes but finally lets out a small smile. His energy starts to switch, and he de-escalates a little bit.

"I gotta tell you, there are times when it's a little weird being back." He looks away and seems to get very introspective. "The sounds, the people, the entitlement . . . It's a lot to take in all at once. Over there it's different, like I have purpose. Here I just feel like I sit and take up space. I sometimes wonder why I was allowed to live and Jacobi and Smitty were the ones who died."

"Oh my God, are you serious?" I blurt out, stunned beyond belief. "What does that mean?"

"It means I just wonder why it was them and not me."

"How can you say that? What would we do without you?"

"You seem to get along just fine without me," he states, very matter-of-factly.

"Mike! Stop! We cannot do this without you. We *rely* on you, we *love* you . . . Yes, I do it all while you are gone. It's because I *have* to, not because I *want* to. We *want* you here. We *need* you here. I can't imagine Jordan and Parker growing up without you. *Please*, stop this negative talk."

"You're the one who wanted to talk," he reminds me, throwing this back in my face.

"Oh my God, I can't do this," I say as I forcefully run both hands through my hair. I stand up and start to walk out of the room.

Just then someone knocks loudly on the front door. *That's weird. I wonder why they didn't ring the doorbell.* I storm out of the kitchen and quickly open the front door. My mouth gapes open when I realize it's Chad on the other side of the screen door.

"Mandy?" he says enthusiastically.

"Oh my God. What the hell are you doing here? I told you to leave me alone." I half-close the door, blocking Mike's view so he won't see who it is. A wave of fear surges through my veins.

"I knew you didn't mean it. I thought I'd surprise you, you know, for old times' sake," he says with a smug grin on his face.

"No. Please leave. This is not a good time." My mind is racing. I have no idea what to do. I cannot believe this is happening.

"Who is it?" Mike yells out from the other room.

"No one!" I yell back. *Holy shit. Oh my God. Please, please, please go away.*

"Is that Mike? I thought you said he was overseas?" Chad asks in a hushed voice, trying to peek into the room. I close the door just a little bit more.

"Please, Chad, you have to go. Please leave." *Please.*

Just then, Mike appears behind me and abruptly opens the door and sees Chad.

"What the fuck is this?" he asks, shooting me a harrowed, questioning look.

"It's nothing, he—"

"Mike, ole buddy! How's it going? Damn, did you take a hit or something?" Chad sings out, sounding as much like the asshole he has always been.

"Seriously, what the fuck is this?" he asks again, even more pointed.

"It's nothing, Mike. I told him to leave me alone. I had no idea he knew where we lived." I try to explain, knowing it's futile.

"This isn't the first time you've seen him?" Fire darts from his eyes.

"No, it is! It's the first time I've seen him. He's been texting me. I told him to stop. Tell him, Chad," I plead, hoping he will have some mercy.

"I just thought I'd stop over and see my old friends. It's been such a long time, what like five years or something?"

"Have you been texting my girl?" he questions, starting to step towards Chad.

"Clearly I've interrupted something," he says as he starts to back down the sidewalk. "Looks like the two of you need to talk." Mike follows him out.

"What the fuck have you been doing, asshole?" he says in a protective, angry voice.

"Nothing man, I just . . . I gotta go." Chad starts to run down the driveway and quickly gets into his car. He backs out of the driveway and squeals his tires as he speeds off.

"You stay the fuck away from my family!" Mike screams as he runs down the driveway chasing after Chad as he peels off down the road.

My God, what just happened . . . I feel like I'm having an out-of-body experience as I pace around the living room. Mike storms back into the house. "Mandy, what the hell was that?"

"I don't know, Mike. He just showed up." He was angrier than I have ever seen him in my life.

"Have you been seeing him?"

"No! Of course not. He started texting me a few months ago. I told him to stop multiple times and he just wouldn't stop. Here, check my phone."

"How did he get your number?"

"I don't know! He just randomly started texting me. I seriously do not know how he got my number."

"Why didn't you tell me?"

I burst into tears. "Because I didn't want to worry you while you were over there. I'm so sorry, Mike. I didn't think it was a big deal."

"What would have happened had I not been here? Why would you hide this from me?"

"I don't know. I'm so sorry. I didn't know what to do."

Just then Lorraine gently raps on the door. "Knock, kno-ock!" she says in her sing-songy voice she always uses when she stops over. We have completely forgotten she was coming over to watch the kids so we could go to Veronica and Thatcher's for dinner tonight. She quickly realizes she has just walked into something tense and we all freeze, not knowing what to say.

"Jesus Christ," Mike says under his breath and walks out of the room, slamming the bedroom door behind him. I stand there, bewildered, not knowing what to say to his mother. Our eyes meet and tears stream down my face. I open my mouth to speak and nothing comes out. I run down the hallway into the bathroom and lock myself inside. I bury my head in my face and let out a sob.

A few moments later I look up and see little fingers wiggling underneath the doorway. "Mommy? Are you okay?"

301

`·.,,.·´¯`·.,><((((º>`·.,,.·´¯`·..><((((º>`·.,,.·´¯`·..

Melody

On my drive south to the San Luis Valley I stop at the cabin. I decide to leave Rose and the girls a note there telling them of my whereabouts just in case something crazy happens and I don't return. I find a post-it note and write the name of the trail, coordinates for the parking lot, and the words "Gone fishin', see you next Tuesday. —Melody." Seems like enough information to find me if they need to; plus, they won't find the note until Friday when they gather at the cabin and today is only Wednesday. This way, no one can try to talk me out of it or try to tag along. I need this trip to be just for me. If they don't find out about it until it's half over, then they won't worry about me for more than a few days. And it's not like they could talk me out of it even if they tried. If they've learned anything about me, it's that I am pretty strong-willed. Once I get my mind set to something, there is no stopping me.

It's a six-hour drive from my luxurious loft to this barren parking lot. That's a lot of windshield time for self-reflection and self-doubt. Here I am, sitting in a parking lot at the trailhead pondering my decision. *Am I ready?* I feel ready. *Do I just get out and start walking?* I guess so. What's that saying? *A journey of a thousand miles begins with the first step*? I am going hopefully to find myself or at least some answers on this trail. My mindset going in is not to worry

303

about who I have been or who I'm supposed to be, but to focus on who I want to become.

I get out of my Honda Civic, open the hatchback, and unclip the top of my backpack. I pull out a few things so I can clip in my keys to the inside. Nothing would be worse than getting back to the car after five days and not having your keys. That would royally suck. I also hid a key under the car in a hide-a-box shaped like a fish, just in case. After packing everything back up, I strap on my pack. It feels much heavier than when I was wearing it around downtown. *Could the altitude make it feel heavier? Or is this just me doubting my decision to do this?*

I lock the car and look around to check out my surroundings. A port-o-let, two other cars, a few hungry chipmunks, and a narrow opening to the trail. It doesn't look all that inviting. But it does look worn, indicating that I'm not the first person to take this journey. The thought of this makes me smile. I take a sip of water, inhale a deep, cleansing breath, and start walking.

`` `..,.·´¯`..,><((((º>`..,.·´¯`...><((((º>`..,.·´¯`... ``

The trail starts out with a rocky incline up a tree-lined hill. My boots hit the gravel, and I feel a surge of energy rush through my veins. A smile washes over my face as I start hiking up the narrow trail towards the top, shuffling and quickstepping as needed. The sounds of the forest are cool—birds chirping, the wind wisping through the branches, and gravel crunching under my boots. *Adventure!* I am on a mission, and this is going to be so fucking cool.

After several minutes of walking I pause to look behind me to see where I have been. My car is the size of a Matchbox car, and it now sits looking solemn and lonely in the parking lot. I

304

feel in my gut a ping of uncertainty and excitement all at the same time as I turn and hike on. *No turning back now. I've got this.*

The trail starts zigzagging up a steeper part of the hill, and I can feel the weight of my pack pulling on my shoulders. I tighten the waist straps on my pack to allow more of the weight to rest on my hip bones than on my shoulders. I can feel the blood surge across my shoulder muscles and a cooling sensation race down my arms. *The hiking part of this journey is definitely going to be harder than I thought.* The flat streets of Denver are nothing compared to this uphill hike. I guess I should have known this, and the reality of how difficult this is going to be is starting to hit me. *You've got nothing but time. Just do it.*

The first hour of my hike is pretty good. The sky is blue, there aren't a lot of bugs, and I've encountered a few deer scampering through the trees. My pace is pretty steady, and my pack seems to be wearing better after I shifted the weight from my shoulders to my hips. I stop to catch my breath at the top of the switchbacks and to take sips of water as needed. Overall I feel pretty good. *I wonder how far I have gone?* Hard to tell with all the squiggly lines on the map.

The trail is narrow but well-worn through the woods. *I wonder if this trail is man made or if it started out as a migration trail for the elk herds.* I'm sure that early hunters would track the elk for food, and these trees would provide excellent cover for them.

About two hours into my hike the sun starts peeking through the treetops, casting some shadows across my face. *Oh, cool photo op.* I can tell I'm getting closer to the top of the first big hill as there is an opening in the trees. My pace quickens as I near the top, my pack bouncing along behind me. As I breach the top of the mountain, the view explodes in front of me. *Holy shit, that is gorgeous. Look at all of this!*

305

Big-ass meadow full of intoxicating wildflowers. The colors seem to burst across the horizon as I stand and marvel at it all. I pull out my phone to take a few quick pics as I don't want to unpack my camera gear just yet. I take picture after picture of this lush landscape. I can tell there had been a wildfire in this location many years ago as the remains of blackened tree stumps litter the meadow. The scars of the fire are still evident, and you can see exactly where the path of the fire stopped. A fallen log beside the trail now blooms with purple Columbine flowers growing all around it. I kneel down and bury my face in them. Suddenly, my pack shifts its weight, catches me off guard and quickly topples me to the ground. *Fuck!* I fall hard, land solidly on my hands and knees first, then the weight of my pack forces me forward, and I feel my whole body thud to the ground. Hard. *Shit . . .* I lay there facedown in the dirt, assessing the damage. *Any injuries? No noticeable pain . . .* I move each extremity and don't feel anything out of the ordinary. *I think I'm good.* I laugh as I roll my ass over into a seated position. *Damn, this pack is heavy.* I smile as I realize I have just learned my very first lesson on this journey: carrying extra weight on your shoulders will definitely bring you to your knees. Or in my case, my ass. I sit for a few minutes to rest and let the sun warm my face.

I pull out my water bottle to rehydrate and soak in the scenery. The view is spectacular. *Now that I'm on my ass, I might as well get my big camera out.* Snowcapped mountains surround me in every direction. The clouds look so close I feel like I can reach out and touch them as they drift across the blue sky. The air smells crisp and cool as I take big, deep breaths, soaking it all in. The only sound I hear is a faint breeze whispering through the tree branches. I know that fishing remote waters is my primary focus on this trip, but the scenic view all around me is a nice bonus. I'm glad I brought one of my lighter cameras with me to capture as much of this trip in my viewfinder as I do in my mental photo album.

The map I'm following indicates that I should hit my first stream about ten miles in. I figure that is far enough away from the trailhead that most people would not hike that far for the fishing. I might see some day hikers to begin with and possibly some backpackers along the way, but for the most part I should be pretty far removed from civilization. Ten miles is a decent distance to hike on a mountainous trail, so I'm not sure I will make it to the stream tonight. I'll hike several miles or until the sun starts to dip behind the peaks, and then I'll find a place to set up camp for the night.

I ate a big breakfast this morning hoping to maximize my energy and get as far as I could on a full belly. I packed all kinds of freeze-dried backpacking food that I purchased at REI. *I've never tried any of it, so I hope it doesn't suck.* "Just add boiling water and in a few minutes you'll be enjoying the delicious meal you worked so hard for," says the back of the package. *Let's hope they are right.* I also brought along lots of dried fruits, nuts, beef jerky, and some banana bread that Rose baked for me. The guy at REI talked me into buying a few 3,600-calorie energy bars as well. That's more calories than I usually eat all day, but I threw a couple in at his strong suggestion. I typically don't eat a whole lot anyway, so I'm not too worried about running out of food. I packed enough water for two days. I brought my water filtration system to pull water out of the river for the rest of the trip. Giardia is prevalent in Colorado mountain streams, so I need to filter any water I will drink. I definitely do not want to get sick.

Getting back into a standing position with my pack on is equally as humorous as my fall. Lucky for me there was no one around to witness this comedy.

As my hike continues, my feet start to feel hot. I bought top-of-the-line boots hoping to avoid major blisters. I ordered them online and they seem to fit okay. I stop and look in my backpack for my first aid kit. *Shit, where is it?* I know I packed it, but I must have briefly taken it out when I was figuring out what to clip my keys to. *Damn. Hope I don't need that.* I tried to break in my boots on the few downtown hikes I did getting used to the weight of my pack. *Maybe I didn't do enough.* Hopefully I don't get any bad blisters as I need my feet to get back out of here in a few days.

I toss my pack onto my shoulders and start out again. *Damn, this incline sucks.* I start chanting, "Up-sucks-up-sucks-up-sucks," with each step. This hike is much harder than I thought it would be . . .

Several hours go by, my feet taking me step by step farther away from my car. Walking through the tall trees does seem to awaken all my senses, though. *I love the smell of the forest.* Every time the sun falls behind a treetop, it seems like a kaleidoscope of light and color. *I wish I could capture on film what I see with my eyes.* The sunlight seems to fight its way through the treetops. Each time a beam of light hits my face, I feel my face gravitate up towards the light—like it's searching for the direction and warmth. A soft breeze inspires the thousands of leaves to flicker and dance in the filtered sunlight, with a perfect rhythm and sound that no camera can capture.

About eight hours into my hike, I can really feel myself slowing down. *I'm getting really tired.* I've developed several blisters, and I can tell one of them is now oozing blood. I decide to start looking for a place to set up camp for the night. I've come a long way today, most of it uphill. I check my map and it looks like there's a small lake coming up. *Cool, I can make it that far.* Several minutes pass and then the trail opens up, and I catch the first glimpse of the crystal-blue lake. A feeling of elation and joy washes over me, and the weariness seems to lift off my shoulders. I find a flat spot near the water and set up my campsite for the night.

What a good day today. Countless feet have pounded this trail smooth long before me. The feeling of accomplishment is awesome. The excitement of seeing this mountainous country for the first time, the thrill of exploration and doing something adventurous on my own. I feel rich with good fortune of my experience. I will never own this water or the peaks and valleys, but the sunset and the view will belong to me as I have purchased this experience with my own sweat and blood. I look up at the stars and thank the universe for such an awesome first day.

`·.,,.·´¯`·.,><((((º>`·.,,.·´¯`·..><((((º>`·.,,.·´¯`·..

The next day I hike the rest of the way to my destination and camp next to the river for a few days. The first few days I've passed the time by fishing, taking pictures, and just enjoying the solace of being alone.

Tonight, however, I'm having a hard time falling asleep. I'm getting frustrated that I'm not really finding much clarity out here. Sure, I'm catching a lot of fish, but I guess I had different expectations for what my mind would do while on this journey. I thought I'd have some answers by now, although I'm not sure how they are supposed to come to me. *Am I just supposed to wake up one morning and know this shit?*

I sit up in my sleeping bag and pull out my journal and start penning my thoughts to paper. As I sit here and write, I can hear the Conejos River playing music with the rocks, and it is peaceful, similar to the sound an ocean makes, a sound that lulls one to sleep. *Well, someone except me.*

I wonder how one finds clarity. I've always heard of people finding themselves out in the wilderness. Maybe I'm not lost enough to find myself. That sounds cheesy. I really want to figure out what I want to do with my life. I love my photography, but is that what I want to do for my profession? What is my purpose?

Money is something I have never had to worry about. I know there is a shit-ton of money in my trust fund that I can tap into when I'm twenty-five. My grandparents bought my loft for me, so I really don't have that many expenses. I sell some of my photography pieces from time to time for a little extra spending money. I really haven't had to "earn my keep" yet. Nor will I ever have to, for that matter. As long as I don't get stupid with my spending, I should never have to worry about being homeless or starving. I guess I am fortunate in that way. What can I do that will make a difference in this world? Make a difference to me? There are days when I just feel useless, like it wouldn't matter if I didn't exist. I'm not suicidal by any means, but I feel a desire to matter to someone or something.

The other girls do such amazing things with their time. Amanda seems to be an amazing teacher and mother. She doesn't have a lot of money, but it doesn't seem to bother her. She makes the best of what she has, and she seems so happy all of the time. Sophie has set up so many programs for youth at her greenhouse; she definitely has a giving heart and thinks of others before herself. She donates all of that food to help feed the hungry, and she does that Military Appreciation event at the pumpkin patch. Veronica's whole business career is to transform business leaders. Can't get much cooler than that. And Rose is just Rose. She is one of those people you just feel lucky to know. Everything she does is in the best interest of others. Being a part of this group has really made me want to do more with my life than the path I am currently on. I find myself literally at a fork in the trail, and I am trying to figure out which path will be the best one to take.

I sit here in my tent tonight listening to the river and the sounds of the natural world around me. All of a sudden I hear the wind picking up, the leaves rustling in the trees, and the river sounds like it is running faster now. It has gone from a peaceful sound to almost sounding angry. I wonder if something is brewing upstream. *I'm gonna check it out.*

The moment I step outside my tent I can tell there is one hell of a storm headed my way. I quickly make sure my tent stakes are securely in the ground and that the rain fly is securely fastened. This tent is the only shelter I have, and everything I own is on the inside. I hope the reviews I read online for this tent are right. Otherwise, I'm going to be up shit creek. Flashes of lightning expose extremely black, threatening clouds. A few raindrops begin to fall, so I quickly climb back into the tent. I knew that weathering a storm was a possibility on this trek. I just didn't know how bad it would actually get.

`·.,,.·´¯`·.,><((((º>`·.,,.·´¯`·..><((((º>`·.,,.·´¯`·..

At home in my loft, I really enjoy thunderstorms. I've always been intrigued by the beauty, brightness, and destruction of lightning. I love to watch each shiny strike slither out from the black clouds and snake across the sky. It's mesmerizing and I find myself getting lost in the storm. Watching a storm from my loft is fun. Weathering a storm in my tiny tent is not.

At an elevation of ten thousand feet, lightning seems just inches overhead—and in reality, it probably is. This storm is making me nervous. Okay, not nervous—terrified. My fingers wrench together as I sit helplessly in my nylon dome. My breath quickens with each loud strike. I am by no means an experienced outdoorsy type, and I am feeling grossly unprepared for what is happening outside. This tent feels like a parachute ready for liftoff in the wind. My tiny body is no match for what mother nature is brewing outside. It is so loud I can hardly even hear myself think. The thunder vibrates through my chest and through my bones as it echoes forever in every direction. My tent sways violently in the wind, and it is freaking me out. So far the ropes are holding firm, as taut as violin strings with each wind gust. I pray that they hold and that I do not end up catapulting down this mountain as a nylon burrito. I hear tree branches swirling close and picture them bending to and fro with each assault.

I try not to think of all the stories I've heard of people being struck by lightning. What did I read online? The chance of getting struck by lightning in any given year is one in a million. With as many lightning strikes that are happening around me, I definitely do not want to be that one. As the wind roars around me like a freight train, I picture the bending trees nearby crashing down on me. The rain attacks my tent like a relentless army. I sit, bewildered and alone in my small nylon space, wishing I was somewhere else than on the side of this mountain.

It's pitch black; I can't even see my hand directly in front of my face. Then lightning strikes, and it lights up like daylight for mere nanoseconds and then it is pitch black again. I swear it is striking right outside my tent. The thunder is so loud and terrifying. I turn my headlamp on to look around. At what I'm not sure. Just to reassure myself that I'm okay, I guess. I turn it back off and lay there wide-eyed and terrified. Then another burst of lightning strikes, and it temporarily blinds me with the contrast from dark to light. I keep my eyes shut tight and curl up into the fetal position in my sleeping bag.

I lay there for hours. The storm does not seem to want to subside or let up. I beg Mother Nature to show me some mercy. *Please stop, please stop . . .* Tears prick the back of my tired eyes as my fatigue starts to get the best of me. Horrifying winds, deafening thunder, and a long wait in a small space is an exhausting combination. I see rivers of water stream down my rain fly. *This is not a field test, this is the real deal.* Each gust of wind beats the tent with gusts of water. I feel small rivulets of water start to creep beneath my sleeping bag. I can see the small stream of water making a new river underneath my tent. Thank goodness I spent the extra money on a good tent. I'm still bone dry on the inside despite the buckets of water dousing the outside of my tent.

The constant flow of lightning strikes wears on for hours because the storm cell is all around me. *I might enjoy this more if I weren't so scared.* I can hear the river roaring beside me. I'm glad I set up camp a good hundred feet away from the water. I can tell the water has swelled up and over the banks with the amount of rain that has fallen.

My headlamp casts eerie shadows on the tent walls. The nylon is flapping in the wind so hard it sounds like a kite taking a beating on a ferocious wind. It's deafening as it's only twelve inches from my head. The wind switches direction, and it feels like the storm is heading back my way. *Will this night ever end?* The sound of all this rain makes me have to go pee. There is no way I am going outside in this weather, though. *I will hold it no matter what.*

I can't sleep even though I am completely exhausted. All of a sudden one of the tent walls slams into my face. My tent stakes have finally given way to the relentless wind and softening earth. I gasp as I scramble to push it back into place. I know I have to go outside to fix it, but every ounce of my being wants to stay inside where it is safe and warm. Mustering up every ounce of courage I own, I quickly get out of my sleeping bag and shove it into the farthest corner of the tent so it won't get wet when I unzip the door.

I would much rather be watching this storm instead of living it. I have never seen or heard anything like this before. I'm cold and scared and would really like to go home now.

`·.,,.·´¯`·.,><((((º>`·.,,.·´¯`·..><((((º>`·.,,.·´¯`·..

As soon as the lightning and thunder finally subside, I go to sleep almost immediately and don't wake until dawn. I wake up groggy and feel a little hungover. I finally crawl out of the tent and assess the damage from the storm. There are leaves and branches everywhere; however, the earth seems to look a bit refreshed. Every leaf and pine needle is glistening with dew, the rocks shine brightly in the sun, and the leaf debris looks like a soft blanket covering the grass.

Overall I was spared any harmful consequences.

I have survived the storm . . .

`·.,,.·´¯`·.,><((((º>`·.,,.·´¯`·..><((((º>`·.,,.·´¯`·..

Veronica

Because I travel so much, I'm definitely a travel snob. I get irritated when things don't go as planned: flight delays, novice flyers making rookie errors, waiting in lines, rude wait staff. I know I should be more patient, but knowing the shortcuts and being used to the free upgrades, the longer it takes me to get from Point A to Point B, the more irritated I get.

I lost my romance for airports a long time ago. At one point, I actually enjoyed flying: the people watching, the new destinations, the occasional crazy flight attendant. Now that I log over a hundred thousand frequent flier miles a year, I have a love-hate relationship with flying. Tonight emphasizes another reason why I have lost my love of flying: flight delay.

I get out my phone and begrudgingly text the bad news to Thatcher.

V: Ugh, flight delayed 2 hrs.

T: What? No! That sucks.

V: Yes, most likely will not make dinner with the gang. Are you OK with hosting without me?

T: Can probably handle it.

V: Thanks, love. Wish I could beam myself there.

T: If you could control it I'd be mad. But since you can't I'll deal with it.

T: What's the delay?

V: Storms in the Midwest stretching from North to South.

T: Guess there's no alternate route.

V: Unfortunately, no.

T: Sucks.

V: Yes it does, sorry hon.

T: I'll manage. I just want you home.

V: Soon enough.

V: What's on the menu tonight?

T: You might not want to know.

V: Crap, that means you are making mussels, my favorite.

T: I aim to please.

V: And please you do. :)

T: I'll make you some when you get here.

V: Sounds divine. Can't wait.

T: How was your day?

V: Pretty good. Great audience today.

T: I'm sure they are on inspiration overload after your keynote.

V: Aw shucks. Hope so.

T: How could they not? You're the best! Proud of you.

V: Thanks. Means a lot.

V: How was your day?

T: Pretty chill. Looking forward to you being home.

V: Me too.

T: I love waking up with you.

V: That made me smile.

T: Good.

V: Can't wait to snuggle up with you tonight.

T: You might not get much sleep.

V: Oh really? Why is that? lol

T: You've been gone for four days. You know why. Ha-ha

V: Well, I look forward to being sleep deprived.

T: Me too.

T: Kitchen is calling. Gotta go.

V: OK, have fun tonight.

T: Will do.

T: Travel safe, bae. Text me when you land.

V: I will. Tell everyone I say hello. Love you baby.

T: Love you too, Bae.

I reread our conversation one more time and then throw my phone in my purse. Tears prick the back of my eyes as my frustration grows with the thought of missing tonight's fun. I am usually a take-control kind of person, and flight delays falls into the you-have-no-control department. I pull out my *O Magazine* and leaf through the pages while I hopelessly sit and wait . . .

`` `·.¸¸.·´¯`·.¸ ><((((º>`·.¸¸.·´¯`·..><((((º>`·.¸¸.·´¯`·.. ``

Three hours later I am finally sitting on the plane. Although I will definitely miss dinner with my friends, I still get to see my gorgeous husband tonight. That is enough incentive for me to get this flight loaded as quickly as possible and in the air. I take my aisle seat in first class, buckle in, don my earbuds, and prepare for takeoff. I smile at the older lady seated in the window seat next to me. She is nervously clutching her purse and gives me a flustered smile in return. A novice flyer, no doubt, so I pull my earbuds out and strike up a quick conversation with her.

"Fly often?" I ask, already knowing the answer.

"Oh no, my son bought me this ticket so I can meet my grandson. This is my first plane ride ever."

"Well, congratulations, Grandma. Nice of your son to put you in first class for your first flight."

Distracted from her nervousness, she smiles. "Oh, thank you. Yes, he used his miles or something."

"Ah, he must fly a lot then."

"Yes, he travels for work," she says. "I'm very excited to meet my grandson. He's just two weeks old now."

"Oh, still brand-new! I'm sure you are excited. Is this your first grandchild?"

"Yes, I just have one son and this is his first child. Do you want to see his picture?"

"Of course." Not really, but I oblige.

She fumbles into her purse and pulls out an envelope addressed to Grandma Lillian. She pulls out five or six snapshots and hands them to me.

"His name is Ethan."

"Well, Ethan is a real cutie. I think he has your nose, Grandma," I say as I shuffle through the photos. His eyes are beautiful and look to be the same color as mine.

"I think so too." She smiles as she takes the pictures back and gazes lovingly at them again.

"Well, I fly almost weekly, so I'm an old pro."

"I don't know how you do it every week. My stomach is in knots."

"You get used to it when you fly as much as I do. Pretty soon you'll be a pro with those monthly flights to visit Ethan," I say with a smile and playfully nudge her with my elbow.

"Oh, I don't know about monthly, but I would like to see him as often as I can so he knows who his grandma is."

"He'll know you. I can tell you will be one of those grandmas that will call or FaceTime, and send letters and visit as often as you can. Grandmothers are special people."

She smiles and gazes down at her pictures again. "Yes, I already love him more than words can express," she says softly. "What do you do that has you flying so much?"

"I'm an executive coach for women CEOs, and I speak at several conferences a year. My clients are all over the country, so I rack up several frequent-flyer miles each year."

"That sounds really interesting. What does your husband do?"

"He owns a restaurant in downtown Denver. Have you ever been to Noire?"

"I don't believe I have, but I bet my son has."

"Well, you'll have to check it out sometime. It's a pretty amazing place, if I do say so myself."

"I'm sure it is. I'll be sure to look it up."

A momentary silence happens, so I adjust my seat belt and tuck my water bottle into the seat pocket in front of me.

"Let me know if you have any questions about the flight and I'll be happy to answer them."

"Thanks for being nice to me."

"Oh, you're welcome," I say as I place my hand on hers and give it a squeeze. "My name is Veronica."

"I'm Lillian," she says as she squeezes my hand back.

"Good to meet you, Lillian."

"Likewise."

With that I put my earbuds back in and turn the TV channel to HGTV and start redecorating my loft in my mind. Once in the air I'll get my laptop out and get a little work done on the way home.

I wrote a lot of my book sitting in an airplane thirty-five thousand feet above the earth looking out the window at the distant, hazy horizon. I do my best work on airplanes, as no one can bother me. No phones, no distractions, and I can always turn the TV off if I want to get some work done. Even though some planes have internet access now, I can always claim that it wasn't working and get away with a little internet research and Facebook stalking while in the air if I want to. Looking out the window of an airplane always inspires me. To see all of the vast land below me, knowing that someone owns each and every little acre of it, is amazing to me. The square fields and irrigated crop circles always tell me there are farmers working hard to provide food for people they will never meet. The bustling cities and long highways stretching across America mean growth and opportunity. The distant storms I fly through are always fascinating to see how tall the cloud structure is, which makes me wonder what is happening below. Tonight, however, we seem to be flying right through a storm system, and it is the bumpiest plane ride I have ever experienced.

After ninety minutes into the flight, the flight attendants are finishing up their first beverage service as the turbulence begins. They wheel the noisy cart back up the aisle and get it secured back into the galley just as the plane jolts back and forth. Both flight attendants grasp the walls next to them as they struggle to maintain their balance. I look over at Lillian and she has fallen asleep. She has her head propped up against the window and I'm hoping she stays asleep so I don't have to soothe her through the rough ride.

The turbulence continues for a good thirty minutes and is consistently bumpy. The lady behind me has already been through two "complimentary bags," and the man across the aisle from me is white as a sheet and looks to be frozen with fear. The airplane has jumped many times causing me to grab hold of the armrests with a death grip and gasp out loud a few times, which is rare for me. Someone a few rows back is crying, and the overall passenger mood is very solemn. Thankfully Lillian is still sleeping, although I'm not sure how with all of the jostling. I've been through some doozy flights before, and landings into Denver are always a little bumpy with the mountain altitudes and weather, but tonight's storm seems to be quite severe. The dark, black clouds are ominous, and the lightning off in the distance is blinding when it lights up the sky. I can see the rain streaking down the window by the illumination of the blinking safety lights of the plane. For the first time in a long time, I am actually a little bit scared of this upcoming landing.

Trying to take my mind off the weather, I close my eyes, take a deep breath, and think about fishing with Rose last week. We were up at a high mountain lake and I caught a Golden Trout. It's a pretty rare fish in Colorado, only found in a few higher-elevation lakes and streams here. The whole experience of catching this fish has had my mind buzzing. I'm certain I have never told Rose about how I supported myself after college, and yet the details she gave me about the Golden Trout were uncanny. A California native . . . no parental care . . . known for laying its eggs and leaving . . . These statements pretty much sum up my childhood and hit me harder than I thought they would.

First off, I grew up in southern California. My grandmother raised me, as my parents were very young when they had me and made some really poor decisions early on. The State terminated their parental rights when I was four years old, and my grandmother was granted custody. She took me in as her own and I haven't seen my parents since. Neither one of us know where they are or if they are even alive. I suspect they have been in and out of jail on drug charges, but I'm not certain. My mother came back once when I was seven asking my grandmother for money. My grandmother could tell she was high and told her to leave and not come back until she was clean. We haven't seen or heard from her since.

Secondly, after college I had had a hard time finding a job right away. When my student loans kicked in, I was still unemployed and struggling to make ends meet. I heard an advertisement on the radio for a fertility clinic paying for egg donations, and they were looking for women in my demographic and education level. I decided to give it a try. I worked with a fertility clinic and received $7,000 per donation and ended up donating six times. I had my student loans paid off in one year and was able to make ends meet until I landed my first job in Human Resources for a natural gas line. So essentially, I laid my eggs and left—a little ironic if you ask me. The fact that this fish has a similar life cycle pattern that I had in my past is a little odd. What's even weirder is that Rose pointed out these facts in particular to me. Rose either has uncanny intuition or maybe I have mentioned my childhood to her in the past. I really don't remember telling her details about growing up, other than telling her she reminds me a lot of my grandmother. She perplexes me sometimes.

The plane suddenly leaps and my stomach lurches into my throat. We seem to be dropping out of the sky as if we were on the downhill of a roller coaster. The plane rapidly pitches left and then right, throwing us violently from side to side. Lillian lets out a blood-curdling scream, and I realize she has

323

hit her head on the cabin wall. Fear pierces her eyes as she looks to me for help. She was thrown so violently into the side of the cabin wall that it cracked the plastic that houses the window. She starts bleeding profusely from the head, and I spring into action grabbing every spare drink napkin I can find to help stop the bleeding.

"Lillian! Oh my gosh, you have hit your head."

"What is happening?" she says bewildered.

"You've hit your head, we need to stop the bleeding," I say, springing into Girl Scout mode.

"My head hurts. What is happening to the plane?"

"We've hit some turbulence, which is usually pretty normal. Tonight it seems to be a little more severe than normal." I quickly ring my call button for a flight attendant to get some assistance.

"Medic! We need some medical attention here!" I yell out, trying to keep my voice calm so I don't escalate her fear.

Everyone around me starts shoving their beverage napkins at me when they see that I have applied mine to Lillian's forehead. Their small size is hardly keeping up with the amount of blood spurting out of the gash. Streams of blood gush down her face, and she reaches up and wipes her face. Seeing the blood on her hands she freaks out.

"Veronica! I'm bleeding!" she says in terror.

"Yes, I know. We need to apply pressure to the wound. You hit your head on the side of the plane when we went through some turbulence. I've called the flight attendants to come and help so we can get you taken care of. We'll get you fixed up here.

"Oh, look at your shirt, you have blood on it."

"Oh, that's okay. It will wash. Don't you worry about a thing." I say with a smile, trying to keep her calm.

The flight attendants still haven't come and I start to worry. I can see the goose egg on her head expand in size by the second. She needs an ice pack and quickly.

"We need some help here!" I yell out again.

"The pilot has indicated it is not safe for the flight attendants to be up out of their seats. If you have a medical emergency, please ring your call button again," the voice coming from the intercom says.

Irritated, I ring my call button several more times. "Yes, we have a medical emergency! Bring a first aid kit now!" I scream, losing my patience.

I hear one of the flight attendants unclip her seat belt and carefully make her way down the aisle to us, steadying herself by learning on the overhead bins.

"What seems to be the—Oh good Lord!" she exclaims as she glances at Lillian.

"We need an ice pack and some bandages," I order.

"I'll be right back," she says as she darts down the aisle. She picks up the intercom receiver and says, "Is there a doctor on board? If there is a doctor on the plane, will you please make your way to the first-class cabin?"

"See Lillian. We'll get you taken care of. No need to worry," I say, trying to keep her as calm as possible.

She closes her eyes and leans her head back against the back of her seat.

"Lillian, I need you to stay with me. Keep your eyes open for me." She blinks her eyes back open and gives me a nod. My arm starts to fatigue from holding the bloody napkins to her forehead. My frustration grows with how long it seems to be taking for the first aid kit to arrive.

Finally the flight attendant returns with the first aid kit and a doctor in tow.

"Ma'am, can you please move to the empty seat in front of you so the doctor can take a look at her?"

"Of course," I say as I spring out of my seat. I am glad I am only going to be one row away so I can see what is happening with Lillian.

The doctor belts himself into my seat and springs into action with gloves, bandages, and ice packs. I try to watch what is happening through the narrow crack between the two seats but have a hard time seeing. The doctor calmly asks Lillian questions. "What is your name? How old are you? Where is your pain?" She is able to answer everything coherently, so I take that as a good sign. The plane continues to bounce and shudder through the turbulence and it feels like it has been set to vibrate as it rattles through the sky. I'm sure it doesn't make the doctor's job any easier, and I wish we could find a smooth spot to fly in.

I look around me to assess my new surroundings, and the man sitting next to me is writing hurried notes on a piece of paper. He has tears streaming down his face, and it dawns on me that he is writing a letter with his final thoughts to his family. I look around and other people are doing the same thing on whatever paper they can find, including the barf bags. An eerie silence has fallen over the passengers, and you can almost smell the fear in the cabin. Nobody is saying a word. I white-knuckle the armrest of my chair and close my eyes and think of Thatcher. Tears stream down my face as my fearful mind starts to create the worst-case scenario. Death by plane crash. I've always wondered if this would be my fate with as much as I fly. The thought of never seeing Thatcher again rips at my heart, and a floodgate of tears opens up as I let out a sob.

The man across the aisle from me must not have had his seat belt on, as he suddenly ejects from his seat when the plane takes another harrowing drop. He slams into the bulkhead and lands hard in the aisle. Dazed and confused, he scrambles back into his seat and fumbles to get his seat belt fastened. Our eyes meet and without saying a word he looks at me as if to say, "What the hell just happened?" Screaming and chaos ensue. The oxygen masks drop from overhead and plastic drink cups fly through the air, showering everyone with ice and random cola products.

The captain comes over the intercom and instructs us to tighten our seat belts and put on the oxygen masks. Suddenly, the cabin lights and TVs flicker on and off several times, and everything in the overhead bins start shifting back and forth. The plane starts bouncing, jerking, and even shuttering. One of the overhead bins explodes open, and the contents come crashing down on the man below. Screams and sobs erupt from the cabin as we all try to wrap our heads around what is happening. Someone behind me yells out, "This is it! We're all going to die!" I tighten my seat belt a little tighter and hold on as we shake uncontrollably through another rough patch. Everyone is panicking and praying to God, both silently and aloud. I am terrified beyond belief.

`·.,¸,.·´¯`·.,¸><((((º>`·.,¸,.·´¯`·..·><((((º>`·.,¸,.·´¯`·..

Amanda

The tension in the car is palpable, like you could cut it with a knife and feed it to a pack of wolves. We both stare ahead out the windshield, neither one of us knowing what to say. The hour-and-fifteen-minute drive to downtown Denver feels like an eternity, the road stretching on forever in front of us. I look out the driver's window at the mountains and see some dark, scary clouds start to form over the front range. "Wow, that looks ugly," I mutter. He glances over, acknowledges, but still says nothing. I shake my head and let out a big, frustrated sigh. We ride the entire way in silence.

We pull into Veronica's parking garage and park. We just sit there, not really knowing if we should talk first or just go in. Finally I muster up the courage to speak and whisper, "I'm so sorry . . . I don't know what else to say."

"I can't believe you didn't tell me."

"I didn't want to worry you. I wasn't trying to hide it, I just didn't want you to freak out."

"Well, now I'm freaking out. I'm over there, defending our freedom, and you're over here keeping secrets from me."

"That's not it! I was just trying to avoid it becoming an issue. I told him to stop, he didn't, so I quit replying to him altogether. Here, please take my phone and read through the texts. You *have* to see that I was doing nothing to encourage him or provoke him. *Please.*"

I open my texts from Chad, scroll all the way to the beginning and shove my phone at him. "*Please.* Read them. You *have* to read them."

We sit in silence as he scrolls through the messages. He shakes his head back and forth multiple times as he runs through the conversations. "What a fucking asshole," he states hotly as he continues to scroll. "I don't know what I would have done if you would have told me, but this just makes me mad as hell."

"See? I told you. I told him to stop—multiple times. Would you have told me if it were the other way around?"

"That's different. I'm supposed to protect *you*, not the other way around."

"We're supposed to have each other's back."

"Which is why you should have told me. How am I supposed to protect you when you don't tell me this kind of shit is going on?"

"How would you protect me from way over there?"

"I don't know, I could have had some buddies from another unit stop in and keep an eye on you. I could have figured out how to find Chad and had him beaten to a bloody pulp."

"Oh Jeez, like that would have made the situation better."

"I'm just sayin', Mandy, next time something like this happens, I want you to tell me. You're my girl, it's my responsibility to take care of you, even when I'm not around."

Just then Rose walks up and knocks on my window.

"Well, hello!" she exclaims. "Fancy meeting you here!"

"Hey, Rose," I say through the closed window, not entirely sure she can hear me.

"Wanna go up together?" she says.

"Of course," I reply, shooting Mike a look, and we abruptly switch gears and get out of the car.

"Oh, Mike, it's so good to see you! How is your shoulder doing?"

"It's doing fine, ma'am. On the mend."

"Well, good. You gave us quite a scare."

"Yeah, I know. Sorry about that."

"It's good to have you home. Let's head upstairs and see what kind of masterpiece Thatcher has cooked up for us tonight." She turns and looks in her car window. "You be good, DJ! Oh, I hate leaving her in the car, but their building doesn't allow dogs inside. She'll be fine in the car for a few hours, won'tcha, girl?" She taps on the window and DJ whimpers inside. DJ's tail is wagging and she looks longingly at us. The window is cracked just enough for her to have some fresh air. "The only thing I'm worried about is this bad storm that seems to be coming over the mountains. Have you heard anything about it?"

"No, I haven't heard anything, but I haven't checked either," I reply. *Yeah, the weather is the* last *thing on my mind right now . . .*

`·.,,.·´¯`·.,><((((º>`·.,,.·´¯`·..><((((º>`·.,,.·´¯`·..

Rose

Dinner tonight was a little off. Thatcher was the most gracious host, as always, and the food was out of this world. We enjoyed a nice night of conversation and fun, even though we were missing a few people from our table. Veronica had a flight delay and did not make it home in time to join us. I know she has to feel awful leaving her husband to tend to all of her friends, but he was wonderful as always. It was nice to see Sophie having so much fun with her new beau, Buck. He seems like a nice fellow, and I hope he doesn't break her heart. He was very sociable tonight and kept up with all of our conversation and sarcasm. Mike and Amanda seemed a little distant tonight. I'm not sure what is going on there, whether it is stress from his injury or something else at play. I think they were in a difficult discussion when they were in the car, but I'm not sure. They sure have a lot going on for being such a young family.

And then there is Miss Melody who skipped out on dinner tonight. When I talked to her a few days ago, she indicated she was joining us. She didn't answer her cell phone when I rang her, so after dinner I am going to go over to her place to check up on her and make sure she is okay.

`., , .´¯`., ><((((º>`., , .´¯`...><((((º>`., , .´¯`...

As the evening wears on, the storm intensifies outside. I decide to leave early as I know DJ would be a skittish mess in the car. Sophie and Thatcher vehemently protest me leaving, and both of them offer to give me a ride. I strongly decline, not wanting to be a nuisance to anyone. By the time I get back to the car, DJ is a complete wreck. I can tell she has been pacing back and forth in the backseat, and there are scratch marks all over the seats and back door. Poor thing.

"There, there, girl. You're just fine. I'm so sorry I left you out here alone."

I get in the car and DJ instantly crawls on my lap. I hold her tight and can feel her tremble with every crack of thunder. Her eyes dart from left to right as she lets out a few soft cries. Lightning strikes again and she buries her nose under my arm.

"You're okay, girl. Mama's got you. Let's just sit here for a minute."

We sit in the car for a few minutes before I decide I need to get home. The storm seems to be getting stronger, so I want to get home before it gets even worse. Even though the rain is coming down terribly hard, I don't want to sit in the car all night long.

"Come on, girl. Get into the backseat and let's get on home." She refuses, so I set her firmly in the passenger's seat. "If you're a good girl, you can sit in this seat. You need to stay put, though." Her eyes are full of fear and my heart just breaks for her. "It's okay, girl. Let's get home where you'll be more comfortable and safe."

I start the car, back out, and slowly pull out of the parking garage. We immediately get pelted by the torrential

334

downpour, and I can barely see the road. *Oh, this is not good.* The sides of the streets are swollen with rushing water and the rain is pouring down hard. My windshield wipers can barely keep up with the unrelenting rain. I manage to get out of downtown and head towards our neighborhood. I was several miles down the road when all of a sudden, my steering wheel doesn't feel right. I try to brake and my car is not doing what I want it to do. I start to pump my brakes and yell out, "No, No, No! I'm hydroplaning!" I scream as my car skids out of control on the rain-slicked roads. DJ yelps and gets tossed from side to side. Suddenly my tires catch and I quickly recover. I pull over to the side of the road, my hands trembling on the steering wheel. My heart is beating out of my chest, and I notice my breathing is rapidly irregular. DJ whimpers and appears to be okay, just shaken up a bit. I look over into the drainage ditch and see a massive amount of water being slammed into a guardrail. Several downed trees have started to pile up, and the water and debris are smashing into them.

I instantly flash back to Clara's death . . . my poor, sweet baby girl who slipped and fell into a raging river at the age of nine during a flash flood. We were watching the floodwaters together when she jumped up on a rock to get a better view. She slipped and fell and went tumbling into the current. I screamed in horror and desperately tried to grab ahold of her. She instantly went under and was lost in the current. I raced down along the riverbank, hysterically screaming out her name, scanning from bank to bank looking for her red raincoat in the muddy water. She surfaced fifty yards downstream and choked out a blood-curdling scream, desperately calling out my name. "Mommy! Mommy! Help me!" I can still hear her screams in my dreams. They will be with me to my grave . . . They found her body trapped in logs and debris about a mile from where she fell in. A wave of grief as strong as the raging water outside hits me as I relive the last few moments of her life. How horrific and scary that must have been for her, looking desperately for me to save her. *Oh, how I wish I could have saved her . . .*

I stare at the raging water, devouring trash and other debris as it traps it against the buckling trees. The violence of the scene overwhelms me. I bury my head in my hands and let out an intense, primal scream. I sound more like a wolf howling than a woman crying, which communicates everything I am feeling without saying any words. *Why did we get so close to the river? Why didn't we just stay inside? Why was she so fearless?* The familiar gut-wrenching pain overwhelms me.

Just then, the rain dies down, so quickly that it catches my breath. I shake my head and almost laugh as I think about how ironically this storm is like my life of roller-coaster grief since Clara died. Thus is the nature of any tragedy: eventually there is blue sky after a rain. Eventually sunshine returns to your life, although it takes years if not decades to see it clearly again. The crescendo of feelings, the dreams of her still being alive, then waking and reliving the truth all over again. It's been thirty-four years since I buried her. I still can't believe I haven't told Sophie and Veronica about her. I still can't believe I told Amanda that day that Melody fell into the river. I was so in shock seeing this tiny, dark-headed girl bobbing down the river, screaming for help. I went into some kind of weird trance. What's even more strange is that after I told her, there came an immense sense of peace. Like I had emerged from the depths of grief to find a new depth of living and loving and laughter with my girls. Grief is such a weird journey. One that you must walk alone down your own path at your own pace. Sure, there are others on the path with you, but your experience will be unlike anyone else's. Even Bob's journey was different than mine, and he held my hand through much of my journey. Oh, how I miss him as well . . .

I'm not sure if Amanda has shared this story with the rest of the group yet. I don't think she would, but it's a big story. I'm

336

assuming she hasn't or else Sophie surely would have asked about it. The photo on my dresser at the cabin is of Clara, but everyone thinks it's of me as a little girl. Oddly enough I feel like I have allowed them to believe that lie long enough. Maybe it's time I tell the girls . . . I'm not sure why I have never told them before. Probably because it would've been too painful to retell every time someone new entered our group. Ever since I accidentally told Amanda that day, I have a new peace with it. Internally I had some guilt for a few weeks after sharing such a sacred story with Amanda, like I should have shared it with Sophie or Veronica first. Now I feel like it happened that way because I needed permission from myself to open up about it. I'm thankful Amanda stayed back to check on me that day, and that I shared the story with her. I'll have to share that with her the next time I see her. I look over at DJ and she is calmer now that the rain has let up. I pat her on the head and give her a good rubdown. "Come on, girl. Let's move along."

`·.¸¸.·´¯`·.¸.><(((º>`·.¸¸.·´¯`·..><((((º>`·.¸¸.·´¯`·..

Now that the heavy rain has subsided and DJ is content in the passenger's seat, I decide I will run by Melody's loft to check in on her and see why she wasn't at dinner. When she doesn't answer her call button, Girard approaches and asks, "Are you Rose Bradbury, by chance?"

Startled, I reply, "Why yes, I am."

"Miss Hu left this for you," he says as he hands me an envelope with my name on it.

"Thank you, sir," I reply and open the note.

"Dear Rose, please don't be mad, but I decided to go on a solo backpacking trip. Please don't worry about me. I'm taking everything you have taught me and going out to fish a cool river I read about down in the San Luis Valley. I'll leave a note in the cabin telling you exactly which trail and where I'm parking my car. I'm really looking forward to this. Please don't be mad. —Melody. P.S. I'm sorry I lied about coming to dinner, but I knew you would try to talk me out of it. I've got this."

That little rascal. I look over at Girard, still standing beside me in the lobby, and point my finger at him. "Did you know about this?" I ask accusingly.

A little startled, he replies, "Miss Hu just told me to give you this note, and then she left with her large backpack a few days ago. She told me someone would be by to check on her, and to tell you she expects to be back on Sunday."

When I call Sophie and tell her what I have found out, she volunteers to drive up to the cabin and find out where Melody has gone. I tell her to wait until morning, but I'm pretty sure she will try to drive up there tonight.

`·.,,.·´¯`·.,><(((º>`·.,,.·´¯`·..><(((º>`·.,,.·´¯`·..

Amanda

"Damn, this storm is crazy. I wish I could drive so you wouldn't have to," Mike says as we pull out of the parking garage.

"It's okay, baby, I've got this." The windshield wipers squeal as we pull out into the downpour.

"Yuck, we need to get these blades replaced. That noise is terrible," I say as the wipers squeal again.

"Jeez, you're right. I'll see if I can do that tomorrow. I might be able to one-arm it," he says with a smile.

"I bet you can," I say confidently, knowing he can do anything he sets his mind to.

"What did you think of dinner tonight?"

"It was alright. Seemed a little weird without Veronica there. I felt bad for Thatcher having to entertain all of us."

"I don't think he minded."

"Yeah, you're right, but it still would have been nice to have her there." I pull onto the interstate and start our long drive home. After a few minutes of silence, I pipe up and ask, "Are we okay?"

"Yeah, we're okay, baby." *I love it when he calls me baby.* "Life is too short to stay mad. It helped for me to see the text thread, so thanks for letting me read those."

"Of course. I hope you see that I wanted nothing to do with him."

"I do, I get it now."

"I'm sorry, baby."

"Me too."

`·.,,.·´¯`·.,><((((º>`·.,,.·´¯`·..><((((º>`·.,,.·´¯`·..

Sophie

It's probably not the smartest thing, driving up to the cabin in this terrible storm. But I have this sinking feeling in my gut that Melody is out there and needs my help. I'm so glad that Buck is going up with me. I feel safer knowing he will be with me, which is such an odd feeling to get used to since I have been on my own for so long.

On the drive up, there is one point where it is raining so hard that I can't see the road. Heck, I can't even see three feet in front of me. I can barely make out the center line, and I have driven this road so many times that I can almost drive it with my eyes closed. *Almost.* The rain sometimes stops for a brief second, just enough time so I can temporarily get my bearings. The lightning flashes so brightly, it temporarily blinds me. Cars are pulling off onto the shoulder of the road, waiting for the worst of the storm to pass; their brake lights hurt my eyes as I pass them. I feel driven to continue on. When the wind kicks up and blows so hard that it causes my truck to swerve, I decide I should probably pull over and wait a few minutes and let it die down. I find a wide shoulder to pull into and put the truck in park.

"I think we should pull over for a little bit. This lightning and wind is crazy!" I exclaim, squinting my eyes as I try to peer out the window.

"Oh good. I was going to recommend it but didn't want to be a backseat driver."

"Sorry, didn't mean to scare you. I've never seen rain like this before! Have you?"

"Maybe once or twice, but this one is definitely a doozy, that's for sure."

I suddenly catch a whiff of his cologne, and my heart skips a beat. *Oh! A musky, amber combo . . . Melt!* I unexpectedly shiver from a little cold blast of air that creeps into the cab of the truck. "Ooh, I'm cold. Are you? I'm going to turn the heat up a little bit," I say as I mess with the knobs on the dash.

"Here, take my hoodie," he says as he pulls off his sweatshirt. His warmth engulfs me as I slip it on; I naturally hug it as his heat warms my core.

"Oh gosh, that feels good. Thank you!" Instinctively, I curl my fingers around his arm, drawing him closer to me. "You're not cold?" I ask, hoping he doesn't notice my unsteady breathing. This kind of warmth is something I haven't felt in a while.

"Nah, I'm good," he says, as I feel an energy shift in both him and me, his eyes lock in on mine.

"This storm is crazy," I stammer, desperately trying to determine whether to keep talking about the weather or just lean in and kiss him. Unable to form a coherent thought, much less a sentence, I attempt to say something witty. Buck makes that impossible by inching closer to me, leaning over towards me. The storm heightens outside and increases the sensuous suspense of the moment.

"Sophie, I . . ."

I lean into him. Into his kiss. Into the moment.

A deafening crack of thunder and lightning tear through the truck, ripping my lips from his as I let out a scream. Lightning flashes through the windows, and I close my eyes as it's too bright to have them open. His fingers stroke my face and hair, and I inhale sharply. His proximity makes my hormones go crazy. Judging by the look he gives me, he knows this, as he passionately kisses me again. I could feel the blood in my veins pounding in tune with the vibrating thunder outside.

I welcome the sensory overload, even if it's only temporary.

I move my lips so they almost brush against his, teasing him a little bit. I feel his energy shift again, and he edges forward and pursues me. I pull away and he pulls me towards him. I don't mind as I am the one initiating the cat-and-mouse game. He has a smoldering look in his eyes as the storm rages outside. Our first kiss . . . tentative and full of intensity. I can feel the passion, the electricity . . . I haven't felt this way in a long time . . .

He pulls away slightly and cradles my face in his hands. "You have no idea how many times I have thought about you in the last twenty years. I can't believe I found you again." *I can't believe the way my body reacts to the sound of his voice . . .*

His words have an atomic effect on me, sending a heated jolt right through my core. His lips brush along my neck and huge goose bumps radiate all the way down my spine. The smell of cologne mixed with sweat emanates in the air, bringing a sense of euphoria around me. He "accidentally" brushes my breast with his arm. I truly can't tell if it was intentional or accidental.

Instantly I pull away. "I'm sorry. I just . . . Sorry . . ." I feel my face burn bright. My feelings overwhelm me as I get engulfed by an irrational fear that my good, safe life could inexplicably implode all around me at this very moment. The last time I felt this way was with John . . .

"No, I'm sorry. That was an accident. I just . . . I'm sorry." He pulls away back to his side of the truck. He looks at me through the darkness with those big, sapphire-blue eyes.

"It's been a long time for me . . . I just . . . I just need to go slow."

"Of course. Sorry . . . Of course."

Damn it, Sophie. What are you doing?

"I really enjoyed meeting your friends tonight," he says, trying to change the subject. "Thank you for inviting me."

"Of course. They are a huge part of my life, so I definitely wanted you to meet them." *I really wish I was still kissing him.*

The storm continues to rage outside. We both sit in the darkness, not really knowing what to say next.

"Buck?"

"Yeah?"

"Will you please kiss me again?"

He smiles sweetly and brings a hand to my cheek, running a finger down it. He leans towards me and softly presses his lips to mine. It is a sweet and tender moment complete with a short and sweet kiss. He smiles as he pulls away, and I appreciate his willingness to respond to my request to go

344

slow. I rest my head on his shoulder, and he tenderly kisses my forehead. I relax into his arms and get caught up in his touch. He holds my hand and I feel safe in his warmth.

"Is this really happening? Am I really holding you right now?" he whispers.

"Thankfully, yes. Why is that so hard to believe?" I ask in a playful manner, but I don't mind hearing the answer either.

"I just . . . I just really didn't think you were still out there." I can hear the pain in his voice, the pain of longing for something you didn't know you would ever find. I close my eyes and nuzzle deeper into him. I can relate on so many levels.

"You found me. I'm here." *I'm not going anywhere . . .*

`·.¸¸.·´¯`·.¸¸><(((º>`·.¸¸.·´¯`·..><(((º>`·.¸¸.·´¯`·..

Amanda

It takes us two hours to get home because the storm is so bad. The blinding streaks of lightning make it so hard to see, and the deafening cracks of thunder are so loud my ears are actually ringing a bit. My nerves are going crazy by the time we finally pull into the driveway.

We get into the house and spend a little time with Lorraine before she decides to head home. Since it was obviously awkward when we left, we needed to show her that things are okay now. She doesn't live far away, and she insists on going home on her own, even when we protest. I think she figures we need our space in case there is anything else we need to talk about.

Once she leaves I peek in on the kids and give them both a kiss on the forehead. *Sweet babies. I love them so much.* Their rooms smell faintly like their shampoo, and I smile as I think about them splashing in the bathtub. *Jordan is fearless in the water. I cannot wait until she is old enough for me to teach her how to fish.*

The house is quiet and dark. I don't bother turning on the lights as I go from room to room picking up toys and putting them away. I notice that Parker is dangerously low on diapers near his changing table and make a mental note to add them to my grocery list. Mike plops down on the couch with a cold beer and turns on the TV. It is obvious he needs a mental break from the day.

I decide to take a shower and wash off this long, strange day. I am exhausted in every way possible—mentally, physically, emotionally—and I know a good, hot shower will do my mind and body good. As the water washes over my body and pools at my feet, my mind starts to wander to Mike's appointments next week, both his physical and his psych eval. I hope that things are progressing nicely, and that he's able to start doing more with his arm. He is bored out of his skull, so being able to do more would be good for him. He's been very good at doing his physical therapy, even if it is painful for him. I also hope that talking things out today helped him, although he still hasn't talked much about what happened.

When my fingers start to wrinkle, I decide it's time to get out. I dry off and wrap my hair in a towel and stare at myself in the mirror. I try not to notice the lines that are beginning to collect in the corners of my eyes. *Great, getting crow's feet at the ripe ole age of twenty-three. Awesome.* I let out a big sigh as I think about all of the crazy events that unfolded since I last looked in this mirror this morning. What a whirlwind of a day.

I throw on a pair of sweats and an old T-shirt and join Mike out in the living room.

"Hey, Mike?"

"Yeah, babe?"

"I was thinking about your appointments next week. Do you know when they are supposed to let you know if they want you to go back?"

"No, it depends on what the doctors say. If they think I'll be able to return to combat in the next few months, they may send me back."

"Seriously? That's a possibility? They might send you back?" My mind starts racing again. *But I just got him back.*

"Yeah, you know that. Just because I got injured doesn't make me immune from returning to duty."

"Oh God, I can't even think about that right now. Do they ever give you the option of whether you go back or not?"

"I'm not sure, but I'd probably go if they did."

"Um, what?! Are you serious? What do you mean you'd probably go?"

"Mandy, this is my job."

"I know, but we almost lost you."

"I know that, but if they need me back there, I have to go. That's the end of it."

"But we need you here too."

"Can we please not get into this right now? Seriously, haven't you had enough today?"

"I just can't believe it's not open for discussion, that you would just elect to go back and not even think about us."

"Of course I would think about us. I'm doing this for us."

"Whatever," I say hotly.

He stands up from the couch and puts his beer on the table. He takes my face in his hands. I try to pull away, but he won't let me.

"Mandy, stop." Slowly he tries to turn my head, but I won't meet his gaze. A wall of silence builds up between us. "Look at me, *please.*" I can't look at him; I am fuming inside. My damp, tangled hair falls across my cheek. "Let's not do this now, Amanda. We have all day tomorrow to talk. For now, let's—"

"So you'd go back and leave us again. Even if it was a choice."

Finally, I let his gaze meet mine, and in his blue eyes I see the kind of sadness that makes my breath catch. "I have to go back, Amanda."

The tears fall, streaking down my cheeks. I angrily wipe them away.

He throws his good arm around me and tries to embrace me. *No, you can't do this. I need to get away.* I pushed him away.

"This is impossible. YOU are impossible! I'm going to the store."

`·.,,.·´¯`·.,><(((º>`·.,,.·´¯`·..><((((º>`·.,,.·´¯`·..

Section 8: Striking, Playing, and Landing

"Most fish lost in fly fishing are lost either at the moment you strike or when you attempt to land them. Playing a fish on a fly rod is a relatively simple matter of making the fish work against the spring of the rod until he gets tired. A fish lost on the strike or at your side is usually caused by operator error, and a fish lost in the middle of a fight is often due to a bad knot or because the fish was just not hooked securely in the first place."[xi]

The Orvis Fly-Fishing Guide
by Tom Rosenbauer

Amanda

I storm out of the house, Mike chasing after me. "Mandy, stop!" he yells.

"No, Mike, *you* stop," I scream. I turn and point my finger at him. "I just need to clear my head!"

"Please come back inside. This is a crazy storm. I'll leave you alone."

"I'm just going to go and get Parker some diapers. I'll be right back!" I shriek, completely out of my mind.

"I can go first thing in the morning. *Please*, *Mandy*."

I slam the car door, whip the car out of the driveway, and tear off into the night. The rain relentlessly pelts the car, making it terribly hard to see. Luckily the grocery store is not far, so I shouldn't be out very long.

I hear the squelch of the windshield wipers in between my sobs.

Why does he have to make this so hard? I'm so tired of the fight, so tired of the stress. Why can't he just stay home with us?

Tears flood my eyes and temporarily blur my vision. I wipe them from my eyes, still so angry.

All of a sudden I see a flash of headlights and feel my car slam into another car. My windshield explodes around me and the glass pelts my skin. The airbag explodes and slams into my face, disorienting me. My steering wheel and dashboard make an eerie sound as they are instantly crushed into a mangled mess. I feel an intense pain in my lower gut. The passenger door rips from its hinges and flies through the night. I feel like I'm doing rapid summersaults as I get thrown from side to side, completely disoriented about what is happening. As if I'm in slow motion, I can see shards of glass mixed with rain swirling all around me as lightning briefly lights up the interior of the car. It feels like an out-of-body experience, as I hear myself shrieking, yet it doesn't sound like me either. I've never heard sounds like this come out of me before. I catch a whiff of oily smoke in the air, and there is a coppery taste in my mouth. After what feels like an eternity, I finally feel the car groan and shudder as it falls slowly onto its roof.

I'm hanging upside down and I feel the blood rush to my head. I try to look around but I'm so disoriented. The rain is crashing down all around me. I look down and see my cell phone lying on the ceiling. The screen lights up and I can see that Mike is trying to call me. It's too far away for me to reach . . . I close my eyes and try to take a deep breath but can't . . .

I briefly open my eyes and see my keys dangling from the ignition, with a keychain picture of Parker and Jordan in the swimming pool together. It's getting soaked by rain . . . Their sweet faces smiling at me . . .

Rain is pelting around me . . .

I'm so cold . . .

This seat belt is cutting into my shoulder . . .

I can't feel my legs . . .

Jordan . . .

I have this weird sensation in my chest . . .

Is that rain dripping down my face?

It's so loud and the lights are so bright . . .

So bright . . .

I'm so tired . . .

Parker, my sweet, baby boy . . .

I just want to sleep . . .

I'm so sorry, Mike . . .

I'm just going to close my eyes for a moment . . .

`·.¸¸.·´¯`·.¸><(((º>`·.¸¸.·´¯`·..><(((º>`·.¸¸.·´¯`·..

Veronica

The pilot finally comes on over the intercom and announces that we are experiencing what is called a wind shear and he is doing his best to find smoother air. He asks us to remain seated and make sure our seat belts are securely fastened. I'm sure the pilot has no idea that the dumbass next to me just ejected into the bulkhead a few moments ago, so his timing was impeccable. I glance over at Mr. Dumbass, and I see him tug on his seat belt a little tighter. I smirk at the experiential lesson this man just learned and wonder what the hell he was thinking not having it on earlier.

We finally start flying into smoother air, and thirty minutes later the pilot announces we are descending into the Denver area. He explains we will be circling for a few minutes, as the runways are backed up with multiple flights delayed by the storm. I am so ready for this flight to be over and be safely back on the ground. I am also thankful I am seated in first class and not squeezed between two football players back in coach.

The pilot came back over the intercom and announced that he knew it had been a scary flight and he assured us that he was confident that we would land safely.

As soon as the wheels touch down and we can feel the plane slow down naturally, a huge outbreak of cheering and clapping erupts from the cabin, not to mention the huge release of tension. Tears and screams of joy flow as we give each other virtual high fives for being safely back on the ground. The flight attendant praises all of us for being calm and cooperative through a very tense experience. She indicated that Emergency Services would be greeting us at the gate to assess any injuries that were sustained during the turbulence. I peek back at Lillian, and she has a large bandage wrapped around her head. She still looks rather pale, probably from the significant amount of blood she has lost. Poor thing is probably scarred for life from flying and won't be getting on another airplane anytime in the near future. The doctor is still sitting next to her, and she is thanking him over and over for helping her. I'm glad he has been able to sit with her for the remainder of the flight.

Once the plane comes to a full stop and the seat belt sign goes off, we all unbuckle our belts and cautiously rise to our feet. Some people immediately embrace the person seated next to them. Some have been holding hands with a complete stranger for the last two hours. Everyone gingerly opens the overhead bins where luggage, coats, and everything else comes cascading out in a disheveled mess. Everyone is more than willing to help one another out, as we have become immediately bonded through this experience. The absolute fear of falling out of the sky and crashing to our most certain deaths seems to have brought a kindness and new perspective to everyone.

As we deplane, we are greeted at the gate by Emergency Services. There is a blur of people rushing around inside the terminal. As I step through the terminal door, I stop for a brief moment, draw in a big deep breath, and slowly exhale. I am alive. I am safe. Praise be to God.

A medic approaches me and says, "Ma'am, are you bleeding?"

Puzzled, I respond, "No, why?"

"You have blood all over your hands and shirt."

Oh, Lillian. "Oh, no sir, I was seated next to a lady who sustained a head injury. I helped her until the doctor could see her."

"Please have a seat here and let's make sure you are okay. What is your name?"

"Veronica Reed."

"Where are you from?" he says as he shines a bright light into my eyes checking my pupils.

"Denver."

"Welcome home then. I understand you hit a little turbulence on the way here?" he applies a blood pressure cuff to my arm and starts the squeezing process.

"Just a little," I retort, my voice dripping with sarcasm.

"Sarcasm is a good sign of having your wits about you," the medic replies with a smile.

I offer a smile back as he quickly runs through a smattering of quick vital tests.

"You seem to be fine, Miss. You are free to go unless you have any other concerns."

"No, I'm good. Thanks." I stand up and start to walk towards baggage claim.

I look around to assess the other passengers. There are lots of bumps, scrapes, and bruises, but overall everyone looks pretty good. Several people look visibly shaken and a little wobbly in the knees. Some passengers actually fall onto the ground and kiss the carpet as they enter the terminal sobbing and praising whatever God they worship. As far as I can tell, Lillian seems to have the worst injury, and they immediately put her on a stretcher and start to wheel her away. The doctor from the flight is right there with her, giving status updates on her condition. I run up alongside her stretcher to say a quick good-bye.

"Bye, Lillian. Enjoy that grandson of yours," I say, louder than usual just to make sure she can hear me.

"Oh, thank you, Veronica. Thanks again for all of your help," she replies.

"You get better quickly," I say as I give her hand a squeeze.

"I will, thank you."

They wheel her away and I head off towards baggage claim. All of a sudden it dawns on me that I have not turned my phone back on yet. Thatcher! I immediately hit the power button and impatiently wait for the Apple icon to disappear and for my screen to light up. I instantly call Thatcher and burst into tears the moment he answers.

"Hey gorgeous, welcome home."

"Thatch, I . . ." I cannot complete my sentence before a sob erupts from my throat.

"Whoa, what's wrong? Are you okay?" he replies with concern.

"Oh, Thatcher, it was terrible."

"What, what is going on? Are you okay?" I can hear the panic settling into his voice.

"Yes, I'm fine . . . My flight was just the most turbulent, scariest experience I have ever been through. We flew right through a storm and the plane was like a roller coaster."

"Oh my God . . . Are you sure you're okay?"

"Yes, I'm really okay. There were several injuries, though. The lady next to me slammed her head into the wall so hard she had a massive contusion."

"Shit, is she okay?"

"I think so. Ironically, it was her first flight ever."

"And most likely her last."

"Probably so."

"I'm so glad you are okay."

"I love you, baby."

"I love you too, V."

"It's crazy the things that go through your head when you think you are going to die."

"Damn girl, it must have been bad to have you talking like this."

"It really was that bad."

"Are you okay to drive home? Should I come and get you? It is still raining like crazy out there."

"Do you mind coming to get me? I'm still pretty shaken up, and I don't want to have to maneuver through this storm. Plus, I just need to see you and be wrapped up in your arms."

"I'm on my way. I'll leave now and we'll meet at our usual spot. I'll call you when I am close."

"Thanks, baby. I love you so much."

"I love you too, bae. I'm on my way."

I learn later that the National Weather Service reported that there was a line of strong thunderstorms extending from Minnesota all the way to southern Texas. There were updrafts of up to one hundred miles per hour, and there was not a good place for the pilot to fly around the storm. That will go down in the record books as the craziest flight I have ever been on.

`·.¸¸.·´¯`·.¸><(((º>`·.¸¸.·´¯`·..><(((º>`·.¸¸.·´¯`·..

Melody

When I set out on this journey, I brought enough food for a couple of days and then figured I'll just cook up a few fish that I catch. Simple, right? The catching part comes easy. These trout seem like they have never been fooled before with an imitation fly. I have never caught so many fish in my life! The killing part, on the other hand, has been a lot more difficult than I expected. I have never killed anything before. It looks pretty easy in the fishing video I watched on YouTube. Catch a fish, pick up a rock lying nearby, and bash it in the head. Done. Dead fish. Fillet him. Cook him. Eat him. Simple. I thought it would be easy when the fish being killed was for sustenance. Strangely enough, when it comes right down to it, it is a hard concept to swallow.

On the fourth night, when all I have left is a few cashews and a handful of dried cranberries, I know I have to have some protein before I can hike out ten miles tomorrow. I am dreading the thought of throwing out my line, knowing that one of those unsuspecting, beautiful creatures will end up as my supper. My stomach growls loudly just thinking about it, so I grudgingly tie on my first fly of the day.

The first several fish I land are beautiful brook trout. None of them are very big, and I can see the extreme fear in their eyes as they gasp for oxygen. It almost makes me sick to my stomach, so I quickly release them back into the water. Four fish later I decide I'm not cut out for killing any of my fish friends and just decide to hike out hungry. Since it is already getting dark, I know I must wait until morning to depart. Going hungry for one night is not going to kill me. Or any of the fish . . .

Now that I've decided I'm not going to kill any of the fish, I start enjoying the sport of "standing in a river and waving a big stick," as Rose calls it. I truly do enjoy this sport. It is so peaceful and relaxing, and I'm actually getting better at it. It's like a symphony of movements, all orchestrated together in perfect time. At first I thought I was hopeless. There is a lot to learn in fly fishing. Even Rose says she has more to learn about the sport, although I don't know how that is possible. She is such a natural and so knowledgeable.

I throw my line out one last time and get a bite right away. It looks like a big rainbow on the line. I love the fight that comes with a big fish. They really make you work for your prize! I fight this one hard. *"Come on, big guy. Come on, big guy,"* I say to myself as I reel him in. *Wow, this is a strong fish!* He is shooting from side to side, then racing up and downstream. I know I have to keep it taut or he might get away. About fifteen minutes pass, and I am still fighting him. My arms start to tire from the constant tug at the line.

Finally he gives in, and I pull him into a small pool and net him. He is huge! He has to be sixteen inches or more. I marvel at his size and beautiful color. "Thanks for the good fight, buddy!" I say out loud to him as I gaze at all of his scales and gills. This is truly an amazing creature. The greens and yellows shimmer against the reflection of the sun on the water. His black speckles jump out like pepper. After gazing longer than I should, I thank him again for the good fight and gently put him back in the water.

At first he just sits there, not moving. Usually a fish of this size would dart away as soon as he has his wits about him again. I put my hands back in the water, cup him from below, and point his head upstream, forcing the current and water back into his gills. Still nothing. I start to panic that he isn't going to regain his wits. I work him for a long time and start begging him to breathe again. *"Come on, big guy. Come on, big guy,"* I say out loud again, although this time I want him to breathe instead of give up the fight and come to me.

I start to notice that the glistening greenish gold of his scales when first caught are becoming an eerie, shadowy silver. I talk to him as if he were a friend in need: *"Oh buddy, come on! Come on, big guy, come on. You can do it!* I bend his body back and forth trying to force oxygen back into his gills. *I'm so sorry. Oh Jesus, please start swimming! It will be alright if you will just start swimming!"* I start to choke up and almost cry. Several minutes pass, and the fish is not showing any signs of movement.

He rolls over and becomes listless in my hands. I just stare at this huge, lifeless fish lying in my hands. He is such a beauty, and now he is gone, just lying there belly up in the water. An intense wave of sadness overwhelms me. I pull him out of the water, lay him on a rock, and sit on the side of the river just staring at him. I can't believe something that so strong a few minutes ago is now dead.

I have killed my first fish.

And hated everything about it. Part of me wants to offer him back to the river as a watery grave for his final resting place. Another part of me wonders if this fish gave himself up for me because he knew I couldn't do it myself. The intense guilt that washes over me is overwhelming. The hunger pains in my stomach now make me feel nauseous. I leave him on the side of the river while I go to find my knife and kindle the fire.

`·.,,.·´¯`·.,><((((º>`·.,,.·´¯`·..><((((º>`·.,,.·´¯`·..

That night I lie awake in my tent. My belly is full, but I do not feel nourished like I thought I would. This trip has been good, but I'm not sure I have found the clarity I was hoping for. Maybe a good night's rest will open my eyes to new things in the morning.

`·.,,.·´¯`·.,><((((º>`·.,,.·´¯`·..><((((º>`·.,,.·´¯`·..

I'm not sure what time it is, but I know I have been lying here for hours. I'm frustrated with how exhausted I am, and yet it seems impossible to escape my thoughts and turn off my brain. It's colder tonight and I am hunkered down in my sleeping bag trying to will myself to sleep. I've tried every force-yourself-to-sleep method I can think of, and yet I am still wide awake.

I left my rain fly off the tent on purpose so I could stare at the stars for a while before I went to sleep. It was really nice for a while, but now the stars seem too bright to me and are distracting me from my goal of slumber. Maybe the stars are trying to tell me something. What is right in front of me that I cannot see? It's also a full moon tonight, and it's blinding me, staring me down.

I can still faintly smell smoke from the remaining embers of my nearly extinguished fire where I cooked up my friend earlier. The chill in the air has me snuggling deeper into my down sleeping bag, wishing I would have put on one more pair of wool socks. I toss and turn over and over; my mind keeps drifting to earlier in the day when the life went out of that beautiful creature. Finally, frustrated out of my mind, I sit up and throw open my sleeping bag.

Fuck it, I'm going fishing.

Pissed off I climb out of my sleeping bag, and a blast of cold air invades my soul. "Holy shit, it's cold!" I scream out loud even though there is no one around to hear me. I turn on my headlamp and start piecing together all of my fishing gear. My fingers turn to immediate icicles, which makes it even harder to get my crap thrown together. It's amazing how hard it is to assemble your fly rod when your hands are shaking like you are having a seizure.

I finally get my boots pulled on, throw on a hat that has a few flies hooked in it and head to the stream. I have never been night fishing before. The moon is bright enough I don't really need my headlamp. I'm sure I will, to tie on a fly, but after that I'll turn it off and see what happens. Maybe fishing in the dark will shine some light on this trip. Who hasn't had a night where they sit up late, looking up into the darkness of the sky, and wonder if the path they chose was the right one? I'll just do it while fishing.

The river sounds different at night, darker and more mysterious. It reminds me of a song my parents often play in the symphony when the baritones get low and slow. The bugs also sound different, like they can be themselves without having to worry so much about the predators that are seeking to devour them during the day. *No wonder I like the nightlife . . .*

I begin to cast out into the darkness. I rely on feel due to the darkness and trust that my inner sense of putting the fly in the right place is correct. I can vaguely make out my strike indicator as it reflects off the water and tumbles downstream. I cast multiple times and feel at one with the water. *I don't even care if I catch a fish.*

All of a sudden something jumps out of the river and makes a huge splash about fifteen feet away from me. *What the hell?* That didn't sound like a regular fish to me. *What was that?* I could feel the hair on the back of my neck start to stand. I get a shiver of goose bumps up and down my arm that almost hurt they are so large. I move slowly and methodically, careful not to make a sound as I shift towards the splash. I definitely feel a sense of something very different near me. *I don't know what this thing is, but I want to catch it . . .*

I can hardly contain my excitement as I carefully false-cast twice and then carefully lay down my fly in about the same area that this creature rose. I wait . . . Nothing . . . I wait some more . . . Nothing . . . My first cast falls a little short. *Maybe I should do a quick roll cast and flick my fly back to the spot where he rose . . .* Hesitation . . . Doubt . . . I want to snatch it back but patiently let the fly float through, hoping it will at least catch this creature's attention. *What do I do?... I don't want to scare it away . . .* I pick up my rod tip and quickly roll cast the fly back into position—this time right on—but again nothing. A third cast . . . nothing . . . More doubt . . . Fourth cast . . . Strike! The strike of this beast is telegraphed to my hands like a jolt of electricity. "Holy shit, this thing is strong!" I scream out. It moves in ways that are unfamiliar to me from catching other fish. It is difficult for me to maintain my footing. My heart races and I let out a scream. This is the biggest creature I have ever hooked, and it is now taking all the line it can get. My rod bends, my reel is screaming from the rapid pace the line is pulling out, the line rips through the water like a razor—I am in ecstasy. I realize this fish has taken out so much line that I am starting to get into my backing. I know that I will have to act fast or this beast is going to get away from me. *Not if I can help it.* Everything Rose has taught me is critical in this culminating moment in time.

I start stepping downstream, moving towards her. I try to maintain my footing on the round, slippery rocks beneath my feet. My rod is bending and shifting with the crazy movements pulling from the other end. *Dang, this is fun.* I am holding my own. I start reeling in little by little, coaxing this beast over to the riverbank and out of the current. I feel a rush of excitement pulse through my veins as I reel it in closer and closer.

After a long, drawn-out fight, I finally get this thing close enough where I can see, and it leaps out of the water shaking its whole body, trying to dislodge my fly. I can feel her jerking her head vigorously against the line. Reeling her in, I see flashes of black and blue and a long eel-like shape. I still have no idea what this creature is. *I hope it doesn't attack me once I net her . . .* Fear creeps into my thoughts, and I feel a cooling sensation run down my spine. Another leap in the air displays her razor-like teeth reflecting in the moonlight. I have definitely never seen anything like this fish before. I can hardly wait to net her and take a picture of her. *This is so fucking cool.*

After a good thirty-minute battle, this brute finally starts to tire. I reel her in to the small pool of water my feet are standing in. Immediately I flash back to earlier that day when that beautiful rainbow lost his fight. *I'm not sure if I could handle another experience like that the very next time I wet a line.* This time everything has gone right. I wait the necessary moment, tighten the line, and bring her in.

Strangely, once she is in my net she does not put up a fight. I am expecting something completely different from this strong, odd fish. It's almost as if she knows this is a special experience, one I need badly. Maybe she knows she will be released, that my intention is not to harm her.

Once in my net I turn on my headlamp to get a better look at her. *What the hell?* This isn't a fish at all! This is some sort of

369

eel! I marvel at her long, sleek body. It has a huge mouth and piercing black eyes. She is gasping for air as her head moves from side to side. Her gills pulse in and out as I lift her out of the net to get a closer look. She stares at me, lying quietly in my hands. I've never seen anything like this in a river before. *Man, I wish Rose was here.*

I keep her wet and partially submerged to keep her alive. Luckily, I have my waterproof phone in my coat pocket. I clumsily fish it out so I can shoot several pictures of her before releasing her back into the wild. I know these pictures will not be the print quality that I'd like, but just to have a permanent picture of her will be worth it. I know the picture in my brain will be etched in stone forever. I can't wait to show it to Rose and find out what it is.

I decide it's time to let her go. As I turn to grab my hemostats, the eel lurches and bites off the line, leaving the hook in her lip. *Damn, this is cool.* She starts flailing back and forth, and I know there is no way I can get the hook out before she jumps out of my hands. I smile as I think about her having a piercing in her lip, just like me. As she rushes away, a wave of sadness washes over me. This has been a cool moment, one I surely will not forget. As she slithers away, I see her stop and pause in the water. She turns and faces me, almost staring me down before she darts away into the black water. I have definitely made a connection with this eel. One of those connections that dips right into your soul. *I don't know what it was, but I'm sure she felt it as well.*

`·.,.·´¯`·.,><((((º>`·.,.·´¯`·..><((((º>`·.,.·´¯`·..

The next morning I wake to the warmth of the sun on my face and the sound of the river water playing music with the

370

rocks. It is peaceful and I feel fulfilled. What an amazing experience last night! All of the experiences this trip has granted me have me thinking with fresh perspective. I know I will need a few days to soak it all in and to make sense of everything that has happened.

There is a part of me that is excited to hit the trail today and start my journey home. There is another part that will be sad to leave this pristine wilderness. I crawl out of my tent and walk straight to the river where I caught the eel last night. There is no sign of any life form as the sun shines its brassy brightness onto the water.

I look down into the water and catch my reflection. *Who are you?* I stare at myself for a few minutes. The reflection of myself in the water is not the same person I saw yesterday. Instinctively I get my camera set up to do a photo shoot. I take off my clothes and enter the water for an epic photo shoot. It's like I know myself better today than I did yesterday. The confidence, the bravery, the strength I feel . . . *I have never felt so full of life.*

I think I will see a whole new person when I take time to process this experience.

```
`·.,,.·´¯`·.,><((((º>`·.,,.·´¯`·..><((((º>`·.,,.·´¯`·..
```

After I have my campsite cleaned up and packed in my backpack, I stop and stare at the river one last time. I stoop down and pick up several flat rocks and build an inukshuk like I have seen Rose do so many times. Seems fitting to leave something marking the journey I have been on. *I'm not sure what all of this means yet, but I feel like I'm on the right path.*

Sophie

We finally get to the cabin. It is still raining, although the worst of the storm seems to be over. As I pull up into the driveway, I can see that there are no lights on inside. *Damn, she's not here. I was hoping she would have changed her mind.*

We get inside and I find a note from Melody on the kitchen table. It's a post-it note with the name of the trail, the coordinates for the parking lot, and the words "Gone fishin', see you next Tuesday. —Melody." *That rat knew she wasn't making dinner the whole time!*

Since there is nothing I can do about it at this time of night, I give Buck the quick tour of the cabin. As we're standing in Rose's room, it dawns on me that we're both going to be staying here tonight. Why that hadn't crossed my mind until now is beyond me. *Guess I really am out of practice at dating.* He stands in front of the dresser and looks at all the pictures and knickknacks that Rose has displayed. He picks up a photo of Rose and me, and glances up at me through the dresser mirror. "This is a fantastic photo of you two."

"Thanks, she really is something special."

"I enjoyed meeting her tonight. The banter between the two of you was hysterical."

"Yeah, we have the silliest relationship. One minute she's giving me solid life advice, and the next she's insulting me like she was my sister."

"I hope she made it home okay in that crazy rain. Have you checked in with her since she called you?"

"Oh jeez, no I haven't." *I hope she's okay.* "Let me get a fire going in the fireplace and then I'll text her."

Pleased with my one-match fire, I shoot Rose a quick text. She texts right back and says she and DJ made it home safe and sound. *Thank goodness.* I let her know that Melody indeed left the note and I know where she is. I tell her I will drive up there in the morning and make sure she is okay. After we are finished talking, I toss my phone to the side so I can concentrate on this cute guy sitting next to me. I open a bottle of wine to share, and we both crash on the couch. We snuggle up under one of Rose's quilts and just relax, watching the flames of the fire dance in the fireplace.

I tell him stories from some of our weekends here at the cabin, and how Rose and Bob built it with their own two hands. He shares how he has drifted by this place multiple times while guiding and always wondered what the story behind it was. It feels good just to hang out. We talk into the wee hours of the night laughing and getting to know one another better.

I wake up about two in the morning still curled up next to him on the couch. I decide to move back into my bedroom, and carefully stand up as to not wake him. I smile as I cover him up and gaze at how handsome he is. I pinch myself to make sure I'm not dreaming.

I tiptoe down the hallway into my room and shut the door quietly behind me. I sit on the bed and let my body fall backwards. My hands graze the embroidery of the comforter Rose made for me and a smile washes over my face. It has been a long time since I have felt this way, and I am so grateful for it. I crawl under the covers and drift off to sleep, feeling as blessed as I have in a very long time.

`·.,¸,·´¯`·.,><((((º>`·.,¸,·´¯`·..><((((º>`·.,¸,·´¯`·..

The next morning I wake early and pad out into the hallway and peek around the corner. He's still asleep and looks handsome as hell curled up on his side. I can't help but smile as I quietly make my way over to the fireplace and gingerly add a few logs to the fire. There are zero embers left from last night's fire, so I attempt to get another started as quietly as possible. In true Sophie form, just as I have the fire going at a steady roar, I clumsily drop an extra piece of firewood on the floor. It bounces off the hardwood floor, making a horrible, loud noise. Buck startles awake.

"Oh, I'm so sorry," I loudly whisper. "I was trying to be quiet and get a fire going to take the nip out of the air."

He looks around the room, a little disoriented. "Oh hey. What time is it?" He yawns, rubs his eyes, and stretches awake.

"About six thirty. You can go back to sleep if you want."

"Nah, how can I sleep knowing there's a gorgeous girl in the same room with me?" He grins and melts me with those beautiful blue eyes.

"You expecting someone else?" I joke back, giving him a coy smile.

"Not even a little bit. Come here, you," he says as he opens up his blanket and motions for me to join him. I crawl up next to him and snuggle deep into the warmth of his embrace. "Good morning, gorgeous."

"Good morning," I reply, resting my head on his chest. We sit in the quietness of the morning and watch the fire. It feels good to be in his arms. We watch for several uninterrupted minutes.

"The only thing that would make this a little more perfect would be a cup of coffee. Want one?" I say as I hop up off the couch.

"I definitely won't turn one down."

"How do you take it?"

"Black."

"Perfect. You're easy." I fiddle around in the kitchen and inspect the refrigerator to see if there are any signs of food. *Oh good, eggs.* I make myself a latte and bring Buck a steaming cup of Joe.

"So this morning, I'd love to go to the trailhead where Melody indicated her car is. I'm not sure we'll even see her, but I think I'll feel better if I know that she at least made it to the parking lot. That okay with you?" I ask, realizing he doesn't have much of a choice since he rode up with me.

"Yeah, I'm game for whatever. I'm enjoying just hanging out."

"Well, good, me too," I say as I clink his coffee cup with mine.

Just then my phone rings. "It's Rose," I say to Buck as I put the phone to my ear. "Hey, Rose! What's up?"

Section 9: Catch and Release

"It is spring now. The afternoons are beginning to linger. Rod and creel and ashes wait with me for summer, for the long light, when they will enter the stream at the riffles. Sometimes I wonder if the creel is his permission for me to keep what I catch. Right now, it seems more important that he taught me how to release.

This summer I will carry the creel, empty, and bear the wicker weight of his absence. They say death comes as an invitation to the light. I hope so. I would like to think of life as a progress from light to light."[xii]

"The Long Light"
by Le Anne Schreiber
in *Uncommon Waters:
Women Write about Fishing*
edited by Holly Morris

Sophie

I've done a million flower arrangements for funerals in the past. Most of them for people I don't know. It's so different doing this for someone you loved . . . Amanda's favorite kind of flowers were daisies. Beautiful, cheery daisies. The vibrant yellow and white flowers will add charm and whimsy to an incredibly sad day. They seem too happy for a funeral, but that pretty much sums up who Amanda was. She always had a smile on her face, even if she was scared or sad on the inside. She was one of the tough ones.

Whenever I do an arrangement for a funeral, I try to give some kind of expression to the grief, as if it's my last opportunity to say good-bye. I usually make sure that each and every flower is handpicked and fresh; however, for Amanda I'm doing an artificial arrangement—that way Mike can keep it forever. As a greenhouse owner I don't dare say that out loud, but I have something special in mind for Amanda. I actually prefer it when people choose living plants to send to a funeral, instead of a fresh arrangement. Fresh flowers just die about a week or so after the funeral, which in my mind is just another reminder of the loved one they lost. My dad's favorite flower is a yellow rose, so I always send a yellow Knock Out rose bush to the family on their first Mother's Day, Father's Day, or anniversary after their loved one has passed. I know that the first year of "firsts" without a loved one is the hardest. First birthday, first anniversary, first Christmas . . . Families receive so many cards and flowers at the time of death that receiving something on these special days that are also hard lets them know that they are still being thought of and that their loved one is still missed.

For Amanda, I'm doing a large wreath for her urn to sit in. Mike decided to have Amanda cremated, so there is no casket. He didn't want Jordan and Parker to have the last memory of their mother lying lifeless in an oversized, shiny box. He wanted them to remember her as being the vibrant, amazing woman that she was. I've decided to do a nice, big wreath full of daisies and hackle from her fly tying supplies. Mike gave me a big box of her colorful hackle yesterday, so I have an enormous amount of colorful material to work with. Mike collapsed on me yesterday when we embraced. The enormous grief and guilt he is carrying is overwhelming.

Amanda knew that each one of us had specific flies that we liked to fish with, so I'm going to tuck in one fly that represents all four of us. I'm also going to add some silver ribbon for sweet little Jordan and a San Juan Worm fly for Parker. That boy loves to dig in the dirt for worms, and this simple fly is in every fly fisher's fly box.

Arranging flowers is a very therapeutic process for me and where some of my best internal thinking happens. There is creativity and meaning in each placement decision. I love the way my mind can wander freely, and I can make connections between the items I'm arranging to meaningful real-life scenarios. As I was gathering items for Amanda's wreath, it dawned on me that our little group of women is very much like a fly fishing outfit, each of us bringing unique personalities and purpose to one another. Once I get the foundation of greenery, daisies, and ribbons placed, I take a deep breath and I start to choose a fly for each of us. This will probably be the hardest flower arrangement I have ever made . . .

I decide to start with Rose.

For Rose I choose the Parachute Adams fly. I pick up the fly and examine all the intricate details of this historic fly. I think I've heard her tell the story a hundred times of how the Parachute Adams fly got its name, and it could be argued that it's the most widely used fly out there. It was the first dry fly that Rose taught Amanda how to tie and one we all use frequently. I use some of Amanda's tippet to tie the fly onto one of the green sprigs. Rose also gave me a section of one of her old bamboo rods to add to the wreath. As I work it into the greenery, I can't help but think of how this piece really does represent who Rose is to all of us. She is the one we all look up to, and in reality the bamboo rod is the traditional symbol of the sport. Incredibly resilient, beautiful inside and out, she always seems to be there when we need her. What a gift she is to each of us.

As I reach for my fly, the Beadhead Pheasant Tail Nymph, I feel hot tears well up in the corners of my eyes. Whenever I catch a fish on this fly, it makes me feel like my dad and brothers are right there with me, a fun reminder of our past pheasant hunts together. Now I will think of Amanda every time I tie on a fly. She made me a few special ones with some light-blue thread, my favorite color. Her thoughtfulness and customization of our flies will never be forgotten. I still can't believe she is gone . . . I'm so glad she was at the pumpkin patch that day we met. I am going to miss her so incredibly much . . .

If I had to pick a part of the fly fishing rod that is most like me, I'd say I'm most like the reel. Tough on the outside, attached to Rose in a beautiful way, and overly protective of Amanda, who in my mind is very much like fly fishing line. Bright on the outside with a level, braided core on the inside. I let out a big sob as I weave some bright-yellow fishing line through the wreath. It pains me a bit to reflect and admit that

I know I'm good at taking care of other people's needs more than my own, which is exactly the purpose of the reel. I smile as I make this connection and another tear rolls down my cheek. I see myself carrying on this role as I will help Mike take care of Jordan and Parker for the next few months through this tough transition.

Veronica's favorite fly is the Elk Hair Caddis, as she loves to fish with dry flies. Trout tend to fall for its distinctive and realistic appearance almost every time, and in Colorado where we mainly fish for trout, it's a no-brainer. The colors on this fly also seem to match her brown, silky skin. I'd say Veronica is very much like the leader of the fly fishing outfit. The leader is the nearly invisible fishing line that is responsible for the transition from the fly line to the fly. It also helps complete the transfer of energy built up in the fly line through the casting stroke, through the line, and down to the fly so that the line rolls over and straightens itself out in a fairly straight line. If you cast and your fly and line land in a giant bird's nest on the water, you won't have much luck enticing those fish to take your fly. I laugh as I think about Veronica's first few days of learning how to cast. I'm so glad she stuck it out and didn't give up. I also love that V has been so instrumental in helping Melody get connected to Thatcher and the rest of our group, which is exactly what the leader does for the fly.

I've chosen a Bunny Leech fly to represent Melody. It is a vivid black-and-purple fly made with rabbit's fur, which actually matches her hair right now with the purple stripes she had put in last week after she got back from her hike. There are really no flies more visually impressive than rabbit fur flies, and if humans think this, you can bet that the fish do as well. I smile as I tie it onto the wreath as it actually looks like Melody with all of her tats and piercings.

Once I finish, I step back and take a look to make sure it properly represents who Amanda was, and that it's not too gaudy or overdone. Everything is beautifully and tenderly nestled in just the right place. To me it's just perfect.

Suddenly a wave of grief hits me, and I double over the table and sob uncontrollably. Tears rain unhindered down my face as I just let it all out. I am going to miss my friend so, so much . . .

`·.¸¸.·´¯`·.¸><(((º>`·.¸¸.·´¯`·...><((((º>`·.¸¸.·´¯`·..

Rose

I arrive at the church a little early and find a nice bench to sit on while I wait for the girls to arrive. I don't like attending funerals, especially for the young. At my age I've been to my fair share, and I know there will be many more as my friends and siblings continue to age. There is a certain beauty in the celebration of someone's life, but when it's cut so short, it just seems more tragic. Even though I am well aware that death is a part of life, the living part is my favorite. It's a lot harder to enjoy living when someone you love is no longer around to live it with you.

I look down and see a little memorial plaque that reads "In memory of Cecil and CeDoris McMullen." *Lovely people, I'm sure.* I remember, when both Clara and Bob died, that feeling of needing to do something with the money that people so generously gave. For Bob I donated generously to Colorado Parks and Wildlife in the Arkansas River Valley. Seemed fitting to donate to an organization that would help protect the river that runs right by our little cabin. I was also older when he passed, and we had more time to prepare for it. Clara's death was so sudden and tragic. I did nothing with Clara's memorials . . .

I don't even remember the year after Clara's death . . . Life seemed meaningless, and I was in a hazed fog most of the time. The hours and days seemed to drag on for eternity. There were days, even weeks, that I couldn't even get out of bed. The life had literally been sucked out of me. The horror of losing a child is nothing I would wish on anyone. The unnatural order of bringing something into the world and then having it ripped from you is more than any human should bear. It was a good thing that breathing was involuntary, as I'm certain I wouldn't have remembered to do it. I always wonder what she would have been like as a teenager. Would we have gotten along? Would she have gotten good grades and been courted by boys? Would she have worn her hair long or short? Where would she have gone to college? Would she be married by now and have a family of her own? Would she have lived close by or would she have had an adventurous spirit and traveled the world? So many questions left unanswered. So many dreams cut short. I would have loved to have been a grandma. There are days that I ache to have her run and jump into my arms again and hold her close to me. She had the best laugh . . . It's impossible for anyone to understand the depth of pain you experience when you lose a child. Losing Amanda is a stark reminder that we aren't promised anything, and those poor babes of hers . . . growing up without their sweet mama. A painful void they will feel for the rest of their lives. I shudder just thinking about it and let out a big sigh.

I look up and see Melody walking towards me. *My goodness she owns a dress*. "Hello dear. Don't you look lovely."

"Hi, Rose. How, um, how are you?"

"Oh, I'm fine. A little sad, but doing okay." Melody looks down and kicks at the grass a bit. I could tell she had no idea what to say or how to act. "How are you?"

"Um, I'm good, I guess. I rode with Veronica and Thatcher."

"Oh wonderful. Are they inside?"

"Hey, Rosie, don't you look beautiful," Thatcher says as he scoops me up into a hug, his cologne a little overpowering.

"Oh goodness, you startled me!" I exclaim, surprised by their sudden appearance. Veronica, dressed in a smart, black suit also welcomed me with a warm embrace.

"Hey there," she says, tears welling up in the corners of her eyes. "Sorry about that, I thought you saw us coming."

"Oh, no worries." I gently squeeze her arm, acknowledging her pain. "Have you seen Sophie and Buck yet?"

"I saw Sophie's truck in the parking lot, so she must be inside making sure the flowers are just right."

"Oh yes, I'm certain that's where she is."

"Or not," Sophie says as she and Buck sneak up behind us. We each take turns giving each other hugs. "I've been looking for you, Rose. Mike has a special place he wants us to sit, so I was supposed to find you and show it to you."

"Well, alright then," I say as I grab Sophie by the hand. I hesitate, wanting to talk to the girls for just a moment alone. "Boys, can you give us just a moment?"

"Of course," they say in unison and walk a few steps away, giving us a little space. I take Veronica and Sophie by the arm and Melody does the same. The four of us stand in a little huddle, not really knowing what to say. I pull out my tissue and capture a tear trailing down Sophie's cheek. "Here, dear," I say as I hand her a wad of tissues. "I brought an entire purse full." She takes them from me and crumples them in her hand.

"I don't even know how to do this," Sophie squeaks out, choking back a flood of tears.

"Well, no one really does. That's the thing about death, we're not really taught what to do or how to handle it. You don't know how it will affect you until you lose someone you love."

"It just seems so unfair," Veronica chokes out. "Why Amanda? Why so young?"

"Death doesn't care your age." I pause and immediately think of my sweet Clara. A huge lump forms in my throat, and my voice cracks just a bit. "Girls, today our hearts are broken, and we will be sad without apology. We will cry, be weak, and reminisce about the good times we had with our Amanda. Let's try to be strong for Parker and Jordan, but also let them know that it's okay to be sad and miss their mommy."

We stand together, arm in arm, under an old oak tree next to the little bench that has been my welcome respite. Our little group of five has been reduced to four. My goodness, we will miss that girl.

I draw in a big deep breath, give them each one more squeeze, and say, "Okay, girls, it's time. We *got this*."

We quietly walk down the sidewalk and head into the church.

The church is full of people coming to pay their respects to a beautiful young woman who has died too young and too soon. She was only twenty-three. Her entire fifth grade classroom of students are all there, sharply dressed in their clip-on ties and summer dresses. Many of them are holding each other's hands and crying. It is heartbreaking. I'm sure Amanda was an amazing teacher. Sophie has arranged for the entire class to do a butterfly release after the service. This will serve as a special way for them to know when Miss

Amanda is thinking about them each and every time they see a butterfly. So sweet.

Parker and Jordan are sitting with Amanda's parents. Mike wants us to sit right behind the family, so we all take turns passing the kids back and forth over the pews during the service. Jordan clings to Aunt Sophie through most of the service, and Parker falls asleep on his Mimi's lap. Mike wears his military dress uniform, his arm still in his sling. He looks very solemn and numb.

Mike gave me a small portion of Amanda's ashes yesterday to take to the cabin and release in the river. He said that fly fishing awakened a part of her soul that he wanted to honor in her passing. The four of us are going up to the cabin next weekend to say our final good-bye.

After the service, there is a lovely meal provided by Thatcher's restaurant. We all mingle with Amanda's family and friends for a while before we part and go our separate ways.

`·.¸¸.·´¯`·.¸ ><((((º>`·.¸¸.·´¯`·..><((((º>`·.¸¸.·´¯`·..

Melody

The day before we are to go to the cabin for the weekend, I stop by Rose's house so I can show her my pictures from my trip. I hope she can tell me more about that weird fish thing I caught the last night of my trip.

"Hey, Rose, can I show you something?"

"Of course, dear. What is it?"

"I caught something out on my trip that I have never seen before." *I really hope she knows what it is.*

"I'm still a little mad at you for going and not telling me, ya know."

"I know, I'm sorry. I did feel bad about lying to you." *Like, really bad.*

"Well, good. At least I have that," she says with her ornery smile that I love so much. "What did you find out there?"

"I couldn't sleep one night, so I decided to do some night fishing. It's the only thing I caught that night, but it wasn't a fish."

"Really? What was it?"

"I'm hoping you will know."

Fumbling with my iPad, I finally get my photos open to the folder with my trip pics in it. "Here it is. What do you think it is?"

"Hmm, it's a little dark," she says as she squints her eyes at the screen.

"Yeah, I caught it at night, and I only had my phone on me." I flip to the next picture in the folder. "Here, here is a different one. Can you see it better in this one?"

"Oh yes, this one is better. Well, look at that." She sits back and stares at the picture. She puts her hand up to her mouth and shakes her head.

"What? What is it?" I try to read her face but can't decipher what she is thinking.

"I've always heard there are a few of these in Colorado, but I've never seen one. Do you know what this is?"

"Um, no. That's why I asked you." *Tell me!*

"I'm pretty sure this is an American eel."

"A what?" *I knew it was an eel.*

"Pretty sure this is an American eel, really rare."

"Oh yeah? How rare?"

"Very, this is really something special."

"Really? Why?"

"This fish has only been seen or caught by about six people in Colorado in the last twenty years."

"For real? Holy shit!"

"How did you catch this?"

"It was really cold and I couldn't sleep one night. I tied on whatever I had stuck in my hat. I turned my headlamp on just long enough to tie my fly on, then I shut it off and just tossed my line out. I heard it rise about fifteen feet away from me, so I casted a few times to where I thought it rose. I wasn't expecting much, but all of a sudden, a jolt of electricity shot through my line as she struck. I fought her for a good thirty minutes before she finally tired and I netted her. I was a little scared she would attack me once I had her in my net."

"Oh my goodness, it sounds so exciting! Where were you?"

"I went down to the San Luis Valley. I was hoping to find some remote water, away from people, with some rare fish."

"Indeed you did. You know, the only reason this fish is even in Colorado is because it escaped an aquaculture facility that was once in Conejos County."

"Really? Wow . . ." *What's an aquaculture facility?*

"Yes, this fish is found in three places in the world: near Chesapeake Bay and the Hudson River, some freshwater rivers that feed into the Gulf of Mexico, and one river in Colorado—the Conejos River."

"That's the coolest thing I've ever heard! I can't believe I caught it." *Epic!* "What else do you know about it?"

"I'd have to reference my favorite Colorado fish book to recall all of the details, but I remember reading about it one time. If my memory serves me right, it's very active at night and pretty dormant during the day."

"I caught it at night, so that makes sense."

"That's also why I've never seen one. I don't think I've ever been night fishing."

"It was pretty awesome. Cold, but awesome."

"What I do remember, though, is that this fish is in Colorado because it escaped an aquaculture facility. It escaped a life it didn't want and it survived by adapting itself into its new environment," she says as she stares at me over the top of her glasses. "Kind of like you, eh?"

"Um, what?" *What's that supposed to mean?*

"Think about it, how are you like this fish?" She pulls out that crooked-finger-point thing that she does when she's trying to get you to think about something.

"Um, I don't know." *What is she talking about?*

"Sure you do, think about it."

"Because I like to come out at night?" Judging by the look on her face, this was not the right answer.

"Maybe . . . what else?"

I sit there quietly, making connections between me and this fish.

"You're the one who wanted to find some clarity out on that trail, aren't you? Of all the fish that are in the Conejos River, why did you catch this one?"

The more I think about it, the more connections I start to make. I can escape whatever parts of my life that I don't like and adapt to my new surroundings. I don't have to go to Julliard because my parents want me to. I can be a Suicide Girl and be proud of it. I can create my own path by mixing my love of music, food, my online life, and photography. I don't have to live up to anyone else's expectations of me, as long as I'm living up to my own. I don't have to be like anyone else. *I can be a cool motherfuckin' eel.*

We sit and chat for another hour about every possible metaphor we can think of. I tell her more about the trip: the parts I loved, the parts I hated, and how hard it was at times. She reminds me that we usually learn the most about ourselves in our most difficult times and not the easy times. I'm loving the new perspective she gives me and the things that are opening up for me now that I've met my fly fishing friends. I haven't realized what a loner I've been for the last several years. Had I not fallen in the water that day, I'd still be doing the same thing, every day. I'm now starting to see the value of having a connection with someone or something outside yourself, and I need to do a better job at this. Had I not opened up and gotten to know the girls better, I would have lost out on some really cool opportunities. I have a connection now to Rose that is deeper than any I've ever known.

One that will be even deeper since she has just suggested we both go and get tattoos of the American eel together.

`·.¸¸.·´¯`·.¸><((((º>`·.¸¸.·´¯`·.¸><((((º>`·.¸¸.·´¯`·..

Sophie

Today I left home early so I could get to the cabin before everyone else. I snagged a big bunch of daisies from the greenhouse and want to put them into several vintage blue mason jars and set them out all over the cabin, a sweet reminder of our girl. Rose is bringing the small glass vile of Amanda's ashes up with her. Tonight at sunset we will release them into the river.

I will miss not being able to hang out with Buck this weekend. I just love being around him. Hearing him say my name; seeing him use his charm to make me feel sexy and beautiful; feeling privileged he lets me in just a little bit more each time we see each other; trying desperately to fall asleep when thoughts of him are keeping me wide awake; when he makes up silly lyrics to well-known tunes; those few moments when I'm brave enough to let him in a little more; the moments when my heart skips a beat just from seeing his face: these are the things that I love.

```
`·.¸¸.·´¯`·.¸¸><((((º>`·.¸¸.·´¯`·..><((((º>`·.¸¸.·´¯`·..
```

One by one everyone arrives at the cabin. We mostly wander around the cabin in silence, busying ourselves with putting our things away and eating a quick bowl of Rose's stew—Amanda's favorite. Just before dusk we all put our waders and boots on and head down to the river. We each step into the water, and Rose pulls out the small glass vile. DJ finds a spot on the riverbank and lies down, head on her paw. She looks just as sad as the rest of us.

"Oh girls, I still cannot believe we are here," she says as she looks around the circle at each of us. She stares at Amanda's ashes for a moment and takes a big deep breath. "Miss Amanda was something special, and each of us had a different relationship with her. I thought it would be nice if we each said a few words or told a little story as we release her ashes into this beautiful river. How does that sound?"

We all just nod back in acknowledgment. The color of the sky darkens just a bit as the remaining clouds cast a beautiful pink glow on the Sangre de Cristo Mountains. Several moments of silence pass by; then surprisingly Melody speaks up first.

"Okay, I'll go. Um, I didn't really know Amanda as well as the rest of you, but she was a cool chick. This fly right here is the fly I watched her tie the first night I spent with you all in the cabin." She points to the fly on her vest, and we all smile remembering Melody's naked baptism into our group. "When she gave it to me, I thought that was the coolest thing and I'll never forget it. She instantly made me feel like I was a part of this group, and stuff like that is hard for me. I'll definitely miss her."

Rose reaches up and puts her hand on Melody's shoulder, forgetting that this is the exact spot where she got her new tat. "It will be hard to get rid of us now," she exclaims as she gives Melody's shoulder a squeeze. Melody winces yet says nothing. We all smile and nod in agreement.

"For me, Miss Amanda was such a bright, happy part of our group," Rose says. "She always had a smile and knew when

398

we needed a laugh, even if she was hurting on the inside." Just then a butterfly lands on Rose's shoulder. Everyone smiles as Rose looks down at it. "See! It's like she's right here with us. She's not gone forever, just a little further away." Rose reaches up and the butterfly transfers to her hand. We all watch and smile as tears roll down our cheeks.

Veronica pipes up next. "I loved her laugh. She had the best laugh! And I also loved her hunting spirit, how she managed to piece together the best fishing gear out there on a shoestring budget—all while taking care of and providing for her family at the same time. Completely amazing. And the way she learned how to tie all those flies . . . She didn't let the complexity of the task get in her way. She was bound and determined to be an equal part of this group and this sport and not let any barriers get in her way. I will not be able to tie on another fly without thinking of her every time."

"Me either," Melody chimes in.

"Me too," I add.

"Girls, we are all so lucky to each have a fly box full of 'Amanda flies.' She will be with us each time we step into the river for years to come," Rose says.

"Agreed," we all say at about the same time.

Well, I guess that leaves me. "Well, for me, this week has been filled with a lot of tears and pain as I learn how to say good-bye to one of the most beautiful souls I've had the privilege to know. I had the hardest time making her wreath for the funeral. I've made thousands of arrangements for funerals in the past, but this is the first time I have bawled through the entire process. I still can't believe that Mike gave it to us to hang here at the cabin." I pause and look around at the beautiful surroundings, regaining my composure as the lump in my throat swells. "Today on the drive up here, I decided I want to focus on this moment being more of a celebration of Amanda, rather than a good-bye. I feel like she is going to be with me every time I step into a river, like she's not far away. I'd like to honor the short but *beautiful, important,* and *impactful* life that she lived by not saying good-bye, but to keep a part of her alive by always having some 'Amanda flies' in my fly box. She was such a gift to each of us, and the gifts she gave us will be around for a long, long time. I will miss her *so* much."

"Well said, Sophie," Rose says.

Then, for the next several minutes we stand there in silent reflection, tears flowing down our cheeks as the river flows past our knees. Rose eventually uncorks the small glass vile of Amanda's ashes and pours a small amount into the palms of our hands. In unison, we each silently scatter them into the water and watch them slowly float downstream. We gather next to one another and put our arms around each other's shoulders and watch the ashes until they are out of sight. The sounds of the river are the only thing you can hear.

It was a beautiful release . . .

`·.,¸,.·´¯`·.,¸><((((º>`·.,¸,.·´¯`·..><((((º>`·.,¸,.·´¯`·..

Section 10: The Present and Years Ahead—Ethics and Manners

"Once you've learned the basics of fly fishing, you're ready to reap the rewards. You'll find that fly fishing will greatly multiply your pleasure of the water; you'll enjoy the process of casting itself, and you'll enjoy the special thrill of tempting a really difficult fish to your fly—perhaps one you've tied yourself."[xiii]

L.L. Bean Ultimate Book of Fly Fishing
by Macauley Lord, Dick Talleur,
and Dave Whitlock

Sophie

We make our way out of the river and back up to the cabin. We hang our waders on the front porch, and I head out to the fire pit and get a campfire going. Veronica brings out a bottle of wine and four glasses, and we all plop down into one of the five Adirondack chairs to enjoy the fire—yet another reminder that Amanda is gone. We sit and tell stories, both happy and sad, for a few hours. It feels good to be at the cabin, in a comfortable place where we all feel safe and loved. As the sky darkens and the fire is the only light left in the day, we all get quiet and just stare into the fire. Campfires have a way of putting you in a trance, as if they transport you into a different time.

Eventually Veronica breaks the silence and says, "I wish this was a bad dream, that we will all wake up tomorrow and she will still be with us . . . I just can't believe she is gone."

 "Yeah, we'll be saying that same thing for the rest of our lives. I said the same thing for years after my Clara died . . . ," Rose says. We all look at her quizzically.

"Who's Clara?" I ask, completely dumbfounded.

"Girls, I have something I need to share with you," Rose says as I see her lip quiver just a bit. "I've been meaning to share this with you for a little while now." She stops and

403

closes her eyes and takes a big deep breath. I feel my heart skip a beat, as I can tell whatever she is about to say is going to be hard for her.

"Clara was my daughter. I lost her when she was nine years old."

"What?" we all gasp.

"Oh my God, Rose, what are you talking about?" I ask. My head starts spinning. We all lurch upright in our chairs. *Why would she not have shared this with me before now?*

"It was a horrible accident. I've . . . I've never told anyone about it because . . . well, *grief . . .* ," she says, tears welling up in her eyes. "I don't ever talk about her, because the pain is sometimes still so unbearable, even thirty-four years later." I look around the circle; everyone's mouth is wide open, mine included.

"Rose, I . . . I don't even know what to say," I stammer, completely and utterly speechless.

"You don't have to say anything." We all sit there in utter disbelief, no one knowing what to say. "She accidentally fell into some floodwaters and drowned . . . I couldn't get to her in time . . ."

I look around at Veronica and Melody, everyone's eyes and mouths wide open, frozen in shock and disbelief. Several moments pass, and I suddenly remember that day with Rose on the riverbank. "Oh my gosh, that day by the river, when Melody fell in . . . you . . . you were in shock."

"Yes, a horrifying flashback for me . . . She was so tiny and had long black hair just like Melody's. It was strikingly similar . . ."

"I'm so sorry, Rose. I didn't mean to . . ."

"I know, Melody. You had no way of knowing. And I'm so glad it had a different ending."

"Rose, my God, I . . . I just can't believe this," I falter at finding any words to describe what I am feeling.

"I know . . . I've been holding on to it for so long . . . and that day by the river, when Amanda stayed back to check on me, I told her what had happened that horrific day. It was the first time I had told that story in a few decades, and once I got it out, I felt an incredible peace about it, as if I had finally learned how to release part of the pain . . ." The silence is deafening; we all just sit and stare at our dear Rose. I can't imagine the lifetime of pain she has kept bottled up inside for so long. "I share this with you now because it's important for you to know that grief is a funny thing. It's an emotional process of letting go of that which is already gone, and it's not an easy process. Especially when a life gets cut so short, like both Clara and Amanda."

I stand up and walk over to Rose and throw my arms around her. I hold her as tight as I possibly can. "I'm so sorry, Rose. Thank you for telling us."

"Is that picture of the little girl on your dresser a picture of Clara?" Melody asks, and, by the look on her face, maybe immediately regrets it.

"Yes, that is my sweet girl."

"I always thought that was a picture of you," Veronica says.

"Well, I led you to believe that. Otherwise, you would have asked too many questions I didn't want to answer."

"I'd love to know more about her sometime. Whenever you are ready to share more," I say.

"Thank you. I most definitely will tell you more about her sometime." Rose takes a big deep breath and lets out an audible sigh. "I don't mean to be a damper on the evening, but it felt like the right moment to share this with you. I'm so thankful for Amanda that day on the side of the river. She helped me release a part of my grief that I have held on to for so long. I will be forever grateful to her." She raises her wine glass and motions for us to do the same. "To Amanda."

"To Amanda!" we say in unison, and toast to the life of our dearly beloved friend.

`·.,,.·´¯`·.,><((((º>`·.,,.·´¯`·..><((((º>`·.,,.·´¯`·..

Veronica

The rest of the weekend is spent as a group of four: laughing, crying, eating, drinking, telling stories, and fishing on flies that Amanda tied for us. She is still very much a part of our weekend together.

As I reflect on Amanda's life, I can't help but think of Jordan and Parker, and how those poor kiddos now have to grow up without their mom. *Just like I did.* It also has me thinking about whether I have any children out walking this earth from my egg donation so long ago. I've never really had a strong maternal instinct. I think deep down I have always been scared that I would turn out like my mother and not be there for them. I told Thatcher when we were dating that I didn't want kids. I wanted to give him every opportunity to back out in case that was a priority for him. He always says he has no regrets about this, but I sometimes wonder if he does. We like our simple, carefree life, so it would be a major life change for us. I will admit I have a little internal juggling going on with it now. Funny how death can make you rethink your whole life.

`·.¸¸.·´¯`·.¸><((((º>`·.¸¸.·´¯`·..><((((º>`·.¸¸.·´¯`·..

Rose

Friendship is a great gift, one that should never be taken for granted. The capacity of a woman's heart for her friends is vast, so vast it is hard to comprehend sometimes. Like the river transforms the land, the bond of friendship can transform your life. Trusting the currents, navigating the terrain, and figuring out how to read the water are all skills that take patience, time, and love.

We hold the friendships not only of the ones who are still with us but also of the ones who are already downstream. Life changes like water in motion. The love and loss of the bond that once flowed is still a powerful force, just further away than it once was. I will miss our sweet Amanda, but I will find her whenever I see a doe and two fawns or a butterfly in the meadow, or feel a gentle evening breeze. A piece of her will forever be imprinted in the vast ocean of my heart.

Every angler will tell you a story of the one that got away. They will also tell you some lucky tales of the ones that didn't. Modern-day fly fishing is generally catch and release. There are definitely some lessons in the catching, but more important are the lessons in learning how to release.

`` `..,,.`´¯`·..,><((((º>`·.,,.·´¯`·..><((((º>`·.,,.·´¯`·..

Book Club Discussion Questions

- Which character did you relate to the most, and what was it about her (or him) that you connected with?

- What was your favorite moment in the book? Your least favorite?

- What was your favorite quote or passage?

- If you could invite one character over for dinner, who would it be and why?

- What surprised you the most when you were reading the book?

- If you had to choose one lesson that the author hopes to teach us with this story, what would it be?

- How did the characters change throughout the story? How did your opinion of them change?

- Would you consider going fly fishing after reading this book?

- What do you think the author means when she says, "What are you wading for?"

- If you could rewrite the ending, how would you have ended the story?

- Who is your "Rose," or the person you look up to in your life?

- Would others describe you as someone who is good, like Sophie, at taking care of other people's needs and not necessarily your own? Give an example.

- Has the book inspired you to try something new or to push yourself outside of your comfort zone, as many characters do in the book?

- If you were in charge of casting the movie version of this book, who would you cast as each character?

- We all weather storms in our lives very differently. Who is in your support system when you need to reach out to someone?

Resources for Women
in Fly Fishing

Breast Cancer Fly Fishing Retreats for Women

Casting for Recovery
www.castingforrecovery.org

Fly Fishing Retreats for Veterans, both men and women

Project Healing Waters Fly Fishing, Inc
www.projecthealingwaters.org

Rivers of Recovery
www.RiversofRecovery.org

Magazine Dedicated to Women Fly Fishers

DUN Magazine
www.dunmagazine.com

Fly Fishing Nonprofits for Children

Mayfly Project
Mentoring Foster Care Children Through Fly Fishing
(both girls and boys)
www.themayflyproject.com

Family Tyes
3049 Amy Drive
South Park, PA 15129
Youth Development and Environmental Conservation
Through Fly Fishing
www.familytyes.org

C.A.S.T for Kids — Catch a Special Thrill
Serving children with special needs
www.castforkids.org

Fly Fishing Clubs for Women

United States Nationwide:

Sisters on the Fly
www.SistersOnTheFly.com
info@sistersonthefly.com
(Michelle is Sister #2204)

Trout Unlimited
Women's Initiative
www.tu.org

United States by State:

Arkansas

Damsel Flyfishers
33 Turnberry Court
Mountain Home, AR 72653

The River Runners Women's Fly Fishing Club
https://rrwfclub.shutterfly.com

California

Golden West Women Flyfishers
790 27th Avenue
San Francisco, CA 94121
http://www.gwwf.org

Colorado

Colorado Women Flyfishers
PO Box 101137
Denver, CO 80250
www.colowomenflyfishers.org
info@colowomenflyfishers.org
(Michelle is a member!)

Pikes Peak Women Anglers
Colorado Springs, CO
http://www.anglerscovey.com/get-connected/women-anglers/pikes-peak-women-anglers

Braided
www.braidedflyfish.com

Connecticut

Connecticut Women Anglers on the Fly
24 Dryden Drive
Meriden, CT 06450

Delaware

Delaware Valley Women's Fly Fishing Association
1501 Charles Road
West Chester, PA 19382
www.dvwffa.org

Florida

The Bonefish Bonnies
32 Cardinal Lane
Key Largo, FL 33037
www.BonefishBonnies.com

Georgia

Georgia Women Flyfishers
325 Spring Lake Terrace
Roswell, GA 30076
www.georgiawomenflyfishing.com

Idaho

Women Flyfishers of Idaho (WFFI)
600 S Walnut Street
Boise, ID 83712
www.wffi.club

Indiana

Reel Women-Reel Men of Indianapolis
www.reelwomen-reelmen.com

Kansas

The River Runners Women's Fly Fishing Club
317 South Spruce Street
Garnett, KS 66032
https://rrwfclub.shutterfly.com/

Maine

Maine Women Fly Fishers
https://www.facebook.com/groups/MaineWomenFlyfishers

Maryland

Chesapeake Women Anglers
PO Box 296
Phoenix, MD 21131
http://www.chesapeakewomenanglers.org/

Massachusetts

Mass Women Fly Fishers
19 Abbott Street
Beverly, MA O1915
www.masswomenflyfishers.org

Michigan

Flygirls of Michigan
7315 Altadena
Royal Oak, MI 48067
www.flygirls.ws

Minnesota

Fly Fishing Women of Minnesota
PO Box 24592
Edina, MN 55424
www.flyfishingwomenmn.com
(763) 639-4887

Missouri

The River Runners Women's Fly Fishing Club
317 South Spruce Street
Garnett, KS 66032
https://rrwfclub.shutterfly.com/

Montana

Gallatin Valley Wad'n Women
13840 Kelly Canyon Road
Bozeman, MT 59715

New Jersey

Delaware Valley Women's Fly Fishing Association
1612 Pine Street
Philadelphia, PA 19103
http://www.dvwffa.org
info@dvwffa.org

Joan Wulff Fly Fishers
PO Box 893
Ramsey, NJ 07746
www.jwffclub.org

Nevada

Sierra Nevada Women Fly Fishers
294E Moana Lane #14
Reno, NV 89502
sierranevadawomenflyfishers@gmail.com

New York

Juliana's Anglers Sporting Club
PO Box 1143
New York, NY 10185
www.julianasanglers.com

North Carolina

Women on the Fly
400 Robmont Road
Charlotte, NC 28270

Ohio

Buckeye United Fly Fishers
PO Box 42614
Cincinnati, OH 45242
http://www.buckeyeflyfishers.com

Oklahoma

The River Runners Women's Fly Fishing Club
317 South Spruce Street
Garnett, KS 66032
https://rrwfclub.shutterfly.com/

Oregon

Stonefly Maidens
PO Box 1451
Lake Oswego, OR 97035-3401
http://stoneflymaidens.org/

Pennsylvania

Delaware Valley Women's Fly Fishing Association
1501 Charles Road
West Chester, PA 19382
www.dvwffa.org

South Carolina

Women in Waders
109 Country Club Court
Spartanburg, SC 29302

Charleston Angler Reel Women
654 St. Andrews Boulevard
Charleston, SC, 29407

Texas

Texas Women Fly Fishers
5609 Fort Benton Drive
Austin, TX 78735
http://www.twff.net

Utah

Wasatch Women's Fly Fishing Club
9430 S 670 W
Sandy, UT 84070
www.facebook.com/groups/wwffc

Vermont

Braided
www.braidedflyfish.com

Virginia

Reel Ladies
2756 Avenel Avenue SW
Roanoke, VA 24015

Chesapeake Women Anglers
PO Box 394
Lisbon, MD 21765
http://www.chesapeakewomenanglers.org/

Washington

Spokane Women on the Fly
http://www.spokanewomenonthefly.com/

Washington, DC
Chesapeake Women Anglers
http://www.chesapeakewomenanglers.org/

International Fly Fishing Clubs for Women

Australia

Girls Gone Fly Fishing
https://www.facebook.com/groups/1607386592840267/

Canada

Alberta

Calgary Women Fly Fishers Club,
26 Beddington Gardens NE
Calgary, Alberta T3K 4N9
www.calgarywomenflyfishers.com

British Columbia

Broads with Rods
Box 2277 Main Station
Merritt, BC V1K1B8

Ontario

Ottawa Women Fly Fishers
c/o 2659 Ayers Avenue
Ottawa, ON Canada K1V 7W7

Reel Women Flyfishing Club
2039 Chrisdon Road
Burlington, ON L7M 3 W8 Canada

Ireland

Dublin

Irish Ladies Flyfishing Association
irishladiesflyfishing.com/index.html

Japan

Tokyo

Japan Fly Fishers Women
1-24-10 Asagayakita Suginamiku
Tokyo, 166, Japan

Sweden

Fjallorna
Brannkyrkagatan 105
117 26 Stockholm, Sweden
www.fjallorna.se

United Kingdom

Rotherham

England Ladies Fly Fishers
Rotherham, England S65 3BG

Stoke-sub-Hamdon, Somerset

The Damsel Flies
East Stoke Cottage
Stoke-sub-Hamdon, Somerset
Welsh Ladies Angling Division
Newport Pembs West Wales, SA 42ORJ Great Britain

Outfitters that Specialize in Fly Fishing Gear for Women

ANGLHer
Fish Like a Girl
www.ANGLHER.net

Athena & Artemis
Women's Flyshop
www.womensflyshop.com

Cabela's Women's Collection
http://www.cabelas.com/category/Womens-Fishing-Clothing/104816880.uts

Damsel Fly Fishing
Fishing/Fashion/Function
www.damselflyfishing.com

Fishe Wear
Anchorage, AK 99503
www.fishewear.com

Orvis Women's Fly Fishing Collection
www.Orvis.com

Patagonia Women's Fly Fishing Collection
www.Patagonia.com

Rods, Reels and Heels
www.RodsReelsAndHeels.com

SaraBella Fishing
Customized fly rods for women and girls
PO Box 201720, Denver, CO 80220
www.Sarabellafishing.com

Simms Women's Collection
https://www.simmsfishing.com/shop/womens.html

Fly Fishing Blogs for Women by Women

www.SheLovesFlyFishing.com

www.TheCoutureFly.com

About the Author

Michelle Cummings started writing *The Reel Sisters* in 2009 and it has been a labor of love ever since. She has authored five books in the team-building field. She took her first fly fishing class in May 2009 and has been hooked ever since. This is her first novel.

Michelle has her Bachelor's degree in Psychology and her Master's degree in Experiential Education. At her core, she loves to provide opportunities for people to step outside their comfort zones and learn something new about themselves. She hopes this book does the same thing, and encourages more women to take up fly fishing. She is the Big Wheel and founder of Training Wheels, a team-building organization, and Chief Creative Officer and co-founder of Personify Leadership, a leadership development company.

Michelle grew up on a farm in Norton, Kansas, and currently lives in Littleton, Colorado, with her husband and two sons.

Learn more at www.TheReelSisters.com

Notes

[i] Jim Casada, *Beginners Guide to Fly Fishing* (Hauppauge, NY: Axis Publishing Limited, 2006), page 11.

[ii] Monty Python, *The Lumberjack Song* (Work House, London: Label: Charisma, 1975) Written and composed by Terry Jones, Michael Palin, and Fred Tomlinson. Produced by George Harrison. Appeared in the ninth episode of Monty Python's Flying Circus.

[iii] Cecilia "Pudge" Kleinkauf, *River Girls: Flyfishing for Young Women* (Boulder, CO: Johnson Books, a division of Big Earth Publishing, 2005), page 81-83.

[iv] Margot Page, *Little Rivers*, (New York, NY: Lyons and Burford, Publishers, 1995), page 5.

[v] Sandy Rodgers, "Shows, Events, & Schools," in *The Elements of Fly Fishing: A Comprehensive Guide to the Equipment, Techniques, and Resources of the Sport, by* F-Stop Fitzgerald, (New York, NY: Simon and Schuster, 1999). Page 209.

[vi] Dr Seuss, *Mr Brown Can Moo, Can You: Dr. Seuss's Book of Wonderful Noises* (New York, NY: Random House, Inc., 1970, 1996),

[vii] John Bailey, *John Bailey's Complete Guide to Fly Fishing: The Fish, The Tackle & The Techniques* (Guilford, CT: The Lyons Press, 2001).

[viii] Joan Wulff, *Joan Wulff's Fly Casting Techniques* (New York, NY: Lyons and Burford Publishers, 1987), page 233.

[ix] Norman Maclean, *A River Runs Through It* (Chicago, IL: University of Chicago Press, 1976), page 7.

[x] Rich Osthoff, *Fly-Fishing in the Rocky Mountain Backcountry* (Mechanicsburg, NY: Stackpole Books, 1999), pages 9-10.

[xi] Tom Rosenbauer, *The Orvis Fly-Fishing Guide* (Guilford, CT: First Lyons Press, 1984), page 200.

[xii] Le Anne Schreiber, "The Long Light," in *Uncommon Waters: Women Write about Fishing,* ed. Holly Morris (Seattle, WA: Seal Press, 1991, 1998), pages 8-9.

[xiii] Macauley Lord, Dick Talleur, and Dave Whitlock, *L.L. Bean Ultimate Book of Fly Fishing* (Guilford, CT: First Lyons Press, 2005), page 129.

CPSIA information can be obtained
at www.ICGtesting.com
Printed in the USA
LVHW03s1926200918
590803LV00027B/520/P